STEPHEN EDGER

Stephen is the author of nine books and four short stories and has been writing since 2010. He was born in Darlington and raised in London, but has lived in Southampton since studying law at University over a decade ago. He is one of the most exciting thriller writers to emerge in the UK.

Stephen has worked in financial services for more than a decade and it is his detailed understanding of this industry that adds authenticity to his work.

Stephen regularly tweets about his work on Twitter.com and can be followed as @StephenEdger.

Learn more by visiting www.stephenedger.com

STEPHEN EDGER

Crosshairs

Hi Alan,

Thanks for reading. Enjoy!

Stephen

Copyright © 2014 Stephen Edger

ISBN-13: 978-1500111939
ISBN-10: 1500111937

<u>THANK YOU</u>

This is my opportunity to say a big 'Thank You' to those who have helped / inspired me to write and have given helpful ideas and feedback on this story.

But special thanks as always needs to go to Marina Dear, Hannah Edger, Tim Ford and Jo Taylor for proof reading my final draft, reminding me not to use hyphens and semicolons so frequently and for pointing out when I just don't make sense.

I would also like to recognise my faithful Facebook and Twitter followers for helping me devise the cover for this book (you know who you are!).

Final thanks should go to everyone who has downloaded or purchased a paperback copy of *Integration*, *Remorse*, *Redemption*, *Snatched*, *Shadow Line*, *Trespass*, *Crosshairs*, *Complicit* or *Double Cross*. It has truly inspired me to continue writing and to tell the stories that run through my imagination every day.

Until the next time, keep reading.

PROLOGUE

D.C.I. Janet Mercure was in Mobile Command Unit Two, biting her nails. She was on the phone to her superior, Detective Superintendent Peter Gulliver. 'Silver Control to Gold Commander: I need a decision, sir. There are two minutes and counting until the device will detonate,' she said.

There was silence on the other end.

'Silver Commander to Armed Response: do we have all targets in sight?' she said, holding the walkie-talkie close to her mouth; on the other end: the officer in charge of the team of snipers, currently positioned on the roof of the building across from the bus.

'Armed Response to Silver Commander: we have eyes on all targets. They are still standing at the window with their hands raised. Waiting for your orders, over,' replied the sniper commander.

'Jan, are you there?' asked Gulliver.

'Silver Control receiving, over.'

'We want you to provide an update on the targets again,' Gulliver instructed.

Mercure sighed and began to recite the information she had already shared three times in the last thirty minutes: 'Target-one is Retourget: a French-Arab male, early forties, in dark clothing.

Target-two is Nazir Ahmed: an Asian female in her late twenties. We know she is a legal secretary in the city, as I met her earlier. Target-three refused to give his name when asked. He is a white male in his thirties, who has a bulge beneath his traffic warden's coat. Target-four is Aaron Cross: another white male in his thirties, dressed in a black naval uniform. Target-five is Tracey Reed: a white female in her late forties, dressed in business attire. We have learned from those on board that the bus driver was executed on arrival. We believe Targets one and five are just in the wrong place at the wrong time. I need a decision on Targets two, three and four, over.'

The line was muted once more, while Gulliver and the Chief Superintendent discussed their options.

Detective Sergeant Kyle Davies knocked on the door and entered Mobile Command Unit Two. 'Any decision yet, Guv?'

Mercure shook her head.

'What did the bomb disposal team find?' he continued.

Mercure frowned. 'Nothing! They've pulled back now and reported that there is no bomb outside of the vehicle; it must be inside with one of the passengers. They have checked the holds beneath the bus, as well in the engine compartment, but there's no trace of any explosive. They also reported there is no obvious transmitter or receiver, which they would have expected if the bomb was to be detonated remotely from outside of the bus.

'That means that the bomb is either on a timer, connected to a remote inside the bus as the terrorist has claimed, or doesn't even exist,' Kyle reasoned. 'I mean, Guv, have we even considered that possibility? What if this whole thing is a ploy to get the police to shoot an innocent victim, even though there is no real threat to life?'

Mercure shrugged. 'What choice do we have? Rely on the word of a crazed madman or ignore it? We're screwed in public regardless. If we shoot the wrong person and the bus explodes, he wins. If we shoot nobody and the bus explodes, he wins.'

'I cannot believe we are even considering this!'

'Gold Commander?' Mercure shouted into the phone. 'This is Silver Control, deadline is sixty seconds and counting. I need your decision now, please.'

'Received, Silver Control,' Gulliver's voice boomed back. 'No decision has been reached yet, over.'

'Silver Commander to Armed Response,' Mercure said into the radio, 'do you still have eyes on all targets? Any changes?'

'Armed Response to Silver Commander,' the radio crackled. 'we still have eyes on all targets. We...wait...there's movement on the bus, Silver Commander. The naval officer has moved away from the window and is walking to the front of the vehicle.'

'Do you have a shot?' Mercure shouted.

'Negative, he is out of view...the traffic warden has moved forward too and appears to be shouting at him...wait...the traffic warden is still in scope...'

'What is the naval officer doing?' Mercure cried, exasperated. Is he about to detonate that bomb?'

'Can't say, Ma'am,' the radio crackled. 'He is out of sight.'

'Then get round so that you can see him. I want eyes on him. What the fuck is he doing?'

'Gold Commander to Silver Control,' Gulliver said into the phone. 'What is going on down there?'

'The man in the naval uniform has moved from the window, sir,' Mercure fired back. 'We've lost sight of him.'

'Armed Response to Silver Commander,' the radio crackled. 'The traffic warden is now moving to the rear of the vehicle with his arms over his head. He is shouting something. Should we take the shot?'

'Stand down!' Gulliver shouted into the phone. 'I repeat: stand down! Do not take that shot!'

'Armed Response to Silver Commander, should we engage? Twenty seconds till deadline. Ma'am? We need a response...'

12 HOURS AGO

07:00

Southampton M.P. Eve Partridge lowered the paper and removed her glasses, allowing them to hang between her fingers.

'Is everything okay, Eve?'

She glanced up.

'My God, your face is ashen. What's happened?'

She didn't answer, not sure how to explain what she had just read.

Paul, her Press Secretary, P.A. and unconventional confidant for the last ten months, walked over and placed a reassuring arm around her shoulder.

'Tell me what's happened, dear,' Paul urged, flapping his hand as a makeshift fan.

She ignored his fussing and began to read the letter again.

Counsellor, as an elected official it is your duty to represent the people of this city. You were chosen to debate our causes and to fight for our rights. But what have you done for your people?

You have failed them.

For too long the people of this city have striven for parity whilst the law makers tread on their broken bones. I cannot sit idly by whilst the governance of this city remains in such unsafe hands. I have witnessed your corruption and the time is coming when you will pay back what you owe.

I am one of you.

I walk amongst you but you do not see me.

The restorative process will commence today and by the time the moon is at its height you will know my words are true.

I am in the city.

I am ready to do whatever it takes.

I will not fail.

You have been warned. There is nothing you can do to stop me. I will be in touch when the time is right.

You have brought this on yourself!

'What's this?' Paul asked, reading the start of the letter over her shoulder. 'Fan mail?'

Eve folded the letter carefully and placed it on her desk, before standing quickly and moving to the window. The sun's rays were already breaking through the early morning May cloud.

'It's a warning,' she said finally, her voice breaking with the strain.

'A warning about what?' Paul asked, unable to hide the confusion in his voice. 'Eve, what's going on?'

Paul was the most organised and loyal person she had ever met, but it did frustrate her when he failed to see the obvious.

'I received that letter at my house this morning. It had been hand-delivered and posted through my letter box. It was in a white envelope with just my name on it. I had assumed it was a note from a neighbour or something, so I grabbed it on my way out but didn't open it until I arrived in the office. It's a warning, Paul. Something bad is going to happen today.'

'Like what?'

'That's just it…I don't know.'

Her hands were trembling.

'I'll get you a cup of tea,' Paul said, leaving the room.

'No,' she called after him, 'coffee, please: black coffee.'

She wasn't sure if he had heard her. She returned to the desk and sat back down. Her G.P. had warned that her stress levels were dangerously high and that she needed to reduce some of her workload or risk an early grave.

Easier said than done, she thought.

Her name had rarely been out of the headlines for the last six months, ever since news of her expenses scandal broke. She had been an elected Member of Parliament for six years and, in all that time, nobody had ever told her she couldn't claim for certain items; quite the opposite in fact. On more than one occasion, she had witnessed her peers claiming expenses for items they hadn't even purchased.

'We do so much for our constituents, we deserve these little luxuries,' one of the party had quipped, while shovelling caviar into his mouth.

She hadn't realised that what she was doing was so wrong: everybody did it! She was practically an angel next to some of the more established members. When she was first elected, nobody seemed to be monitoring what was claimed. It became second nature to only book Business Class flights and to stay in five star hotels. Then suddenly, two years ago, a story had broken in the national press about one M.P. who had claimed expenses for a night with a prostitute. The change was epic!

Overnight, it was as if the shutters at the bank had been pulled down. Suddenly every receipt had to be accounted for; every drink and meal had to be justified. It became a nightmare to manage. Of course, Eve should have done the sensible thing and hired an accountant to monitor her expenses, but she couldn't justify the cost of an accountant out of her staffing budget. She had done her best to keep hold of receipts, and keep personal purchases separate, but, with all the pressure she was under, mistakes were inevitable.

Six months ago, it had been her turn to have the auditors come in and analyse the previous year's claims. She had spent three weeks working with Paul to get everything sorted out, but they had failed miserably. A team of three auditors examined every receipt and transaction, working ten hour days until their report was ready.

She had expected a slap on the wrist for some meals that probably shouldn't have been claimed but, compared to her peers, she had expected a good report.

The year before, she had attended the Cannes Film Festival. A documentary maker from the county had been nominated in the 'Best Documentary' category and he had invited her to attend as a thank you for all the support she had provided during the project. She had been so excited to attend and had bought three dresses for the awards ceremony: not sure which colour to wear. She had been booked to stay in a plush hotel and, on the night of the ceremony, she had decided to treat herself to an all-over body massage. She had felt so relaxed afterwards. The cost of the massage had been added to her room bill in error, but she had not realised until after she had checked out. The auditors found the oversight.

Unfortunately for Eve, two months after she had stayed at the hotel, the owner of the chain had become embroiled in a scandal of his own when the police raided several of his hotels and had discovered gigolos and prostitutes in bed with hotel guests. The charge on each of the client's bills showed as 'Le Massage'.

News of Eve's indiscretion was revealed in the press hours before the auditors advised her of their findings. She didn't have the time to offer an explanation before the story went viral on the internet. It was a scandal she didn't need and, in her eyes, didn't deserve. Her husband, Neil, had publicly stated he would stand by his wife but, behind closed doors, he had been sleeping with a neighbour for months and it wouldn't be long before they would be headed for the divorce courts.

Paul placed the mug of coffee on the desk before her.

'Can I see the letter?' he asked.

She handed it to him without looking up. She didn't want him to see her anxiety.

'It all sounds a bit apocalyptic. What do you think it means?'

She shrugged.

'Who do you think sent it? You know what; I bet it's one of your unelected rivals. It's just a scare tactic.'

'But what if it's not, Paul? What if it's something far more serious?'

'What; you think someone wants to kill you?'

'Maybe. It says I have failed my people. The threat is against me.'

'Or worse: it could be a threat against the city itself. You don't know what kind of mad people are out there. Remember last year?'

How could she forget? Last summer a young Asian student had attempted to detonate a bomb in the West Quay shopping centre. The incident had been successfully resolved without loss of life, but it had shocked residents and, when the expenses scandal broke in the same year, loyal constituents had started calling for her head. The last thing she needed now was another nutcase threatening the city.

Her city.

07:23

Nazir Ahmed pushed the duvet cover back and welcomed the cool breeze. She felt so warm and her back felt like somebody had been walking over it all night. The room was dimly lit, only a few rays of light managing to peek through the gap under the curtains. She glanced at the clock on the bedside table and groaned when she realised she had woken up ahead of her alarm for the umpteenth time that month; what was wrong with her body clock these days?

She sat up and swung her legs over the edge of the bed. She felt light-headed and took several breaths to compose herself. A sudden sharp pain in her belly caused her to yelp out as her body instinctively rolled onto its side. The pain eventually began to ease but then returned twice as hard; it felt like somebody was stabbing her with a long knife, the pain erupting throughout her lower abdomen.

'Make it stop,' she pleaded to the empty room.

Nazir tried to roll onto her back, hoping to shift the pain but that only made it feel worse. There were tears in her eyes now as she shifted uncomfortably back onto her side. How she longed for her overly-warm duvet and sleep right now.

Two minutes passed and finally the pain started

to subside. She waited as long as she could and sat back up, knowing that too sudden a movement would bring the pain back swiftly. Her forehead and lower back were covered in a cold sweat and a feeling of nausea was rising rapidly in her throat. Conversely, she could feel her bowels moving as the stomach cramps simmered under the surface.

She made her way unsteadily to the small bathroom adjacent to the bedroom, uncertain whether she should sit on the toilet or kneel in front of it. The sweat continued to pool on her face as she swallowed uncomfortably. Her gaze moved from the toilet to the basin and then back again. She knew something was going to happen sooner or later.

Which end is it going to come from?

She collapsed to the floor just in time to lift the toilet lid and throw up a mixture of bile and water into the bowl. Her body twisted and turned as she retched until there was nothing else coming up. She reached out and ripped a piece of toilet paper from the roll and wiped her mouth. Her throat was on fire but the sweat was dissipating.

She allowed her body to slump next to the bowl for a moment before clambering up to the sink and staring at the sad face in the mirror. Her dark brown eyes looked swollen and were filled with tears. Her usually shiny and straightened black hair had a matt and unkempt look to it.

You look like shit!

She splashed some cold water on her face and brushed her teeth twice to try and cover the stale taste in her mouth. She could hear her mobile phone vibrating in the bedroom so she made her way carefully back, vowing that she wouldn't rush and that if she was too late to answer it, it would be fate's way of giving her a break.

No such luck.

'Hello,' she said, answering the call.

'Nazir? It's Simon; I didn't wake you, did I?'

Simon Denby: one of the partners at the solicitor's firm where she worked as a legal secretary. Technically they were one big team but Simon was her functional manager and as such she tended to work for him more than the other partners.

'No, Simon, you didn't wake me. How can I help?'

'I'm going to work from home this morning. I've got someone coming round to fix the lock on the patio door, so it seems easier to work here until he is done. I was wondering if you have finished typing up the latest notes on the McKenzie case yet.'

'Nearly,' she replied. 'I'm just over half way through yesterday's dictation?'

'Okay, well I need you to get it to me as soon as you can. I've got the Stadler case file with me so I can work on that until you get over here.'

'I've got a doctor's appointment this morning, Simon. Remember? I should be in the office by ten, hopefully, so I'll finish the notes as soon as I arrive and courier them across.'

'No. Don't courier them; bring them yourself,' he said urgently, but then his tone softened. 'Doctor's appointment: are you okay?'

'It's nothing to worry about,' she lied. 'Just a check-up. It shouldn't take too long.'

'Good. Okay. Any problems, I'll have the mobile

on.'

She thanked him and hung up. Returning to the bathroom, she gargled some mouth wash and brushed the knots out of her hair. When she looked back at her reflection, her naturally olive-coloured skin had turned ashen and it was all she could do to stumble to the toilet before throwing up more bile.

The tears were flowing as she gasped for air and eventually was able to stand once again.

Is it all worth it?

She had asked herself the question a dozen times a day for the last five months. Rubbing her hand over the small, yet now noticeable, baby bump she couldn't hide the smile spreading across her face. She knew it was worth it. Growing inside her was the most precious gift she had ever received and she would do whatever it took to carry this child full-term. She hadn't told Simon yet or anyone else at work for that matter. She had been wearing loose-fitting blouses and always had a file to cover her abdomen whenever she walked around the office. She knew she wouldn't be able to hide the bump for much longer. She wasn't scared about what they would think, but she wanted to secure the bonus she would receive for the McKenzie case before she revealed her secret. She was concerned that she might be switched to a different case if they thought she couldn't handle the stress, but she needed the money.

She had always been a sensible woman, saving a percentage of her salary each month for a rainy day such as this. Originally she had planned to use the money for a deposit on a house, but that was before she had fallen pregnant. She had had to do a lot of reprioritising since her GP had confirmed the news, but she was determined to see it through. After all, abortion was against her religion, even though they had turned their back on her. Feeling a little better, she dressed in a grey trouser suit and black blouse and looked at her reflection in the full-size mirror in the hallway.

You'll do.

Her appointment for the twenty week scan wasn't until half past nine, so she had plenty of time to relax and ready herself for the day ahead. As she wandered to the small kitchen, she examined her cupboards, hoping to find something edible that wouldn't make her want to rush back to the bathroom. Finding nothing, she decided to drive to the supermarket, hoping it would take her mind off other matters.

If she had known how her day was to progress, she would have phoned in sick and returned to bed.

08:20

'I want to speak to Detective Chief Inspective Janet Mercure. Now!' Eve Partridge demanded.

She was standing at the front desk of the police headquarters building on the edge of the city. Her hands were still shaking; they had been since she had first read the hand-delivered letter in her office. She had read it a dozen times since and, the more she considered the vocabulary used, the more it scared her.

You have failed your people.

'Do you have any idea who I am?' she challenged the officer behind the partition. She didn't like to use her Parliamentary position for gain, but she was determined to get her own way this morning. Besides, if the writer of the letter was to be believed, she wouldn't hold her position for much longer.

The scandal had all but destroyed any political aspirations she may have clung to. Sure, she had run for office to make a difference, but that didn't mean she hadn't dreamed of the benefits of joining the P.M.'s Cabinet would have brought.

The younger Eve had left Southampton to attend Kings College London and, from there, had worked her way through the management structure of 'General Financial', the global investment bank.

Then, nine years ago, her father, nearing retirement, had been made redundant from a large tobacco company in the city; losing the pension bonus he would have received had he still been employed on his sixty-fifth birthday. The company had decided to minimise its operation in Southampton and had switched its manufacturing arm to existing plants in Korea and Singapore. It had dealt a major blow to the city; leaving thousands looking for work.

Her father had had no chance of securing additional employment and had been forced to make do with the pitiful redundancy package the company had pulled together. The incident had affected him badly, and his health had also taken a turn for the worse, resulting in his death two years later. The city's Labour M.P. had done very little to convince the company to remain loyal to the city. He could easily have stepped in and helped negotiate a lower rent for the Millbrook site; but he hadn't. He had been more interested in lunches at the golf club than fighting for his people.

'You should make a bid for his seat,' her father had quipped after one of their many conversations about the state of the country.

She had been unable to think of a reason why she shouldn't put her name forward for election. The following morning, she had joined the local Conservative Party association and, within two years, she had an electoral campaign behind her. She was skilled in influencing those around her, a knack she had learned during her time with the bank, and it was this that had aided her swift rise.

She had been beaten quite convincingly by her

Labour counterpart, but that had only made her more determined to win the next time. She ran again, four years later, but this time she focused on meeting as many of her potential constituents as she could, attending local fêtes, speaking on radio and television news programmes, and holding open coffee sessions for the public to attend and ask her anything.

She had won by a narrow margin and, up until the scandal broke last year, she had proved a reliable and popular choice. She had been spending half her time in Southampton and the rest of her time in Westminster. She had made a number of powerful allies as well and, it had been mooted that she would have a place in the next coalition cabinet, if she kept her Southampton seat. Such whispers had grown increasingly quiet in the last twelve months and her dreams, of becoming the second female Prime Minister, had all but diminished. Thatcher had been a strong, determined woman; but that was where their similarities ended.

'This could be the answer you've been looking for,' her P.A., Paul, had said on analysing the letter an hour earlier.

'What are you suggesting?' she had naively asked.

'Think about it…city in siege saved by serving M.P. If you play this situation right, it could be worth a million pounds of positive publicity.'

'That's sick, Paul. Besides, it might be nothing…' Even as she had said the words, her gut instinct had told her that she was wrong. 'You think I should phone the police about the letter?'

'No,' Paul had said shaking his head and gently

massaging her shoulders as a coach would do for a boxer in the ring. 'I wouldn't report this to any two-bit uniform who doesn't know his arse from his elbow...forgive my bluntness...you need to take this to the top.'

'Who? The Chief Superintendent?'

'Heavens, no! Trying to get a meeting with him is difficult at the best of times. What's the name of the D.C.I.? You met her at a fundraiser last month...'

'Jan Mercure?'

'That's her. Ultimately, she'd probably head up any investigation into this threat so you might as well take it straight to her.'

'And then what?'

'Well...make sure she keeps you updated with progress reports. It needs to appear to the public that you are in control of this situation, even if, operationally speaking, you're not. It's all about perception, Eve. We've been looking for something to shift the focus from that Cannes-debacle. This could be it. The people of Southampton will forgive what happened with the audit if you can prove you are fighting for them.'

'Why would Mercure be willing to keep me in the loop? I've met her once, but we're hardly friends. I'm just a politician; I don't have any influence over police matters.'

Paul swivelled the chair around so she could see his expression.

'Eve, my dear, you're the victim! A threat has been hand-delivered to your home. Some madman is targeting you as well as the city. You have every right to know what progress is being made.'

A grin had spread out across Paul's face and it had made Eve's stomach turn. She had always known he was ruthless, but she had never realised quite how Machiavellian he could be.

Eve was now ushered through the station to the third floor and to a door with Mercure's name and rank stencilled onto it. The officer, who had escorted her, knocked on the door before opening it and introducing Eve to Mercure. He closed the door as he left.

'Mrs Partridge, it's good to see you again,' Mercure said offering her hand to shake.

'It's Eve, please?' she said accepting the gesture.

The two women sat down, before Mercure said. 'How can I help you?'

Eve carefully removed the piece of paper from her handbag and placed it on Mercure's desk.

'I received this letter at my house this morning.'

Mercure scooped up the paper and read the contents.

'I see,' she said when she had finished. 'You think it's a prank?'

'I don't know. Do you?'

'In my experience, there are two types of threats: those that write about them are usually just attention-seekers. Real threats don't give a warning. Have you any idea who might have written the note?'

'No, none.'

'Where did you find the letter?'

'Okay,' Eve began, recounting the morning's events. 'I got up at half past five, showered and dressed quickly and was in my car by quarter past six. As I left the house, I saw a white envelope sticking through my letterbox, so I grabbed it on my way out. I thought maybe it was a note from the neighbours or something.'

'Did you notice anybody suspicious hanging around the street as you left your house?'

'Not that I can recall.'

'Is there any chance the letter was posted late last night, rather than this morning?'

'I don't think so. I went to bed at eleven last night and I would have noticed if the envelope was in the letter box then. It wasn't.'

'That gives us a six hour window. Do you have any kind of security cameras at your property?'

Eve blushed slightly. 'We do, but they're out of action at the moment. Some kids were throwing stones at them about a month ago and we haven't had anyone out to repair them yet.'

'Has anyone else touched the letter or the envelope?'

'Just me...oh and my P.A., Paul.'

'Okay. We'll make a copy of the letter and send the original for forensic examination and see if there are any other fingerprints present. I doubt there will be as the perpetrator would have worn gloves if they had any sense. What do you make of the letter's tone?'

'I'm not sure what you mean'

'It strikes me as...I don't know...apocalyptic? It reminds me of the sort of thing you might read in the New Testament. Do you know what I mean?'

'That's funny...that's what Paul said too.'

'It seems quite wordy too. I don't think it's

anything serious to worry about.'

'With respect D.C.I. Mercure, what is your assessment based on? Just because the person who wrote this is educated doesn't mean he or she isn't a real threat.'

Mercure didn't like Eve's tone, but tried to remain calm. 'My assessment is based on decades of detective work and experience. I'm not saying that this letter isn't a real threat. What I'm saying is: in my experience, this type of threat is usually unrealised. We'll investigate it, of course we will, but unless the forensics team find something, there's little we can do until the writer makes another move.'

'That's not good enough! This person has threatened my life and maybe the lives of my constituents.'

'I beg to differ. The writer says the restorative process will begin, but that could mean anything. He hasn't said he wants to end your life, nor has he said he will terrorise anyone else. I think…maybe you're reading too much into this, Eve.'

Eve shot her an angry look.

'Look, if you believe your life is in danger, then I'd suggest you maybe stay at home today, or go somewhere familiar with lots of people. The chances are it's just a disgruntled constituent trying to scare you. Surely you must receive threats and abuse quite frequently, given your chosen profession? What makes this one different?'

'This one was delivered to my home.'

08:30

Tracey Reed thumped her fist on the door.

'Lewis, you'll be late for school again. Get up!'

She thumped the door a second time and, as she did, she caught sight of her watch.

Oh shit! I'm going to be late myself.

Tracey rushed to the bathroom and covered her tight blonde curls in hair spray. The reflection staring back looked tired. Despite a good seven hours sleep the night before, she felt exhausted. It had been a long time since she had had a holiday. She desperately needed a break from reality, but with barely enough income to pay the mortgage and bills, a holiday was something she simply could not afford.

Tracey lived in a small three bedroom terraced house in the Freemantle area of Southampton. Work was a twenty minute walk across the city to a small furniture factory on an industrial estate. She was paid slightly more than the minimum wage to attach handles to custom-made kitchen cupboard doors. It wasn't a particularly challenging role and it certainly didn't improve the monotony of her everyday life. The only thing she enjoyed about work was the chats she had with Joanne and Holly, two of her colleagues and now closest friends. Joanne had started a book club, six months ago, where each member would read the same book and then meet up to chat about what they had enjoyed and what they had disliked. The club had started with a dozen members, but it was now down to a core of five people. The group had started by reading the classics: Austen, Brontë and Dickens, but that had since given way to erotic fantasy books: 'Mills and Boone with whips and chains,' is how Holly described them.

It was all a bit of fun and the discussions the ladies had on a fortnightly basis was a damn sight more exciting than Tracey's own love life. She hadn't had sex with Ian in nearly a year.

Ian, her husband for some nineteen years, was the Deputy Headteacher at a local primary school. Their sex life had never been particularly passionate, even before marriage, but since their son Lewis had been born, it had all but dried up. He was a good man and, maybe if he were a bit more forward with her, they could rekindle things a bit, but he hadn't made a move in so long. She could still remember the last time they had had sex: his birthday. Given that he was due to turn fifty in a month, it really hit home just how long it had been.

Ian had already left for work. It seemed like he was leaving earlier and earlier these days and getting home later and later. She wished he was here now to help get Lewis out of bed. She walked back to his door and thumped again.

'Bloody hell, Lewis!' she shouted. 'If I get a phone call from your school again, there will be serious trouble. You hear me? I'll confiscate your

Playstation. Get your bum to school. Now!'

She checked her watch again and cursed. Mr Bletcher would be cross if she clocked in late again. It was always Lewis' fault. He had never been an easy child. Even his birth had been difficult, as the umbilical cord had caught around his neck and an emergency caesarean section had been performed to deliver him. But since his seventeenth birthday, he had distanced himself from family life. He displayed nothing but disdain for Tracey and she was reaching the end of her tether with him.

Why can't he understand that I just want what's best for him?

She listened at the door and heard the bed creak. Satisfied that her message must have got through she turned and headed for the front door. She longed for excitement in her life, but for now, work would have to suffice; she wouldn't be waiting too long for her wish to come true.

08:41

Nazir Ahmed placed the car park ticket in her purse and put it away in her handbag. One of the other secretaries at the law firm had lost her parking ticket recently and was charged for a full day's stay at Southampton's General Hospital. With her mind all over the place at the moment, Nazir didn't want to suffer such a penalty.

This was the second ultrasound scan her GP had sent her for, the first, two months ago, had been to confirm the baby was present. However, due to her slight frame and family history of miscarriage, he had told her he would be taking every precaution with her and, that meant regular ultrasound scans and blood tests.

She still hadn't eaten yet, as her appetite had yet to return since the morning's vomiting. The trip to the supermarket had only served to worsen the nausea, rather than improve it. She was dreading the pint of water they would make her drink on arrival, which would provide a clearer ultrasound picture, but it was an inevitability she could not avoid. As she made her way to the reception desk, she was surprised at how busy the waiting room seemed. In her mind, it was still early in the day and she found it odd that so many other women were lined up for appointments at the same time. She handed her appointment card over and moved to the seating area, as instructed.

She had been thumbing through a housekeeping magazine when a woman she recognised sat down opposite her.

'A'isha, how are you?' Nazir asked, trying to make eye contact. 'I didn't know you were pregnant too.'

The woman in the hijab smiled when she saw who it was speaking to her, but then quickly looked around, as if checking to see if anybody was watching them.

'Oh, Nazir, you are looking well. It has been too long since I have seen you. You have not been at the mosque.'

The first person Nazir had confided in, when she had discovered she was pregnant, had been the Imam at her local mosque. She had felt sure that he would offer sympathy for her predicament, and offer to help manage the uncertainty the future had to offer. If she had suspected what would actually happen, she would have kept quiet.

The Imam had been deeply disappointed that she had allowed herself to fall with child outside of a loving marriage and that, by consenting to sex with a man who was not her husband she had breached the sacred teachings of the Qur'an. The Imam had told her to attend the evening's prayer session, which she had agreed to do, thinking that he would offer up prayers for her. Instead, she had been brought before her brothers and sisters, and publicly denounced. The Imam had banished her from the mosque, and warned that she was not to be contacted by any of them.

She had run from the mosque in tears, incredulous that her religion had shunned her. She accepted that she had made a mistake, but she had expected forgiveness and care. What made it worse was that she knew her Islamic brothers and sisters were hardly pure of soul.

'I am not allowed back to the mosque, A'isha. The Imam has banished me,' Nazir explained.

'Oh,' replied A'isha, nervously looking around once more. She had been away visiting her husband's family on the night of Nazir's shun, but had heard the rumours.

'It is really good to see you, A'isha,' Nazir continued, eager to prolong the conversation. 'Are you here alone?'

'No, Qasif is parking the car. If he sees...'

'So how many months do you have left?' Nazir interrupted.

'Baby is due in three months,' she replied, looking to see if there were any other seats available. There were not.

'That's good. You will give birth two months before me. I wonder if we'll both have boys, or if one of us will have a boy and the other a girl. Who knows, maybe they will marry one day and we will be sisters.'

'A'isha!' said an angry looking man, from the edge of the waiting room.

Both women looked up to see Qasif glaring at the two of them.

A'isha stood up immediately and apologised. 'I better go. Good luck, Nazir.'

She hurried off to her husband, fully expecting him to chastise her for daring to speak with Nazir.

It frustrated Nazir to see Qasif acting in such a way. The Imam had made such a big deal of her being pregnant without a husband but, if that was the way a husband was going to treat her, she felt better not having one. She had always been an independent woman, making decisions that would affect her future. It was why she had allowed Samir to seduce her.

She had met Samir at a party her firm had held at the start of the year. They had hired the recently refurbished Waterside hotel, down by the city's docks. All the partners had been there, as had several clients. The party was being held to celebrate the end of a very successful year for the firm and the champagne had been flowing; all on the house. Nazir had been sipping from a flute when her phone rang. She had stepped out of the party for a moment to answer it, but it had been a sales call from a double glazing company, so she had quickly hung up. She had been about to return to the party when a young Asian man, in a bright white suit, had approached her.

He was very handsome and she had thought she recognised him, but hadn't been sure from where. He had told her he thought she was beautiful and that he wanted to take her somewhere quiet where they could chat. He had told her that he was a Bollywood actor, in the city to purchase a new yacht. When she had realised exactly who he was, she had become star struck and would have done anything he had suggested. He had taken her to the yacht he had bought and had promised he would take her away with him, if she so desired. They had spent the entire weekend in his hotel room, making love and dreaming about the future life they could have together.

When she had woken, slightly hung over, on the Monday morning, he had already left. He hadn't even left a note. She had found it odd and kidded herself that he would return and keep the promises he had made. After the first week had passed, she knew he would not be in touch. It had been an incredible weekend but now she felt used, and wondered just how many other women Samir had seduced in the same way.

When Nazir had discovered she was pregnant, it had come as a massive shock. She had considered trying to get in touch with Samir to tell him, but had assumed that he would not want to know. He was young and enjoyed a playboy lifestyle, he certainly wasn't the type to marry and raise a family. As the weeks had passed, she had grown more determined to carry her baby and raise it alone. She had felt certain that Allah had a plan for her; she just didn't know what it was.

Yet.

08:45

The assassin known as Ophion was dreaming.

Although he was not yet awake, his subconscious had allowed him to realise that it was a dream. He tried to ignore the feeling of disappointment and enjoy the memory he was reliving. He could see the deep blue of the Mediterranean to his right and the old boat they used to use to go out fishing and for chats. Special chats.

His dream ego must have been about ten or eleven at this point, as his uncle still had both arms. Uncle Giorgio had lost most of his left arm to an incendiary device whilst serving abroad somewhere. The young Ophion did not know exactly where his uncle had spent his war years, only that it was something the older man did not like to discuss.

They were in the wooden fishing boat now; its paint peeling and with more than just one splintered edge. He was sitting at the bow and his uncle at the stern, controlling the small outboard motor. They had oars too but his uncle preferred to traverse the water quickly.

A ruffling noise to his left disturbed the dream and his mind let the memory drift away. He desperately tried to cling onto the image of his uncle in that boat, but the dream was over. He kept his eyes closed and willed sleep to return, hoping that he could pick up where he had left off, but it was impossible. Frustrated, he rose and moved to the bathroom.

At a little over six foot, he was taller than the average fifty year-old Greek. He had his father to thank for this: a former Romanian bodybuilder, his father had taken care of his body and had lived into his seventies, until the cancer had taken him. Ophion had been raised to look after his body too; eating a diet of oils and vegetables, never drinking alcohol and avoiding passive smoking. He stretched his biceps and triceps whilst admiring his reflection. He knew how powerful he was and it was often people's under-estimation of him that gave Ophion the upper hand. In fact, his last job had required him to execute a strong and well-trained former naval Commander. The assignment had required him to make it look like the target had accidentally fallen from his yacht and drowned. He had succeeded with the objective, although it had taken slightly longer than he would have preferred.

He checked his phone, but the client had not made contact yet this morning. It didn't matter; Ophion knew the plan and understood the objective. He was sure the client would want regular updates of his progress throughout the day, hence the untraceable smart phone he had been sent. He put the phone in the pocket of the jacket hanging on the back of the door as he returned to the bedroom. The hotel was adequate for his needs. It had a bed, warmth and a kettle. He did not care for television much and had not even switched it on.

He heard groaning behind him.

'Wh-what time is it?' said a young man's voice.

Ophion was surprised to find the youth still in bed; he had expected him to have left by now.

'It's nearly nine,' Ophion replied.

'Nine? Whoa, man, that's way too early. Come back to bed and wake me when it's eleven.'

'No,' he replied matter-of-factly. 'I have meetings today. You must go.'

The young man pushed the duvet back so he could make eye contact with the olive-skinned man standing naked in the middle of the room.

'What the fuck?' the young man said. 'Did you not enjoy last night?'

The young man's face looked hurt, but he was probably just acting, Ophion thought. He ignored the question and removed a freshly pressed white shirt from the wardrobe and began to put it on. He had managed to fasten three buttons when he felt the young man standing behind him.

'You know you paid enough for the whole night,' he said, placing his hands around Ophion's waist. 'My morning doesn't start until eleven, so...'

The young man swivelled round to face him and then tried to pull his face into a kiss. Ophion could feel himself becoming aroused, but fought the urge, pushing the young man away.

'No,' he said simply. 'I have meetings.'

The truth was: he needed to have his instincts on alert today, and he never had sex on the day of an operation; only on the eve.

'Come on, man,' said the young man grabbing Ophion's penis in his hand. 'Surely you've got time for a little tug of love?'

'No,' said Ophion, walking away again and fastening the rest of the buttons. 'I have no need for you now. You may go.'

He had picked the young man up outside a club in the city the night before and they had agreed a price for what he wanted, before returning to the hotel room, down near the docks. When he had carried out this practice before, the rent boy was usually gone by the time he woke up, so he managed to avoid this kind of awkwardness.

'Fine then,' said the young man in a strop. 'It's your loss.'

Ophion finished dressing in the bathroom, hoping that the young man would be smart enough to leave before he returned. The phone began to vibrate in the inner pocket of his jacket. He answered it, knowing that only one person had this number.

'Yes?' he said.

'Is everything ready?' said the voice.

The phone was fitted with a voice-scrambler, disguising the age, sex and nationality of whoever used it. The client had an identical device.

'The plan is in place and it is good.'

'Excellent! And you are in the city already?'

'Yes,' he replied. 'I arrived yesterday.'

'Good. I will be in touch again soon.'

The call ended. Ophion opened the bathroom door and was disappointed to see that the young man was back in bed, watching television.

'Who were you speaking to?' the young man asked.

I gave you a chance, why didn't you leave?

Ophion moved to the door to leave.

'Just ignore me then! Don't say good bye or anything,' the young man mocked without looking up.

Ophion removed a small calibre pistol from his shoulder holster and pointed the tip an inch from the man's head. It was fitted with a noise-suppressor and, when Ophion squeezed the trigger, it sounded like someone swatting a fly on a wall. The young man's body slumped forward on the bed.

Ophion felt for a pulse, knowing he wouldn't find one. The bullet had exited through the young man's forehead, having passed clean through the brain. He found the bullet on the floor, a foot from the edge of the bed. He picked up the tip and placed it in his trouser pocket. A large crimson stain was already spreading rapidly across the white bed sheets. It didn't matter. He had the room booked for the rest of the week, but wasn't due to return to it, so the body would not be found until long after he had left the country. He pushed the head back to the pillow.

Ophion re-holstered his weapon and ensured he placed the 'Do Not Disturb' sign on the door handle as he closed it and walked towards the lobby. In twelve hours' time he would have completed his mission and would be on his way to safety.

08:50

D.C.I. Mercure could not help but sigh as she opened her inbox and saw the thirty new emails that had arrived since she had logged off the night before. She had stayed late again last night, trying to respond to as many of the previous day's requests as she could before her brain had told her it had had enough. There had been twenty emails when she had left and that had been too many. The fifty now staring back at her was enough to make her wish she had stayed at home today. The truth was: she had been battling a strong head cold all week and she felt physically drained. But she was a stickler for good attendance and didn't believe she could chastise her officers for sick days if her own record wasn't impeccable. The last thing she had needed on arriving this morning was that panicked M.P. Mercure had taken her down to the canteen for a tea and told her to wait there while she tried to arrange for an officer to escort her home.

The job wasn't what she had imagined when she had joined the force straight out of college. Her friends had thought her crazy for wanting to join such a male-dominated organisation. She had told them they were wrong to doubt her strength. It had been 1981: Thatcher was in power, inspiring women everywhere that they too could reach the higher echelons of power. Mercure had decided that she could make a difference too. The job these days was more about shuffling paperwork, providing high-level operational updates to the Detective Superintendent and attending local community initiatives. She spent more time in her office than she did fighting crime. In many ways, she missed the buzz of day-to-day policing.

She minimised her inbox and was about to go and arrange Eve's escort when her desk phone rang. She sighed again before lifting the receiver.

'Mercure,' she said, recognising the dial tone as an internal call.

'Janet, it's Peter,' said the Detective Superintendent. 'How are things this morning?'

'Morning, sir,' she replied, trying to make herself sound more awake than she was feeling. 'Everything is okay here. We are making real progress with Operation Fortress. We carried out a raid yesterday morning at a house in Bitterne. We managed to recover cannabis with a street value of a quarter of a million pounds. The house was being used to grow and package the product. We arrested six on site and a further ten based on intelligence discovered at the scene. We questioned residents at neighbouring properties, but no further narcotics were discovered.'

'That's a great result, Jan. You must be pleased.'

''It's another victory, but it's just the tip of the iceberg.'

'Have you got any further with identifying who is bringing these drugs and weapons into the county?'

'We've issued arrest warrants for three known

dealers, but we believe there is one major player controlling the trade overall. We've heard this man could be South African, but that's as close as we are to identifying him at the moment. It won't be long until we discover his name.'

'You think this man is based in the city or London?'

'We believe he is here and there is a rumour he is looking to expand his range by importing a large quantity of cocaine. I'll let you know more when we do.'

'Good, good. And are you any closer to finding a replacement for D.I. Vincent?'

Mercure was getting fed up of him asking this question. He had asked it at least once a week since the Detective Inspector had left last year. She had never particularly liked Jack Vincent. His approach to policing had been old-fashioned and he was always prone to jumping to the wrong conclusions. It had been a relief when he had said he had decided to take early retirement and move abroad. It had left a hole in the team but she had to credit the team for pulling together and continuing to succeed.

The operation to recruit his replacement was one she had approached with caution. She had now been in her position for three years and was looking to move onto something different in the next year. She wanted to bring in somebody who could potentially cover her role in the interim before she was replaced, which would thus expedite her own move. She had received a number of applications from Detective Sergeants who were undertaking the Inspector's review board but she didn't want to promote for the role. She wanted someone with experience of making difficult decisions and running a large C.I.D. team.

She had even received an application from one of her own team: D.S. Kyle Davies. Davies had only been in C.I.D. for a couple of years and hadn't had his sergeant's stripes for very long. Whilst he had performed well since Vincent's departure, he was still a number of years from being ready for the position. She liked Davies' attitude and didn't like the idea of disappointing him but he just wasn't what she was looking for.

'Not yet. The post is still being advertised internally, but I had a call from a colleague in Northumbria who reckons he has the D.I. I'm looking for: someone with a bit more experience.'

'Sounds interesting. What do you know about this man?'

'Not much, other than a name and his length of service. The D.C.I. I spoke with tells me the candidate is just what we're looking for.'

'Will you undertake a formal interview?'

'Probably. I'm sending one of my team up there to meet with the candidate today and start the transition. The transfer will initially be on a secondment basis and if he proves to be a success I'll appoint thereafter.'

'Good. There was another reason for my call, too. All counties are being advised to watch out for an international suspect, who goes by the name of 'The Serpent', apparently. There is an open warrant for his arrest in several European countries and Interpol believe he may be attempting access to the UK.

There isn't much detail for us to go on, unfortunately; a couple of aliases and an e-fit photograph, but that is all.'

'What is he wanted for?'

'He's an assassin by all accounts; a hired killer. I'm not sure why Interpol think he's on our soil, but all areas are being briefed to watch out for him at ports and airports. I've forwarded the details in an email but I need you to update your squads as soon as possible.'

'Will do, sir.'

'I need to go, Jan. There is one more thing I need from you: the Chief Superintendent is due to attend a meeting with the other division heads tomorrow and needs details of all operations relating to the Stratovsky family. I know your team had some minor involvement with the operation run by the National Crime Agency and I need you to treat this as top priority for today.'

The D.S.I. ended the call. She again longed for the days when she could get out of her office and make a difference. Little did she realise that her wish would soon come true.

08:51

Jean-Paul Retourget tore the plastic wrapper from the carton and pulling a cigarette out, placed it between his lips. He struck a match and lit the cigarette. The initial inhalation of delicious nicotine caused him to cough; the first of the day always did this. He drew on the cigarette several times in quick succession, welcoming the light-headed giddiness that followed. He hadn't eaten yet, but this would suppress his appetite for an hour or so while he made the call.

He checked his watch again. The UK was five hours ahead of Colombia but Señor Santiago Hernandez preferred to do his business on Western Time, believing that any local drug enforcement teams, potentially listening in on the conversation, would be in bed. Retourget flipped the packet of matches open again and looked at the telephone number he had been given. He lifted the handset and tapped in the digits. When he heard it connect, he inserted a couple of coins and uttered the password. The voice on the other end whispered the corresponding passphrase.

'Hola, Santiago, como estas?' Retourget offered.

'Estoy bien, Jean-Paul. Y tu?' replied Hernandez, his deep voice belying his age.

'I'm good, amigo. Gracias.'

'Good, good. What time is today's meeting?'

'Ten o'clock. Are you still happy for me to conclude the deal based on what we discussed last week?'

Retourget was a 'fixer'; someone who connected those with a demand to those with a supply. A former member of the Foreign Legion, he could speak eight languages, including English, Spanish and his native French. He was born in Djibouti to white parents delivering foreign aid in the country; he had never felt like he belonged. His parents had returned to France shortly before his fifth birthday, and the change of culture had been a shock. At sixteen he had run away from 'home' to join the Foreign Legion, but they had rejected his application due to age. He had spent the next two years working his way around the globe: taking jobs on fishing liners and cargo ships. It was this experience that had ultimately shaped his future career path. The Legion had accepted him on his eighteenth birthday and he had fought for them until his thirty-fifth birthday: the day his parents had died in a car accident. He had returned to France for the funeral, but something had changed in him when he had seen how loved his parents were by the number of people who had turned up at the service.

He had briefly settled in Marseille, spending time working at a local market. It was here that he transacted his first drug deal. A couple of traders, in the port on business, had approached him, to see if he knew where they could score an ounce of cocaine to celebrate the successful conclusion of their meeting. He had known who the local players were, and had scored the product for them, charging twenty percent more than he had paid the dealer. It was quick and easy money.

He didn't only transact narcotics deals. He had earned a reputation for being able to deliver almost anything. If you needed to find a friendly politician, in a foreign country, who could grease judicial palms, Retourget could introduce you. If you wanted to make a problem disappear, he could introduce you to an exterminator. He was good at what he did and he was rewarded handsomely, as he had never failed a client yet. It was the very reason he found himself in Southampton today.

On a visit to the UK a month before, he had been introduced to a local trader in Southampton, a South African, who was looking to set up transportation links with a foreign country to supply wholesale quantities of cocaine. He had met the man and discussed the risks involved with such an enterprise and the likely costs of the product. The businessman had taken the numbers discussed in his stride and the two had agreed on a price. Retourget had approached Hernandez, as he was the biggest exporter of white powder in Colombia, and Retourget believed the price the businessman was to pay would be sufficient to satisfy the kingpin.

Santiago Hernandez was the kind of man you didn't want to make an enemy of. He had risen to the head of the family business when his father had been executed by a rival family from Bolivia. He had sworn he would avenge the death, but instead of hiring an assassin to exact his revenge, he had undertaken it himself. Arriving at a meeting of all the heads of family to seek resolution to the conflict, he parked a Land Rover, packed with semtex, outside the window of the meeting and had excused himself to use the toilets. The blast killed everyone in the room, leaving him with a broken collarbone. He quickly claimed that they had been attacked by the US government, and he had vowed he would lead the families to seek retribution. Of course, the other, now leader-less, families agreed to unite beneath him and a new group had formed. Hernandez had been twenty years-old. Fourteen years on, this group was responsible for seventy percent of the cocaine exported from South America.

Retourget had spent last week at Hernandez's home in Bogota, observing the Colombian's set-up, so that he could give assurance to the UK businessman that the Colombian could handle the quantities required. Hernandez had accepted the price on offer, minus the Frenchman's cut.

The phone line crackled.

'I want ninety thousand per kilo.'

Retourget was afraid this would happen; Hernandez had a reputation for changing the deal at the last minute.

'Santiago, we agreed on eighty-five last week. My client is not going to be happy with the increase.'

'Last week is the past. The cost today is ninety.'

'Santiago, don't do this. We shook hands on eighty-five thousand dollars. What has changed?'

There was a pause.

'I have looked at the transportation issues between here and there and the risk is greater for me.'

'What risk?'

'I have to drive the product from Bogota to Barranquilla, take it underwater via Haiti to Senegal, then drive it to Morocco, before crossing to Spain and shipping it through the Bay of Biscay to English waters. A lot could go wrong!'

'Sustantivo!' Retourget challenged. 'You own border control in each of those places: that's the reason I came to you first. You are the biggest exporter of snow in South America! Eighty-five a kilo is a fair price.'

'I don't care what you say. The price is ninety a key and that is final!'

The phone began to beep to indicate he would have to add more money to continue the conversation.

'Forget it,' Retourget said and slammed the handset down.

Hijo de puta!

He looked at his watch again. There was no way he could cancel the ten o'clock meeting. He had never failed to deliver, and he wasn't about to let a greedy Colombian crush his reputation. He lit another cigarette to give him time to think about whom else might be able to deliver the product. A couple of names came to mind, but he wasn't certain they would appreciate him phoning in the early hours of the morning to arrange a last minute transaction. He smoked the cigarette to the tip before squashing it underfoot.

He was worried: it was one thing to stand by his client, and refuse to re-negotiate the deal, it was quite another to snub Colombia's leading cartel. If Hernandez found out that he had approached an alternative supplier, it could mean the end of their working relationship. Literally: the end. Retourget knew a lot about the Colombian's other business deals, particularly those in Europe, and that meant he was a risk to Hernandez's operation. He didn't have time to consider what Hernandez would do but he made a mental note to phone the Colombian back that day and smooth any ripples.

Retourget lifted the handset again, and punched in a different number. He had no idea of the significance of the deal to the South African or those he ultimately reported to. If he had, he would have been more concerned about the snub to the Colombian.

09:14

The Serpent answered his phone, angry at being disturbed again so soon.

'How are you progressing?' the client asked.

I'd be progressing much quicker if you stopped pestering me, he thought.

'I am on my way to the first target,' Ophion lied, having arrived five minutes before.

'Good,' said the client. 'I want all the loose ends tied up. Is that understood? I don't want any of...this...coming back to me.'

Is there no trust these days?

'You hired me because I am the best. I will deliver what you have instructed. You have my word.'

'Good,' said the client again. 'I will send you the next address once you have completed this first task. How long do you think it will take you?'

'I will be done within the hour.'

'Excellent. I have deposited half of your fee in the Swiss account you nominated. I will deposit the remainder upon completion. How do you plan to leave the city?'

That is none of your business!

Ophion never liked to share his exit strategy with a client. If the client knew the means of his escape, there was a danger that the client might let it slip to the authorities. He usually evaded the question, where possible, but, if the client was insistent on knowing, he usually gave them a false plan.

'I have a flight booked for this evening. Once I have handled matters fully, I will be gone.'

'I assume you are going to a country without an extradition policy with the UK and US?'

'I'd prefer not to say where I am going.'

The truth was: he had no intention of fleeing the UK by plane. He had secured several disguises and false passports over the years and on this occasion had decided he would stay in the country long after the consequences of his actions had become clear. There was something about this client that he did not trust.

'I understand,' replied the client calmly. 'I'll send you the address in an hour. Be sure to take your time on this current job. It needs to follow the plan to the letter. Any slip-ups now would be disastrous for both of us. Am I making myself clear?'

'I know the plan. I will carry out all your instructions,' Ophion replied evenly.

The client hung up and Ophion placed the phone back in his jacket pocket. He was sitting in a car he had acquired earlier that morning and it gave him the perfect vantage point. There were still several people moving up and down the street, so it was important for him to bide his time. He expected the road to quieten imminently and when it did, he would make his move.

Satisfied that he had time to reach the target without being seen, Ophion opened the car door and closed it quietly behind him. He was carrying a small black bag, which contained all the tools he needed. He approached the beige four by four carefully and, with his back touching the spare tyre attached to the boot, he slid down to a crouching position. He stretched his legs out and lowered his head so that he was lying flat on his back on the road, then, very carefully he placed his gloved hands on the car's bumper and slid underneath it. The chassis of the vehicle was barely four inches from his face, but he had just enough space to open the small black bag he had been carrying and remove the contents.

The device was encased in an aluminium tin, about the size of a tablet device. Inside the tin was enough semtex to destroy the car and anything within a thirty foot radius of it. He had been tempted to detonate it remotely, but such devices became more unreliable the further away the detonator was. He didn't want to rely on a radio wave transmission, when it was just as easy to attach a digital timer. Ultimately, the client had been quite specific about the time he wanted the device to go off, so it was in everyone's best interests to use the timer.

Ophion had made the device himself. He found it such a cowardly way to end life. He much preferred to look his victim in the eye, so that they would know who had ended their life. He felt his victims deserved to know they had been killed for a valid reason. Most times, the clients who hired him really didn't care how he chose to dispose of the target. It was better that way as it gave him the freedom to choose the most effective way. But this client was different. This client was very prescriptive about who should die and how. It didn't matter to Ophion as he was very adept with a number of weapons and explosives were just another weapon.

Ophion removed the second item from the small black bag: a tube of superglue. He had considered magnetising the box to attach it to the car, but there was a danger that the magnetic field could misalign the timer so he had ultimately decided to rely on a strong adhesive instead. He now opened the tube, pierced the nib with the lid and squirted the transparent liquid liberally on the tin, taking care not to spill any on himself. He pushed the metal tin up onto the chassis and held it in place while he counted for two minutes. He lowered his hand and was pleased when the tin did not fall down.

Ophion heard footsteps passing the car. He remained still until he could no longer hear them, and then he carefully slid out from under the vehicle. He remained crouched so he could check that nobody was around to see him, and then he returned to the car he had arrived in. He waited and watched the four by four for another minute, wondering exactly what the client was hoping to achieve by detonating an explosive at this location. He appreciated it was hypocritical for him to judge the motivation of a client who had hired a professional assassin, given his chosen profession, but it did not sit well with him.

A bell rang in the building the four by four was parked outside of, indicating that assembly was over and that it was time for the children to return to their class for registration. Ophion shook his head as he started the engine and pulled away from St. Mark's Primary School.

What kind of sick bastard wants to hurt children?

09:24

'Would Tracey Reed please proceed to Mr Bletcher's office,' said the public address system.

Tracey put her screwdriver down on the workbench in front of her and glanced up at Holly opposite her.

'Oh shit,' Tracey muttered, certain he was about to tell her off for being late to work again.

'What's Bletcher want with you?' Holly mouthed.

Tracey leaned across her bench and whispered. 'I was late clocking in again this morning. My bloody son wouldn't get out of bed again.'

Holly pulled an empathetic frown and mouthed 'Good luck,' as Tracey made her way to Bletcher's office. She knocked politely and waited to be invited in.

'Come in,' Bletcher bellowed from behind the door. 'Your son's school are on the phone for you,' he continued, when she had closed the door and taken a seat across from him.

She shouldn't have been so surprised, but she had been convinced he had called her in for a telling off. She picked the telephone receiver up from the desk and asked who she was speaking to.

'I'm Mary Pierce, the Admissions Secretary from Lewis' school. Is Lewis okay? It's just...he's not turned up today and we hadn't heard from you…'

'He's sick,' Tracey quickly lied, frustrated with having to cover for him.

'Oh, he's sick. It's just nobody phoned to say…'

'Sorry about that,' Tracey quickly interrupted, conscious that Bletcher could probably hear both ends of the conversation. 'I meant to phone you before I left for work, but it must have slipped my mind.'

'What's wrong with Lewis?' the attendance secretary persisted.

What is it to you? Tracey thought, but quickly tried to think of an excuse for her son's mysterious absence.

'He's got food poisoning. He was very sick in the night. We think it's something he ate.'

'Food poisoning? Oh I see. What did he eat?'

Does it really matter?

Tracey blurted out the first thing she could think of. 'Chicken.'

'Are you and your husband okay?'

'We're fine,' Tracey replied, certain she didn't want Bletcher to think she had brought any kind of sickness into work.

'How come? Did you not all eat the chicken?'

What the hell is this? An inquisition?

'We ate out last night…at a restaurant…my husband and I didn't have the chicken.'

Why am I lying for him?

'Oh I see. You really should report the restaurant to the local health service if you think the food poisoning stemmed from there.'

'Great, yes, I will do,' Tracey muttered, pleased

that the secretary had believed her lies.

'Well I hope Lewis feels better soon, Mrs Reed. He has missed a number of days' school already this year and I'd hate for him to fall further behind...'

'Behind? Is he behind in his work?'

'Oh...didn't you know? I thought the Head of Sixth had written to you about Lewis' coursework?'

'I haven't received any...' Tracey began before the realisation dawned on her.

That little shit!

'It's not really my place to say but, from what I understand, Lewis has yet to hand in any of his three pieces of AS Level coursework, and they are already two weeks overdue. If he doesn't get them in within the next week, he is liable to automatically lose twenty percent of his grade for them.'

Wait till I get my hands on him...

'He was a good lad, your Lewis,' the secretary continued. 'Is everything alright at home? It's just...he doesn't seem like the same boy sometimes.'

'What do you mean he was a good lad?'

'Well, it's just since his suspension; he's just not seemed the same.'

'His suspension?'

'For smoking on school grounds...he was excluded for two weeks...it was just after Christmas?'

'Thank you for your concern, Mary, but everything is fine at home. I remember seeing the letter you're talking about now. Lewis will hand the coursework in this week, I assure you. As I said, he is sick today, but I'm sure he will be better tomorrow.'

'Okay, thank you, Mrs Reed. Take care.'

Tracey was fuming when she handed the phone back to Bletcher.

'Everything okay?' he asked, noticing her decidedly flushed face.

'It's fine,' she sighed, determined to phone home on her break and give Lewis a piece of her mind.

'You were five minutes late clocking in this morning, Tracey,' Bletcher continued, as she was about to leave.

Oh God, he noticed!

'I'm really sorry Mr Bletcher, I won't...' she began, before he raised his hand up to silence her.

'Tracey, you know I like to run this factory more as a family than as a place of employment. It was the way my father started the company and the way he taught me to run it. It's not easy sometimes. I have various overheads to handle, contracts to negotiate with our major clients and it causes me no end of stress, I can assure you. But the one thing I count on is the moral integrity of every person who works here. You need to have respect in a family; mutual respect. I need to know that I can trust each and every one of you out there.'

Would you pay your family such a low wage?

'This isn't the first time you have been late clocking in. In fact, it is the third time in the last month. How do you think it looks to your colleagues? Hmm? What would happen if everybody decided to turn up late? Nothing would get done, that's what! We wouldn't fulfil our orders; we'd let down our clients and our customers. What would that mean for our reputation? I can't be seen to let your poor timekeeping go by without reprimand.'

'Look, Mr Bletcher, you're right. I understand what you're saying. I promise you I will be better. I'll stay behind tonight and do an extra hour to make up for it. I really am sorry. I won't let it happen again, I promise.'

'The thing is, Tracey, you're a good worker and the quality of your output is second to none, but that's why I can't be seen to let it slide. I don't want it to look like I have favourites. Besides, you've made these promises to me before and yet here we are again. I'm sorry to say it, but you can now consider yourself on a verbal warning. If you are late again for any reason that I don't consider reasonable, I'm afraid I will have to take more formal action with you. Do you understand?'

Tracey nodded, feeling the blood rising in her cheeks again.

Just you wait, Lewis!

'Right, well that is all. Let's see a new attitude from you please, Tracey. You can return to work now.'

Tracey left the office and stalked back to her workbench.

'What happened?' Holly whispered, when Tracey had sat down again.

Tracey was about to answer when she felt the tears start to fall from her eyes. She buried her face in her hands and allowed the emotion to flow. Holly walked over and wrapped an arm around her shoulders.

'What is it?' she said and listened as Tracey explained what had happened and how she had lost her patience with her son. Holly went and fetched them both a cup of tea and they chatted quietly as they both returned to work.

'If he won't listen to you, you should get your Ian to have a word,' Holly suggested.

'Can I tell you a secret?' Tracey asked.

Holly nodded.

'I think Ian is having an affair.'

With that, Tracey began to weep again.

09:30

Jean-Paul Retourget dropped the butt of the cigarette to the floor and crushed it under foot. He had been standing at the same pay phone for over an hour. As he reached into the packet for another cigarette, he found it was empty.

Merde!

He looked around but there were no obvious shops nearby to purchase a new packet. He had phoned four narcotics exporters since he had hung up the phone on Santiago Hernandez, without finding a solution. It wasn't that his contacts were unhappy with the price; eighty-five thousand dollars for a kilo of cocaine was the going wholesale rate. The problem was: they couldn't supply the volume of snow that was in discussion. That and, nobody wanted to undercut Hernandez.

Retourget was due to meet the local businessman in a little over an hour and he still needed to make his way to the rendezvous. His reputation depended on him being able to deliver what he had promised. He had never failed a client to date and the thought of doing so now made him anxious.

He picked up the handset and punched in a final number. It belonged to a Moroccan that he had not spoken to in a number of years. Retourget dropped coins into the slot when the line connected.

'Mohammed, it's Jean-Paul. How are you my old friend?'

Retourget had met Mohammed Al-Batani while serving in The Legion. The service had been called to disperse civil unrest in Rabat, Morocco's capital. When they had arrived, they soon learnt that it was more of an uprising than merely a few unhappy protesters. Al-Batani was leading the revolution against a tax increase of fifty percent on fishermen. The increase was being applied across the country and protests were beginning to spread all over. However, the most significant groups were in Rabat and nearby Temara.

The Legion was asked to keep the protesters in check. Officially that meant they had to keep the angry crowd back from the Parliament buildings. Unofficially, that meant infiltrating and undermining the group. Because of his Algerian ancestry, Retourget was one of three men chosen to penetrate the group and get close to its leader. Having no real cultural identity of his own, Retourget found it easy to adopt the role of a disgruntled Moroccan fisherman. In fact, he actually enjoyed being united with men fighting the same cause, even though it wasn't particularly close to his own heart.

He had met Al-Batani during a violent outbreak, instigated by The Legion, with the intention of putting the two men onto the same course. Retourget rescued Al-Batani from a beating and the two men escaped to a quieter part of the city where they shared backstories and became properly acquainted. To his credit, Al-Batani came across as a man ready to fight for the rights of his people. He spoke passionately about his disdain for the corruption in government office and how he wished to lead a revolution against the King and his oppressive government. Retourget found himself empathising with Al-Batani.

The uprising lasted a week, during which time Retourget demonstrated how useful an ally he could be to the young Moroccan. Then, one evening, an attempt was made on Al-Batani's life. A pressure-switch attached to two sticks of dynamite was placed under his bed. The explosion tore through the outside wall of his small house and robbed him of his left leg. He had been sitting on the edge of the bed when the device had detonated; had he been lying down, he would surely have died.

Al-Batani was rushed to hospital, where the bleeding was stemmed and the stump bandaged. He sustained several lacerations to his face and upper torso, but, considering how bad the impact could have been, he escaped well. The following night he called his closest friends together to understand who might have attempted to kill him. Retourget attended the meeting too. Various theories and ideas were debated and it was eventually concluded that it was The Legion who had acted. Retourget knew this was the wrong conclusion and, once the others had left for the night, he came clean to Al-Batani and told him who he was.

Al-Batani had been shocked and upset at first, but had eventually accepted Retourget's statement that The Legion would not have made an attempt on his life. It was at this point that Al-Batani had revealed that he was part of the 'Directorate de la Surveillance du Territoire', a branch of the Moroccan Intelligence Service. He explained how he had been placed undercover in an effort to identify political corruption in Rabat, but that this attempt on his life meant that it was likely his cover had been blown. Their meeting ended with Al-Batani promising to meet with Retourget the following day. He never saw Al-Batani again.

It was vital for Retourget to keep up to date with the current political climate and to understand who the players were in each country across the globe. Al-Batani had gone off the grid and the rumour was that a second attempt had been successfully made on his life the day after the explosion. Retourget knew differently. During a recent operation in Eastern Europe, where he was helping orchestrate a hostile takeover of an international investment firm, Retourget had come across a photograph of Al-Batani. The man in the picture was referred to as Abdullah and was described as the firm's secret banker, meaning he was one of the men using the firm as a front to launder money.

Retourget had been tempted to contact him straight away, but had resisted the urge, unsure whether Al-Batani was still part of the DST or whether he had changed vocation. Either way, he was a man who might be able to help Retourget out of this mess.

'Jean-Paul. Ça va, my old friend?'

'I am well, Mohammed, how is your leg?'

There was a pause on the line before Al-Batani eventually said. 'What do you want?'

Retourget knew he was taking a risk in contacting Al-Batani after so long, but proceeded to explain what he needed and the price he was prepared to pay for the trade.

'Why do you think I could help you?' Al-Batani asked, when he had finished explaining.

'Mohammed, you were always resourceful. I have heard rumours that you are the man who controls the north coast of Morocco. Tell me if I am mistaken.'

'Continue.'

'I have a trade in place; I just need you to put me in touch with a supplier.'

'If I could do it, why should I?'

Retourget considered the question, before responding. 'Because I can give you the name of the man who put a bomb under your bed.'

The answer surprised Al-Batani. 'Okay, Jean-Paul, I accept your terms. I will supply what you want for the price you will pay and, in return, you will give me the man who took my leg.'

Retourget hung up the phone and resisted the urge to punch the air in delight. The deal was back on, and it was unlikely that Hernandez would ever find out. He pulled the smart phone from his pocket and punched in the postcode of where he would be meeting the local business man. The directions suggested it was a thirty minute walk. He hoped he would pass a shop on the way where he could buy some more cigarettes and something to eat.

Al-Batani weighed up his options before calling his superior. 'Hernandez is trying to forge links with the UK narcotics market,' he reported. 'I have a chance to infiltrate at the ground level. Do you wish me to proceed?'

There was a pause on the other end of the line as the Director-General considered this new intelligence.

'Is there evidence of The Cadre's involvement?'

'They must be involved,' Al-Batani replied. 'They are moving the pieces around the board. Hernandez is just the first step. More will follow.'

'Okay. Proceed with caution. We don't want to do anything to spook the operation. Is your cover still in place at the investment firm?'

'Hernandez doesn't suspect a thing.'

'Interpol have advised that The Serpent may be in the UK. It cannot be a coincidence. Do you know their next move?'

'Not yet, but I'm pretty sure we'll know more before the end of the day.'

09:52

Nazir was skim reading the obituaries of the local newspaper when a nurse approached and said they were nearly ready for her and that she should finish the water she had been given to drink. She had been so upset by her earlier encounter with A'isha and Qasif that she had forgotten all about the water. Her attention had been caught by the drowning of a former naval Commander who was due to be buried that afternoon. She didn't usually read things like that, but something had compelled her to do so. She eagerly drank the water as the nurse walked back to the examination room. She had nearly finished the drink when she heard her mobile phone ringing in her handbag. She avoided the disapproving looks of the hospital staff who grew tired of patients ignoring the 'No phones' signs.

She recognised Denby's home phone number from earlier that morning.

What does he want this time?

'Hello again, Simon,' she said calmly.

'Nazir? Good, you're there,' he began, something strange in his tone that she couldn't quite place. 'Are you in the office yet?'

Nazir glanced at her watch. She had hoped the appointment would have been finished by now and that she'd be on her way into the office.

How can they be so far behind schedule already?

'Not yet, I'm afraid. I'm still at the hospital...'

She instantly regretted confirming her location.

Why didn't I say I was at my local surgery?

'Hospital? I thought you said it was a check-up?'

'It is...sort of,' she lied, hoping that he wouldn't push her if she remained vague.

'I need that McKenzie file urgently, Nazir. When can you get it to me?'

'Is everything okay, Simon? You sound anxious.'

'Please, Nazir, it's best you don't ask any questions. Just get that file to me.'

'I will, Simon. I'll finish typing the dictation as soon as I'm in and bring it over...'

'Forget the dictation!' he interrupted, urgency now in his tone. 'Just get the bloody file across as it is.'

This was what she had feared. He must have suspected she was pregnant, despite her precautions, and now he was eager to move her to a less-stressful case.

Why did I say hospital?

'I can handle this, Simon. I've read the file; I understand the ins and outs of it. I've learned enough down the years to interpret what is going on. You don't need to worry,' she reassured.

He was silent a moment and then said. 'You've read the file?'

'Well...yes...I thought if I understood the background of the case it would help me better understand your dictation...'

'Oh God, Nazir, you shouldn't have read the file.'

'Why not? I do it with all the cases I support you with...and the other partners...I mean, it is better for me to know who is who and what legal points are being challenged.'

'Just get the file to me, Nazir. As quick as you can, okay?'

He paused to await her acknowledgement, but another thought hit him before she had responded. 'You haven't discussed the case with anyone else have you? The other legal secretaries? Anyone else at the firm? Friends? Family?'

'No, Simon, of course not,' she replied, hurt by the suggestion that she would breach client confidentiality or his trust.

'Good. Good...that's good.'

'What's going on, Simon? If you doubt my abilities, please just be honest with me...I'm good at my job and I deserve your respect.'

'Miss Ahmed, we're ready,' said the nurse behind her.

Nazir lifted a finger to indicate she would be a minute. The nurse tutted as she returned to the examination room.

'Simon? Are you there?'

'You're a great worker, Nazir: the best I've worked with. Nobody's questioning your ability...I just need that damn file. Okay? Get it couriered to me at home. Now, please.'

The line went dead.

It was nice to speak to you too!

She knew the nurse would probably be growing impatient, but decided to fulfil Simon's wishes. She found the number for the office and began to phone it. The line was engaged.

It'll just have to wait, she decided.

Nazir entered the examination room, where she removed her blouse and lowered her trousers before lifting herself onto the examination table.

'Will the father not be joining us?' the nurse enquired pleasantly enough.

'No,' Nazir replied evenly, determined not to get into a debate about why not. She began to wonder just how many other illegitimate children Samir had unknowingly fathered.

The sonographer squeezed a transparent gel onto Nazir's bump. It felt cold but she couldn't help tingling with excitement. The sonographer then placed the small probe onto the bump and used it to spread the gel around until there was an even covering. Nazir remained quiet while the probe's echoes were translated onto a small screen. The sonographer spoke quietly and quickly to the nurse, who was sitting at a nearby desk, scribbling notes. It was as if Nazir wasn't even there.

After ten minutes of this, the sonographer turned to face her. 'This is your baby. Can you see? It looks like the baby's waving.'

Nazir could see two ball shapes, one larger and more elongated than the other, with what was presumably an arm protruding. The arm was moving ever so slightly. It was enough to make Nazir well up. She moved a hand to her mouth in shock.

The sonographer moved the probe around and then pressed it more firmly into Nazir's abdomen.

'Can you hear that? That's your baby's heartbeat.'

Nazir listened to the thudding noise, a smile

breaking out across her face.

'Is everything…' she began, but found it hard to finish the sentence.

'Okay? Yes, everything appears to be fine. Your baby has a strong heartbeat and the organs and limbs are developing as they should be. You've every reason to feel positive.'

Nazir wiped a tear from her cheek.

'Would you like to know the sex of your baby?'

The question surprised her. 'You mean, you can tell?'

'Well, these things are never one hundred percent accurate, but I'd say I'm pretty confident I know what you're having.'

Nazir hadn't even considered whether she might be carrying a boy or a girl; until this point it was just a baby.

'I don't know,' she replied honestly.

'In my experience, some mothers prefer to be surprised on the day. Others would rather know so they can plan for what types of clothes to buy, whether to paint the baby's room pink or blue, that kind of thing. It's entirely up to you. No pressure!'

Nazir considered her options, but she couldn't really think straight.

'Yes,' she eventually said.

'Okay, well, judging by the placement of your baby's limbs, I count only four appendages attached to the torso.'

'What does that mean?'

'I count four…not five. I believe you're having a girl,' the sonographer smiled.

Nazir caught her breath as her heart skipped a

beat. It was the single most enjoyable moment of her short adult life.

'A girl? Are you sure?'

'Well, as I said, we can never be one hundred percent accurate with these things, but I'd say I'm pretty certain you're having a daughter.'

Nazir reached out and grabbed the sonographer in a warm embrace. It wasn't that she had any feelings towards her; she just needed to share the moment with somebody.

At that moment, she vowed, she would do whatever it took to secure a bright future for her daughter and would protect her at any cost.

10:10

Where the fuck is he?

Retourget had never been patient and the fact that the South African businessman was now ten minutes late for their rendezvous was vexing him. He had made it to the industrial estate, just off a fairly busy stretch of road, in plenty of time. He had even managed to procure himself two more packets of cigarettes from a shop he had passed. He took out the bottle of water he had also purchased at the shop and took a long swig. The industrial estate looked virtually abandoned, with no vehicles parked nearby, and the shutters drawn down and locked on each of the tall hangar-like buildings around him. He was beginning to wonder whether he was in the wrong place.

He pulled out the mobile phone he carried for emergencies. All of his communications with the South African had been conducted using public phones, for security reasons. However, the last thing he wanted was to mess up the deal because he had misread the directions. He dialled the South African's number. A woman's voice informed him that the number had been disconnected.

Odd, he thought, but then it was probably a smart move for both parties to vary the phone numbers they used. He had met Richard Eksteen a month earlier. Eksteen had contacted him, claiming he wanted an intermediary to help him import cocaine for distribution. Retourget had carried out his usual checks on the man, to ensure it wasn't part of a police honey-trap operation. He spoke to contacts he had made in Britain, who were able to confirm that Eksteen was not currently being investigated for drug trafficking by any UK force, nor was he an undercover operative. It was scant consolation, but at least it gave him confidence about meeting the man.

Eksteen had arranged for the meeting to take place on a car ferry crossing from Southampton to the Isle of Wight. The journey had lasted an hour, but it had been plenty of time for the intricacies of the deal to be discussed. The location meant that no unwanted radio waves would have been able to pick up their conversation. It made Retourget think he was dealing with a clever man.

He put the phone away and looked around for any sign of life. He spotted a large dark van pull into the slip road that ran down to the entrance of the estate. The van meandered slowly and then pulled into the estate. It had to be him.

Not the most inconspicuous of vehicles!

The van gradually approached the building that Retourget was leaning against. The Frenchman lit another cigarette and exhaled a cloud of smoke.

Get a move on, he willed.

As if the driver suddenly recognised him, the van sped up and arced around with a screech of tyres, until it was facing in the opposite direction. In no time, the rear doors of the van sprang open, and Retourget saw two masked men lying on the floor of the van, pointing automatic weapons at him. His eyes widened as a flurry of bullets erupted from the guns. He ducked for cover and managed to fling himself over a small wall of concrete that separated the parking bays from the neighbouring building. He stayed crouched down as he heard bullets ricocheting off the other side of the wall.

What the holy fuck!

He dared to raise his eye level just above the top of the wall as the men in the back reloaded their weapons. It looked like just the three men in the van: the driver and the two shooters.

More bullets thundered against the wall, causing him to duck down again. He figured he had two choices: remain where he was until he ended up full of holes and dead, or he could adjust his own position and return fire. It was simple: kill or be killed.

Retourget pulled out the small calibre pistol he always carried just in case. He knew it held eight bullets in the magazine and one in the chamber, but it was no match for the two SIG Pros that his adversaries were using. It was also no use from this distance. He would need a lot of luck to hit either of them from where he was. He needed to get closer.

The wall stretched for twenty metres but it reduced in height the further it got from the building, meaning he would barely get to the midpoint before they saw him. He could get further if he crawled on his belly and that would have to do. Moving the pistol to his right hand, he squatted onto all fours and then stretched his body out. He had crawled over far less comfortable surfaces in his time. Placing one hand in front of the other he moved forward, making it to the midpoint in a matter of seconds. He continued three metres more and then rolled over so he was now facing the spot which was still the focus of the gun fire. He took three quick breaths and then sat up immediately, his gun arm extended towards the rear of the van. The gun men were protected by the left hand side door so a shot wasn't possible. He considered his options again, but there was no decision to make: he had to move closer.

He lifted himself over the now much smaller wall and kept low as he walked in the direction of the van. He was about eight metres from the rear doors, when he heard the driver shout something unintelligible and suddenly the van's tyres were screeching again, as the driver attempted to pull away. Retourget poked his gun arm out towards the van and fired wildly, hoping to hit either shooter before they could return fire. He saw the hooded head, of the masked man furthest away from him, drop. The van was moving again, pulling away far quicker than when it had arrived. The second gunman was ducking for cover behind the lifeless body of his colleague. Retourget steadied his arm and aimed, shutting out the noise of the van's engine and the traffic still passing on the busy road. He fired three shots in rapid succession at the rear tyres of the van and, as one bullet connected with its target, the tyre burst and the van flipped up into the air. The rear doors were still open and it gave

Retourget a view of the second gunman being flung against the inside wall of the van as it landed, nose first, onto the concrete ground.

The sound of the crash echoed around the estate. Retourget lit a new cigarette, as he began to walk towards the van. He had no idea if either of the remaining two men were alive or dead so he kept his gun arm extended towards the rear of the van, ready to fire in an instant. Adrenalin was rushing through his veins and he began to wonder exactly who had hired the three to kill him.

Would Eksteen be so stupid?

He wasn't certain, but there was one man he did suspect: Santiago Hernandez.

10:15

It had been an hour since Bletcher's reprimand, and Tracey was still seething. The news from the school that Lewis had been playing truant hadn't helped. Nor had the news that he had been suspended earlier in the year, something she'd known nothing about. She had tried to focus on her work and ignore the multitude of thoughts racing through her mind, but even she would admit: it wasn't working. She had already threaded two screws because she had used the wrong screwdriver head. She had to concentrate, but all she could think about was her son laughing at her behind her back.

Admitting Ian's possible infidelity to Holly had brought some respite. She had no proof, but her instincts told her that he was probably seeking pleasure elsewhere.

Why else does he work such strange hours and have no interest in sex?

Holly had done the kind thing and reassured her that she was probably just jumping to the wrong conclusions. That's what friends were for, although Tracey had seen through the ploy. The more she thought about it, the more certain she was that her assumption was correct. But that still left her with a decision to make: what should she do about it?

The obvious response would be to confront him about it and find out who she was, how long the affair had been going on and the reasons why. But she wasn't sure she wanted to know the answers to those questions. What if he came clean and told her he was leaving? She couldn't afford the mortgage payments on her own, and she certainly couldn't deal with Lewis unaided. She wasn't unhappy with the current set-up. Sure, she missed the physical side of the relationship, but he wasn't a bad man. He still knew how to make her laugh and he made an effort with her birthday and Christmas presents, so what was the harm really? Could she tolerate his behaviour for the sake of securing her future?

It was a tough decision and one that she wasn't ready to make right now. She would have plenty of time to make it, and she was sure that speaking to Holly and Joanne about it would help. They wouldn't judge her, regardless of the decision she made.

'You can go for your break now,' Holly said, returning to her seat.

'Great, thanks,' she replied, snatching her mobile phone and stomping to the small staff room. It was more like a walk-in wardrobe, but it included a kettle and a cupboard with tea-making facilities. She closed the door behind her and dialled her home telephone number. She didn't expect Lewis to pick up on the first ring, and when the answer-machine cut in, she knew he would be able to hear what she was saying if he was in fact at home.

The machine bleeped.

'Lewis, it's mum, I know you're there, so please

do us both a favour and pick up the phone so that we can talk like adults…'

She paused, waiting to see if he obeyed.

'I know you didn't go to school this morning…the admissions secretary phoned me at work and said you hadn't made it in…do me a favour and just pick up the phone…Lewis?…I'll keep phoning until you answer…'

The phone line went dead as the answerphone disconnected her. She dialled the number again and waited for the bleep.

'Lewis, I will keep phoning…we need to talk, please pick up the phone…'

'Alright, alright, what do you want?' a groggy sounding Lewis said, on lifting the phone.

'About time! Now, why aren't you at school?'

'I tried to tell you this morning, I'm not feeling very well so I stayed home.'

'Not well? What's wrong with you?'

'I don't know…I just feel ill.'

'Ill? Tell me your symptoms.'

'I don't know…I have a stomach ache…and I feel really hot…'

'Have you been sick?'

'No, not yet, but I might be.'

'Have you made a doctor's appointment?'

'No.'

'Why not? If you're ill, you should visit the GP.'

'It's probably just one of those twenty-four hour things.'

'Why are you lying to me, Lewis?' she sighed. 'You think I can't tell when you're lying? I know there's nothing wrong with you. Why have you got to be so difficult?'

'Jesus, mum, get off my back…I'm ill.'

'Bullshit!'

Tracey's use of an expletive caught him off guard.

'I know that you've been skipping a lot of school this term. Do you really want to throw your education away? Hmm? What about university? I thought you wanted to study law? You think any university will consider you if you don't pass your exams? Have you handed your coursework in yet?'

'Yes…'

'Don't lie to me, Lewis!' she interrupted. 'I know that your coursework is already several weeks overdue. What happened to the letter from the Head of Sixth? Hmm? Forget to give it to me, did you? And when were you going to tell me and your father that you'd been suspended from school? You are in so much trouble young man. You can forget about going on the school skiing trip next year.'

'You can't do that, mum! You've paid the deposit…'

'I don't care! Give me one good reason why I should pay for you to go away? Huh? Your coursework is late, you're skipping school, and you are acting like a spoilt child. What would you do in my position?'

'Mum, you're overreacting! I've missed a couple of days of term, that's all.'

'Do you want me to go to prison? Is that it? If you skip school, your father and I could end up in court and in prison. Is that really what you want?'

'That's school, not sixth form. The police aren't interested in sixth form and college. Check it out if you don't believe me.'

'That's not the point, Lewis. Your father and I work very hard to allow you to get qualifications.'

'No you don't! You work in a shitty factory and dad does anything he can to get away from the house. You two are a joke!'

Tracey took a deep breath. 'How dare you! You inconsiderate little shit! You want to throw your fucking life away? Go ahead! I'll expect to see your things packed up and you gone from my house before I get home tonight. I have never felt so betrayed in all my life! To think of all the love and kindness we have given you and this is how you choose to pay us back. You'll never amount to anything! I hope I never see you again!'

Tracey ended the call before Lewis could hear her burst into tears.

He stared at the phone in his hand.

Was she serious?

He had had arguments with his parents in the past but it had never gone that far before.

Surely she wasn't serious?

He slumped down on the sofa. He was tempted to return to bed, but he knew he wouldn't manage to get back to sleep. School was out of the picture now too, since his mother had lied to the Admissions Secretary. That meant he had the day to himself. Those few friends he had would most likely be at school, so he pulled the mobile phone from his pocket and called someone he knew would be available.

'Yo, Billy, it's Lewis Read. You got any gear you can bring over? I'm in the mood for getting high.'

'You got cash?'

Lewis wandered into the kitchen and climbed up onto the counter top. Carefully stretching his arm to the top of one of the cupboards hanging from the wall, he pulled down a small, rectangular cake tin. He opened the tin and found a stack of twenty pound notes, estimating there to be about five hundred pounds.

'Yeah, I got funds.'

'Where you at?'

'I'm at home. You think you can pick up some beer and crisps on your way over? I'll settle up when you get here.'

'You got Rizlas?'

'I've got nothing here to be honest…bring what we need and I'll pay you to skin up enough for the two of us. That cool?'

'I'll be over soon.'

Lewis hung up the phone and wandered back to his room to get dressed.

10:29

'Bonjour,' Retourget mocked, as the driver of the van started to regain consciousness. The driver winced as he became aware of the sudden pain in his head. He looked around to try and get his bearings. His eyes focused on the Frenchman who was looking down at him with a big smile on his face. It was at this moment that he remembered the rear tyre bursting and the van flipping into the air: they had failed in their assignment.

The driver tried to put his hands on the ground so that he could adjust his seating position and it was then he realised that his hands had been tied together with his own shirt.

'I hope you don't mind,' Retourget offered, as he continued to look down at his quarry. 'I had to improvise. There was no rope in the van, so...'

The van driver felt movement behind him and the groan that followed confirmed it was the surviving shooter who was pressed up to his back.

'Your friend's hands are tied together too,' Retourget continued.

'What do you want?' the driver interrupted.

Retourget lit a cigarette and crouched down so that his face was only a foot from the driver. He exhaled a cloud of smoke into the driver's face before saying, 'It's simple really. I want to know who hired you to kill me.'

The Frenchman's smile was unnerving the driver. He had no idea who the Frenchman was or why they had been hired to kill him. Clark, the man tied up behind him, had called that morning to say that he needed a driver. The driver and Clark had been friends since school and, usually when Clark phoned, it was because he needed a getaway driver for a robbery. Of course he'd accepted the job; he needed the money. It was only as they had pulled into the industrial estate that Clark had told him the real purpose of the job. By that point it had been too late to pull out.

'I don't know who hired us,' the driver coughed.

Retourget smiled at him again. The driver was starting to sweat heavily.

'That's a shame,' said Retourget, accepting the answer and straightening up again. He placed the cigarette between his lips to free up both hands. With his right, he removed the small calibre pistol he had used to kill the other shooter. With his left, he ejected and checked the magazine. He had reloaded the weapon since the gun fight. He replaced the magazine and cocked the weapon. The satisfying click made the helpless driver shudder.

'For one of you, the end is near, for the other, your day just got a lot worse. You have five seconds to tell me who hired you, or one of you will die here and now. One...'

'Just tell him, Clark,' the driver spat. 'Come on, I don't want to die today. Just tell him.'

'Two...'

'Shut it,' Clark spat back at his cohort.

'Three…'

'Please, Clark, I have a wife and daughter…just tell him.'

'Four…'

The driver stared up at the Frenchman, his eyes pleading for mercy.

'Five…'

Retourget pointed the gun at the driver's sweaty forehead. 'Last chance.'

Clark shook his head, so Retourget squeezed the trigger. The bullet entered the driver's head, causing it to recoil back and knock into Clark's.

Retourget moved around so he could stare down at Clark.

'Your name is Clark?' Retourget asked, hoping that his action would have loosened the man's tongue. 'I'm a reasonable man, tell me what I want to know and I can end all of this quickly.'

'You don't get it, pal,' Clark replied defiantly. 'There is nothing you can do to me that they couldn't do worse. I'm a dead man if I tell you, so do what you need to. You won't get anything out of me.'

Retourget couldn't help but admire the man's obstinance. He had learned, while serving with The Legion, how to avoid cracking under the pressure of questioning. He had also learned how to exert pressure when conducting an interrogation. It wasn't something he particularly enjoyed but he couldn't doubt its effectiveness and, right now, he needed answers.

'You think I won't kill you? Let me assure you: I

will.'

'You do what you need to. If you kill me, you'll never find out who hired me. I guess we have a stalemate.'

'How so?'

'Whether I tell you or not, I'm a dead man walking. If you don't kill me, they will. That gives me a choice as the outcome is the same regardless. So, should I tell you or not…'

'I can help you reach a decision,' said Retourget, inhaling on his cigarette.

In a flash his hand moved down and he squashed the glowing end of the cigarette into Clark's right eye. Clark let out a helpless squeal as he felt a pain like none he had ever known. The Frenchman held the cigarette in place as a thin line of blood ran down Clark's cheek and tears down the other. Clark was weeping uncontrollably by the time Retourget stepped away.

'You…fucking…son…of…a…bitch!'   Clark managed between sobs.

'I told you, I can end this quickly or slowly. Unlike most men, you have the choice of how you die.'

Retourget left the statement hanging in the air and allowed Clark to re-gather his emotions.

'All I want is the name and address.'

'Fuck you!'

'You should know that I have eight bullets left in this gun. I'd rather not waste good ammunition on a worthless piece of shit like you, but if necessary, I will use all eight bullets in the most painful method you can imagine, before I kill you…don't make me prove that to you.'

Clark's right eye was closed and swollen, singed with black and red. The line of blood on his cheek remained, giving him the look of a man who had just lost a fist fight. Clark raised his head so he could look at the Frenchman with his remaining eye, and then he spat in his direction.

'Oh, Clark, that is a shame.'

Again, in a single and calculated movement, Retourget pulled a six inch flick knife from his trouser pocket, opened it and ran the blade against the fingertips of Clark's left hand, pushing down where the nail met flash. Clark let out an anguished gasp again.

'Stings, doesn't it?' Retourget asked, wiping the blood off the blade with the vest Clark was wearing.

'I will never tell you.'

'Okay,' said Retourget, pointing the gun at Clark's right foot and firing.

The end of Clark's shoe disappeared, along with his big toe.

'You believe me now?' Retourget challenged, firing again, this time punching a hole in Clark's left knee cap.

'Are you listening to me, Clark? Give me the name and address and I'll stop...can you hear me, Clark?' he continued, pulling out the flick knife again and running it along the edge of Clark's left ear. He threw the removed lobe into Clark's lap, blood quickly covering the newly exposed area.

Clark was a mess of blood and tears. 'Please,' he pleaded, 'stop!'

'I can make this all go away: give me the fucking

name and address!'

'Okay, okay,' he sobbed, 'it was Eksteen! He gave me ten grand to come here and kill you.'

'Why?' demanded Retourget. 'We had a deal. Why does he want me dead?'

'He is tight with some powerful people. They ordered him to have you killed.'

'Why me? Who are these people? Why do they want me dead?'

'How the fuck should I know? Maybe you pissed off the wrong person…it could be anything.'

'Hernandez? Was it him? Retourget shouted'

'I don't know who! All I know is: Eksteen was given the order.'

'Where is Eksteen?'

'He's probably at one of his business premises. He has several across the city.'

Retourget pointed the gun at Clark's temple and squeezed the trigger. The body slumped over and the crying stopped. Retourget checked nobody had witnessed the last few minutes, but the passing traffic on the main road continued to hum by, oblivious.

10:30

D.S. Kyle Davies sluggishly opened his eyes and looked at the display on the bedside clock. The sudden presence of light made his head hurt. He closed his eyes again and tried to clear his mind. He knew it was time to get up, but it felt like he had only just fallen asleep. He had under an hour to get dressed and to the train station, but he was determined not to rush. He rolled over, wondering where his wife Megan was and then in answer to his question, the sound of a crying baby grew closer.

The bedroom door swung open a moment later, and the image of Megan carrying their beautiful six-month-old daughter appeared in the doorframe.

'Morning,' she said cheerfully. 'How you feeling?'

'Not good,' he admitted, his stomach churning. 'I think maybe it was something I ate.'

'Ha!' she laughed. 'I'm sure it had nothing to do with all the beer, wine and vodka you probably drank last night, eh?'

'You're probably right,' he replied sheepishly. 'What's wrong with the little 'un?'

'I think it's her teeth again. She's been a bit sick on her blanket. I don't suppose you could wipe it up while I take her down and give her some medicine? Please?'

'Sure,' he said, as she disappeared from view.

Kyle slid out of bed, unsteady on his feet as the pain returned to his head again. He tried to ignore it and walked across the hall to his daughter's bedroom. The smell of baby vomit hit his nostrils like a battering ram, and it was all he could do not to throw up as well. The pink woollen blanket in the cot was covered in a translucent slime.

How can one tiny being create this much mess? he wondered.

He pulled a wet wipe from a nearby packet and started to try and soak up the viscous liquid. The slime clung to his fingers. Once the wipe was sodden, he looked around for a bin, and not finding one, he dropped it to the floor and pulled another one out.

'Oh God, Kyle,' he heard Megan say behind him. 'What the hell are you doing? I'll sort it! Go back to our room and watch your daughter!'

He watched as she pushed past him, rolling the blanket up to keep the liquid trapped inside, and carried it out of the room.

'Kyle! What's wrong with you? Go and make yourself useful!'

She headed downstairs with the blanket, presumably to stick it straight in the washing machine. He looked at the goo on his fingers and moved to the bathroom to wash it off. His head was thumping like a bass drum, and the skin on his face looked pale. He felt bad about allowing Megan to take control of everything, and he knew being hung-over was not the help she deserved.

'Kyle, will you...' she began, just as he leant over

and threw up in the toilet bowl. 'Great! That's two of you. I'll get you some water.'

She returned a moment later with a tall glass of cool water, which he gratefully accepted and began to sip.

'I'm sorry,' he offered.

'Don't worry,' she sighed. 'Do you want to tell me what happened? I'm guessing it was bad news?'

'What time did I get in?' he asked.

'Just after two. I remember because you made that much noise you disturbed the baby.'

'Oh God, did I? I'm sorry, Megan.'

'What happened, Kyle?'

He tried to think back to the night before. He was on the late shift this week and he had been just about to log out at ten when his boss, D.C.I. Jan Mercure, had called him into her office to break the news. The team had been without a permanent D.I. since Kyle's mentor, Jack Vincent, had suddenly retired sixteen months earlier. Mercure had claimed she was waiting for the right replacement to come along. In the interim, she had hired an experienced Detective Sergeant to act up as D.I. as he saw out the months before his own retirement. Kyle had originally approached her about replacing Vincent, shortly after he had left, and she had laughed at the idea. He had accepted her reaction, as he had been a relatively inexperienced D.S. at the time. A year's more experience under his belt had convinced him to apply for the job formally and to put in a request to sit the Inspector's exam, which he was due to take next week.

She had agreed to consider him for the role. A lot

had happened since Vincent had left and he had proved himself to be a very competent officer, making decisions that had a positive impact on cases. The acting D.I. had even given him a glowing recommendation for the role. The truth was that the team liked Kyle and respected that he would one day achieve the promotion he craved. They knew he worked hard and put others ahead of himself. They also knew he was someone who got results.

All this had made him think he had a very good shot at securing the role.

Mercure hadn't even asked him to sit before she quickly said, 'You didn't get it, Davies. The interview panel didn't feel you had enough wider experience, having only served the local community. The board felt you would be wise to spend some time in a different division to understand how other areas operate. It's a recommendation I personally agree with. We will be seconding an existing D.I. from Newcastle to lead the team here and I've chosen you to meet with him tomorrow and help his transition.'

Kyle had missed the rest of what she had said, as the news had sunk in. He had felt gutted. That she had left it until the end of his shift to tell him only served to show just how manipulative she was.

'It'll be good exposure for you,' she had continued. 'That's all. You can go home now.'

Her head had returned to the paperwork in her hands. She hadn't even apologised or said goodbye.

Bitch!

He had headed for the nearest pub with the plan to drink until he forgot. He now remembered sending Megan a text message claiming he was working late. His drunken stumbling in the early hours of the morning had probably convinced her he had lied.

'What a bitch!' Megan said, when he explained what Mercure had said. 'She'd rather bring in a stranger, with no knowledge of the team or area, than promote someone who has worked their way up? It amazes me how people like that reach such levels of seniority!'

Kyle shrugged: it was fair comment.

'You should just phone in sick today and see how she likes that. They can't treat people like that, Kyle. It's not fair. Can you appeal the decision? Y'know: go over her head?'

'It doesn't work like that. She advertised the role, so she's allowed to pick whomever she wants.'

'I always said she didn't like you, didn't I? After she laughed the last time, I said she had it in for you. Do you know much about the new guy?'

Kyle shook his head.

'I wonder why he's decided to transfer down here,' Megan pondered.

'What do you mean?'

'I don't know. It's just…well…I could understand him transferring if it was for promotion, but as he's already got the rank…there's got to be some other reason he's moving.'

'What does it matter?' he said dismissively.

10:34

Nazir parked her car in the only free space in the car park and hurried the short distance to her office. Her appointment had over-run and she was later than she had expected.

She greeted her colleagues, as she entered the building, and headed for the small office that the legal secretaries tended to use when they wanted some peace and quiet. She had been using this room more and more recently and secretly thought of it as her own office; an illusion that worked until one of the others came in to use it too. The room was able to accommodate four medium-sized oak desks and hers was the one furthest from the door. She slipped her handbag over her head and allowed herself to fall into her trusty leather chair. She took a couple of moments to allow her breath to return. She hadn't realised that the walk, coupled with the two flights of stairs up to the firm's lobby, would be so strenuous. She dismissed it as a symptom of her present condition.

Denby had sent her a text message since they had last spoken, demanding to know why the file had yet to arrive. She had been unable to respond as she had been driving.

'Simon's been on the phone, asking for the

McKenzie file,' said a voice from the doorway.

Nazir looked up to see one of the other legal secretaries hovering at the entrance of the room.

'Simon phoned? Here? When?' Nazir replied.

'About ten minutes ago,' the woman replied. I had a look for the file, but it wasn't in the cabinet. He seemed a bit annoyed and said he had been asking you for it all morning. Do you know where it is?'

Nazir nodded. 'I was working on it yesterday and have some notes to finish up this morning, so I figured it was easier to lock it in my desk drawer, you know, to save myself some time?'

'Oh I see,' the woman nodded. 'Well, he wanted me to tell you that he requires it urgently. Can I leave it with you to get it couriered?'

'Sure,' she nodded.

Nazir waited until the woman had left, before unlocking her desk drawer. The McKenzie file was one of three she had in the drawer at the moment. She had studied law at college and had hoped to continue her studies at university, but her mum had not been able to afford the fees, so she had had to give up on that dream. She had undertaken a number of jobs before landing the chance to train up to become a legal secretary with her current employers. She had worked hard in the years since she had joined, and liked to read the case files she was involved with, imagining how she might have fought the case had she been in charge. She hadn't given up hope of undertaking a degree course in her spare time, and felt that the more she read and was able to understand while at work, the better placed she'd be if she studied. Of course, the pregnancy had pushed these plans back.

She removed the McKenzie file and flipped it open on her desk. What was it with this case that was making Simon act so out of character?

She read the summary notes at the start of the file. She had read and re-read the file from cover to cover a couple of times already, but she was beginning to wonder if maybe she had missed something before. The defendant in the case was a former partner in an Edinburgh investment firm, who had departed the company for a rival some twelve months earlier. The plaintiff investment firm was seeking damages for loss of earnings and breach of contract. It was alleged that the ex-partner had joined a private investment company based in Europe and North Africa, and so the case was against the defendant and his new employers. The plaintiff claimed that the defendant had taken a list of his former clients and encouraged them to follow him to the new company.

Nazir had read many cases over the years and this was one of the least exciting she had set her eyes on. Ultimately, the question to be debated was whether the defendant had encouraged his clients to move, or whether they had done so of their own volition. Denby had been appointed to act on the plaintiff's behalf: McKenzie Investments. Nazir had been surprised that the client had contacted the firm, given the vast distance, but Denby had told her that he had been friends with one of the current partners at university, and it was she who had contacted him. Because the case involved international parties, finding a precedent for such a case was a challenge, but there was nothing Denby liked more than a challenge.

Nazir read the shorthand notes she had compiled following the last meeting with the defendant's legal representation. The conversation had revolved around which country's legislature would be relevant to the lawsuit. Both sides had made suggestions but the meeting had ended with no concrete decision made. She closed the folder when she had finished reading the contents.

'Nazir? Simon's on the phone again. Do you want to take it?' said the legal secretary, who had returned to the doorway.

Why is he so desperate to see it?

'Tell him I'm going to bring the file over myself. Tell him I'm leaving now,' Nazir replied, rising and scooping the file up under her arm.

The woman seemed satisfied with the response and returned to the telephone. Nazir headed for the exit, still not fully recovered from her last jaunt on the staircase. She took the stairs carefully, ensuring that the file and her bag remained in front of the bump. She walked back towards the car park and cursed when she arrived back at the spot where she had left her car not even ten minutes earlier.

The front passenger-side tyre was flat. On closer examination she found a nail poking through the top of the tyre. She spotted a nearby building covered in scaffolding and builders in high visibility vests. She had driven right past the building on her way into the car park and that must have been when she had driven over the nail.

That's all I need, she thought, as she looked up at the sky and asked for help.

She was in no condition to attempt to change the tyre herself, not that she really knew how anyway. She was pretty certain there was a spare tyre in the boot, as this wasn't the first time she had suffered a puncture. She pulled her mobile phone out and dialled the number for her breakdown service.

'Hi,' she said into the phone. 'I've got a puncture, I'm pregnant and I'm stranded. Please send someone to my location.'

10:48

Lewis Reed had known Billy Patterson since they were both twelve, and back then the young Billy had been a wholesome choir boy. Lewis wasn't exactly sure what had happened, but there was a rumour that Patterson had fallen in with the wrong crowd, had ended up in a young offenders' institute and it had been downhill from there. He had been expelled from college earlier this year for threatening a fellow student with a gun on college premises. He hadn't seemed bothered by it, and judging by the fancy sports car he was pulling up in, he was clearly doing well for himself with his extracurricular activities.

The two embraced when Lewis opened the door. Patterson was holding a plastic bag stuffed with cans of lager and bags of crisps.

'Where you want me to skin up? Your room?' Patterson asked, aware that Lewis still lived with his parents.

'No, that's fine. Head through to the living room; there's more space in there anyway.'

'Won't your rents notice the smell when they get back?'

'Don't care!'

Patterson followed Lewis through to the living room and placed the plastic bag on a coffee table near the sofa.

'How much do I owe you?' Lewis asked. He had hidden some of his mother's savings in a sock in his room, but had kept half of it in his pocket.

'Let's call it ten quid for the beer and crisps...as for the other thing you wanted, it depends on what you want to smoke. I've brought a small range with me, depending on the kind of high you're looking for.'

Lewis grinned. 'A joint's a joint, isn't it? I just want to feel calmer and forget about the shit I'm dealing with.'

'Y'know, that's like saying wine is just wine...there are different varieties of high these days...'

'And I'm guessing the prices vary too?' Lewis interrupted.

'You catch on fast. You ever smoked weed before?'

'I spent a summer as a club rep in Ibiza...I've smoked and supplied...but it was only whatever I could get my hands on...we never discussed types of high.'

'Okay, well I'm not going to lecture you on the intricacies of marijuana...you said you wanted to forget your troubles, right? Then I'd recommend this batch,' he added, pulling a small plastic bag from his pocket.

Lewis watched in awe as Patterson emptied a quantity of the stems into a small grinder before rolling it and some tobacco into a joint.

'You ever rolled a joint?' Patterson asked, passing the joint over.

Lewis shook his head as he put the tip in his mouth and lit it. He inhaled the sweet-tasting smoke and coughed as he exhaled. He began to feel a little light-headed almost immediately.

'It's good, right?' Patterson laughed.

'Oh yeah,' Lewis grinned back, taking another puff before passing it back.

'It's a pretty mellow high, but shouldn't make you feel paranoid or anything.'

Lewis moved across to the bag and pulled out two cans of lager, opening both and passing one to Patterson.

'Business is good I guess? I liked your ride outside.'

Patterson nodded. 'It's harder work than people imagine, but the rewards are pretty good. The real money is in supplying though...I get my supply from the person who is supplied by the person who imports the gear. So, by the time it reaches me, two people have taken their cut of the price, meaning my mark-up is much smaller than it could be. If I could score gear straight from the importer, I'd be minted!'

'So why don't you?'

'It doesn't work like that...it's like the military: there's an order to who you deal with. I can't just rock up to the importer and strike a deal...you've got to be introduced, and my supplier won't introduce me, as he'd lose my business. You see?'

'Don't you worry about being caught by the police?'

Patterson shrugged. 'I'm very careful about who I sell to and where I do it. It's getting harder to stay out of trouble in the city at the moment. The fuzz are cracking down on the industry a lot. They've got this major investigation going on at the moment. They call it Operation Fortress or some shit.'

'Doesn't it worry you?'

'It's a risk I take for sure, but I've been inside before and lived to tell the tale. Besides, it beats doing some office job for a faceless corporation. Think about it: I'm free to come and go as I like. I own my own flat, work when I want to work and don't get shit from anybody. I was in London last weekend, Bournemouth last night and I'm going up to Scotland for a music festival in a couple of days. I'll probably spend the summer supplying abroad, where I've got connections already in place…it's just a good life.'

'It sounds it,' Lewis admitted. 'I wish I didn't have to put up with shit from my parents.'

'Let me guess: they're on your back about going to university or whatever?'

Lewis nodded. 'Yeah, my bitch of a mum wants me to study law; she thinks I could be a rich barrister one day, but it's just not me. I want to live my life, while I can still enjoy it!'

'I understand, bro, I really do. I was just like you…I can't remember the last time I spoke to my mum…good riddance!'

Patterson passed the joint back to Lewis and started to prepare another one.

'How much do you want for this?'

Patterson considered him for a moment. 'You want to come and work with me today? I've got to pick up some gear from my supplier in a bit, but then I'm going to be hitting the pubs and clubs...you can come and watch how it's done...what d'you say?'

Lewis exhaled again and remembered his mother's words: You'll never amount to anything!

'Fuck it! Why not! What time you meeting your dealer?'

Patterson glanced at his watch. 'Not for another hour yet, so we got a bit of time to chill until then. You got anything we can watch?'

'I'll bring my PS3 down,' he replied, leaving the room, pleased with how the day seemed to be shaping up.

10:50

'He's not there, Guv,' yawned D.S. Danny Strong.

D.I. Tony White ignored him and continued to stare out of the dirty window at one of the many shops with its shutters pulled down firmly. The venue his eyes had been fixed on for the last hour was a former bookies in the heart of Newcastle's city centre.

'Guv?' Strong asked, hoping the D.I. would call off the operation and release him to go and get some much needed sleep.

'Give over! You got somewhere you'd rather be? Don't let me stop yeez. Leave your warrant card on the dashboard on your way out.'

His tone was testy, thought Strong; it was always testy.

'That's not what I meant, Guv, it's just…'

'Just what?' White demanded, facing his colleague.

Strong knew he was about to be on the receiving end of one of Tony White's infamous denouncements. They were legendary in these parts and he had witnessed his colleagues feel the boss' wrath on a number of occasions. He didn't like the idea of experiencing it himself.

You need to be firm with him, Strong told himself; hoping that echoing his wife's words would give him the courage he needed.

'David Hoxley is a degenerate gambler, pimp and drug dealer, sir. He can't be trusted.'

Hoxley was the reason they were here.

Nearly a year ago, White had learned of an underground gambling scene in the heart of his beloved Newcastle and he had sworn he would close it down, one way or another. There had been countless surveillance operations since, trying to gather as much intelligence on the operation as they could. The problem was: nobody was willing to talk. White knew who was behind it, though: Jock McManus.

McManus was a legitimate businessman by day, donating regularly to charitable causes, playing golf with the Chief Constable and dining out with the local MP. He was the city's sweetheart, even though he had only moved here from Glasgow five years before. He had been responsible for huge improvements to some of the city's most-deprived areas. He was the poster boy for the well-off to give something back to the needy. He had even paid for a box at the city's football stadium, which he raffled off on the eve of every match for one lucky person to take their friends to the game in style.

He was untouchable.

But where did all the money come from? How could a university drop-out, with no family wealth to rely on, rise to become so rich and powerful?

'He controls all the crime in the city,' Hoxley had confessed as White had dangled him from the balcony of Hoxley's council-owned flat. 'Anything that goes down has to be agreed by McManus first.'

Half an hour later, and with gravity causing Hoxley's face to look like a plum, White had finally pulled him back over the edge and sat him in a chair. Hoxley had spilled the beans on everything: the offices McManus used to conduct his extra-curricular meetings, the derelict shops behind which illegal casinos were run, the small factories where narcotics were cut to distribute to the masses. White got it all: names, places and dates. He took a fortnight's leave to verify the information, skulking in dark corners and quietly watching the inner workings of the city. At the end of the two weeks, he handed a well-written and researched file to his D.C.I. and explained how he wanted to proceed.

The D.C.I. had listened intently whilst White had explained how it all worked and had then said, 'I'll need to take this up the line to get the go-ahead. Leave it with me.'

A week had passed and White had heard nothing. Eventually he had knocked on the D.C.I.'s door and asked what was going on. The D.C.I. had handed the file back. 'It's not strong enough. We can't just pull him in on a hunch.'

White had been incredulous. 'A hunch? It's more than a hunch! Look at the photos and the logs of activity. Look at Hoxley's statement. What more proof do you need?'

The D.C.I. had looked him square in the eye before adding, 'I said it's a no. Leave it alone, Tony.'

The D.C.I. should have known better. It had been like waving a red rag in front of a raging bull.

White had stormed off to the nearest bar and after his eighth bottle of Newcastle Brown Ale, he had sworn that he would catch McManus in the act. Strong had been there that night and after much negotiation he had manhandled White into a taxi cab and sent him home. White had continued to investigate the cases that came across his desk but he was always looking to see how it could be tied back to McManus. He kept his own file on him at home. It had started as a couple of hundred pieces of paper, but had now taken over the spare bedroom; there were photographs pinned on each wall as well as pieces of twine linking the shots to a timeline that he had drawn above the picture rail. To an ordinary person it looked like a mess, but if you asked White to explain the connections, he would talk for hours and it would all make sense.

Hoxley had been arrested for assaulting one of the prostitutes he 'cared for'. She didn't want to press charges but as the assault had been witnessed by a plucky Police Constable walking her beat, they had been able to pull him in regardless. White had heard about Hoxley's arrest but had waited until the pimp had been bailed before paying him a second home visit. This time, he hadn't used the balcony to extract a confession.

Hoxley was so battered and bruised by the end of their 'conversation' that he could barely speak, let alone lie. He swore that the information he had given up on McManus was legitimate and said that the Scot had invited all his captains for a special meeting to discuss distribution of a large shipment of crystal meth that was due to arrive at the docks the following week. Hoxley identified the bookies they were now sitting outside of as the location for the meeting. They had agreed that, if the meeting was in progress, Hoxley would make his excuses to leave and that would be the signal for White to storm the building.

'He might be the scum of the earth,' White said angrily to Strong, 'but the prick ain't stupid enough to lie to me! If that bastard McManus is in there with his crew, then I'm going to see what the little shite is up to. Understood?'

'Yes, Guv,' Strong humbly replied.

'And if he thinks he can stop me by having a quiet word in the Chief Constable's ear, he's in for a big surprise!'

'What about the D.C.I.? He'll have you kicked off the force if you go against his instructions?'

'Fuck the D.C.I.! I'm going to have McManus if it's the last thing I do!'

'Guv, look,' Strong suddenly said, pointing out of the window.

White's gaze followed the finger. David Hoxley was standing outside the bookies, lighting a cigarette. The metal shutter in front of the door had been raised. Hoxley nodded towards them and casually strolled off down the street.

'Go, go, go!' White shouted into his radio to the two D.C.'s who had been parked in a Transit van behind the bookies.

I've got you, you bastard, White thought as he purposefully strode across the road to the doorway.

10:53

Retourget was in a small coffee shop, nervously tapping his fingers on the table top. He was using his phone to search for Eksteen's businesses across the city, and so far he had located five, but all were in different areas of the city. With no transportation, he had to think smart about the order he would visit them in, until he found his prey. The reason for the nerves was something Clark had said right before Retourget had shot him: they ordered him to have you killed.

But who were 'they'?

His role as a fixer had brought him in touch with several very powerful individuals across Europe and the rest of the world. In fact, his last job prior to this narcotics deal had been aiding a hostile takeover of an investment company, a front for money laundering in the heart of Europe. He didn't know names, but he did know that some of the people involved were incredibly powerful and well-placed in governments around the continent.

Is that who Clark meant? But why would they want me dead?

Of course, Clark's reference to Eksteen's powerful friends could just have been bluster, and it was just as likely that Hernandez had ordered the execution for the morning's snub. Either way, with the deal now off or a death sentence hanging over him, Retourget knew he should probably warn Al-Batani about what had happened.

The coffee shop had a small public phone at the back, near the kitchen; it was why he had chosen to stop here to gather his thoughts. He always preferred to use public phones for such delicate conversations, but he was concerned about who in the kitchen might overhear and how they would handle the topic of murder, drugs and money laundering.

He waited patiently, until the cook looked busy with a breakfast order, and then he quietly rose and moved across to the phone, dropping coins in while dialling the number he had phoned just over an hour ago. Al-Batani answered on the second ring.

'Mohammed, it's Jean-Paul again. The deal is off.'

'Off? Why?'

'My contact here in the UK tried to have me killed. I think Hernandez might have ordered the hit. If he knows you went behind his back, he may come after you too.'

'Merci mon ami,' Al-Batani replied, but didn't sound overly concerned.

'Did you hear what I said? Your life might be in danger now too.'

'I heard you, Jean-Paul, but there is no reason for Hernandez to suspect my involvement as I haven't spoken to anybody since we last talked.'

'So how could he know I had decided to go with another supplier?'

'I don't know. Are you sure it's him?'

'It has to be him. Unless you know something I

don't…'

Al-Batani recalled his conversation with the Director-General, but knew he was not at liberty to share the details of his DST assignment.

'Of course I don't,' Al-Batani lied, wondering how this latest development would impact the operation. 'All I mean is: in your line of work, you make a lot of enemies…maybe it's not Hernandez who you should be worried about. What has your local businessman said about the hit?'

'I am on my way to speak with him now. His name is Eksteen, a South African in the city.'

'What if he doesn't talk?'

Retourget laughed. 'They always talk, Mohammed, you know that.'

'Well be careful, my friend. It sounds like there is more going on there than you understand. What will you do if Eksteen names Hernandez?'

'I will get my revenge one way or another…of course, I might need some help getting into Columbia unannounced…do you think you could assist an old friend?'

'You want me to help you kill Colombia's biggest supplier of cocaine? Do you realise how crazy that sounds?'

'You owe me,' Retourget whispered loudly into the receiver.

'Let me think about it,' Al-Batani whispered back. 'An unsanctioned operation against someone like Hernandez is not easy to keep quiet; it will need careful planning.'

'You've done far worse in your time, Mohammed…we both have.'

Al-Batani hung up, promising he would be back in touch when he had looked at the logistics of the operation. Retourget returned to the table and finished the now cold coffee. He looked at the list of addresses on his phone and decided to head to the nearest one: a vehicle repair shop in Sholing. He only had five bullets left in his gun, with one additional magazine in his pocket, but that would have to do; he was confident Eksteen wouldn't be as obstinate as Clark.

10:55

Simon Denby was pacing around the living room of his luxury Ocean Village apartment. The adjoining balcony afforded him a view of the sea, which this morning was glistening under the sunlight. Not that he was admiring the view. His gaze was aimed at the floor as his mind raced with a whir of thoughts and possibilities. He was still wearing the previous day's clothes and there was an odour emanating, which was growing more noticeable. His shirt sleeves were rolled up and he had long since abandoned his neck tie. That said, his current state resembled a banker at the height of the 1920's stock market collapse. He was a man on the verge of losing his mind.

He picked up the half empty bottle of scotch and took a swig. It burned as he swallowed but it helped snap his senses back to the current predicament.

Where is she?

He had already phoned and spoken with his legal secretary, Nazir, twice that morning.

Why isn't she bringing me the file?

He took another swig from the bottle and placed it down on the sideboard. He had tried phoning the office to see if one of the other legal secretaries could get it couriered over to him. The one he had spoken with had told him she couldn't find the file in the cabinet.

Where is the bloody file?

He'd phoned the office back for an update and been advised that Nazir had the file and would get it over to him. He started pacing the room again. He felt tired. He hadn't slept a wink in nearly thirty hours and his body ached. There was no point in trying to invoke sleep, though. There was no way his mind was going to let him sleep. Not now, anyway.

He took some deep breaths.

Calm down! If you give them the file, this will all go away!

The week had started as any normal week did, working ten hours day at the office on the variety of cases he had. He had still been tipsy from the previous evening when he'd woken yesterday morning. She had told him to come back to bed and fuck her again, but he'd been firm and declined the offer.

'My clients are depending on me,' he'd said.

He'd met her at a bar on the wharf and they'd hit it off immediately. Sure, she was younger than him, but she had come on so strong that he'd been unable to turn down her advances. She'd made a beeline for him on the dance floor, and they had soon been engaged in a long and powerful kiss. She'd whispered that she wanted him to tie her up and punish her for being a naughty girl. He'd told her his apartment was nearby and they'd run from the bar just before midnight. They'd barely made it in through the door, before she was tearing his clothes from him. He'd welcomed it.

She had told him to use his tie to fasten her

hands to the bedframe and he'd duly obliged. The sex had been mind-blowing and they hadn't stopped until three-ish, which was the moment he'd passed out. He'd been surprised that she was still in bed when he'd woken yesterday morning, but he had made sure she was gone before he'd locked up. He'd taken her number and she'd suggested he should phone her again when he'd finished at work that evening. He'd promised he would and had meant it at the time.

He had sensibly caught a taxi to work, buying a strong coffee at the café on the corner before breezing into the office. His mood had been the best it had been in ages. He'd attended each of his meetings and had achieved a positive result in all bar the last one: the McKenzie case. The defendant's lawyer, a snooty man in Madrid had failed to confirm which country's legislature would be adopted for the lawsuit. It was a blot on an otherwise perfect day. That meeting had ended at four p.m. and he had told Nazir she could knock off as soon as the notes were typed up. He had returned to his office to find a brown A4 envelope on his desk. His name had been scrawled on the front in lipstick.

Bemused, he had opened the envelope and had felt physically sickened by its contents. There were a dozen black and white photographs of him with her. There were pictures from the bar of them dancing and kissing, of them in his bed, her hands bound and him on top. There was even a picture of her bent over the bed while he screwed her from behind. The most disturbing part was: these photographs had been taken from within his apartment, meaning they had not been alone that night. The most disturbing image of all was a photocopied page of her passport: she was fifteen years old.

He had walked to his office door, to see if there was any sign of who had left the images, but there were no faces that looked out of place. He had asked Nazir if she knew who had left the envelope on his desk.

'What envelope?' she'd replied, so he'd told her to forget about it.

He had returned to the desk and reviewed the photographs again, looking for clues as to who might have sent them. His mobile had started to ring: a withheld number. He had answered it and heard a voice he didn't recognise.

'You've been a naughty boy, counsellor,' the voice had taunted. 'Sex with a minor is a criminal offence. You're facing at least a decade in prison if it ever gets out. Not to mention, losing your licence to practise law. Imagine the humiliation!'

'What do you want?' he'd managed to whisper.

'I'll come to that. First, I need you to understand that if you don't do exactly as we say, copies of the images you are looking at will be sent to the local press, the police and your employers. You'll notice how scared she looks in the images where she is tied up; she really is a talented actress. She's destined for great things if you ask me. Do you understand what I am telling you, Mr Denby? We will ruin you if you do not do as we say. Now, tell me you have understood my terms.'

'How do I know that you won't renege once I've

done as you've asked?'

'I am a man of my word, Mr Denby. If you do as you are asked, we will send you the original copies of the photographs, along with a signed statement from the girl that she will never tell a soul.'

'That's not good enough.'

The voice laughed. 'You really are a tough negotiator, Mr Denby. I tell you what, meet my demands and I will handle the girl for you personally. I'll send you her decapitated head as a souvenir if you like…now, do you accept my terms?'

'It's not like I have a choice.'

'Of course you have a choice, Mr Denby. You can contact the police and explain that you engaged in a number of sexual acts with a fifteen year old girl last night, and now you're being blackmailed by a man you cannot identify, for a reason you don't understand. I'm sure they'll be lenient…'

'Okay,' he had grunted. 'I'll do whatever you want.'

'That's the spirit, Mr Denby. There's nothing I like more than cooperation. I will phone you again this evening and tell you what you are to do.'

The call had come early this morning.

'You are to locate all the paperwork relating to the McKenzie case you've been working on and give it to me.'

'Is that it? Why?'

'Yours is not to question why, Mr Denby. You are just to do as you are told. You must have all the paperwork; if anything is missing, our deal is off. Do you understand? I will contact you again at midday and tell you where to bring the file. If you try and double-cross me, you will regret it!'

Denby had wasted no time, and had headed to the office immediately. As a partner, he had a set of keys and knew the alarm codes, so was able to enter the building undetected. He had headed straight for the filing cabinet where the McKenzie file should have been, but it had not been there. It was then that he had realised that Nazir must have locked the file away in her desk drawers, so he had returned home and waited till six before phoning her to advise he needed the file. He had tried to sound as calm as possible when speaking to her, anxious not to make her suspicious of his motives. She had said she should be in the office by ten, but there was still no sign of the file.

A knock at his door caught him by surprise and, as he peered out into the corridor, he saw a courier in a helmet staring back.

'I have a parcel for a Mr Simon Denby,' the courier shouted through the door.

At last! It's here.

He opened the door and took the cardboard box from the courier.

'I need you to sign here, here and here,' the courier said, pointing at three boxes on the form on the clipboard.

'Sure,' replied Denby scrawling his signature.

He turned to pass the clipboard back to the courier and was surprised to see the end of a sound suppressor pointing at his head.

'What the…'

'Sit down at the table, Mr Denby,' the courier interrupted. 'Take out your mobile phone and a piece of paper and begin to write what I tell you.'

He knew better than to argue with an armed man. Pulling out a piece of white paper he began to write what he was told. With his back to the courier he did not see the man in the helmet remove a piece of nylon cord from inside his jacket, and slowly start to tie it to the ceiling rose.

THE BIG PICTURE

11:00

Eve Partridge had made something of a small nest for herself in Mercure's office. Mercure had been gone for an hour and a half already but had encouraged Eve to remain at the station if she was worried about her safety. Eve had accepted the offer and had said she could spend the day working through email correspondence on her laptop. She had advised Paul to cancel all the afternoon's public engagements, citing ill health. He had told her he had already rearranged all her meetings for the next week as he suspected she would be busy with other matters.

Eve still wasn't certain if the threat in the letter was real or, as Mercure had suggested, just someone trying to scare her. Her P.A. had been on the phone again, asking her how she was getting on with 'asserting her authority.'

'It's not that easy,' she'd told him.

'Nonsense!' he'd rebuked. 'This is your time, Eve. You need to seize the bull by the horns and take control of what is going on. If the threat is real, the city will need someone it can turn to in its hour of need.'

She had hung up the phone, promising she would take a more pro-active approach when dealing with

Mercure.

The office door opened and Mercure strode purposefully in.

'Eve, you're still here? I thought you might have gone by now.'

'I'm not in the way am I? I can move if there's a spare desk somewhere. I'm up to my eyes dealing with emails from constituents.'

Eve had taken the brave decision of making her work email address available to the people of the city so that they could speak to her directly. More often than not, what she received she was able to delegate to the appropriate council office to resolve. Queries ranged from parking ticket disputes, complaints about striking bin men and the like. On the odd occasion she received a genuine enquiry, but these were the exception to the rule. She had never received a 'thank you' note yet, but she retained the hope of one day doing so.

'I'm not sure that we have any space for you,' Mercure replied dismissively. 'I'm happy with you remaining in here for now. I have an interview with a suspect lined up downstairs and that could last a couple of hours so you should be okay here.'

'That's great,' said Eve smiling. 'I really appreciate it.'

The phone on Mercure's desk rang.

'That's unusual,' Mercure remarked. 'It's an outside call. I've only just had the number changed. Nobody knows what it is.'

Eve shot her a puzzled look.

'This is Detective Chief Inspector Jan Mercure,' she said, lifting the phone to her ear.

'Hi…I…um…' said an anxious voice.

'Hello? Who is this please?'

'A bomb…uh…has been placed in a car…um…outside a school…um…in Southampton…Jesus!…um…the bomb will be detonated at exactly twelve p.m.…oh my God…if you do not locate the device…'

'Who are you?' demanded Mercure. 'What school are you talking about?'

'You must listen carefully if…um…I will only relay this…uh…information once. I am one of you…uh…I walk amongst you…oh, God, please…you do not see me…the restorative process has begun…um…I am in the city. I will not fail…there is nothing you can do to stop me…'

'Listen, I hear what you are saying. We will do whatever it takes, please, just tell me the location of the device.'

'Uh…you have brought this on yourself…there are approximately thirty primary schools in the Southampton area…the device is at the home of the winged lion…uh…you have one hour. Good luck.'

With that the line went dead.

Mercure slammed the phone down and marched out of her office to the incident room where her CID team were working.

'I need someone to trace the number that just phoned my office.'

'I'll do it Guv,' shouted a voice from somewhere in the room.

'Good. Listen up, people. Some lunatic just phoned and said he has planted a bomb in the city. The device is allegedly outside one of the city's thirty primary schools, and is due to detonate at midday today. The bomber has said we are allowed to disarm the weapon if we discover it. Someone get onto the Royal Navy bomb squad and get them over here pronto. I want a list of all the primary schools up on this wall straight away. Drop whatever you are currently working on. Locating this device is number one priority. I need to report this up the line. I'll be back in here in five minutes and I want your full attention.'

Mercure returned to her office.

'Did I just hear you right? There's a bomb in the city? Jesus Christ!'

'Eve, now is not a good time. I'm going to need you to vacate my office. A threat such as this is...' Mercure paused and stared at Eve as she recalled something. 'Your letter,' she said holding out a hand. 'Give me the copy we made.'

Eve passed the piece of paper over, a baffled expression on her face. 'What is it?' she asked.

'The man who spoke...he mentioned...yes, here it is: I walk amongst you but you don't see me. It was as if he was quoting from the letter. The language he used...'

'You think the two threats are related?'

'I don't know...maybe. The man I just spoke to sounded nervous, anxious, there was something edgy about his voice. And the way he spoke, it was...as if he was reading what he was saying. He sounded scared.'

'Did he say which school it was?'

'No. He gave a clue to its identity: the home of the winged lion. That means nothing to me.'

'Me neither. Is there anything I can do to help?'

'Just sit down. I need to phone the Chief Superintendent and then speak with my team. I'm going to get one of my team to interview you about this morning. It seems I may have underestimated the gravity of the letter you received.'

11:02

'Right, team,' Mercure began when she was back in the incident room. 'We are on the clock. The names of all the primary schools in Southampton are written on the board behind me. We are looking for one that would be described as the home of the winged lion. Does that mean anything to anyone?'

There were anxious head shakes around the room.

'Come on, people. What do you think of when you think lion. Shout some stuff out; don't hold back!'

'Richard the Lionheart?' shouted D.C. Oliver Capshaw.

Mercure scanned the list of schools but none referenced King Richard.

'Good, but it's not that. Anybody else?'

'Leo? As in the zodiac?' shouted another voice.

Mercure shook her head. 'No Leos but good try. What else?'

'Maybe it's a school near the airport at Eastleigh? You know, like the winged lion could be a plane?'

'I like the idea. Do me a favour and write the location of the school next to each name on the board. Any other ideas?'

'Guv,' interrupted D.C. Emma Jarvis. 'I've got

the bomb squad on the line. They want to speak to you.'

Mercure moved to Jarvis' desk and accepted the phone.

'Hi Jan, it's Sid Travers, what have you found and where is it?'

It wasn't the first time that a bomb threat had been received in the city, and Mercure had made an effort to develop a good relationship with the Royal Navy's bomb disposal unit for exactly this kind of situation.

'Hi Sid, it's too early to say right now. What we've been told is that the bomb is in a car outside a primary school somewhere in the city.'

'There really are some sick bastards out there, right? How close are you to discovering the location?'

'We're working on it as we speak. We've got till midday to find and disable it.'

'That doesn't give us long. Right, I'll get my team over to you straight away. We'll travel by helicopter as you never know how bad the roads between Portsmouth and Southampton will be. Can you seek permission for us to land on the grass at the Common?'

'I will.'

'I'll also need a couple of cars waiting for us there so that we can get to the location as quickly as possible.'

'Consider it done.'

'Great! I'll contact you when we're up in the air and give you our E.T.A.'

Mercure hung up the phone and returned to the

front of the room. 'Any progress on the winged lion yet?'

D.S. Roger Gillespie approached the board to review the list of names. 'I might have it, Guv,' he answered excitedly. 'I did an internet search for winged lion and allegedly St. Mark the Evangelist is sometimes referred to as the winged lion.'

Mercure stared at the board. 'St. Mark's C of E Primary is on Stafford Road in Shirley, less than ten minutes from here. Get two units over to that school now! Tell them to check out any cars parked near to or in the school grounds. They are to look but not touch. The rest of you, keep checking for winged lion references in case it's not St. Mark's. Good work, Roger.'

Mercure returned to her office, keen to speak to the Detective Superintendent as soon as possible. She had tried and failed to get hold of him once, but he would want to know about this immediately so she would have to keep trying.

'Is there anything I can do to help?' asked Eve, who had followed her back.

'No, Eve, there isn't!'

'Have you any idea who might be behind all this?'

Mercure shook her head.

'Have you thought about leaking the story to the press?'

Mercure shot her look that was a mix of astonishment and loathing.

'Hear me out,' Eve continued. 'At the moment, this bomber, or whoever he is, has the power of anonymity. We don't know who he is or where he is and that gives him the upper hand. If we got the local press involved, suddenly it throws the spotlight on him. Suddenly it will feel like the walls are closing in on him and anyone who is helping him.'

'Are you crazy? The last thing I need is a city plunged into fear because there is a lunatic on the loose! How many parents will demand to know what is going on if they discover someone is targeting schools in the area? There would be pandemonium! No, we have to keep this quiet at the moment, try not to draw any unnecessary attention to what we are doing. For all we know, thrusting the spotlight, as you describe it, onto our bomber might push him over the edge and cause him to actually detonate a device, rather than just threatening. Leave it to my team; we're very good at what we do.'

Eve blushed slightly. She had carefully thought about how she could justify getting the press involved. She had been about to volunteer to coordinate media efforts before Mercure had declined the suggestion.

'Guv,' said Gillespie from the doorway. 'You were phoned from a mobile number. The phone is now turned off so we can't triangulate where the call came from, however, it is a registered number so I'm just waiting to hear who it belongs to.'

'Good. We'll send a unit to the address as soon as we have it.'

11:12

Eve stomped from Mercure's office and headed for the canteen downstairs. She was pleased to find it virtually empty, although a couple of men were playing pool in a far corner. They were deep in conversation and didn't even notice her enter the large room and move out of sight behind a wall. She pulled her phone out and pressed redial. Paul answered a moment later.

'How's it going down there?' he asked cheerily, excited by the prospect of their clandestine activities.

'Not well...I can't seem to get Mercure to open up to me. She keeps shutting me out.'

'Ah, hang in there, Eve. I'm sure we can still manipulate the situation so you come out shining. We have to believe that's why you got that note this morning: it's a sign that someone wants you back on top.'

'You'll never guess what's going on down here now. A bomb has been planted in a car somewhere...outside a school of all places.'

'Jesus Christ! What kind of sick bastard would do that? Which school is it?'

'That's just it: they're not sure. The person who phoned it in gave some cryptic clue to its location and from that they believe they know which school, but they're not certain.'

'So what are they doing about it?'

'They've called for the Royal Navy's bomb disposal unit to be flown in to attempt to diffuse the device.'

'So they're putting all their eggs in one basket with this school?'

'It would appear so, yes.'

'What if they're wrong?'

'Exactly! I can't bear the idea of a bomb exploding and killing innocent children.'

'Which school do they think it is?'

'St Mark's in Shirley. It's a Church of England primary school.'

'Sounds like you know it well; have you ever been there?'

'I attended the school's harvest festival last year. It was quite sweet actually.'

'So you know the Headteacher?'

'Yes. Why?'

Paul was quiet for a moment.

'Paul? Are you still there?'

'I was just thinking is all…'

'Thinking? What about?'

'How quickly could you get to the school?'

'I don't know. Ten minutes if I caught a taxi. Why?'

'Well, Mercure's probably not going to let you tag along with her…but, what if you had an appointment with the Head? Let's say your meeting ends as the bomb squad arrives…you'd be on hand to answer any questions that the local press might have…'

'Press? What press? The media are out of the loop on this: Mercure's orders. I suggested to her that we could leak the story to the local media, to help turn the spotlight on whoever is behind all this, but she made it perfectly clear that that was not an avenue she wished to pursue...'

'You could leak the story,' Paul interrupted. 'You've got contacts at BBC Radio. Give them an anonymous call and give them a tip-off in exchange for an exclusive interview with you in return.'

'Mercure would go berserk if she found out I leaked it.'

'That's why they will have to agree that the tip-off is anonymous. You see? They are not obliged to reveal their sources to the police.'

'I don't know, Paul...it all seems so underhand...'

'Eve, listen to me; none of this is your fault. It's not your fault that whoever is behind all this chose to leave a letter at your house this morning, nor is it your fault that he has decided to plant a bomb at a school...but this is your opportunity. Sure, it's sneaky, but nobody ever said you could win without getting your hands dirty.'

'Okay, Paul,' she sighed. 'You're right. I'll do it...I just hope this doesn't end up backfiring later on.'

Eve hung up the call and located the number for Karen Pallot at the local BBC radio station. She had known Karen for a number of years, and had used the journalist to help her launch her political career, agreeing to a series of interviews about how she would change the city for the better. Unfortunately their relationship had cooled somewhat since the expenses scandal.

'Karen? It's Eve Partridge. Can you spare me two minutes for the biggest story of the year?'

'This better be good, Eve. I'm not willing to let you use me to justify what happened at that hotel.'

'No, no, listen, I've got a great scoop for you; nobody else knows about it...this could really help you secure that role in London you've always dreamed about...'

'Okay,' Karen yielded, 'what is it?'

'First, you need to agree to treat this as an anonymous tip-off. If the police find out I've spoken with you, I'll be out of the loop.'

'This doesn't sound good, Eve. I'm not sure I want to be involved...'

'It's nothing bad, I assure you, well, not like you're thinking anyway. Look, agree to keep it as anonymous and I'll tell you what is going on. If you don't like what you hear, you can still walk away. Okay?'

'Okay. Continue.'

Eve quickly looked around to make sure nobody could hear her; the two officers playing pool had left the canteen, so, for now, she was alone.

'The city is under siege,' she began. 'We think a lunatic has planted a bomb in a car outside of St Mark's Primary in Shirley. He has warned the police by phone and it is due to detonate in...' Eve checked her watch. 'In forty-five minutes. The D.C.I. in charge has called in the Royal Navy's bomb disposal unit, but this might just be the first of a series of calculated attacks on the city.'

'Where are you getting all this, Eve?'

'I've been at the police station all day. The lunatic sent me a letter this morning warning that he would attack the city. If you want this exclusive Karen, you need to act fast.'

'Okay, okay. So are you prepared to go on the record?'

'Not yet. Meet me at the school in the next half an hour. If the bomb is there and if it is successfully diffused, I will tell you everything I know…on the record.'

'I'll need to run this past my manager, first…'

'There isn't the time, Karen,' Eve interrupted. 'It's now or never. Tell him you're going out for an early lunch and come and meet me. He'll understand when he realises what is happening. We need to keep this between ourselves for now; I don't want anyone else becoming aware. Is that understood?'

'Okay. I'll be at the school in fifteen minutes. Won't it be cordoned off? How will we get close?'

'The police don't want to alarm anybody unnecessarily so their investigations will be brief and limited. If they start cordoning the area off, it will draw attention to what is going on and that is not what Mercure wants. She is hoping to keep this whole crisis under wraps.'

'So why are you telling me?'

'I believe the public deserve to know if their lives are in danger. It's in the public interest.'

Eve wasn't even sure she believed the line she had just spun, but she hoped Karen bought it.

'I'll meet you there,' Eve said, disconnecting the line and placing the phone back into her handbag.

She took a couple of deep breaths, to control her nerves, and then walked hurriedly from the police station to a nearby taxi rank. She really hoped Paul's idea didn't make matters worse.

11:20

White looked around the dark room, an increasing unease growing. Five men had been rounded up and were currently facing the back wall of the room, their hands secured behind their backs whilst identification was established. The small table in the centre of the room was covered in cards and cash with a cloud of smoke hovering just above it. The shutters at the front of the shop had been secured with a padlock as they had started the raid, choosing to barge in through the back to catch their rats in the trap. A group of five men playing poker and smoking cannabis joints was hardly the picture of the illegal casino that Hoxley had painted.

'There's no sign of him, Guv,' Danny Strong yawned.

White cursed under his breath. Hoxley had given them the agreed signal outside of the shop to indicate that McManus was inside with his captains discussing the crystal meth deal. McManus was not one of the five restrained men against the wall. Neither was Hoxley.

'Where is the little shite?' White shouted.

Strong wasn't certain if the D.I. meant Hoxley or McManus.

'I think Hoxley bolted as soon as we had

padlocked the shutters. As for McManus, there is nothin' here to suggest he was ever in the room.'

'Who are the five twats we found?'

'Lowlife gamblers, Guv. I recognise a couple of them from previous arrests, but I don't think any of them are part of McManus' network.'

'I want this room turned over; do you hear me? I want every drawer emptied, every sneak hole found. We are not leaving here until we have looked at everything. Is that understood?'

'Yes, Guv,' Strong replied, rolling his eyes behind White's back, frustrated that his shift just got extended further.

White approached the small table. He emptied the contents of the ash tray onto the green table cloth and picked through the butts with a biro. McManus tended to smoke cigars rather than cigarettes, but White was eager to learn whether the Scot had ever been in the room, or whether Hoxley had dared to lie to him. It was impossible for him to see whether there was cigar ash amongst the tobacco and cannabis, so he called one of the P.C.s over and asked him to bag it up and get forensics to take a look.

He next moved over to the five men at the wall.

'I want to know if Jock McManus was here earlier. I have a hundred quid for the first of you to speak and confirm it.'

There was no answer. The five continued staring at the wall.

'Did you bastards not hear me?' White bellowed. 'There's a hundred quid for the first one to squeak. Was McManus here?'

The wall of silence remained. White grabbed the wrists of the man closest to him and shoved, causing the man's face to knock straight into the wall. White continued to exert pressure until the man started to groan.

'Where is McManus?' White sneered.

'I don't know who that is,' the man winced.

'Don't bullshit me! I know he was here, I just need you to confirm it.'

'It was just us lot. We was only playin' cards and havin' a smoke.'

White released his grip but repeated the gesture on the next man in line, this time twisting the man's wrists as he pushed.

'Ah, shite, you're gonna break m'arm,' the man yelped.

'Tell me what I want to know and I'll let you go.'

'Your man's right: he wasn't here!'

'Ah, but you know him?'

'Who doesn't know him? He wasn't here!'

White released the man's wrists and stomped over to Strong, who was examining the contents of a desk in the opposite corner of the room.

'You found anything?'

'Nothing illegal, Guv,' Strong replied, holding up some papers. 'There are some blueprints for a factory down south, but there's nothing wrong with that.'

'Unless they're planning a job.'

'There's no other evidence suggesting a job. To be honest, Guv, I think Hoxley has stitched us up. I don't think McManus was ever here, besides, all we've got is a group of delinquents smoking a bit of pot behind closed doors. There isn't even enough here to do them for intent to supply.'

White examined the blueprints briefly before passing them back and telling Strong to bag them up for closer inspection later.

'I need a breath of fresh air,' White said, excusing himself and walking outside. He lit a cigarette and exhaled his feelings of frustration. The D.C.I. would want to know why he had sanctioned a surveillance operation without permission and, the fact that it hadn't yielded any leads would not go in White's favour. He thumped his hand down on the roof of the car. It was at that point he spotted the skulking figure of David Hoxley no more than a hundred yards away. White spat out the cigarette and set off after Hoxley who duly began running in the opposite direction.

White was in no shape to be chasing down a suspect. Thankfully, Hoxley was in no shape to be running from a policeman, and White had soon made up the distance between them. He tackled Hoxley to the ground and secured his wrists with a plastic strip. White lifted him back to his feet and tried to get his breath back.

'You bastard!' he began. 'You set me up, you little shite. People have died for less than that.'

'I'm sorry, Mr White,' Hoxley sputtered. 'I didn't have a choice, like! The meeting was supposed to be there today, but someone tipped McManus off that you were heading there. He cornered me, like, and accused me of talking t'you. He said if I didn't play along, he would kill m'sister's kids. I had no choice!'

White lashed out, landing a punch in Hoxley's

midriff. 'You cannot be a slave to two masters. You have another important choice to make now, David: are you going to help me or help McManus? The first way is guaranteed to end in pain and prison, but if you help me, you may live through this mess.'

'You know I want to help you, Mr White…but m'sister's kids, like…'

'McManus is full of piss and wind! He won't hurt your family…I won't let him. Help me nail the bastard and he'll never bother you again.'

White released the plastic strip and put an arm around Hoxley's shoulders. 'Find out where the shipment is coming in and tell me. That's all you have to do. If I can catch him with the crystal meth, it'll force my superiors to look into all his other illegal activity. He'll go away for a long time, I promise you.'

'Okay, Mr White, I'll try and find out where and when. Can you get, like, a police car to sit outside m'sister's place? Y'know, to make sure she's safe, like?'

'I will,' White lied, before allowing Hoxley to go on his way. White slowly made his way back to the bookies, where he found Strong standing by their car, holding more papers.

'What's all this?' White asked.

'I found a loose floorboard under that poker table and this stuff was inside. It doesn't tie McManus to anything here, but it's copies of more blueprints.'

'And? Another building?'

'Well you're not going to believe this, Guv: they're blueprints for a bus.'

11:25

Aaron Cross brushed a piece of white lint from his sleeve and watched it float slowly to the ground. He checked his watch again. He'd been awake and wearing full dress uniform since seven o'clock!

Discipline, son: that's what you need.

His uncle's words. No man had had a more profound impact on his life than his uncle.

The navy will make you a man.

Those words seemed so ironic now.

Aaron had been conceived twenty-nine years earlier in the back of a builder's van. His mother: a young and naïve sales assistant walking home alone one cold and dark December evening. His father: a cruel bully who preyed on defenceless women. Aaron's conception was not the result of love.

Subsequently raised in a variety of halfway houses and care homes following his mother's demise, Aaron's early years saw him cautioned for shoplifting, criminal damage and assault.

'It's not his fault,' his aunt would plead. 'He needs a chance.'

Aunt Marilyn: a kind and gentle woman, but not someone you wanted in a crisis. He did miss her.

On his sixteenth birthday, Aaron learned that the man who had raped his mother all those years ago had been released from prison. He had decided to pay the old man a visit and found him celebrating his newly found freedom in the corner of a dark and dingy pub.

He had approached the table in an effort to engage the old man in conversation but, he had lost his nerve at the last minute and had continued past the table to the toilets. When he had re-emerged, the old man was gone. Aaron had hurried out of the pub and caught a glimpse of him stumbling up the road. It hadn't taken Aaron long to catch up.

'You okay, mate?' the youngster had asked.

'Fuck off!'

That was it. The first exchange between father and son.

'You remember Annie Cross?'

'What? Fuck off!'

The old man's words were slurred and he was incapable of walking in a straight line. Aaron hadn't felt empathy; not even pity. He saw the man for what he was: a despicable human being.

'Annie Cross was my mother,' he had continued.

It had done the trick. The old man had stopped still and eyed the youth cautiously.

'And? I don't know her,' the old man had protested.

Aaron's blood had begun to boil. 'Don't do that! Don't ignore the role you played in her demise. I know you know who I mean.'

'Look kid, you don't want to mess with me, you hear. I just got out of prison. Why don't you just beat it before I get angry?'

Aaron could remember launching himself at the

older man, but had no recollection of what happened next, until his uncle dragged him off the beaten and bloody body slumped on the floor.

'Stop, Aaron,' Uncle Troy had commanded. 'Step away. Now!'

Aaron had obeyed immediately; such was his uncle's tone.

'I know you're angry, and you have every right to be. What this…scum…did to your mother was unforgiveable but you can't do it like this. One more arrest and you'll be locked up yourself. Go and wait in my car.'

'But…' he had started to say, the look his uncle had given him had been enough to end the protest.

Aaron had walked over to the car. His uncle had joined him five minutes later. Watching him climb into the driver's seat, Aaron had observed his uncle wipe a line of blood from his trusty penknife. He knew not to ask what had happened.

'That scum won't trouble this family again, Aaron. It's time to put it out of your mind and start your own life. Your aunt and I have always looked out for you since…Annie passed away…but we're not going to be around forever. Discipline, son: that's what you need.'

On the journey home, Aaron had listened to his uncle speak candidly about life in the military.

'It's not a job. It's not even a career. It's a way of life. The navy will make you a man. You want to make something of yourself? I'm giving you the chance. I can pull some strings and get you an interview.'

Aaron had been uncertain, but had respected his

uncle's wishes and signed up. Twelve years on, and now a Lieutenant, his life was very much on the straight and narrow. He was due to give a eulogy at this morning's funeral and was still not sure why he had been asked instead of Troy's son, Harry. He decided he would ask Harry when they met up later.

He looked down at his uniform and wondered again whether it was right to wear this to his uncle's funeral. Whilst Troy had once preached the naval way of life, his opinion had changed somewhat in recent years. Returning from active duty in the Middle East in 2005, Troy had instigated an ugly confrontation with an Admiral, whom Troy believed had not acted in the best interests of the service. Troy had ended the disagreement by punching the Admiral in full view of his peers, a crime that had led to a formal disciplinary committee demoting him. Troy had served his notice the moment the decision had been read aloud, no longer prepared to put up with the hypocrisy he had witnessed.

Aaron had read all about the incident and had feared that his uncle's actions might stand in the way of his own promotion hopes, but thankfully, that had not been the case. Aaron had never spoken to Troy about the real reason he had assaulted the Admiral, but he was pretty sure his uncle wouldn't have acted without a good reason.

Troy had taken what savings he had had and invested it abroad, spending half his time in the UK and the remainder travelling across Europe. They had lost touch in the last couple of years, although Aaron had still received a card at Christmas and on his birthday.

Aaron was considering changing into a civilian suit and tie when his mobile phone rang. Recognising Harry's caller ID, he answered it.

'Morning, Harry. How you holding up?'

'Yeah, I'm as well as can be expected, cuz. Did I wake you?'

'Ha! Don't worry about that; I've been up since six. It's the training.'

'Oh yeah, sure.'

'What couldn't wait till later? You need me to do something?'

'No, no, nothing like that. Sorry, Aaron. I…do you…do you think we could have a catch-up after…well, y'know…at the wake?'

'Sure, sure, of course we can.'

'Good, good. You sticking around for a while?'

'I'll be here till the weekend but then I need to get back to base.'

'There's something I need to talk to you about.'

'Is everything okay, Harry? You don't sound like yourself.'

'Everything's fine. We'll chat later. I'll see you at half twelve.'

Harry hung up. Aaron put the phone back in his pocket, wondering exactly what his cousin had phoned up for.

11:41

Royal Navy Commander Sid Travers did not look pleased as he stepped out of the squad car and walked over to where D.C.I. Mercure was waiting.

'The press, Jan? You really think they're a good idea?'

'Press? What press?' Mercure replied looking around for whom the man in dark Kevlar was referring to.

'There,' Travers said, pointing at M.P. Eve Partridge and a skinny looking woman next to her, eagerly scribbling into a note pad.

'Sid, I didn't...I'll deal with that later. In the meantime, we've not found anything suspicious yet. I've had four of my officers looking for anything odd in the cars parked in the vicinity of the school.'

'Is there a chance we're at the wrong place?'

'The bomber's clue points to this school so I don't believe so...we've considered all the other Primary schools for links back to the 'winged lion' but haven't found anything. My gut tells me this is the right place.'

'Okay, well, I'll disperse my men out to join the search. We need to clear the immediate area. Depending on the size of the device, we need to ensure there is no immediate danger to anyone. That includes evacuating the school. Have you spoken to the Head yet?'

'Not yet. I've only just arrived on scene and, to be honest, I was hoping to avoid telling the school anything.'

'With respect, Jan, that move is both reckless and against the rule book. If we don't find the device, or we're unable to disarm it and it detonates...let's just say I wouldn't want to be in your shoes.'

'Okay, okay, I'll go and speak with her.'

'Skipper, I think I've found it,' said one of Travers' men, rushing over to them. 'There's a device and timer under a four-by-four parked opposite the school. The hood is cool so the vehicle has been there at least an hour.'

'Good work! Get Malky working on disarming it, the rest of you double-check for secondary devices under the remaining vehicles. We need to move quickly: the school has yet to be evacuated.'

The man nodded and jogged off, shouting orders at two of his team.

Travers checked his watch. 'Jan, we've got eighteen minutes until boom, which gives you five minutes to get that school empty.'

Mercure rushed over to the school. She scowled at Eve as she did.

'Clearly, there's a woman you've pissed off!' Karen Pallet observed. 'Is that the woman leading the investigation?'

'It is,' Eve confirmed. 'Where were we?'

'You said you received a letter this morning warning of calculated attacks.'

'That's right. I was shocked by the nature of the

letter and took it straight to the police.'

'And what was their reaction?'

'If I'm honest, Karen, I don't think the threat was considered serious. In fact, it was dismissed out of hand as the writings of a lunatic. Perhaps if it had been taken more seriously, we wouldn't be in this situation…'

'And you said someone phoned the police station to give a warning about this device?'

'That's right. I was there when the warning was relayed.'

'And what was the police response to the phone call?'

'Oh that's when panic set in, I think. Suddenly they realised what I had known all along: the threat was serious. It was like all hands to the pump.'

'And the bomber didn't actually state it was this school where the bomb was planted?'

'Not exactly, no. He hinted that it might be this school, but gave nothing concrete.'

'So what you're saying is: the bomb could actually be located at a different school? A school with no knowledge of what might be awaiting them?'

'Yes. How many innocent lives could be taken today because the police have made the wrong call? It sickens me, Karen, it really does.'

'Well it looks like they might have found something,' Karen observed, nodding towards the four-by-four.'

'Hopefully they've been lucky,' Eve continued. 'But what happens if they're not so lucky next time?'

Karen continued scribbling notes. 'I'd better call my editor and tell him exactly what is going on.

Mercure was headed towards the school so this story is going to leak out soon enough, so it's best if we get the scoop. Thanks, Eve. Once I've spoken to him, we'll get some audio clips to use on the radio. That okay?'

'Sure.'

The Royal Naval Captain known as 'Malky' was stretched out on his back, beneath the four-by-four. He had carefully examined the box and could not find any kind of tamper-contingency, meaning he could remove the lid of the box and take a closer look at what lay beneath. It was a warm day, and, whilst the Kevlar outfit he was wearing would provide some meagre protection should the device detonate, it was raising his body temperature, causing him to sweat. In all, he had disarmed fifty bombs of one shape or another, both home and abroad. He was the most-experienced member of the team, but that didn't mean he was feeling overly confident at the moment. He was filled with feelings of anxiety every time he got close to a bomb, but the adrenalin that he also felt was an addiction he was not prepared to kick.

The device was made of some kind of steel or iron, and it looked like a strong adhesive had been used to attach it to the vehicle's chassis, meaning he would have to diffuse it in situ. He picked up a pair of pliers and studied the wiring from the small amount of semtex, to the circuit and then to a cheap digital watch face. The timer was counting down and told him he had fifteen minutes to figure out how to disarm it.

'What are we looking at?' he heard Travers ask

from the side of the car.

'Right, skipper, I've got about two hundred grams of semtex conventionally wired to a small circuit board. There are three wires: red, blue and black. It looks like the circuit is using the timer's battery for power, so I think we'll need to bypass that in order to remove the timer. The device looks homemade and is the least complicated device I've seen for a while. I'd say whoever built it has some knowledge of bomb-making but the device looks like it wasn't supposed to be discovered as even a novice could disarm it.'

'That's odd. If it wasn't supposed to be found, why the tip-off?'

'No idea, skipper. Can you pass me the battery pack and the rest of my tools? I should have it disarmed in the next two minutes. Removing it is going to be a bit more of a challenge, but I'll see what I can do.'

Travers climbed to his feet, confident the captain would do as he had said.

Mercure reappeared at the school gates and Travers walked over to her.

'I've spoken with the Head and she is moving the children and teachers out through the back of the school. They have a substantial sports field so they will wait at the far side of it until we tell them all is okay.'

'How did she react to the news?'

'To her credit she was calm and collected. Has your man made any progress?'

'Luckily, he should have it dismantled in the next five minutes. I should warn you though we found two hundred grams of semtex under the vehicle, which is enough to destroy anything within a one hundred metre radius. It wouldn't have killed many in the school, but there certainly would have been some casualties.'

'So you think the school wasn't the target?'

'I'm not saying that. I've no idea what this lunatic's motivation is. What I'm telling you is that he will strike again.'

'How can you be so sure?'

'Semtex traditionally comes in kilogram blocks. He's only used a fifth of one block. For all we know, he may have more than one block, in which case, I think we should be prepared for further devices.'

Travers allowed the statement to sink in, before continuing. 'There's another thing: I think the only reason we found this device is for the bomber to prove how serious he is. I can't think of any other reason that you were given the warning. Jan, this threat is real. I think it's time to activate the Gold protocol: there's a terrorist on the loose and he has a reason to hurt this city.'

'Guv,' yelled a D.C. from one of the squad cars. 'We've got an address for the owner of the phone used to make the warning call.'

11:48

Lewis Read crushed the empty can of lager with his hand. Patterson warned him not to spill any dregs on the leather upholstery. They were in the car and had nearly reached their destination.

'My supplier lives just up here on the left,' Patterson commented.

Lewis wasn't really paying attention; the three beers he had consumed, along with the two joints he had shared with Patterson, had put him in a dream-like state.

'Hey, what's going on?' Patterson asked rhetorically, as he saw a friend flagging the car down. He pulled over and wound down the passenger window. 'What's up, homes?' he asked the youth who had been waving frantically. The youth got in the back of the car, shouting, 'Just drive, dude. Keep going. Don't stop at the house.'

Patterson did as he was instructed. He drove to the end of the road and turned right, before speeding up to put some distance between them and the road they had just been on.

'We missed the house,' Lewis observed, oblivious to the newcomer in the back of the car.

Patterson had spotted the police cordon tape as they had driven past the address. 'Why are the fuzz at the house?' he asked the youth in the back.

'Shit, man! You ain't heard the news? The house was raided yesterday, man. It's all part of that Operation Fortress shit. They're monitoring whose coming and going from the place still. If you'd stopped, they'd have had you in for questioning too.'

'Where's Archie?'

'They arrested him, man. He was there when they stormed the place. He's gone, man. He's looking at serious time inside. They found a shit-load of gear and some weapons that he was holding onto for his supplier. You're gonna have to find yourself a new dealer.'

'Ah shit! That's all I need. I was due to pick up a bulk score for this weekend.'

'It's all gone, man. The house is empty.'

Patterson's mind was racing as he continued to put distance between them and the house.

'Yo, you can drop me up here, bro,' the youth said. Patterson pulled the car over and thanked the youth for his help.

'Who was that?' Lewis asked, as he heard the back door close.

'Just a friend; we scored gear off the same dealer.'

'Are we not collecting any weed now?'

Patterson considered Lewis for a moment. 'You're wasted, man! Shit, you're even drooling a bit.'

Lewis wiped his mouth and tried to clear his mind. It felt like his head was in a bubble. He didn't expect Patterson to slap him around the face, but the jolt helped his senses.

'What you going to do?' Lewis asked once the car

was moving again.

Patterson shook his head. 'I'm not sure. Archie was my supplier. I'd already paid him for what I was due to collect, but now the fuzz have it. Son of a bitch!'

'Well why not just go to your supplier's supplier? Y'know: the importer.'

'I told you: it doesn't work like that! Archie would have to introduce me.'

'But Archie's been arrested and owes you gear, so go and tell the importer. If your mate Archie was one of his regular dealers, there must be a vacancy in the operation. You said yourself that you wanted to move up the ladder; maybe this is your chance to do so.'

'I'm not so sure.'

'Look, do you know who the importer is or where he is?'

'I think I know who he is...Archie has mentioned his name before, and I think I know where he operates...he is a South African with a number of legit businesses in the city.'

'Great! Well let's go and see him then.'

'Us?'

'Sure, why not? I can be very persuasive when I want. Besides, maybe he'll take us more seriously if we are a team.'

'You want me to cut you in on my operation? You don't even know how to roll a joint!'

'I'm a fast learner. You want to make more money and I want to make money. I want what you have: a car, a place of my own. Come on, you could teach me the ropes. Think about it: two of us means we could shift twice the load. I may not know much about drugs, but I have good business skills.'

'You're serious, aren't you?'

'Deadly. You have the contacts and the street-smarts, but I can help turn it into a real business; one where we both make bucket-loads of cash.'

Patterson pulled the car into a parking space outside of a fast-food establishment, advertising kebabs and burgers.

'I need you to understand what you are proposing. Buying and selling dope is against the law. If you're caught and charged, mummy and daddy won't be able to bail you out of it. You'll be charged and may go to prison. You sure your skinny ass can handle that?'

Lewis looked him in the eye. 'I understand the risks. I'm not just saying this because I'm stoned. I want in.'

'Okay, well let's say we do go to see the South African, and he refuses to do business with us. What then?'

'At the very least, he can put you in touch with another dealer at Archie's level who can arrange what you need for this weekend.'

Patterson considered his options for a moment. 'Okay, okay. We'll go and see the South African, but before we do, you need to sober up a bit. We'll get some food and pay him a visit after.'

'Great,' Lewis beamed. 'I'm starving!'

11:57

Nazir Ahmed opened the door of the taxi and clambered out. She had visited Simon Denby's apartment on only one previous occasion: his house-warming party. Despite having worked with him for the last four years, she really knew very little about him: he worked at the firm; his apartment had a sea view and was in the popular and luxurious Ocean Village, not far from the city's shops. He obviously earned a decent wage to be able to afford the rent or mortgage on this place!

The RAC man had arrived within half an hour of her discovering the punctured tyre at the car park. He had reminded her that his primary role was to fix engine troubles and that the company was not to be misused for changing flat tyres. She had been quite taken aback by his attitude, but, once she had explained she was pregnant, and in no fit state to be changing tyres, his mood mellowed slightly and he said he would see what he could do. Thankfully he had a jack in his van and soon had the car raised sufficiently to remove the now flat tyre.

He had asked where her spare tyre was and she had guided him to the boot. However, upon opening the boot, she was disappointed when he pointed out that her that her spare tyre was also flat. It was only at this point that she remembered she had not bought a new tyre following the last time she had had a puncture.

'There's nothing I can do,' he told her. 'You're going to need to buy a new tyre and a spare and get them fitted. The car cannot be driven in this condition as it's illegal. The best thing I can suggest is phoning a friend and asking them to tow you to your nearest tyre centre so they can fit them.'

'Can you not get me there?'

'I'm afraid not. I can't even offer to tow you myself. Sorry.'

Frustrated, she had watched him drive away, but, conscious of the urgency of delivering the McKenzie file to Simon, she had decided to abandon the car in the car park until she could figure out what to do with it. She had called a taxi and now here she was: Simon's apartment.

She approached the main door to the building and located Simon's name on the doorbell panel, before buzzing for him to let her in. There was no response, so she buzzed again; surprised that he might have gone out when he should have been expecting the file. She checked her mobile to see if she had any new missed calls from him, but there were none.

Strange, she thought. Surely he would have phoned to chase me up again.

She pressed the buzzer again, but he still didn't answer. She was about to try and phone him when another resident appeared at the main door and opened it to leave.

'I'm here to see Simon Denby in apartment

twenty,' she said, hoping the man would take pity and let her in. It didn't matter as he didn't seem to care as he held the door open for her.

Some security!

Nazir caught the lift up to the fourth floor and, as she neared Simon's apartment, she was surprised to see that his front door was ajar. She pushed it open wider with her foot and called out his name as she entered.

'Simon? It's Nazir. I've brought you the McKenzie file,' she repeated, a little louder this time. 'Simon?'

She pushed open the door to the living room and screamed as she saw him hanging from the ceiling rose. She didn't move at first, unable to comprehend what she was witnessing. His body was still and his face was a dark red colour.

Is this some kind of sick joke?

She didn't know whether to approach him, so phoned for an ambulance instead.

'Hello? Yes…ambulance please…and police…it's my boss, he's…I think he's committed suicide…Oh God.'

Nazir collapsed to the floor as she broke into sobs. She managed to relay the address to the operator on the line. As she rocked back and forth, she didn't hear the sound of someone else entering the apartment. It wasn't until she heard the crackle of the policeman's radio that she realised she was not alone. She caught her breath as he crouched down next to her.

'Miss? Can you tell me what happened here?' the officer asked.

Nazir pointed at the body. 'That's my boss. His name is Simon. I think he's...'

The officer helped Nazir to her feet and led her through to the kitchen and sat her down on a chair. He asked her who she was, how long she'd been here and whether she'd called an ambulance.

'Yes I did,' she replied. 'I told the operator to send an ambulance as well as the police. You got here fast!'

The officer observed her for a moment before admitting, 'We weren't called here about the suicide, Miss. Someone made a phone call from this apartment earlier this morning and told us that a bomb had been left in the city.'

'What? Why? You think it was Simon?'

'I'm not at liberty to say at this time. The number that called was withheld, however, we were able to trace the number to this address.'

'What? But Simon's not...there must be some kind of mistake...he wouldn't...'

Another uniformed officer appeared at the door and asked his colleague to follow him to the bedroom. Nazir was asked to remain in the kitchen. The two officers walked into the bedroom and found a dozen or so black and white photographs scattered across the bed sheets. The photographs showed the victim with a young girl in several compromising positions. On top of the photographs was a handwritten suicide note, signed by Simon Denby.

12:01

Aaron Cross handed a twenty pound note over to the minicab driver and told him to keep the change. He climbed out of the cab and walked towards the crematorium, flattening some small creases from his uniform. For a moment he wondered whether he had come to the right place. He didn't recognise any faces and it looked more like a business conference than a funeral. Men outnumbered women by two to one at least, and those men were dressed in tailored business suits. He was about to phone his cousin, when he recognised Harry's younger brother at the door welcoming guests. Aaron walked over to him and offered a hand.

'Toby, I'm your cousin, Aaron, I don't know if you remember me?'

The fifteen year old looked up and smiled when he recognised Aaron's face. He reached out and hugged him.

'I was so sorry to hear about your dad's passing,' Aaron offered. 'How are you holding up?'

Poor kid, Aaron empathised, only fifteen and he's lost both parents.

'It's not easy,' the youth began, choking back tears.

'Is Harry around?'

Toby looked around and then shook his head. 'I saw him earlier, but I'm not sure where he is now. Maybe he's talking to the funeral director.'

'Okay, that's fine, I'm sure I'll see him later. If there's anything you need, please just ask.'

The young lad nodded and Aaron decided he should head into the building and give him some space. On entering, he heard several voices speaking in a host of different European tongues and it surprised him that his Uncle Troy had known so many people. He was disappointed, though not surprised, that there were no former naval colleagues present.

'You must be Aaron?' asked a woman from behind him, her accent Italian.

He turned and saw a strikingly beautiful woman with dark brown hair smiling at him.

'Do I know you?' he asked, smiling sheepishly.

I really hope I do.

'My name is Victoria, I was Troy's...I knew your uncle very well. He spoke of a nephew called Aaron who is in the navy. You are the only man here in uniform, so I presume you are him?'

Aaron offered a hand, which she duly shook. Her face really didn't fit with the rest of the room. She couldn't have been much older than thirty-five; her face looked virtually wrinkle-free. Her hair was thick, wavy at the edges and shone beneath the lights above. She could have been a model and her curves were accentuated by the knee-length black dress she was wearing.

'How did you know my uncle?' he asked.

She glanced around to check that they could not

be overheard and then whispered, 'we were lovers.'

The surprise admission caused Aaron to choke on his own saliva and he duly coughed.

'Please don't tell his sons; Troy hadn't told them we were dating, and I'm not sure how they would take the news.'

'How...when...why?' Aaron began, not sure what he wanted to ask first.

'I met your uncle two years ago. He was staying at a hotel in my village. He was very charming and he had a zest for life that was infectious.'

'Where is your village? Your English is very good.'

'Thank you. I was born and raised in Bacoli, on the coast near Naples, but I studied at university here in the UK.'

'How did you meet Troy?'

'We were introduced at a party in my village. He told me I was the most beautiful woman he had ever met and he wanted to spend the rest of his life making me happy. I thought he was cute and I agreed to spend some time with him whilst he was in Naples. He was so romantic and kind and I fell in love with him.'

Aaron was surprised to hear about this softer side of his uncle. He remembered back to that fateful night when Troy had executed the man who had raped Aaron's mother Annie.

'You don't believe me?' asked Victoria, noticing his frown.

'What? No, sorry,' he offered. 'The way you describe him, he doesn't sound like the man I knew, that's all.'

'He told me you two had not spoken for a few years. You should know he was very upset to lose contact with you. He thought of you like a son and he was very proud to hear you had become a lieutenant.'

I missed you too, Uncle Troy.

'Who are all these people?' Aaron asked. I don't think I recognise anyone.'

'Troy knew a lot of people. He was always meeting with bankers and politicians. He will be greatly missed. He just had a way with people. Do you know what your uncle did when he left the navy?'

'Not really, no. It was because he left the navy that I think we lost touch. I don't think he wanted to remember what he had left behind.'

'Troy was a very important person. Do you understand what I am saying?'

Aaron shrugged. 'No, not really. He was an investor, or something?'

'Oh God, you really don't know…forget I said anything.'

Victoria turned and walked away.

'Wait,' said Aaron, chasing after her. 'What's going on? Why did you walk away?'

'Please, Aaron, I thought you knew. Forget I said anything. We should go in, the casket will arrive soon. It was nice to meet you.'

Aaron grabbed her wrist as she tried to walk away again.

'Listen, I don't know you and I don't know what you know about my uncle, but clearly there's something going on here.'

Victoria glanced around again, before removing a white envelope from her handbag. Aaron saw it had his name scrawled in Troy's handwriting.

'I found this amongst your uncle's things,' she said. 'I assume he wanted you to have it.'

'What is it?'

'I don't know. Your uncle kept his...work life...private from his personal life. I don't know what it contains, but don't open it here. Wait until you are alone. Put it away quickly.'

Aaron did as he was instructed and placed the envelope in the inside pocket of his suit jacket. When he looked up for Victoria, she was gone. Before he could begin looking for her again, he saw the crowd being directed in to take their seats. The casket had arrived.

12:25

D.I. Tony White was angry by the time he reached the art gallery. This morning's failed bust at the defunct bookies had left him more than a little frustrated. Hoxley's admission that someone had tipped Jock McManus off about the raid didn't sit comfortably either. The only people who had known about the bust were his closest confidant D.S. Danny Strong and the two uniforms they had collared at the last minute. Strong had been in the car with him all day so it couldn't have been him, but could it really have been one of the P.C.s? It didn't feel right but there was no other answer.

He had been chasing McManus for so long now, yet he didn't feel any closer to nailing the bastard than when he had first caught wind of the illegal activity operating within the city limits. McManus was like a snake: slithering from one crime to the next, avoiding detection and without getting his hands dirty. Yet, to the average person in the street, he was still regarded as the city's saviour: the man who had helped put the Geordies back on the map!

White had always despised the kind of person who walked between the raindrops without ever getting wet. It was one of the reasons he had first joined the force. He had wanted to serve. He had wanted to protect his beloved city, but now the challenge was beginning to take its toll. He was approaching his fiftieth birthday, and he wasn't certain he would live long enough to witness retirement. The truth was, he secretly dreaded the idea of waking up in the morning with nothing to do. Even on his days off, he would spend most of his time thinking through his pile of ongoing cases. Being a policeman was in his blood; there is nothing he wouldn't do to see justice served. Of course, this cavalier attitude had got him in hot water on more than one occasion in the past. This latest one-man vendetta with McManus had already put him in hot water with his D.C.I. but the truth was: he knew he was right. He knew there was something very shady about McManus' behaviour and he was determined to prove it, no matter who he pissed off.

McManus had purchased the art gallery, and the building it was housed in, when he had first moved to the city. It was widely known that the Scot loved his personal art collection, but would be willing to sell any of it for the right profit-margin.

'He'd sell his own granny too,' Hoxley had mentioned in the original interrogation. 'I heard a rumour he put her up for auction once!'

McManus could usually be found in his office at the back of the gallery, when he wasn't out and about schmoozing with councilmen and the Chief Superintendent, of course.

White meandered from painting to painting, looking at the artists' names and the estimated valuation of the work. He didn't recognise any of the names, and all bar one of the paintings was more than his annual salary.

'Does anything catch your eye?' the young blonde gallery assistant enquired politely.

'Do you have any Picasso's?' White asked glibly.

The blonde giggled surreptitiously, shaking her head as she did.

'What about Monet? Van Gogh?'

'This is a modern art gallery,' she pointed out. 'Do you have a budget you are looking to spend? Perhaps that would be a good starting point.'

White smiled back. 'Do you have anything by artists from down South?'

'I'm not sure,' the woman frowned. 'Is there a particular artist you are looking for? Or a certain form?'

White ignored the response. 'Is your boss around, love? Y'know: Mr McManus?'

'Mr McManus? I'm not sure if he is due in today to be honest. Do you have an appointment to see him?'

'The only people I make appointments with is the doctor and the dentist. I don't do it with robbing little shites like the man who pays your wages.'

The woman looked nervous. 'Can I take your name, and I'll see if he is available.'

'Oh, my name...I'm Detective Inspector Tony White from Newcastle Constabulary.'

'Can I ask what you want to speak to Mr McManus about?'

'You could, but I'm not going to tell you...if these CCTV cameras work, I'm pretty sure the little bastard knows I'm here,' White added, pointing at the small cameras in the corners of the room.

The woman made her excuses and headed through a door marked 'Staff Only'. White continued to wander around, wondering if McManus would have the guts to confront him. An elderly couple who had been considering what looked like a painting of a woman's vagina swiftly made their way towards the exit.

'That's probably for the best,' White shouted after them. 'You wouldn't want to get caught up in this man's money laundering activity.' The couple scuttled away.

'Is it Detective Inspector White?' a Scottish voice boomed from over his shoulder.

'That's correct,' White shouted back, turning to see McManus at the same door the woman had used.

'Would you follow me?' McManus said, holding the door open. 'It's probably best if we talk in my office, before you frighten off any more of my customers.'

White was surprised McManus had come down personally but wasn't prepared to pass up this opportunity. He grasped the edge of the door, allowing McManus to move ahead of him. They walked down a narrow corridor and then up a small flight of stairs to an office marked 'Private'. The office was far bigger than White had expected and included an oak desk in front of a large collection of monitors, each displaying an image from one of the cameras downstairs. There was a sofa against the far wall.

'I caught your performance,' McManus, said nodding towards the bank of monitors. 'You really do have an active imagination, Detective Inspector.'

'Thank you for noticing,' White replied flippantly. 'I witness so much crap in the city that films just don't seem real enough for me.'

'What can I help you with?' McManus offered, indicating for White to take a seat.

White ignored the invitation and began to walk around the office, trying to see anything that might help him nail the Scot.

'I thought I'd give you the opportunity to confess your crimes and maybe bargain for a reduced sentence,' White said, noticing a calendar behind the desk, gradually moving towards it.

'My crimes? What am I accused of?'

'Oh I think we both know the answer to that. In fact, I wouldn't be surprised if you weren't up to far more than I even know about!'

McManus laughed cordially. 'Are you here on official police business, Mr White? It's just…I would have thought the Chief Superintendent would have been kind enough to inform me if he had any doubts about the legitimacy of my charitable works.'

'I'm not here under any official authority, no. You see, the thing is…I was given a tip off this morning that you would be meeting with some men to talk about the import of a shipment of crystal meth, but when I arrived at the meeting, you'd scarpered. But now I've found you so if you want to come in with me now, I can make your arrest and detention much easier.'

'Can you hear yourself?' the Scot laughed. 'Clandestine meetings? Drug importing? I am a respected businessman in this city. What on earth makes you think I would be involved in such activities?'

White lost his patience and rushed towards the desk. The Scot took a step backwards.

'You're up to your neck in shit, McManus. I know it and you know it! It's only a matter of time until I nail you for your crimes, you understand me?'

'I've had enough of this,' McManus said, scooping up the phone on the edge of his desk. 'I'm phoning the Chief Superintendent this minute and putting in a formal complaint against you.'

'Go ahead! It won't stop me! I am going to track your movements until I have all the evidence I need to see you sent down for a very long time.'

'Hi Jeanette, it's Jock McManus, is Mr Bainton there, please? I have an urgent matter I need to discuss with him.'

'You might have powerful friends in the city, but that won't stop me!' White vowed. 'I know what you're up to and I will prove it!'

McManus lowered the phone to his shoulder and leaned closer to White, whispering, 'You've no idea just how powerful my friends are. You think you understand what I'm involved in? You haven't got a fucking clue, and once I've done speaking with Chief Superintendent Bainton you won't have any chance of ever discovering what I know.'

Just as quickly, McManus raised the phoned back to his ear. 'Hi Roger, sorry to trouble you at work. I'm sure you're hugely busy. The thing is: one of your officers has just barged his way in to my gallery, throwing all sorts of accusations about the place...his name? I believe it's Detective Inspector Tony White. You know me, I don't like to make a fuss, but his outburst was rather embarrassing and frightened off a couple of my best customers...I'm sure you will take care of it...'

White didn't hang around to hear any more, stalking from the office and out of the gallery, vowing that he would get McManus if it was the last thing he did.

12:30

'I should warn you,' Patterson told Lewis, as they pulled up outside of Eksteen Autos, 'this guy is a bit of a hard-ass. Don't get on the wrong side of him or you'll pay for it with your life. You understand?'

'Are you trying to scare me into reconsidering?'

'No, bro, I just think you should know who we are dealing with. Like, he had this guy working for him once: Skinny Pete. Pete was a dealer, selling anything from weed to crack, and Eksteen was his supplier. Pete never let him down; always paid up on time and the two had a good relationship. Then one day, Eksteen hears a rumour that Skinny Pete was picked up by the local fuzz for some reason or another. Rather than waiting to speak to Pete about it, Eksteen jumps to the wrong conclusion, that Pete is colluding with the hogs in blue, and orders a hit on him. Anyway, Pete hears about the contract and goes to Eksteen to explain what happened. Eksteen invites Pete in and then slits his throat with a knife, before Pete's said more than two words. It later turns out that the only reason Pete had been at the police station was to bail out his sister, who had been done for drunk-driving. Apparently someone had spotted him there and put two and two together.'

'Yeah, but did you know this Skinny Pete? How d'you know it isn't just a story made up to frighten people?'

'There's no smoke without fire, bro. I'm just saying.'

The car-lot was bigger than Lewis had expected. For someone who primarily dealt in the trade of drugs and used the car lot to launder his money, there were a lot of vehicles for sale.

You want to throw your fucking life away?

His mother's words still echoed in his memory. He opened the showroom door and saw who he presumed was Eksteen, sitting behind a thick wooden desk in a small office. The man was flanked by two bodyguards: one a tall and very well-built man in a dark suit, wearing sunglasses, and the other a woman, whose toned muscles were clearly visible through the dark suit she was wearing.

'I help you with something, lads?' Eksteen asked.

Patterson pushed past Lewis and extended his hand towards the South African. 'Good afternoon, Mr Eksteen, my name's Billy Patterson, I'm one of Archie's dealers. It's a pleasure to meet you.

Eksteen ignored the hand and continued to watch the two young men.

'This is my partner, Lewis Reed,' Patterson continued. We wondered if you could spare us five minutes for a chat.'

'You interested in a car, sonny?'

'No, Mr Eksteen, sir, not a car.'

'Did I tell you to sit down, sonny,' he barked at Lewis, who had just pulled out a chair.

Lewis casually pushed the chair back towards the

desk and apologised.

'You have sixty seconds to explain what the fuck you want, before I have you thrown out,' Eksteen barked again.

Patterson raised his hands in an attempt to pacify the South African.

'I presume you heard what happened to Archie? That the fuzz have pulled him in and seized all the gear at the house? I just heard about it. The thing is, you see, I was due to collect some gear from Archie today, but with him inside, I'm now out of pocket.'

'Would you mind getting to the part where this is my fucking problem?'

'Well, with all that gear seized, you're out of pocket and down a couple of your regular middlemen. So...'

'What he is trying to say, Mr Eksteen,' Lewis interrupted, 'is that you need us. We're smart, well-connected, and can get this operation back on course.'

Eksteen whispered something to the male bodyguard and then laughed at his own joke.

'I need you? I don't know either of you from Adam. Why the fuck would I want to do any kind of business with you, let alone something so illegal. Are you two cops, eh?'

'Don't be ridiculous!' Lewis chastised, instantly regretting his tone.

'Look at it from my point perspective: two strangers wander into my car-lot and start talking about dealing drugs. I don't know who you are or whom you might be working for.'

'Please, Mr Eksteen, if you supply us on the same

terms you had with Archie, we can help you get back what you deserve,' Lewis bluffed. 'You can trust us.'

'I can trust you, can I? How do I know you're not recording this conversation?'

With that, Eksteen signalled to the woman next to him. She walked around the desk and pushed Lewis towards the wall behind him. She then flattened his hands out so that they were touching the wall. He was shocked at just how strong she was and, as she moved her hands up and down his body, presumably checking for some kind of recording device or weapon, he was nervous and excited in equal measure. As she ran her hands up his inside leg, it was all he could do to stop himself becoming aroused.

'He's clean boss,' the woman said, when the frisking had finished.

Eksteen walked towards the two youths. 'You do realise that the sale and purchase of narcotics is a criminal offence in this country, don't you? What you are proposing is illegal.'

Patterson had remained frozen to the spot, but now decided it was time to get going. 'We're really sorry to have troubled you, Mr Eksteen. We'll be on our way, and leave you to your business.'

Eksteen turned his attention to Patterson. 'Do you work for, have you ever been employed by or are you currently aiding any law enforcement agency, either he in the UK or anywhere in the world?'

'No,' the two of them answered.

'This contract you are suggesting between the two of us: are you fully aware that it is against the laws of this country?'

'Yes.'

'Do you have any intention of reneging on this contract or reporting its existence to any law enforcement agency either here in the UK or anywhere in the world?'

'No, of course not…'

Eksteen opened the jacket he was wearing and removed a small Dictaphone. 'Are you aware that I have just recorded our conversation and will use it as evidence should any legal proceedings be brought against me in this matter?'

The two nodded; amazed at the lengths Eksteen was going to in order to protect himself.

The South African stopped the recording, before adding, 'Are you aware that if I even sense you have lied to me about any of this, I will have you hunted down and killed?'

Lewis gulped hard as he nodded. Patterson was sweating.

The grin returned to Eksteen's face. 'Good, well I'm glad that's all settled. The thing you need to understand about me, lads, is that I only sell to those I know and trust. Archie was a good dealer, but I've been made aware that he could be inside for at least a five to ten stretch, which means there is an opening in my organisation. The house that was raided yesterday was just one of about half a dozen that I am responsible for. Whilst it is frustrating that the gear was seized, it is merely a bump in the road. But, before I can trust you fully, I need you to prove your loyalty to me. Shall I continue?'

Lewis and Patterson quickly glanced at each other and nodded, realising that Eksteen was just as likely to kill them as he was to let them go.

'Good,' he began, returning back to his seat behind the desk. 'I have arranged a meeting later today with a man who claims he can supply me with a regular quantity of crystal meth. Usually, I would attend the meeting personally, but with everything that happened yesterday, I'm apprehensive about the meet. I want you two to go in my place. I will give you the time and location of the meeting and a small satchel of money. All you need to do is turn up on time and make the trade. You think you can handle that?'

The two nodded once more.

The South African grinned and offered his hand for each to shake. As Lewis accepted the hand, Eksteen, pulled him closer, whispering, 'You fuck this up and I will kill you, your friends and your whole fucking family. Is that clear?'

Both youths gulped and wondered exactly what kind of deal they had just made.

12:43

'Miss Ahmed, this is Detective Chief Inspector Mercure. She'd like to ask you a few questions,' said the P.C., who had been with Nazir since his arrival. She nodded and shook Mercure's hand.

'I understand you found the body?' Mercure began, taking the seat the officer had just vacated. 'I appreciate you've already made a statement, but I wondered if you could talk me through what happened: in your own words.'

Nazir wiped a fresh tear from her cheek. 'Where do you want me to start?'

'From the beginning. What contact have you had with...Simon...today I mean?'

'Okay, well, he phoned me at home this morning, asking me to send him over a case file we have been working on.'

'How did he sound on the phone? Did he sound anxious? Nervous? Worried or upset?'

'No, nothing like that. He sounded like...well, like Simon. He asked when I could get the file to him and I told him I had a doctor's appointment but would have it couriered to him once I had arrived in the office.'

'But you didn't courier the file?'

'In the end, no. I was late leaving the hospital and

then I got stuck in traffic, so I decided to bring the file across here myself.'

'What's so special about this file you keep mentioning?'

'That's what I told the other officer: nothing. It is a boring piece of litigation based in mainland Europe. I don't see that it can have anything to do with…this.'

'What do you mean by this?'

'Simon killing himself…I can't believe he would…'

'How would you describe Simon? What kind of boss was he?'

'Pretty good. He worked very hard and demanded high standards, but everyone liked him at work, as far as I'm aware. He's one of the friendlier partners at the firm.'

'Did he have any enemies that you know of? Have there been any cases he has lost where the defendant was disgruntled? Or perhaps he prosecuted someone who might seek revenge?'

'Revenge? Enemies? I thought this was a suicide?'

'Everything suggests that Simon took his own life, but I'm not prepared to rule anything out at this early stage. How had he seemed recently? Was he acting strangely at all?'

'Apart from his desperation for me to get this file to him, no.'

'Desperation?'

'He called me several times and left messages. I've never known him to be so keen to work on a case before. It was as if…'

'As if?'

'I don't know, like he needed to do something with it by a certain deadline...I don't know.'

'So you wouldn't say he was showing signs of depression?'

'No! I mean, we didn't socialise outside of work, but his manner in the office has been as it always is: pleasant.'

'We found a handwritten note in the bedroom. If we showed you a portion of it would you be able to confirm if it was his handwriting?'

'I'm pretty sure I could. What does the note say?'

Mercure frowned. 'I can't really tell you what it says. What I will say is that it does appear to be a suicide note.'

'I still can't believe it...I was only speaking with him this morning and now...'

'I appreciate this isn't easy for you, Miss Ahmed. Did Simon have a girlfriend or partner?'

'I'm really not sure, to be honest. As I said, we didn't socialise outside of work. I don't think he did, but...actually, that reminds me...he did seem particularly chirpy yesterday morning, like he had a real spring in his step. He even let me knock off an hour early.'

'Was that unusual?'

'I wouldn't say unusual. It wasn't a regular thing, but it has happened once or twice before in the last five years. He was a good boss.'

'But he seemed happier than usual yesterday morning?'

'Yes. I can't put my finger on what it was, but if you'd told me that the man who walked into the office yesterday morning would take his own life today, I'd have told you that you were crazy.'

'Miss Ahmed, we found some photographs scattered on the bed as well. They feature Simon and a young lady. I'd like to show you an image to see if you recognise her. Would that be okay?'

Nazir nodded and Mercure showed her the least revealing photograph of Simon with the girl.

'Oh,' said Nazir, when she realised what she was looking at. 'I see...I can't say I recognise her. Sorry.'

She passed the photograph back.

'Miss Ahmed, I don't know if my colleague told you, but I received a telephone call from a mobile phone this morning. The man I spoke to warned me that a bomb had been planted in the city and he gave me a tip-off as to where I could find it. That mobile was registered to this address and we have located it in the room next door. I believe that Simon may have placed that call. Do you know if he has any ties to...'

'You think he was a terrorist? No. No way! Absolutely not.'

'You seem pretty sure of yourself, yet you said you didn't socialise with him outside of work.'

'He just isn't, sorry, wasn't the type. He was a nice guy: he wouldn't hurt a fly.'

'The man I spoke with sounded nervous, and my gut tells me he was reading from a script. The way he spoke, it was as if...as if he didn't want to be saying what he was, but was being forced. That's why I wanted to know if he had made any recent enemies.'

'I really can't think that he has. We don't work in criminal law, so I can't see how he could have become involved in anything like that.'

'Thank you, Miss Ahmed,' said Mercure, heading out of the kitchen. She found D.C. Beth Taylor to ask what the medical examiner had said so far.

'He's said it looks like a suicide. He said time of death is somewhere between ten thirty and eleven thirty. There are abrasions around the victim's neck which are common to death by hanging. We found a chair knocked on its side beneath the victim's body, which would suggest he was standing on the chair to place the noose around his neck and then kicked the chair over.'

'There's something not right about this, Beth,' Mercure said looking down at the victim's body, which was currently laid on the living room floor.

'Guv?'

'In my experience of hanging suicides, the victims tend to do something with their hands, yet his are loose and at his sides.'

'I don't understand, Guv.'

'It is human instinct to survive. Even with the best will in the world, most people would attempt to loosen the noose as they suddenly decide they need one more breath. So, in order to prevent that temptation, most genuine suicides will disable the use of their hands somehow. More often than not, once the noose is tied in position, they will fasten their hands behind their back with rope or cuffs or something. That way, when the body's survival instinct kicks in, the victim will be unable to prevent the inevitable. This guy's hands are untied. He would have needed an iron will not to try and save his own life. As I said, it just doesn't seem right.'

'You think he's our bomber?'

'I think he is the man I spoke to this morning, but I don't think he is the bomber. I have a horrible feeling that he is just a pawn in a more complex game.'

'What about the woman in there? You think she's telling the truth? That she just found him?'

'I want you to verify the handwriting in the suicide note with someone else from his office; to be sure it is his. CCTV at the main entrance will confirm if Miss Ahmed arrived when she said she did, but I've no reason to question her statement. I'm not sure she's telling us everything about the victim's state of mind or about the case he was working on. I think we should tread carefully with her. She says she's pregnant, so I want you to go and buy her some lunch and bring it back up here. Once she's eaten and is feeling more comfortable, I want you to re-question her, focusing on the case file and Denby's mind-set this morning. I don't care how long it takes; question her until she gives us something useful.'

12:59

Ophion had dumped and burned out the Ford and now found himself behind the wheel of a two year-old estate car. He was pretty confident it wouldn't be reported as missing until the owner finished work, which gave Ophion at least a four hour window to do with it what he wanted. He wouldn't need it for that long, and when he was finished with it, the estate would join the Focus as a smouldering wreck.

It had been a busy morning and he welcomed the relief, brought by the sandwich he had bought from a small supermarket on the way to his present location: Fareham. He washed the last crust down with a swig of mineral water, and took a moment to revise the speech he had been formulating for the last hour.

The trip to Denby's flat had gone smoothly. Dressed as a courier, he had easily made it in and out of the apartment block unnoticed. The disguise had been clever, as the motorcycle helmet had kept his face hidden from any of the internal CCTV cameras. He had wondered what sort of man Denby would be. They had spoken the morning before briefly, and that had been the moment he had guessed Denby would be relatively spineless; after all, it hadn't taken much persuasion to convince him to hand over the McKenzie file.

Ophion had entered Denby's flat with the suppressed gun he had used to kill the gigolo earlier that morning, but he had had no intention of using it again, as that would have linked the two deaths. No, he had always intended to see Denby hung; it had simply been a question of whether the solicitor would comply willingly. The sight of the gun had been enough to make Denby bend to his will. The suicide note had been dictated by Ophion, and he had carefully reviewed the handwriting to ensure that the words were suitable. He had then given Denby the telephone number for the woman leading the investigation.

The client had insisted that the police should be allowed to find the first semtex device, so that they would accept the threat was real. That part of the plan had made Ophion nervous as, if a lot of time was spent on examining the device, there was a danger that it could be matched to similar explosions he had orchestrated in other countries. Nevertheless, the client had insisted and had assured that no such connection would be made.

Ophion had handed Denby the message that was to be relayed to the police, under threat of detonating a bomb at the solicitor's firm and killing all of Denby's colleagues. The solicitor, sensing the end was near, had reluctantly agreed to phone Mercure and relay the message. The performance had not been particularly convincing, but once the police identified that the phone was registered to the apartment and found the suicide note, they would have little reason to question the validity that Denby had been responsible for the bomb at the school. Sure, they would struggle for motive, but the copies of Denby in bed with the fifteen year-old would help demonstrate a darker side of his personality.

The only problem he had incurred thus far this morning was that Denby had failed to get hold of the McKenzie file. The client had been adamant that the file needed to be destroyed, and that failure to do so would ultimately impact the success of the day's mission. Ophion had used several techniques to try and locate the whereabouts of the missing file from Denby but the solicitor had stuck to his guns: insisting that one of the firm's legal secretaries had it in her possession. Reluctantly, Ophion had had to believe the solicitor and had managed to extract the legal secretary's name and contact details, before pressing on both sides of the victim's neck below the ear and just above the jaw. Denby had passed out in seconds allowing Ophion to hoist him up to the noose and kick the chair away. Denby had woken as the noose had tightened and it had been all Ophion could do; to keep the victim's hands from reaching up to the noose. Ophion had wrapped his big arms around Denby's waist to secure the hands in place. The solicitor had continued to struggle for nearly a minute, before he had died.

Ophion had undertaken a quick search of the flat, and finding nothing, had returned to the Focus, only to find a cheating traffic warden had given him a parking ticket. Despite efforts to reason with the fat Scot, he had ended up beating the man into submission and had destroyed the ticketing machine.

That had meant he needed to get rid of the Focus, hence why it had ended up smouldering in an unused industrial estate nearby. This had been the second hiccup of the day. He also needed to find the secretary and secure the missing file.

He decided he would not tell the client about these unforeseen hurdles, but would have to make time to deal with them before the day was out. He had planted the second device and it was only a matter of time before the client's true plans would be revealed. He couldn't help but feel a tingle of excitement.

Ophion glanced at the clock display on the dashboard. It was time to place a call. The client had given careful instructions about how the next five hours should play out, and Ophion had vowed to carry them out to the letter; that's what he was paid handsomely to do.

Picking up the phone with the built-in voice scrambler he dialled the number that the client had provided and waited for the phone to connect.

13:01

Detective Sergeant Kyle Davies glanced at the display of his mobile phone, which was laid flat down on the table in front of him. The train to Newcastle had departed Southampton at eleven fifteen and wasn't due to reach its destination until five thirty that evening. He was due to switch to a different train at Birmingham within the hour. He had finished the cardboard cup of coffee he had bought from the on-board trolley service, but at three pounds a cup, he wasn't willing to buy a second.

He was bored. When Mercure had told him he had to go up and meet D.I. Tony White he had been less than enthused. It wasn't until he collected his ticket at the train station that he had really realised just how far Newcastle was from home. Had he known he was anticipating a six hour journey, he would have arranged to travel earlier or later in the day. As it was, he was due to arrive in Newcastle as the new Guv was likely to be clocking off. He was looking forward to spending a night in a hotel at the D.C.I.'s expense, but it did feel like he was wasting the day somewhat. What she thought he would learn by travelling all that way was beyond him.

He had grabbed a copy of the Metro newspaper

at the station, but he had already read that cover to cover twice and attempted the crossword, without success. Now he had nothing to do: he didn't have a book, his phone was basic, with no internet capability, and it looked like there was nothing in the immediate vicinity to occupy him.

The train carriage was packed with people, all making a similar journey to his own. He had been fortunate to bag a table seat, which meant he had slightly more leg room than a standard seat. That said, the man sitting opposite him, who had been asleep for at least an hour, seemed to have incredibly long legs of his own. The woman next to Kyle had earphones in, so the chances of striking up a conversation with her were remote.

Kyle's mobile phone vibrated on the table in front of him. The display said it was from a withheld number, but that probably meant it was a call from the office; their numbers were always withheld. He answered the phone with his cursory, 'Davies. Talk to me.'

'Good morning Detective Sergeant Davies,' said a mechanically-disguised voice.

'Hi, who is this, please?'

'My name, for now, is not important. I have an important message to relay to you, and I wish you to confirm I have your full attention.'

'Alright, who is this?' Kyle said with a grin. 'Dale, is that you? Come on, which of you bastards is it? How did you get your voice to sound so weird?'

'I assure you Sergeant Davies, this is no joking matter. What I am about to tell you carries the upmost gravitas and you would be wise to treat me seriously.'

'Mmhmm. Tell me, what is your serious message? Hmm? Is it to warn me of some great danger that I am heading towards. Ooh, I am scared.'

'Sergeant Davies, you seem to be under the wrong impression about me. I am the man who planted a small incendiary device outside of St. Mark's Primary school this morning.'

The grin dropped from Kyle's face.

'Now, do I have your attention? There will be another bomb detonated in the city in six hours' time. If you wish to identify the location of the bomb before it detonates, you will do exactly as I say. Is that clear?'

'Who are you? What do you want?'

'I told you: who I am is not important. Know that my threat is very real and you are the only man who can prevent catastrophic bloodshed in the city.'

'What do you want? Money?'

Ophion laughed. 'Money is of no interest to me. I am a revolutionary, not a thief. You will learn more about me as the day progresses. The bomb will explode at seven o'clock this evening, unless you do exactly as I instruct. Is that clear?'

'How do I know that what you say is true? I am not aware of any devices being planted at a school.'

'Don't play dumb, Sergeant Davies. You are a serving officer in Hampshire Constabulary. How can you not be aware of what I left for you to discover?'

'I'm not in the office,' Kyle blurted out. 'I haven't been in all day.'

'I see,' said Ophion. 'Well perhaps you should speak with D.C.I. Mercure. I suggest you do this as a matter of urgency.'

The line went dead. Kyle stared down at the phone, but he had a full signal, meaning it had been the caller who had disconnected the phone. He looked around to see if anybody was watching him, just to check this wasn't part of some elaborate prank. Everybody's head was buried in a book, newspaper or tablet device.

Kyle made his way to the toilet so he would not be overheard. He located Mercure's number and pressed the dial button. He placed the phone to his ear and waited for it to connect.

13:04

Mercure was re-reading Simon Denby's suicide note when she felt her mobile phone vibrating.

'Mercure,' she said, putting the phone to her ear without checking who was calling.

'Guv, it's Davies. I need to check something with you.'

'Davies? Have you made it to Newcastle yet?'

'Not yet, Guv. I've not even reached Birmingham yet.'

'It's probably best you take a couple of days with the new guy, I suppose, so that's okay. Boy, how we could have done with your help today.'

'That's what I'm phoning about, Guv. I've just been told there was a bomb left outside a school this morning. Is that right?'

That bloody politician! Mercure thought, as she assumed the radio story had now probably gained national interest.

'It's true, but we found it in time.'

'Oh, good. So nobody was hurt?'

'No. We received a tip-off this morning hinting the location of the device and with a one hour deadline to find it.

Kyle gulped audibly. 'I think I've just received a second tip-off, Guv.'

Mercure listened as Kyle relayed the conversation he had just had and concluded. 'So we have six hours to find the next one.'

'Jesus Christ!' Mercure exclaimed.

'Have you got any leads on who this nutcase might be?'

'The phone used to make this morning's tip-off was registered to an apartment in Ocean Village, but when we arrived at the apartment, the owner had apparently hung himself.'

'Well, the person I just spoke to was very much alive.'

'Did you speak to a man or a woman?'

'I couldn't tell you, Guv; the voice sounded altered, like the person was speaking through a machine.'

'Did the person sound nervous in any way? The guy I spoke to this morning sounded like he was reading a script.'

'Nervous? No. I don't think this person was reading a script. He sounded confident; arrogant even.'

'The guy we suspect made this morning's tip-off was found hanging from a noose by his secretary, shortly before we arrived at the address. We've checked CCTV in the entrance hall of the building and apart from a courier and the secretary, there is nobody suspicious to follow up on. Did your person say anything else that might help us?'

'All he said was: the only way to prevent the second bomb blowing up is if I do whatever he says.'

'Why you?'

'I have no idea. He seemed surprised that I wasn't in the office, so maybe he thought I'd be working the case.'

'Have you ever worked any similar cases? If the bomber knows you then you probably know him too. Can you think of anyone with this kind of M.O.?'

'Nothing springs to mind, Guv, but I'll keep thinking about it.'

'I think you should try and record the calls on your phone if you can. Did the caller say when they would be back in touch?'

'No, just to speak to you to confirm the details of the first device. He said it was left outside of a school; where was the school?'

'It was outside a house near St. Mark's Primary in Shirley.'

Kyle was quiet for a moment.

'Where exactly was the device, Guv?'

'It was glued to the chassis of a four-by-four outside of a house near the school.'

'Which house, Guv?'

'I'm not sure, hold on…' Mercure said, checking the address with D.C. Beth Taylor. 'Number ninety-nine Stafford Road. Why?'

'Oh God!' Kyle exclaimed. 'I know who lives at that house, Guv. My daughter's child-minder.'

'You're kidding?'

'I wish I was. Do you believe in coincidences, Guv?'

'No I bloody don't!'

'Me neither. Why would a terrorist leave a bomb outside of the house where I leave my daughter and then phone me to warn me about another device?'

'I don't know Kyle, but I think we need to try and understand the answer to that question. I suggest you wait and see if he calls back, and at the same time get yourself on the first train back to Southampton. I have a feeling I'm going to need you here today.'

13:10

Kyle was staring hard at the phone in his hands. His bars of signal were fluctuating between two and nothing, and he was panicking that he had already missed the terrorist's return call due to poor signal quality in the toilet cubicle.

Why hasn't he phoned yet?

If he had missed a call, his phone was supposed to send him a text message to advise but, given the intermittent signal, nothing had arrived. He was feeling unusually warm and decided to remove his suit jacket and tie.

If only there was a window I could open. Call damn you!

As if his prayers had been answered, the phone vibrated to life. He answered it immediately.

'Yes?'

'Det...gent...vies...nee...to...sen...flee...'

'What? Hello? I can't hear you,' said Kyle, checking the bars of signal again. It was hovering on one bar.

'Hello? Can you hear me? Hello?' Kyle shouted into the phone.

'Sergeant Davies, can you hear me now?'

'Yes, yes I can,' Kyle confirmed.

'You seem calmer now, am I to understand that

you now believe what I have told you? Do you accept that I am not one of your colleagues?'

'Yes I do. I know that you are very real.'

'Good, then that should save us both some time.'

'Why are you doing this? Who are you? What do you want? Is it about money?'

Ophion laughed long and hard. 'Money? You think I am interested in money? This is about power. It is about rebalancing the scale. The leaders of the country are corrupt and look after their own. It is the same in the cities. The time for change is now!'

'What does this have to do with me? Huh? Why did you leave the device outside of St Mark's school?'

'Who said I left it outside of the school? The device was closer to a house than the school.'

'So the target was a resident in Stafford Road, rather than the school?'

'Have you not figured it out yet?'

'The child-minder my wife and I use. But why? Who are you? What have I done to you?'

'I needed to get your attention, Sergeant Davies. I believe I have it now.'

'What is this to do with me?'

'All in good time, Sergeant Davies. Did your D.C.I. find the man who tipped her off this morning?'

'The suicide victim? Yeah, she found him.'

'He committed suicide did he? Poor man, he did struggle with the morality of his actions.'

'Who was he? What was he to you?'

Ophion laughed. 'Oh please stop asking so many questions, Sergeant Davies. I will give you answers when I am ready.'

'I will find you. You think you're safe? You're not!'

Ophion laughed again, louder this time. 'You will not find me. You don't know who I am, where I am or who I am targeting.'

'You're targeting me.'

'Don't flatter yourself, Sergeant Davies. You are just a small cog in a big machine. You are lucky, I agree, to have been chosen to speak to me, but that is all you are: a communications conduit.'

'So who is the target?'

'All in good time. Now, enough questions. I have left a package in the stands of the football stadium in the St. Mary's area of Southampton. It is hidden beneath a specific seat. If your team can reach and open the package within the hour, they will discover a clue to the puzzle.'

'Which seat is the package under?'

'That would be too easy, Sergeant Davies. I suggest you contact your D.C.I. as a matter of urgency and get her to begin a search of the stadium. If they locate the package, they will need a code to open it.'

'What's the code?'

'Do you read newspapers Sergeant Davies?'

'Sure, sometimes. Why?'

'Do you ever complete the Sudoku puzzles?'

'No.'

'That's a shame. They really are a good tool for improving brain function. They say it can help prevent the early onset of dementia.'

'Well I don't do them.'

'That's a shame. A real shame. You see, the code for the box is hidden in one of the Sudoku puzzles in this morning's edition of The Sun. If you want to know how to get into the box, I would suggest you buy a copy of the paper and start to complete the Sudoku puzzle. You will need to get that code to your superiors as quickly as you can. In the meantime I want you and I to play a little game.'

'A game? You are messing with people's lives here!'

'And if you don't want to witness the death of hundreds, you will do as I instruct you! What I have left at the stadium is just a small part of my plan.'

'There are more bombs,' Kyle concluded.

'Exactly, Detective!'

'Where are they? Why are you doing this?'

'If you complete the Sudoku puzzle, the digits in the four corners of the puzzle make up the code you require. They must be input in the right order starting in the top left corner, and working around in a clockwise direction. Is that clear?'

'Yes.'

'Good. Where is your train now?'

'Just about to arrive at Leamington Spa.'

'I see. For what I have planned, I need you in Southampton…there is a train due to depart that station at one thirty eight, due to arrive in Southampton at three forty-one. Get yourself on that train, Detective Davies.'

'Then what?'

'I will phone you at a payphone at Southampton Central station at three forty-two and give you your next set of instructions. Is that clear?'

'Where is the payphone?'

'On the south-side platform. Don't be late, Detective, or I will detonate another device.'

The line went dead. Davies phoned Mercure and relayed the conversation.

'So you're not the target? What about the child-minder's house?' Mercure asked.

'He said it was just to get my attention. You need to get the team to the stadium straight away. An explosion there will be very public. Also, you need to find someone who can do Sudoku puzzles.'

'Why?'

'He told me that I need to complete the puzzle in today's edition of The Sun to get the code to get into the box.'

'He's right. You do need to.'

'But I don't know how to do them, Guv.'

'Listen, Davies, I cannot spare the manpower. I need everyone I've got to help scour the stadium. You are on a train, so make yourself useful. Find someone who can help you and phone me back as soon as you have that code!'

13:12

Tony White glanced at the clock on the wall across from him. He had been sat in the D.C.I.'s office for exactly four minutes and the D.C.I. had been shouting for exactly three minutes and forty seconds. He wished he was anywhere else right now.

'And the fact you had the audacity to turn up at McManus' gallery and accuse him of all kinds of illegal activity is totally beyond me! I warned you about this little crusade of yours, didn't I? I told you to back off; to stay away. How do you think it makes me look when you defy my command?'

'I'm sorry, sir...' he began but was silenced by a raised hand.

'I've had the Chief Superintendent on the phone for half an hour demanding to know what I think I am doing by commissioning an investigation into one of the city's most respected businessmen. I had to explain to him that no such operation was underway and that you were simply following up on some bad information.'

'Did he believe you?'

'Of course he bloody didn't! You think a man like that makes Chief Superintendent by having the wool pulled over his eyes?'

'Sir, if I can just...'

'Don't, White; just don't…I've heard your excuses before and, quite frankly, I'm sick to the teeth of hearing about your gut instinct. Real police work doesn't happen like that. Not anymore. I get it: you don't like McManus for some reason, but marching onto his property and spouting accusations is not the way to do it! Nor is staking out a bookie's on an unsanctioned surveillance operation!'

'How did you…'

'Know? Thankfully not all my detectives are as stupid as you! Strong came and told me what you were planning earlier this morning. I told him to steer clear but I guess you must have coerced him into compliance.'

So Strong told the D.C.I., I wonder if that's how McManus got tipped off, White wondered.

'With respect, sir…'

'I told you, White: I don't want to hear about your latest theory.'

'But, sir, you read the file I put together. Does your gut not tell you there is something fishy going on?'

'Something fishy? This isn't nineteen seventy two! Writing pages and pages of hunches and suppositions based on, what is at best, circumstantial evidence, is not the answer.'

'Okay, sir, okay, I'll drop the case against McManus,' White lied, hoping the rebuke was now over.

'Oh no, White, it's too late for that kind of bullshit! I warned you what would happen if you persevered with this; the Chief Superintendent wants your warrant card.'

'No, sir, you can't be serious!'

'I'm deadly serious! He wants me to suspend you with immediate effect, pending a disciplinary hearing for gross insubordination.'

'But, sir, I know I'm right. McManus is up to no good...I can prove it!'

'Oh you have proof all of a sudden? Great, let's hear it!'

'Well...' White began, knowing that what he was about to say was thin, 'what made me suspect him to begin with was his sudden rise to wealth. I've spoken to our Glaswegian colleagues and he was a nobody with barely two pennies to rub together until about six years ago and then, overnight it was as if he had won the lottery. Suddenly he began attending invitation-only events, splashing the cash left, right and centre; funding hospital wings the same way you or I would place a couple of quid on the Grand National.'

'And? Maybe he did win the lottery, or maybe he inherited it...'

'Or maybe he met a wealthy backer, or, more accurately, several wealthy backers.'

'What?'

'Hear me out, sir...I know it sounds a bit crazy, but just suppose there is somebody or something else funding his operation.'

'Somebody or something?'

'That's right...one of the things Hoxley told me was that McManus is in pretty tight with a group of rich Europeans who are looking to influence world politics in some way. He was a bit vague, I know, but what if that is what is going on here? Maybe

McManus is just a small pawn in something far grander than we can see right now.'

The D.C.I. roared incredulously. 'Have you heard yourself? Do you know how barmy you sound? A secret organisation? I was wrong, I'm not just going to suspend you: I'm going to have you referred to a psychologist. You've lost it man!'

'No, sir...'

'Enough, White! I thought you said you had evidence. The world is already littered with enough conspiracy theories without you wading in with one of your own. Give me your warrant card now.'

'Please, sir, please, there must be another way. This job is my life; you can't take it away.'

'It's too late, White. You've left me with no other choice.'

'Please, sir, I'm begging you: don't let him win. I haven't broken any laws. Okay, so the bastard has made a complaint against me; I'll accept the punishment for that, but don't take away my job.'

The D.C.I.'s eyes narrowed as he pondered whether to believe White's plea.

'There has to be another way, sir. Please?'

The D.C.I. remained silent for a moment longer, before saying, 'There is one way out of this...'

'I'll do it, sir, whatever it is,' White interrupted.

'I know a D.C.I. in another county who is crying out for a D.I. with your level of experience. I spoke to her about you yesterday as a matter of fact.'

'A transfer? No, sir, that's not the answer.'

'A fresh start, White, that's what you need: a new office with a different breed of criminal to rub up the wrong way.'

'No, sir, come on, I've worked in this city for two decades; nobody knows it as well as me. You need me. You need my experience.'

'Your experience is too costly, White! If I don't get you out of this division, it'll be my arse on the line instead of yours. You have a choice: take the transfer on the same pay and pension or risk losing both by facing the disciplinary hearing.'

'But if I leave, McManus will win!'

'Have you ever considered that McManus might be innocent of your suspicions? He's a rich man with God knows how many enemies, of course his name is going to get slung about by the scumbag snitches you rely so heavily on.'

'You can't force me to accept a transfer, sir. I'll get the Union rep involved.'

'Do what you like, White. I'm sure you'll need your rep for the hearing anyway. It's a pity, though; Southampton really is a lovely part of the country. It's not even that dissimilar to Newcastle.'

'Wait! You said the transfer is to Southampton? As in the bottom of the country? That's miles away!'

'It's about as far from the Chief Superintendent as I can put you. It's that or nothing.'

White didn't want to admit it, but a transfer to Southampton might not be as bad as the D.C.I. thought. He recalled the blueprints Strong had found in the disused bookie's, which were for buildings in Southampton. Whatever McManus was up to, maybe the answer did lie in a different city.

'How long do I have to make a decision?'

'About thirty seconds,' the D.C.I. replied, looking at his watch. 'The D.C.I. I spoke to has just been on the phone. Apparently, they've got a major incident unfolding as we speak.'

'What sort of incident?'

'She didn't want to say on the phone. I told her I wasn't sure if you still wanted the move, so if you do want it, I'll have to phone her back pretty sharpish.'

'It doesn't seem like I have much of a choice,' White replied reluctantly.

13:15

The wake for Troy Cross was being held at the Waterside hotel, a large, plush complex with a striking glass pyramid. Guests had been arriving for the last fifteen minutes, most having driven the short journey from the crematorium. Aaron had managed to squeeze into one of the large black Mercedes that the family were using. He had finally found Harry during the service, but they hadn't had the time to catch up properly. As Aaron now wandered between the small groups of mourners who were chatting, he wondered whether he might bump into the beautiful Victoria again.

She had said that Harry and Toby weren't aware of her relationship with their father, but then who did they think she was? Her good looks and striking figure were out of place with the rest of the business-suited mourners. He chastised himself for thinking about his uncle's grieving mistress in a sexual manner. There was no sign of her, and so he assumed she had decided to forego the wake. The way in which she had spoken of Troy was still troubling him.

He was a very important person...Your uncle kept his work life private from his personal life.

What did she mean? Why was she being so

elusive?

He walked towards the buffet table and placed a selection of canapés and sausage rolls on a small china plate and then wandered around the room looking for any sign of Harry, Toby or the mysterious Victoria.

The various groups seemed more interested in talking about what yacht they were planning to buy next. If they weren't talking about yachts they were talking about the next super-fast sports car they would treat themselves too. Aaron couldn't understand why they weren't reminiscing about the fun times they had had with Troy. He knocked back a glass of wine, his second in the ten minutes since he had arrived, and reached out for another from a waiter who was carrying a tray of glasses.

'I must say: the Prime Minister is doing a fabulous job of uniting the coalition here in Britain,' he overheard one woman remark to a group of five. 'I mean, the tax benefits for us ex-pats are fabulous and it seems like they will long continue. Who knew a Conservative leader with Liberal leanings would be so good?'

The group chortled.

'It's a shame he knows fuck all about running his own country though,' Aaron heard himself remark, before he could stop himself.

'Excuse me?' the woman asked, turning to see who had challenged her.

Aaron watched as the rest of the group turned to see who had interrupted their conversation. He had never been one for verbal sparring in public, but as the group of obnoxious, toffee-noses dared him to speak again, he couldn't help himself.

'I was just saying that the current Prime Minister is spending so much time abroad that he doesn't see what is happening in his own backyard.'

'A Labour supporter? You look the type,' the woman replied dismissively.

'Actually, no,' he challenged back. 'But ultimately, it doesn't make a difference who is in power; they are all as corrupt as each other. Maybe if the current P.M. wasn't so busy snuggling up to his American counterpart, he'd see just what kind of condition his navy and armed forces are in. I've been to Iraq three times and Afghanistan twice in the last decade. I've seen what life is like defending our nation, and I can assure you: it's no pretty picture.'

'A mercenary, no less,' the woman countered, smiling at her friends. It was a look that said, 'Let's humour the little man.'

'I bet you've got three houses and your most troubling thought each day is which servant you should request to apply your body lotion,' Aaron continued, the wine going to his head. 'I bet you've not done a real day's work your entire life. Was daddy rich? Whilst you spend your time championing for better tax breaks for rich people, there are men and women on the frontline, with a lack of supplies and decent weaponry. Do you know how hot it gets in Afghanistan? You think it's easy to work in that heat knowing that this day could very well be your last? You've got no fucking clue what's going on! None of you do.'

'I was merely…'

'You were merely talking out of your arse with no

real perspective from which you can speak. Your P.M., your best friend, has no clue...no clue what is going on. Maybe you should think about that before you start declaring his superiority...'

Aaron felt someone pulling him back and realised he was only inches from the woman as he shouted and spat in her direction.

'Hey cuz,' he heard Harry saying. 'Maybe you should go cool off for a minute.'

Aaron allowed Harry to pull him away and watched as his cousin offered an apology to the small group, who looked as embarrassed as Aaron felt. Harry moved back towards him and ushered him to step outside for some fresh air.

13:18

'Hey, you think I can have one of those,' Aaron asked pointing at the cigarette Harry was smoking.

'I didn't know you smoked.'

'I don't…not really…I used to, but then there's a lot I used to do.'

'Yeah, I remember you were a bit of a hot head once,' Harry grinned as he passed the packet of cigarettes over. Aaron placed one between his lips and allowed Harry to light it for him. He coughed on the first inhale. 'It's been a while,' he commented.

'It's never too late to start again,' Harry added, still grinning.

'So…how are you coping with the whole grieving process? You seem to be taking it in your stride.'

Harry squashed the butt of his own cigarette beneath his foot. 'I've got to stay strong for Toby, y'know. It's hit him really hard.'

'I bet. Was he living with your dad when he died?'

'Toby? No, he's been living with me for the last eighteen months. Dad figured it was better that Toby continue his studies in the UK. When mum died, the mortgage was paid off on the family home so dad said I could live there as if it was my own, on the understanding that he could stay whenever he was back in the country. I figured: a big house, no rent or mortgage to pay, why not? I said I would watch out for Toby, make sure he goes to school, that kind of thing.'

'How much time did your dad spend in the UK?'

'When he first left The Navy, he would spend three months abroad at a time and six months at home, but gradually he began to spend more and more time away. He hadn't been home in nearly nine months I think.'

'And would both of you go and see him?'

'It was too difficult to keep track of him: he was never in one place for too long before he'd move on again.'

'What was it he was doing in Europe? I noticed a lot of bankers or lawyers at the crematorium.'

'If I'm totally honest, I'm not sure what he did. He always had plenty of money, whatever he was doing. I mean: he would send me and Toby money every month, and I'm talking about five grand on average. He said it was to cover the bills: council tax and what not, but I think it was because he felt guilty about leaving us behind.'

'Did it bother you?'

'What?'

'Him being away so much.'

'To be honest: no. You know what it's like in The Navy: we hardly saw him when we were growing up. Mum was our mum and our dad most of the time, and she did a great job. Dad was like some kind of uncle who would turn up for a few months and live with us, but would then be gone for ages when he got posted somewhere.'

'Did your mum never want to go with him? The

navy offers family postings: a home etc.'

'Mum once told me they didn't want to disrupt our school life by moving us whenever his posting changed. They thought it was better for us to remain static so that we'd have as settled an upbringing as possible.'

'I see,' Aaron nodded, coughing as he inhaled again.

'So, yeah, anyway, I'm not sure what he was up to over there. I reckon he had a woman, though.'

'Really?'

'Oh yeah, he was always a bit of a charmer and flirt. I'd be very surprised if he didn't have at least one woman on the go,' Harry laughed.

'And that wouldn't bother you?' Aaron asked, considering mentioning Victoria's earlier statement.

'Why would it? I know he loved my mum, but she's been gone for six years. It wouldn't be natural if he wasn't shagging someone new.'

The two cousins laughed.

'Oh, that reminds me,' Aaron said. 'You said you wanted to chat earlier…y'know, when you phoned me this morning? What did you want to talk about?'

Harry looked around nervously. They were standing on the veranda at the rear of the hotel bar, but some of the guests had come out to enjoy the sunshine.

'I'm not sure I can talk about it here. You never know who might be listening.'

Aaron shot him a puzzled look. 'What's going on? What can't you talk about? Are you in trouble or something?'

'Me? No…not exactly…follow me.'

Harry walked down the veranda and disappeared around the side of the hotel. There was a hedge around the garden they now found themselves standing in, but they were alone.

'Do you know how dad died?' Harry asked.

'Not really,' Aaron shrugged. 'I didn't know he was dead until I received your letter on base. I assumed, given his age, a heart attack or something.'

Harry shook his head. 'You need to promise to keep what I am about to tell you to yourself.'

'Okay,' Aaron nodded. 'You have my word.'

Harry took another glance to his left and right and, when happy that nobody was listening, he said, 'I think my dad was murdered.'

'What? Why? By whom?'

'Whilst I don't know exactly what dad did in Europe, I know that it was something very secretive, and was well-paid. He was always very cautious when he would phone home: never used a mobile phone or his home number. He would always phone us from pay phones, as if he was worried about someone bugging his line. Think about it: what kind of job would a former naval commander be hired to do?'

'What are you saying?'

'I'm not sure, but what if he was an assassin or something?'

Aaron burst out laughing. 'You think he was James Bond?'

'No, not James Bond, you dick! But maybe something in a similar vein. You said it yourself, look at the guests at the wake: all wealthy and all powerful. How do you think people like that get that amount of money and power? They hire people like my dad, to do their dirty work.'

'That's as may be, but what makes you think he was murdered?'

'Right, well, he was apparently hosting a big party on a large boat in Monaco. There were lots of wealthy people on board, allegedly, who said he was the life and soul of the party. Anyway, he tells them all the party is over just before midnight and asks them all to leave, which they do. They said there was something about his demeanour that had not seemed right, like he was upset or worried about something. The last person to leave the party, some aide of the Monaco royal family, said she saw him close up and lock the doors and windows to the boat, and make some kind of phone call. The next day his body is found floating in the water at the port. The physician who carried out his post mortem said he had drowned.'

'Well, maybe he did drown.'

'Oh please, Aaron. My dad was an outstanding swimmer. Hell, he won medals in naval swimming competitions, remember?'

Aaron nodded; he had been to cheer on his Uncle Troy on a number of occasions over the years.

'There is no way he would have drowned, even if he'd fallen overboard like they have concluded.'

'Even so, Harry, it's a bit of a stretch to declare he was murdered. Sure, it seems a bit fishy, but murder? Really?'

'I can prove it,' Harry continued. 'I have something that will confirm it for you.'

'Really? What have you got?'

'I don't want to talk about it here. Let me go and make my excuses and we'll head back to my house. Is that okay with you?'

Aaron nodded, wondering exactly what his uncle had been embroiled in.

13:53

Retourget was growing increasingly impatient with his inability to locate Eksteen. He was now leaving a fourth premises without finding the South African. There was only one place left in his list of possible venues, and that was where he was heading now. The trouble was it was at least half an hour's walk away and there was no obvious public transport he could rely on.

He saw a withheld number was phoning him and hoped it was good news.

'Oui,' he barked into the phone.

'Jean-Paul, c'est Mohammed. Have you killed the South African yet?'

'Not yet; I'm still looking for him. Pour quoi?'

'What I'm about to tell you is very high level, do you understand? It's classified Turkish intelligence and I would be tried as a traitor if it ever came out that I had told you about it.'

'What is it, Mohammed? What do you want to tell me?'

'Have you ever heard of a group known as The Cadre?'

Retourget paused. 'The name means nothing to me. Why?'

'Okay, well let me try and explain: imagine what

would happen if the most powerful people in the world entered into a kind of pact or agreement to work together to take control of the global economy? Suddenly all financial markets would be in the control of a band of people with their own agenda.'

'What are you talking about, Mohammed? You sound nervous.'

'We have intelligence pointing at such a group of individuals, and our mutual friend Santiago Hernandez is a known associate of the group.'

'And? What does that have to do with me?'

'This group have been undertaking small operations for several years but they are growing stronger. They are starting to exercise greater power. The senior politicians in my country believe the threat this group poses is very real. They are setting up a task force to try and infiltrate the group and stop them before it is too late.'

'I still don't understand what this has to do with me.'

'There is a chance that your narcotics deal with Hernandez was in fact part of the group's wider plans. The Cadre is not a group you want to upset or anger. They are known to execute partners that they no longer need or competition they cannot overcome. If Hernandez is involved, then there is a real chance that Eksteen is as well. I thought you should know that there could be far greater repercussions for you yet, Jean-Paul.'

'Okay, Mohammed, I'll tread carefully. I have my gun.'

'There's another thing, Jean-Paul. Have you ever

heard of the assassin called 'The Serpent'?'

Retourget knew exactly who is old friend was referring to. Although they had never formally met, he was aware of The Serpent's work.

'I know of him.'

'Good, well you should know that Interpol believe one of his many fake identities was used to enter UK waters yesterday. We believe he is somewhere in Britain.'

'You think he is in Southampton?'

'It is too much of a coincidence for him not to be involved in whatever is growing in the city. I do not believe in coincidences.'

'You think The Serpent is here to kill me?'

'I'm not sure…if he is, I don't see why Eksteen would have tried to have you killed himself. The Cadre might hire someone like The Serpent to do their business. Is there anything happening in the city that they might be using him for?'

'I have no idea. I am not familiar enough with local matters, to be honest.'

'Will you do me a favour, Jean-Paul? When you find the South African, ask him what he knows about The Cadre before you kill him? I have a feeling we are going to need all the help we can get.'

'Sure, if I ever find him. There is only one place left on my list of possible locations for him: his car dealership. If he isn't there, I'm not sure where to look next.'

'Okay, good luck, mon ami.'

Retourget replaced the phone in his pocket and stopped still. He had lied to Al-Batani: he had heard the name The Cadre before, but it had always been a thing of legend. There had never been any proof that the organisation existed, let alone what they were actually involved with. He had spent the last several months working for people whom he only talked to on the telephone or via electronic mail. Faceless people with lots of money were his stock in trade, but now he was beginning to worry. What if he had been unwittingly working for The Cadre all this time? What if they had decided he was now a loose end they didn't need? There was only one way he could find out: he checked his weapon again and set off at a pace for Eksteen Autos.

13:58

Aaron and Harry arrived at the house in Lowford and, after a brief tour of the four bedroomed property, the cousins slumped down on the sofas in the spacious living room.

'What do you think? Pretty nice, huh?'

'It hasn't changed much since I was last here,' Aaron admitted.

'Are you kidding? I've had the place re-decorated. It was like something out of a seventies horror movie before.'

'Was it? I can't really remember.'

'Let's have a drink; tequila okay with you?'

Aaron glanced at his watch. He had an important meeting later that he didn't want to miss. 'Sure,' he said.

Harry fetched two glasses and a new bottle of tequila and poured them each a generous shot.

'A toast,' Harry continued, raising his glass high. 'To my dad.'

Aaron grabbed his glass and raised it. 'To Uncle Troy: a great man!'

The cousins drank their shots and Harry re-filled their glasses.

'At the party,' Aaron said when the glasses were empty again. 'You said you had proof that your dad was murdered.'

Harry fetched his laptop and tapped a few keys before handing it over to Aaron.

'What's this?' Aaron asked, staring down at a grainy looking video clip.

'Keep watching,' Harry said from over his shoulder. 'There! Did you see that?'

'See what? I can hardly see anything. What am I looking at?'

'Look closely. Tell me what you see.'

Aaron restarted the sixty second video clip.

'Okay, I can see what looks like a boat of some kind. There are lights on inside the hull and people moving about. Two people? They're fighting?'

'Exactly!'

'What? What is this?'

'This clip is from a security camera at the docks where my father's boat was moored in Monaco. What if I told you that the boat in the image is my father's and that the footage was recorded the night of the party?'

'How do you know? Where did you get this from?'

'It was sent to me.'

'When? By whom?'

'It arrived a week after my dad's body was discovered floating in the water. I don't know who sent it to me, but it came with a handwritten note advising it was my father's boat on the night in question.'

'And you believe it? I'm sorry, Harry, but you are basing your theory on the word of someone you don't know, probably with an agenda you don't understand.'

'It's proof, Aaron. Don't you see? The witness said she saw my father close everything up on the boat after the party. If that's true, why is he now fighting with someone on board? Who is this person and how did they get on the boat?'

'That's if they are fighting. This image is so grainy; they could be dancing for all we can see. I'm sorry, we can't even be certain this is your father's boat.'

Harry grabbed the laptop and typed again before handing it back to Aaron.

'What's this?'

'My father sent me an email the night he died.'

Aaron read the note.

Dearest Harry, it is with a heavy heart that I am writing you this email. I desperately want to speak with you and Toby; to hear your voices, but it is late and you are probably asleep.

I believe my life may be in grave danger. I cannot tell you why as I do not wish to put you in harm's way. I do not want you to grieve for me for long. I have had a good life and I was blessed to meet your mother and to raise two such wonderful children. It has been my honour. Truly. There is so much you do not know about me and, if I am lucky, you will never discover half of the things I have done. I need you to understand that everything I have done, I did it for you and for Toby, so that you can lead a better life than I did.

I need you to understand that, if you learn of my passing in the coming days or weeks, no accident has befallen me. If I am dead, know that somebody has caused the situation. I will not die of natural causes or suffer an accident, even if that is what you are told.

I want you to know that you are not in any danger. I have been very careful to keep you out of this. I need you to look after Toby when I am gone. He will find it difficult to cope and he will be reliant on you for support. I need you to be strong for him, and to make it your life's duty to protect him. That is the last thing I will ask of you.

My estate will be split four ways. You will receive thirty percent of all my possessions to do with what you want. Please spend the money wisely. I have placed thirty percent for Toby in trust until his eighteenth birthday. Teach him how to be careful with money and not to abuse the privilege. The remaining forty percent will be split between your cousin, Aaron and a friend of mine who has been loyal to me over the last few years. I will endeavour to get my will forwarded to you once I am gone. Provision has already been made for this.

Whatever you do, do not seek vengeance for what happens to me. That path is laden with trouble that you do not need and would struggle to handle. Grieve for me as you must, and then move on with your lives.

I have been honoured to know you, Harry, God speed!

'Shit, Harry,' Aaron muttered, uncertain what else to say.

'He attached an image to the email,' Harry said. 'Click on that symbol to open it.'

Aaron did as he was instructed. A large, high-quality colour photograph of Troy opened up. He was standing next to a large white boat that was moored at a dock somewhere. Aaron recognised the boat and location immediately.

'It's the boat in the video…'

'Exactly!' said Harry excitedly, as Aaron made the

connection. 'See what I mean? Do you understand now?'

Aaron nodded and passed the laptop back. 'Who is the friend he mentioned? Any ideas?'

'Not sure,' Harry admitted. 'As I said to you earlier, he probably had a woman out there with him, so I'd assume that's who he gave it to.'

A thought struck Aaron. He reached inside his jacket and removed the envelope Victoria had given him earlier. He showed it to Harry.

'What's this?'

'I met a woman at the wake earlier. She told me she was your father's girlfriend and she handed me that envelope. I think it's your dad's handwriting.'

Harry examined the envelope and agreed. 'What's in it?'

'I don't know. She told me to open it when I was alone.'

'Well, you're alone now...well practically.'

Aaron ripped the envelope open. It contained several folded pages. He flattened the paper out.

'It's your dad's will,' he said almost immediately. 'The email said he would get it to you somehow. I guess he instructed her to deliver it in the event that he died.' Aaron continued to read the will. 'It says his estate is worth...Jesus Christ! He was worth nearly one hundred million pounds. Fucking hell!'

Harry snatched the letter up and read it too. Both cousins stared at each other, neither able to hide the look of surprise.

'We need another drink,' Harry said pouring shots for them both.

'What the hell was your father mixed up in, and

who killed him?'

'I have no idea. What on earth am I going to do with thirty million quid?'

Aaron glanced at his watch again. He had two hours until his meeting. Picking up the glass, he knocked the shot back.

13:59

'It's a bit open, don't you think?' Lewis asked as Patterson drove the car into the IKEA car park. 'I always imagined drug deals were done in dark places; under bridges and the like.'

'Hiding in plain sight works well too, bro,' Patterson replied, as the car began to ascend the floors.

'Yeah, but there's in plain sight and then there's just doing it out in the open…this is crazy.'

'It's what Eksteen wanted. We're in no position to argue.'

'You think he'll stay true to his word? I mean, you think he'll let us take Archie's place if we don't screw this up?'

'Look, I don't know, alright? I told you before: Eksteen is a twisted fuck. All I know is: we need to hand over this money and collect the product. That's it.'

Lewis remained quiet until they reached the roof floor of the car park. 'You think he's here yet?'

Patterson pulled the car into a space and glanced around. 'I can't see him.'

'You know what he looks like?'

'Not exactly. The South African said we were to meet with a black fella with a big van. There's no big van, so I'm assuming he's not here yet.'

'How much money do you reckon is in the satchel?' Lewis asked, turning the bag over in his hands.

'It's none of our fucking business,' Patterson growled back. 'What's with all the fucking questions? You haven't stopped since we left Eksteen's.'

'Jeez, I'm sorry...I guess I'm nervous.'

'He's here,' Patterson said, pointing out the window at a large white van that was pulling up at the far side of the car park. You better stay here; we don't want him seeing your nerves.'

'Have you got a weapon? Y'know, in case things turn nasty?'

Patterson reached across him and opened the glove box, pulling out a small handgun. He checked the magazine before stuffing it into the waist belt of his trousers.

'Shit! I was kidding,' Lewis laughed. 'You ever killed anyone with that thing?'

'I told you at lunchtime, you need to understand what you're getting involved with. Have I ever killed anyone? No, not yet. Would I be prepared to do so? If it was a choice between me and someone else, then, yes, I would. Now pass me that fucking satchel and let's get this thing done!'

Patterson exited the car and walked purposefully towards the van. Lewis' heart was racing as he watched a large black man in a leather jacket climb down from the driver's side and walk around to face Patterson.

'You got the money?' Tyrese asked first.

Patterson waved the satchel, at the same time

lifting his shirt to reveal the handgun. 'You got the gear?'

'It's in the van,' Tyrese answered. 'Where's your boss?'

'He was busy so he sent me. That a problem?'

'That all depends; are you able to negotiate on his behalf?'

'What's to negotiate? You and he have already agreed on the price, no?'

'Sure, for this stash, but I mean for another trade. I might be able to supply a larger quantity if he's interested.'

'Oh yeah, how much we talking?'

'That depends on whom I'm dealing with. Am I speaking to you or the South African?'

Patterson thought about whether he would be happy working for Eksteen or whether he'd prefer to trade under his own name.

'That's up to you. If you prefer to deal with a man who doesn't show up for meets, then I guess you're talking to my boss. If you'd prefer to speak to someone with the balls to meet you, then I guess you're speaking to me. How much can you get your hands on and how much will it cost?'

'Let's conclude this trade first. You want to inspect the merchandise first?'

'Sure,' Patterson nodded, pleased with how things were progressing so far. The two men walked to the rear of the van, and Tyrese indicated that Patterson should open the doors. He handed over the satchel and opened the two doors simultaneously.

Lewis' eyes widened when he saw three armed men in Kevlar jump from the van and point their weapons at Patterson. Tyrese grabbed Patterson's arms from behind, and pulled the handgun from his waist belt, forcing him to the floor. Lewis saw Tyrese produce a warrant card from his back pocket and wave it in Patterson's face. Lewis sat frozen as Tyrese ordered two of the armed men to approach the car he was sitting in. In a panic, Lewis clambered into the driver's seat and started the car. The wheels screeched as he tore off towards the car park's exit, nearly crashing in to a parked car as he did. Round and round the exit ramp he drove, sweat dripping down his face. He slammed through the wooden security barrier, cracking the windscreen and leaving a splintered mess in his wake. He didn't know where he was going; he just needed to get away.

14:05

D.C.I. Mercure and her team had been systematically walking between rows of chairs at the football stadium in St Mary's for the last twenty-five minutes without success. They had arrived at the stadium just before half past one but it had taken some convincing to persuade the security team that the threat was very real. Half the security guards on site were currently reviewing historic camera footage to see if they could spot anybody suspicious leaving anything in the stands. The other half of the team was searching the players' dressing rooms and the V.I.P suites under Mercure's instruction, in case the terrorist had misled them.

The last home game had been three nights earlier, and whilst it seemed unlikely that the device would have been planted then, in full view of the public, it was something they had to consider. Without knowing what the terrorist looked like, it would be like looking for a needle in a haystack to see anyone suspicious planting something beneath their seat, particularly as they didn't know what area of the stadium to check. The Hospitality manager had already confirmed that the stadium had been cleaned following the match as it always was and nothing suspicious had been found.

Mercure was determined to make sure. Her team had completed a circuit of the lower section of the Northam stand and had just moved upstairs to start on the upper tier. The terrorist had told Davies that they had an hour to locate the package, giving them only five minutes more.

'I think you and your team should leave,' Travers suggested, as his bomb squad unit had decided to join the search. 'If this device is anything like what we found earlier, it could have serious repercussions.'

'How big would it need to be to flatten the whole stadium?' asked Mercure, as pragmatic as ever.

Travers thought for a moment. 'Something about five times as big as what we found would probably be enough to level most of the site.'

'So we're looking for something bigger than that tin box?'

'It depends on whether he's planning to destroy the whole place or just a small section. Either would probably serve his purpose.'

Mercure was still considering this last statement when she heard an eager voice shout, 'I've found it.'

The voice belonged to D.C. Oliver Capshaw, a thirty year-old detective with less common sense than the rest of the team. Mercure didn't have much time for Capshaw: he served a purpose, but needed a lot of micro-managing to be effective. Capshaw was ten rows higher than her.

'The rest of you keep looking, in case he's left a second device. Sid, let's go take a look.'

Travers and Mercure climbed up over the seats that separated them from where a grinning Capshaw was waiting.

'Thank you, Capshaw,' Mercure said dismissively. 'You continue the search with the others.'

Capshaw reluctantly turned his back and continued to move along the row.

Travers sunk to his knees to get a better look at the item. It was a tin box again, but this one seemed to be reinforced with a titanium alloy, making it a lot more secure than what had been glued to the car earlier. The box was under the chair but was secured in place by the plastic end of the flip-up seat. Travers carefully adjusted the chair and removed the device.

'Be careful!' Mercure shrieked when she saw what he was doing.

Travers turned the box over in his hands and saw a keypad built in the lid.

'Looks like it requires a four digit key code to unlock the box. Any idea what it is?'

Mercure fished the phone from her pocket and hit redial.

'Davies,' Kyle said on answering the call.

'We've found the box, Davies, I need to know the code.'

'One minute, Guv, she's just completing it.'

Davies had disembarked the train to Newcastle when it had arrived at Leamington Spa station. As the terrorist had advised, the next train due south had been at one thirty eight, giving him twenty minutes to locate a copy of the day's Sun newspaper. Unfortunately, the shop at the station had been sold out. He had weighed up the option of leaving the station and venturing out, but knew there was no way he could miss the southbound train and had proceeded to ask each person on the platform if they had a copy of the paper. He was out of luck.

Instead of panicking, upon boarding the train he had found the ticket inspector and asked him to make an announcement; asking anybody with a copy of the newspaper to make themselves known. Thankfully, two people raised their hands. Kyle had approached both and asked them to begin completing the puzzle. One of the volunteers, Sue, was nearly finished.

'Right, Guv, the numbers from the top left corner, working in a clockwise direction are: one, two, three and four.'

'You're kidding!'

'Nope. Seems so silly.'

Mercure relayed the numbers to Travers, before adding, 'What if the code is a trick and actually sets the bomb off?'

Travers shrugged his shoulders. 'Then be prepared to meet your maker.'

He quickly punched the digits in, before Mercure could answer, and listened as the box unlocked and the lid rose slightly. He examined the box more closely and, seeing no sign of a booby trap or cabling, he lifted the lid fully, surprised by its contents.

'Well?' Davies shouted down the line. 'Did it work?'

'I'll call you back,' Mercure said, disconnecting the phone and putting it back in her pocket.

Travers passed the box to her. 'There's no bomb, just pictures. Any idea who the woman is?'

Mercure took the box and began to examine the

photographs and series of newspaper articles it contained. The eyes in each of the photographs had been gouged out, leaving a spooky looking image. The articles that had been cut out referenced the Cannes massage scandal from six months ago. She tried to recall the message Davies had relayed earlier.

How did the terrorist describe the package? Oh yes, a clue to the puzzle.

'Well? Who is she?' Travers repeated.

'She's a local politician. Her name is Eve Partridge and I think she's been the target of this situation all along.'

She found a piece of paper in the box, with a handwritten note. She recognised the words immediately.

For too long the people of this city have striven for parity whilst the law makers tread on their broken bones. I cannot sit idly by whilst the governance of this city remains in such unsafe hands. I have witnessed your corruption and the time is coming when you will pay back what you owe.

'Where is she now?' Travers asked.

'I've no idea. I haven't seen her since the school this morning.'

'Well, if she is the target, you better find her, and quick.'

Mercure nodded her agreement and called for her team to stop the search and join her. 'There was no bomb in the box,' she began. 'This terrorist is playing games with us. We still don't know what his motivation is, but the target is Eve Partridge. I need you to get out there and find her. We need to put her in protective custody as soon as possible!'

14:26

Aaron and Harry had been toasting Troy's passing and any other subjects that Harry could think of, for the last hour. They were both now pretty drunk.

'What's it like?' Harry slurred.

'What?' Aaron replied with a puzzled frown.

'Y'know...The Army: what's it like?'

'I'm not in the fuckin' army, Harry; I'm in The Navy.'

'That's what I meant. What's it like?'

'It's good...it's...I like it.'

'Yeah but what's it like? You ever killed anyone?'

'Oh...the things I could tell you...look, think of it like this...the navy is like family. You meet people that you've never known...from places you've not seen...but you get on. You have a common goal...like...everyone there wants to be there and it's nice. I had a really good friend...he was in my unit...he was like a brother to me.'

'That's nice; what happened to him?'

Aaron's expression turned serious. 'He's dead.' He was suddenly all too aware that he had drunk too much. He checked his watch again; only an hour until the meeting.

'How did he die?' Harry continued unaware of

the change to his cousin's demeanour.

'He died because the NAAFI is under-supplied and left to rot.'

This time Harry noticed the bitter tone and sat up. 'What happened, Aaron?'

Aaron leant back in his chair and closed his eyes to help him picture that day. 'We were stationed outside of Kabul. My unit was there to provide communications support to the troops stationed at the camp. That involved co-ordinating support for insurgencies. Kabul was a TARFU already.'

'What's a TARFU?'

Aaron looked at Harry as if he had just asked what colour the sky was.

'TARFU: it means totally and royally fucked up. It's slang we use.'

Harry grinned.

'Anyway, we were also providing medical support to the camp, cleaning and dressing wounds…that kind of shit. So, a week before we were due to return to ship, one of the patrols was hit by a mortar shell in the middle of the desert outside of Deh-Dana. It was a routine patrol to check the military blockade was intact. At first it was thought that the shell was the result of friendly fire so my unit was scrambled to attend and get the victims back. If there had been any suspicion that the shell had been fired by the enemy, they would have sent tactical support with us, but the analysts said it couldn't be the enemy as they were positioned in the north of the city, not the south. So we suited up and deployed.'

Aaron drained the rest of his glass, before reaching for the bottle and pouring more in.

'So we arrive at the site of the explosion…and I'm telling you it was FUBAR all the way…'

'What's FUBAR mean?'

'Fucked up beyond all recognition. I mean, there were body parts strewn all over. The shell had struck the centre of the jeep and it was now in two parts: the front and the back. The four who had been in the vehicle were gone…I mean, we couldn't even discern who was who. I radioed it in and we were told to collect what we could and return to camp. Next thing I know, Mel, my brother, is screaming BOHICA, BOHICA. I look up and can see the trail of two incoming incendiaries. We all run for cover, running in different directions, desperate to avoid the impact. The two bombs both struck the jeep with a noise like I'd not heard before. I couldn't hear anything for a couple of minutes apart from this piercing noise. By the time, I could function again, it was too late. Mel was nowhere to be seen, but the site of the explosion had doubled in size so I knew straight away that he was gone.'

Aaron threw the drink back.

'That's shit, man. So it wasn't friendly fire?'

'It couldn't have been. What you don't get to see is the number of occurrences where one friendly nation accidentally fires on their allies. It happens regularly, but it's only ever reported when it results in the death of a serving soldier. Friendly fire is like lightning: it never strikes the same spot twice, let alone three times. No, it was clearly a resistance movement in the city who saw us as easy targets. I radioed it in, but still the analysts denied the existence of an enemy group in that part of the city.

Fucking retards!'

'What was your friend shouting?'

'BOHICA?' Aaron laughed. 'Means bend over, here it comes again. It means some bad shit is about to repeat itself. He never had a chance.'

'I'm sorry, man. We should raise a toast to Mel,' Harry said, raising his glass. Aaron copied the gesture.

'We should never been sent out to the jeep without armed response or tactical support. It wasn't the analysts' fault. They were working from funky intelligence. If the government gave the NAAFI the funding it needs to act properly, we would have known about the small resistance group. I'm talking heat-signature maps; I'm talking robotic drones that help pinpoint enemy positions to within an inch. But we had none of that. It's all about scales of war, y'know? Casualties of war are expected in every conflict, so when there is a choice between supplying every camp and unit with what they need to do their job properly, or reducing the budget by accepting that casualties are inevitable, the budget reduction wins every time. I dread to think how many men and women have lost their lives overseas because some tight-fisted tosser kept the purse strings tight. And what for? All so that the politicians can have a second home and a bigger end of year bonus. It makes me fucking sick!'

'But there's nothing you can do, right? Who will listen?'

'Oh they'll listen alright,' Aaron said. 'I'll make 'em listen.'

'How?'

'Let's just say, I have a friend who I'm due to meet soon. He's going to supply me with everything I need to make my point heard. I don't want to say anymore, but know this: my voice will be heard. I will make them understand what I have seen.'

'I hope you're right,' said Harry, finishing his drink and closing his eyes.

Aaron pitied his cousin. Harry had not known the pain Aaron had felt; had not seen the horrors he had witnessed. He knew nothing of the soldier's life, and he would never be able to understand that it had the power to change a man's outlook on life. Aaron allowed his own eyes to close for a moment, as he pictured what he had planned for the evening. He didn't even notice as his mind fell to sleep.

14:32

Ophion pressed a gloved finger to the doorbell and held it there for a second. He was confident that the owner of the flat was not home but, in his experience, it was always better to be safe than sorry. He waited by the door, listening for any noise coming from within, and, on hearing nothing, he removed the small pouch of picks from his inner jacket pocket and set to work on unlocking the door.

The door sprung open inside fifty seconds and he entered casually. He spent the first two minutes moving from room to room, ensuring that the flat was indeed empty and then also searched for any kind of listening or surveillance devices. He checked the usual spots: inside light fittings, behind photo frames and in the fruit bowl. But the place was clean. The various photographs in the flat confirmed the owner was indeed Nazir Ahmed.

Ophion had phoned Denby's firm from an untraceable phone and had demanded to speak with Denby or his secretary. He had been pleased to hear the woman on the other end advise him that Mr Denby was unavailable as was his secretary, Miss Nazir Ahmed. He had hung up and immediately worked his way through the back doors of various social networking sites until he located a picture of

Miss Ahmed. From that he was able to look up her address and contact details. It amazed him that, in this day and age, people were still naïve enough to post so much intimate information online. It was as if she wanted her identity to be cloned. That said, it gave him the opportunity to locate her.

He knew the likelihood was that she wouldn't have left the McKenzie file at home, in fact there was no reason for it to be here in the first place. However he needed to find a pressure point for her quickly. He didn't have the time he'd had to seduce Denby into submission. He had far less time to manipulate Nazir, but it was now equally vital to the day's mission.

He found some opened post on the kitchen counter top and flipped through it. There was a letter from the local antenatal clinic and an appointment letter for an ultrasound scan for that day.

She's pregnant, Ophion observed, smiling slightly. But who is the father?

There were no photographs of men in the flat, and there were no signs of a man living with her: there was only one toothbrush in the bathroom and no dirty socks on the floor. He continued to search the flat, being very careful to return things to the same place where he had found them, so that it would not appear as if anybody had been there. In the bedroom, he eventually found Nazir's diary and settled down to read. It bored him, if truth be told, lots of unanswered questions and general gripes about work, life and the greater good. However, he did also learn the true identity of the father of

Nazir's unborn baby and decided that would be his best shot at getting her to hand over the case file.

The flat looked as it had done when he had entered that morning, so, should Nazir return home unexpectedly, there would be no reason for her to suspect that anyone had been in the property uninvited. Ophion took a second glance around while he considered his options.

Denby had told him that he had contacted Nazir on a number of occasions that day demanding the file. That was bad news. Even if Nazir was the dumbest of legal secretaries who had no clue what the McKenzie case was all about, Denby's demand, followed by his subsequent suicide, would be enough to set alarm bells ringing in the simplest of minds. How long would it be before Nazir told the police about Denby's aggressive desire for that file? That simply wouldn't do.

I have to get rid of her, he decided.

The cogs for tonight's spectacle were already firmly in motion and, but for an unforeseeable hiccup, the big 'Fuck you' from the client to the city, would happen in the next four or so hours.

What if there was a way to get Nazir on the bus, he considered.

A new idea struck him: what if Nazir was held responsible for the bus?

A thin smile began to spread across Ophion's face. He loved it when he had a moment of true inspiration. He felt like punching the air, but discouraged such an immature reaction. He glanced at the time on his watch.

Is it possible? Do I have the time?

It wouldn't be easy.

It would take careful planning...but maybe, just maybe...

Ophion grabbed an open phone bill from a pile of post on the kitchen counter and made a note of Nazir's mobile phone number. He committed this to memory and returned the bill to the pile. He then moved across to her PC and turned it on. He wiped the existing internet history and then accessed a number of known al Qaeda blog sites. After this, he began searching terms including 'bomb', 'detonation', 'IED' and 'Qur'an'. He knew that UK intelligence services had a team dedicated to monitoring internet traffic, and the sites he had viewed at Nazir's terminal would flag up a warning in that team. Her name would probably be passed to some second-grade intelligence newbie to do some additional digging on Nazir; to identify if she was a plausible threat. Not that any of this would necessarily occur before tonight's main event. What it did mean, though, was that in the event of a detective investigating the day's events contacted GCHQ and asked if they had any kind of file on her, the resolute answer would be 'yes'.

Ophion rubbed his gloved hands together. All he needed to do now was to leave some physical evidence hidden from sight and the first part of his plan would be set. He knew he had enough spare gear in the most recently acquired car to give the impression that Nazir was responsible. Ophion made a note of the father's name from Nazir's diary before returning it to the bedside table and casually letting himself out of the flat.

CROSSHAIRS

14:40

It had been forty minutes since Lewis had watched Patterson fall foul of Tyrese's undercover sting operation. He had sped away from the car park, but had soon realised that the damaged windscreen would draw unwanted attention to his escape. He had ended up driving the car back to his parent's house and had hidden it in the garage. He had replayed Patterson's arrest over and over in his mind and still couldn't quite believe he had dreamt the whole thing. He had sat in silence on the sofa until he could no longer ignore the vibrating phone in his pocket. A withheld number had called more than a dozen times, and, when he eventually answered the phone, he was not surprised to hear Eksteen's voice.

'Where the fuck is my meth?' he demanded.

'Tyrese was an undercover cop. He's got your money and he's got Billy too.'

'I really hope you are joking...get your arse over here now!'

Lewis had wanted to shout back that the deal was off; that he had changed his mind and just wanted to go back to being a school kid again, but he knew there was no point. Eksteen had threatened to kill him already and Lewis was pretty sure it wasn't a bluff. Reluctantly, he had climbed back into Patterson's car and driven back to Eksteen's Autos.

The car lot looked as deserted as it had done earlier. His plan was just to come clean with Eksteen; to fall on the South African's mercy, if he indeed had any. Eksteen was still flanked by the bodyguards from earlier and Lewis shuddered as he remembered how the female had manhandled him last time. He knocked on the office door and waited to be ushered in. Eksteen was on the phone and, when he had replaced the receiver, he waved for Lewis to enter. Lewis waited to be invited to sit down and felt physically sick as he sat across the desk from Eksteen.

'Tell me what happened at the meet.'

Lewis took a deep breath and then relayed what he had seen.

'You're saying Tyrese was an undercover policeman? I find that hard to believe! He was recommended to me by someone I trust very strongly.

'I swear to God it's true! Billy was opening the van when three armed officers jumped out and he was wrestled to the ground.'

'And yet you managed to escape. How convenient!'

'I barely escaped. If I hadn't still been in Billy's car, they'd have got me too.'

'Yes, but why were you in his car? Hmm? I thought you two were partners, why didn't you go to the van together?'

'Billy was worried that I looked too nervous and told me to wait behind.'

'That's your version of events, but why should I believe you? How do I know that you aren't a police informant who set Patterson up? Hmm? Or maybe you're an undercover policeman too.'

'I'm only seventeen! I'm not old enough to be a police officer.'

Lewis pulled the wallet from his pocket, removed his driver's licence and threw it towards Eksteen. The South African scooped up the licence and examined it.

'This doesn't prove you aren't an informant though. For all I know, you're the reason the Bitterne house was raided yesterday and caused Archie and two others to be arrested.'

'That's impossible! I wasn't even involved in the drugs industry before this morning!'

'Oh really? But you are Patterson are partners, aren't you?'

'That only happened today...you don't understand, Mr Eksteen.'

'I understand only too well, sonny. You and your friend decided you would try and rip me off so you've kept my gear or my money and made up this crap about Tyrese being undercover.'

'That's not true,' Lewis pleaded.

'I'll give you one last chance: tell me where my crystal meth is! I have a contact in the police who will be able to tell me whether Patterson was arrested or not.'

'Ask your contact. I swear on my life it's the truth!'

Eksteen began to walk around the desk. 'You swear on your life, do you? You know, killing a man is not as easy as they make out in the movies. It takes a lot of courage to look another person in the eye and then end their pathetic excuse for a life. Sure, you can shoot them from behind, that's a bit easier because you don't have to see their pleading eyes, begging you for mercy. I like to look them in the face, out of respect, y'know?'

Lewis didn't like the fact that Eksteen was getting ever closer to him and was talking about murder.

'I reckon I could do it, Mr Eksteen, for you. I mean, if it pleased you, I could do it.' Lewis wasn't sure what he was saying or why, but he was desperate to talk himself out of this predicament.

'Oh, you want to please me, do you, sonny? That's nice to hear. It's good to hear that you're on my side and want to make me happy.' Eksteen was now next to Lewis, who couldn't prevent the sweat forming on his forehead. 'Have you ever sucked a man's cock, sonny?'

Lewis looked up at Eksteen, puzzled by the strange question. 'Wh-what? No. Never. I'm not queer!'

'But didn't you say you wanted to please me, sonny? I thought you were on my side?'

'I am...but...I...'

Eksteen burst out laughing, and slapped Lewis on the back. 'I'm only fucking joking,' he roared. 'Did you see his face?' he said to the bodyguards. 'He thought I wanted him to suck my dick!'

Lewis laughed nervously, grateful that he had seemed to win Eksteen over. After all, if they were sharing a joke that meant they were friends. Right?

Wrong!

Eksteen suddenly lashed out and wrapped his right hand around Lewis' neck forcing the younger man to fall backwards in the chair. He bit his lip as the chair hit the ground.

'What the fuck do you take me for, sonny? Where is my fucking meth?'

Lewis tried to respond but couldn't speak as Eksteen's grip was too tight.

'You thought you could steal my meth? You thought I would believe that some undercover nigger had seized it, when really you've got it?'

Eksteen loosened the grip slightly, expecting to now hear a different version of events.

'But it's the truth!' Lewis gasped. 'Tyrese is in the police. Search me; I have no cash on me.'

Eksteen began to pat him down with a free hand. He found the Lewis's wallet and fished it out. The wallet was indeed empty, save for some coins and cards. He indicated for the woman to take over holding Lewis down, and, when she was in position, he returned to his own seat. He was surprised to find a photograph of Lewis with an older woman.

'This your mother?' he asked, holding the image up high enough for Lewis to see. Lewis nodded.

'I bet she could find the money you owe me.'

'No, please,' Lewis gasped. 'She doesn't have any money, I swear. Tyrese has the gear!'

'Oh please! Stop lying to me, sonny. You have given me no other choice.'

Eksteen picked up the driving licence again and tossed it to the male bodyguard, adding, 'Get Benny over here. I want the two of you to go to this address and deliver a package for me. You understand?'

The man nodded and withdrew a mobile phone as he left the office, presumably to call whoever Benny was.

'She won't give you any money!' Lewis spat. 'She doesn't even like me.'

Eksteen came back around and crouched down, 'Who are you trying to kid, sonny? She's your mother. She loves you. Besides, I have a way to convince her.'

Eksteen smiled as he lifted his right hand so that Lewis could see what he was holding: secateurs.

'Unzip his trousers,' Eksteen told the woman, a huge grin growing.

15:00

It had been five hours since Eksteen's goons had made the attempt on Jean-Paul Retourget's life. The time had done nothing to quell his anger, nor his appetite for revenge; despite Al-Batani's warning about The Cadre's involvement an hour earlier. He was now crouched down across the road from Eksteen Autos, out of sight of anyone inside. He presumed the car lot was a front for the South African's extra-curricular activities, a suspicion that was confirmed by the total lack of trade that had passed through the doors to the showroom while he had been watching.

That had been true until twenty minutes earlier when a youth in a hoodie and skinny jeans had nervously entered the building. The young man's appearance had surprised Retourget, as the attire didn't suggest he was there to purchase a car. The fact that the young man had yet to resurface was, again, suggestive that a car sale was not in process.

Probably one of Eksteen's dealers, Retourget assumed.

His interrogation of Clark and the driver of the van, back at the industrial estate, had left a bitter taste in his mouth. It had been a number of years since he had had to resort to such measures and, whilst he had savoured the power at the time, he knew karma would be out to exact vengeance at some point. Clark had told him that Eksteen had paid ten grand for the execution; a small fee by modern standards, but the recession had hit all areas, not just every day commercial businesses.

Retourget checked his ammunition. His gun had a full clip once again. The three bullets he had left in Clark's smouldering body were untraceable. It had been only right to torch the van and the three victims before he had left the scene. He didn't doubt that the local forensics experts would be able to identify the bodies, but burning them would slow any progress down long enough for him to escape the country. He had one spare full clip in his trouser pocket, but that was the last of his ammunition so, if he needed more than thirteen bullets to dispose of Eksteen, he would be in trouble. He pushed the thought from his mind and the pistol into his waist belt.

Retourget walked as casually as possible towards the car lot. All was quiet inside the showroom, so he carefully opened the large glass door and walked in. He ensured he made as little noise as possible as he approached the small office at the rear of the showroom.

He quickly glanced through the window and was amazed to find a suited man and woman holding down the youth who had entered twenty minutes earlier, while Eksteen waved a pair of secateurs in his face. Retourget looked away so that he wouldn't be spotted, but he pressed an ear against the thin plaster wall so he could hear what was being said.

'Maybe I should cut your fucking pecker off,' he heard the South African say. 'Danielle, pull his fucking trousers down.'

Retourget glanced in to see the woman yanking at the youth's trousers.

'Please, Mr Eksteen,' the young man sobbed. 'I'm telling you the truth!'

Retourget placed his ear back against the wall.

'I don't like people who lie to me, sonny. You hear me? I've killed for far less.'

'I'm not lying! Jesus Christ! Don't cut my dick off!'

'Okay, maybe not your dick…I don't want you to fucking bleed to death before your mother brings me what you fucking owe! Maybe an ear, then. How about that? Or a finger? Maybe I should cut your whole fucking hand off, you motherfucking thief!'

Fucking hypocrite! Retourget thought.

'I swear to God, I'm not lying!' the youth shouted desperately.

'No? Where is my fucking dope then, huh? Where's my fucking money?'

'I told you! Tyrese took it!'

This last statement was followed by a high-pitched scream, like nothing Retourget had ever heard. He glanced back through the window one last time and saw Eksteen, blood-stained sleeves and all, triumphantly lifting a severed middle finger high in the air.

'Brings new meaning to the expression flipping the finger, eh?' Eksteen laughed. The South African threw the bloody digit to a man standing by the door of the office. 'Benny, go with Dieter to the mother's address and leave this with the package.'

'Ya, boss,' Benny replied and turned towards the office door. The man who had been helping hold the lad down stood up and followed him.

Retourget didn't want to get spotted, so he ducked down behind a nearby car and watched as the two well-built men left the office and proceeded out through the showroom. The one called Dieter, who looked like a bodybuilder, was carrying a large brown briefcase in his hand.

What's in the briefcase? Retourget wondered, probably my money!

That left Eksteen in the office with the woman and the youth. Retourget had no idea if any of them were armed, but assumed Eksteen would be stupid not to have at least one weapon hidden somewhere close by. He had a choice to make: get Eksteen now or follow the two goons and get the briefcase.

He could feel the seconds ticking past, as his mind raced for a solution.

Fuck it! Eksteen can wait, he decided.

Keeping low, so that he could scuttle under the office window, he quickly made his way across the showroom floor and quietly slipped out through the large glass door. He could see the two goons about twenty metres ahead, climbing into a dark blue Mercedes that was parked on the forecourt. Retourget looked around and saw an old banger parked in the street. He figured it would be the easiest vehicle to hotwire. He waited for the Mercedes to pull into the road and then ran to it. He used his elbow to smash the window and then poked his hand through to unlock the door. He brushed as much glass as he could from the seat and jumped in.

15:28

Aaron opened his eyes suddenly. He didn't know why, but he had a nagging feeling that something wasn't right.

Where am I?

He glanced around the unfamiliar room and spotted his cousin Harry snoring in an armchair to his left. His memory then kicked in and the events of the day came flooding back. This was swiftly followed by a shooting pain in his head, causing him to blink a number of times as he came to terms with it. He spotted the culprit on the table: tequila. He always suffered after drinking shots of any liquor.

He tried to get up, knowing that the quickest cure would be a couple of pints of water and a slice of dry bread. He stumbled through to the kitchen and located what he needed. He managed to throw the first glass of water down his throat, but the second wasn't so easy; he gave up a third of the way through. He tried to recall why they had started drinking and then remembered telling Harry about his fallen comrade.

Aaron nearly dropped the glass when he suddenly remembered the meeting he was due at. He checked his watch and his eyes widened as he realised he was now late for the meeting. He ran back to the living room and shook Harry awake.

'Harry, where are your keys? Harry, your keys? Where are your car keys?'

Harry stirred but didn't look happy to be woken.

'Harry? Where are your car keys?' Aaron persisted.

'Why d'you want them?' his cousin slurred.

'I'm late for my meeting, Harry. I should be in the city now. Oh God…come on, wake up.'

Harry opened his eyes but, before he could say anything, he threw up. Aaron managed to dive out of the way before his uniform got spattered. Harry's face was a decidedly green colour when he finished retching. 'You can't drive! You're as drunk as me!'

It was a fair point.

'Harry, I need to get into the city. Now! Do you have the number of a taxi company? Maybe a friend who could drive me? Come on, think!'

Harry choked back a second bout of vomiting before offering, 'There's a bus stop two minutes up the road. There's probably a bus due to the city soon. They go from Fareham every twenty or so minutes.'

'Fine. Where is the bus stop?'

'Okay. Go to the end of the drive and turn left. It's about two hundred yards down the road.'

Aaron didn't even wait to say farewell, instead turning on his heel and heading out of the lounge and then out of the front door. He jogged to the end of the driveway and, as he did, he saw a bus drive past. His eyes widened again as he realised he was about to miss the bus. He broke into a sprint as he turned out onto the pavement and began to chase the bus down. He prayed that it would be due to stop, as that would be his only chance of catching it. His head was spinning and a dull ache remained behind his eyes, but he tried to ignore it and focus on his goal.

The bus was still not indicating that it would stop and he was about to give up when he spotted the orange light flashing and the bus pulled to the side of the road. He was gasping for breath as he reached the open doors, but he was able to say he wanted a ride to Southampton Central train station.

'That'll be three pounds please, sailor,' the female bus driver said, smiling at him.

He glanced down and, remembering his uniform, smiled back, slamming three pound coins on the tray before tearing his ticket stub from the machine. He made his way through the bus unsteadily, finding a vacant seat about halfway down. He pulled his mobile phone out and saw he had missed a call from his contact. It must have been this that had woken him from his drunken stupor. He pressed re-dial and waited for the phone to connect.

'Where you been, Aaron?' his contact asked.

'I'm sorry...I was at a funeral. Can we still meet?'

'Where are you now?'

'Lowford I think.'

'How quickly can you get to the city?'

'I'm not sure, hold on...'

Aaron marched back to the front of the bus and asked the driver how long it would take to reach their destination.

'About half an hour depending on traffic, luv,' she replied.

He thanked her and returned to his seat. 'I'll be with you in about half an hour. Have you got everything we discussed before?'

'Of course I have!'

'I want you to confirm what you've got.'

'Are you crazy? I don't know if this line is being monitored…or if your line is clean.'

'Why would anyone be tapping this conversation? Nobody knows what we discussed or my plan.'

'That's as maybe, Aaron, but I'm in an important position; it's only natural that a proportion of my communications are monitored.'

'Paul, don't kid a kidder. You're no more than Eve Partridge's glorified secretary! The fact that you happened to clap eyes on some very confidential files that help my cause was dumb luck! I'm paying you very handsomely for your support today.'

'You can be really rude, you know that? If Eve ever found out what I was doing, she'd be mortified! It would cost me my job and her friendship too! If you weren't paying me, I'd probably be offended…Which bus are you on?'

Aaron looked around for any sign to identify the bus. 'It's a number four I think. My cousin said it travels from Fareham to the city and the driver tells me I'll be there in half an hour.'

'Okay, I know that route. Once you're over the Itchen Bridge, you'll arrive at Ocean Village. I'll wait at the bus stop there. I've placed the files and equipment in a box, wrapped up like a birthday present, so that it doesn't draw unnecessary attention. When you arrive, tell the bus driver you need to collect something and then you can get off the bus at a later destination.'

'It's all very clandestine, Paul. But if it makes you feel better…'

'If you want this package, you'll follow my rules! Clear?'

'Crystal,' Aaron confirmed before hanging up.

15:46

Tracey Reed wasn't sure what to expect as she pushed her front door open. The earlier telephone conversation with Lewis had ended painfully and she had been unable to think of anything else since she had hung up on him. Although she had promised Mr Bletcher that she would stay behind and make up for her lateness that morning, she had been unable to concentrate on work and feigned sickness. She had told Holly what she had said, once her break-time had ended, and even Holly had been surprised at her reaction.

'I didn't mean to say it,' Tracey had confessed. 'It just came out.'

It was true: she hadn't meant to lash out at her son, but what was it they said about hurting those closest to you? It should have been her husband Ian that she had sworn at.

What gives him the right to screw around behind my back?

Holly had suggested that she was suffering with stress and to make an appointment with the G.P. as soon as possible. She was probably right, but Tracey had never been the type to spill her emotions to a virtual stranger. Besides, she didn't want to admit that she might need some kind of therapy to deal with life's challenges.

'Lewis? Are you home?' she called out, as she closed the door behind her. She was surprised at how timid the question had sounded. She had no idea whether he would be here or not. Her statement on the phone had been more than firm, and she desperately hoped that he had stayed true to form and ignored her request.

There was no answer from upstairs, so she crept quietly up to see if he was giving her the silent treatment. She pushed his door open and found that the curtains were closed, the bed was a mess and there were empty crisp packets scattered on the floor. She let out a sigh as she opened the curtains, made the bed and attempted to reclaim the carpet.

She let out a second sigh, this one a sigh of relief, as she opened his chest of drawers and saw all his clothes were still where they should be. He hadn't moved out and that was a good indication that their relationship could yet be repaired. She finished straightening up the room and headed back downstairs to make a well-earned cup of tea. Her thoughts of relief quickly evaporated as she walked past the living room and saw the state it was in. The large sofa had been dragged across the floor and was now sitting directly in front of the television screen. There were a couple of games controllers on the floor, along with more empty crisp packets, crushed beer cans and cigarette butts.

What the...?

She couldn't finish the thought as she hit upon the probable explanation: a party. There was no sign of Lewis in the house, but clearly he had been here today with at least one other person if not more, and wherever he was, he was under the influence of alcohol. The rejection broke her heart. She was about to start picking up the rubbish and tidying the room when she heard the telephone ringing. As she picked up the phone she vowed that, if it was Lewis on the line, she would give him another piece of her mind, and this time she would mean every word of it.

'Yes?' she barked into the phone.

'Is that Mrs Tracey Reed?' asked an unfamiliar voice. She assumed it was some unidentified call centre drone.

'Yes. Yes it is. Can I help you with something?'

'Yes, Mrs Reed,' the voice continued, the accent South African, unless she was mistaken. 'It's about your son, Lewis.'

Oh God! It's the police, she wrongly assumed.

'What's he done?' she sighed.

'Your son has been incredibly stupid.'

'Excuse me? The police shouldn't speak that way about my son!'

The man on the line laughed. 'Oh, I'm not the police, Mrs Reed. Far from it. For now, my name is not important. What you should know is that I am a very powerful man; a very rich man. Your dickhead of a son has stolen something from me and now I am going to hold onto him until his debt has been repaid.'

Tracey almost laughed out loud.

Is this guy for real?

'I'm sorry…who are you?' she demanded.

'I am the man who is holding Lewis prisoner

because the little cocksucker stole some of my drugs.'

'Drugs? Lewis? Oh no, I think you must have him confused with somebody else.'

'I don't think so, Tracey. In fact I'm looking at a picture of you now. My God, you are one ugly…'

'Who the hell…are you one of Lewis' friends? Is that it? He put you up to this? Think you're funny do you?'

'Look in the fridge, Tracey.'

'The fridge? Why would I want to do that?'

'I don't like to repeat myself, Tracey. Just look in the fucking fridge.'

Tracey rolled her eyes as she walked into the kitchen and opened the fridge door. She screamed when she saw a severed middle finger, standing on a plate, on the middle shelf.

'Take my word for it, Tracey: that is Lewis' finger, and if you don't want to receive a different body part every week for the rest of the year, you'll listen to what I have to tell you, and do as I instruct.'

'Where is my son? I want to speak with him.'

'No. You will do as I say! On the table behind you is a briefcase. You are to deliver it to the address I have attached to the handle. Is that clear? It must reach the address no later than seven o'clock tonight, or I will kill Lewis. If you even think about calling the police, you will never see him ever again. Is that clear?'

'You bastard!'

'That's right, Mrs Reed, I am a bastard. Worse than that: I'm a killer. If you want to see Lewis again, deliver that briefcase. Oh, and Tracey, we will be watching you.'

The line went dead. Tracey dropped the phone as the reality of what she had heard dawned on her. Sure enough, there was a briefcase on the table in the kitchen. She looked around, her heart racing from the shock. She half expected a film crew to jump out and explain that she was on some kind of prank reality show, but she was all alone. It was then that she noticed the biscuit tin open on the counter top. She rushed over to it and was disappointed to see her savings gone.

The bastards have robbed me too!

She tried to think of a solution.

Should I phone Ian?

She decided against it as he wasn't much use in a crisis. With little other option, she grabbed the briefcase and studied the address on the label.

15:47

Kyle Davies was eagerly standing by the train's door as it pulled into the station. A signalling fault had meant the train's arrival was two minutes behind schedule. He had no way of advising the terrorist of this fact and he could only hope that the man behind the day's atrocities was patient.

The train came to a halt and Kyle was already pressing the door's release button before the beep indicated it had been engaged. The door eventually opened with a whoosh of air, when the conductor engaged the mechanism, and Kyle bounded onto the platform, heading for the exit. He had to force his way between alighting passengers, all moving towards the station's exit.

'Police business,' he tried to say, but nobody was listening.

He finally got through the crowd and waved his warrant card so that the ticket attendant would allow him through. He ran out of the station and scanned left and right, searching for a bank of pay phones. He spotted it to his left and, as he approached the bank, one phone was audibly ringing. He lifted the receiver and breathlessly shouted, 'Yeah, I'm here.'

'Detective Sergeant Davies, I had nearly given up on you. Did I not make myself clear when we last spoke? I told you what time I would phone. I don't like being kept waiting.'

'Look, I'm here now; that's all that matters.'

'You sound out of breath, Kyle, don't tell me you ran all the way from Leamington?'

'No…I was at the far end of the train.'

'Tut-tut. Did you manage to solve the Sudoku puzzle and retrieve the code?'

'One, two, three, four? Bit childish don't you think?'

'That's as maybe, but I didn't want to make it too difficult for your simple policeman's brain. I would love to have seen your face when you cracked it,' Ophion laughed.

'Why are you doing this? What do you hope to gain? Notoriety?'

'Ah, fame…we don't all crave to be celebrities! In fact, fame is the last thing I crave. Quite the opposite in my line of work. No. I have told you already, there is a message I need to deliver to the city. An important message.'

'Yeah? Why not take out an advertisement in the local newspaper? Better still, buy yourself some radio time. Violence solves nothing,' Kyle fired back breathlessly.

'We'll have to agree to disagree about that I'm afraid, Detective Sergeant. I have known violence to solve many a tricky issue.'

'You won't get away with this…I can promise you that. We'll track you down. Somebody will talk. You'll be exposed for the scumbag degenerate you really are!'

'Where does all this hostility come from, Kyle? I

have done nothing to hurt you. My issues with the city should not concern you.'

'They shouldn't concern me? You threatened my daughter this morning and you are terrorising my city. I will catch you!'

'I look forward to it…but that can wait. There are more pressing matters that we must, alas, deal with.'

'What matters? I've done what you asked of me. I solved the puzzle and I returned to the city. Now tell me what your target is!'

'All in good time, Kyle, all in good time. First, I have something else for you to do.'

'No! Enough of these games! I don't want to see anyone hurt. Where is the fucking bomb?'

'We play by my rules, Detective Sergeant, not yours! You were late getting to this phone. Lateness means a punishment is required to show you how serious I am. I have left an explosive device at the university. It is on a timer, and you don't have a lot of time to locate it.'

'What? You're a fucking psychopath!'

'And? Concentrate on what I am telling you, Kyle. The next bomb will explode at four forty-five. That gives you an hour to find and diffuse it.'

'Where is it?'

'I told you: at the university.'

'Which one? There are two in the city.'

'You'll have to discover that for yourself.'

'That's not enough time. You have to give me another clue to its whereabouts. Anything!'

Ophion paused, while he considered the request. 'Very well, you'll discover the device if you work up enough of an appetite to find it. I'm sure you'll be able to figure out the deactivation code by the time you find it. I will call you in an hour with the next device.'

'Hello? Hello?' Kyle shouted, but the line was dead.

He pulled out his mobile phone and called Mercure.

'You back yet, Davies?' was the first thing Mercure said.

'Yes, Guv. Just.'

'Did you speak with the terrorist?'

'Yes. He wouldn't give me any more information on what his main target is. He told me he has left a device at one of the universities as a punishment for me being late.'

'Late? Why were you late?'

'There was a signalling fault near the airport. Anyway, we need to send teams to hunt for the device; to both universities.'

'Which campuses? There are at least three per university.'

'Shit! Really? I don't know! We'll have to send teams to all of them.'

'How long have we got?'

'An hour.'

'Did he say anything else?' Mercure sighed.

'Nothing helpful. What was at the stadium?'

'It wasn't a bomb, I can tell you that! It was a box full of photographs of Eve Partridge.'

'The politician? You think she's the target?'

'She must be. She received a threatening letter this morning, so I have reason to believe she is connected with this somehow. We have taken her into protective custody for now, and we are running background checks to look for known offenders that she may have inadvertently come into contact with.'

'She was involved in that prostitution scandal abroad, right?'

'Yes.'

'You think she's bent? Like, she's got herself involved in something she shouldn't have?'

'I don't think so. My gut tells me this terrorist is more political than that. Did he definitely say it is a bomb at the university? Did he say the word bomb or did he describe it as a package again?'

Kyle replayed the conversation in his mind. 'He definitely said bomb and explode so we have to assume the threat is real.'

'Right, I'll talk to Sid Travers and we'll coordinate a search of the campuses. We might need to call in support from Portsmouth and any available P.C.S.O.s. Go to the Highfield Campus at the University of Southampton and start searching there. I'll send you a couple of uniformed officers to help. Keep off the phone in case I need to call you.'

Kyle acknowledged the order and headed for the taxi rank.

15:59

Nazir Ahmed felt remorse as she left the apartment block: remorse that she had not made more of an effort to be there for Simon when he needed her. Maybe his demands for the McKenzie file had been nothing more than a cry for help. Maybe it was her that he had needed to see, more than the file; maybe that's why he had kept phoning and messaging her. She wondered how differently the day might have turned out had she not gone for that ultrasound examination first thing. Maybe if she had gone to his apartment with the file instead of to the hospital, she would have been better placed to help him; to talk him out of taking his own life. It made her realise just how fleeting life could be. The police had even suggested that she might have been the last person he spoke to. What made her saddest was that she couldn't even recall exactly what her last words to him had been. They certainly weren't to tell him what a good boss he had been.

Rest in peace, Simon.

The D.C.I. she had spoken to earlier had insisted that Nazir provide them with a written statement of her interactions with Simon that day. Mercure had said the statement should be taken at the station but, owing to Nazir's condition, it could be dealt with at the scene. D.C. Beth Taylor had been asked to sit with her, as she had written the statement, asking pertinent questions to help add as much detail to the statement as she could remember. It was odd: she had read written statements in her time at university, and at the firm, but when she had picked up the pen, she had struggled with how to structure it.

She had never imagined it would take the best part of three hours to write it. She felt physically exhausted as she walked along the street, back towards the city. Taylor had kindly phoned the firm to explain what had happened to Simon and why they required Nazir to be at the scene. Apparently, one of the partners had confirmed that Nazir did not need to return to the office. It was just as well, with only an hour of the working day left; not that Nazir would have been able to concentrate on work.

She had no idea how she would get home that night. With her car still abandoned at the car park near the office, she was without transport and only had a limited amount of change in her purse. How different the world had seemed when she had woken that morning. She could see nothing but despair ahead now.

Stop feeling so sorry for yourself!

She tried to brighten her mood. If anything, Simon's sudden demise should have been a kick up the bum to sort her own life out. She stopped in the middle of the street and closed her eyes, allowing the light rain to splash down on her face.

You need to prioritise, Nazir!

She pulled the smart phone from her pocket and loaded up an internet search page, looking for tow services in the vicinity of her home. She found two possible candidates and dialled the first one.

The man she spoke to said that he couldn't collect her vehicle until the morning and would require her to drop off a set of her car keys. She told him about her pregnancy in an effort to appeal to his softer side. It worked! The man agreed to pick her up from home in the morning and drive to the vehicle's location, before towing it back to her address. It was the best news she had heard all day and she gratefully appreciated his kindness.

She was about to put her phone away when it began to vibrate in her hand. The number was withheld, but that probably meant it was the office phoning.

'Hello? Nazir Ahmed,' she confirmed.

'Hello, Nazir,' said a voice she did not recognise. 'It's Samir Rahul.'

Of all the people that Nazir had thought would call her, the Bollywood playboy who had knocked her up and abandoned her, was the last person she expected to hear from.

'Samir? You sound different on the phone,' she replied evenly. She didn't know how to react: should she be pleased to hear from her former lover or angry that it had taken him this long?

'I'm glad I have found you, Nazir. You have no idea how difficult it was for me to find your number.'

'What do you want, Samir? The last time I saw you…well, in fact, didn't see you, was when you scarpered from the hotel room.'

'I owe you an apology for that. I…I was a naïve

fool to treat you as I did…I don't wish to make excuses but you should understand I was a scared man, back then. I have changed, and I want to make things right.'

'Make things right? Do you have any idea how I felt to wake up and find you gone? I'd thought we had got on well. We made love…I thought…'

'I felt it too, Nazir, that's why I was scared. I had never had a connection with a woman the way I had had with you. It frightened me, so I ran. It is only now that I am able to come to terms with my true feelings. I want you to give me a second chance.'

Nazir couldn't believe what she was hearing. She had spent a lot of time thinking about what she would say to Samir in the unlikely event that their paths crossed again, but she couldn't remember any of it. Her feelings towards him had moved from infatuation to hatred to pity. She had never understood why Allah had allowed her to fall pregnant out of wedlock, and the way the Imam had shunned her since, had left her questioning her faith. None of this would have happened if she had not allowed herself to be seduced by Samir.

'Samir, you have no idea…'

'I know about the baby.'

The statement shocked her.

How could he know?

'But it's okay,' he continued. 'I have spoken with the local Imam here and he has said he will bless our marriage if we promise to raise the child in the Islam faith. I will do whatever it takes to win you back, Nazir, just tell me what I must do to prove myself.'

Nazir's head was spinning. 'I…don't know…I…'

'I'm in England. I have come to see you. I need to see you. Will you meet me? Let me prove to you how much you mean to me. Please, Nazir?'

She didn't know what to say. 'Give me a minute,' she said and held the phone to her chest while she considered her options. The remorse she had felt moments earlier was evaporating; replaced by renewed hope. Her life had hit an all-time low today, but maybe this phone call was the light at the end of the tunnel. If there was any truth in what Samir was saying, it was the future she craved: security for her baby. Besides, what was she leaving behind? A job that didn't pay enough and a community that had turned its back on her in her hour of need.

'Okay, Samir, I'll agree to meet you,' she said reluctantly. 'Where and when?'

'Where are you now?'

'I'm in Southampton.'

'Where exactly?'

'Ocean Village. You remember it? Ten minutes' walk from the Waterside hotel.'

'I can be at the train station in the next hour. Can you meet me there?'

'Sure,' she said. 'I'm sure there's a bus I can catch.'

Nazir walked to the nearest bus stop and looked up at the digital display showing when the next bus was due. 'There's a number four due any minute. I think it goes to the train station. I'll see you in an hour.'

'Perfect. Thank you, Nazir,' said Ophion, disconnecting the line and placing the phone back in his pocket. He had to assume that Nazir still had the file on her person, as the police would have been unable to take it without a warrant. The bus Nazir had referred to was the one he had secured the third bomb to back in Fareham. If he was correct, then the explosion would take care of her. If she caught a different bus, he would take care of her later. He was surprised at how easy it had been to dupe her, but he was pleased the plan was coming together. The client was due to call at any minute, and it would be good to be able to confirm that everything was in place. In three hours, the client would achieve his goal and Ophion would receive the second half of his fee. He leant back in the car seat and allowed his eyes to close while he began to imagine the well-deserved holiday he would soon be embarking on.

RUSH HOUR

16:00

Sally Trexal gently applied her foot to the brake as the bus began its descent down the Itchen Bridge. She had commenced the number four bus route an hour earlier, and she was glad that her break was nearing. She had worked this route for several months and, although the route was quieter than most, there were the regular travellers that she was beginning to recognise. She didn't know any of them by name yet, but a couple did mention her name when they boarded the bus, and that gave her a feeling of appreciation when it happened.

She swung the bus left at the foot of the bridge and pulled up to let a passenger disembark. As she closed the door and pressed the indicator up, she spotted the handsome man in naval uniform, approaching her station from the rear-view mirror.

'Hi,' he said, adding, 'Sally,' when he noticed her name badge. 'I need a favour.'

She stayed silent, while he explained what it was he wanted.

'You see? I am on my way to a birthday party. My friend has had to pull out at the last minute and asked me to take the present he had bought with me. He said he would meet me at the next bus stop and hand it over. Would you be able to let me off for, like, two minutes to get it and then back on?'

'It's against company policy,' she began, 'but as you have such cute blue eyes, I don't see why not. We're a couple of minutes ahead of schedule so I can wait two minutes for you. No more, mind you!'

Aaron flashed his cutest smile as a thank you.

A minute later and Sally pulled the bus over. 'We've arrived at Ocean Village, ladies and gents,' she bellowed to the passengers. We're going to stop here for a couple of minutes before moving on.'

Aaron was still standing by the doors, eager to alight as quickly as possible. In his eagerness to disembark, he almost knocked into the pregnant woman who was boarding the bus. He saw Paul almost immediately. It was difficult to miss the man sitting with a bright red box with a big white bow on top.

'Are you Paul?' Aaron asked casually, when he was in front of him.

'Aaron, right? It's nice to finally meet you in person,' Paul replied, glancing around to ensure nobody was watching them.

'I need you to confirm that everything is in there, Paul. Please?'

'Alright,' Paul whispered. 'I have the three maps of Kabul you requested, including the thermo-signature one. I have saved the pre-redacted emails to the memory stick in here. They really are quite incriminating.'

'And the other thing?'

'The camp's supply list from the period in question. How are you planning on using this information?'

'I'd rather not involve you anymore. Let's just say I have made a friend at an organisation that takes pleasure in revealing people's dirty laundry online. Don't worry, I won't mention you or how I got hold of this information. You've done a great thing today, Paul. You should know that. What I am looking to do is make things safer for our troops serving abroad. If that means I risk a reprimand for exposing the truth, then it's a price I'm prepared to pay.'

'I hope you're right, Aaron. I've enough on my plate today without this additional stress.'

Aaron pushed the box under his arm and returned to the bus. He mouthed a 'thank you' in Paul's direction. The pregnant woman had taken the unoccupied seat that Aaron had been previously using, so he found one further towards the rear of the bus. He couldn't help but notice how pretty she looked, although she was clearly deep in thought about something.

Nazir felt the baby kick and it caused her to wince slightly. She felt exhausted and was relieved to finally be sitting down again. She was still thinking about her conversation with Samir. It had been such a bolt from the blue and she had yet to decide whether she should be happy or angry about his contact.

It bothered her that it had taken so long for him to get in touch. If his feelings were really as strong as he claimed, he should have contacted her sooner. She tried to push the nagging doubts from her mind.

Why am I so pessimistic all the time?

It was time to look at this positively! A man she

had fallen in love with overnight had said he was in love with her and had even discussed marriage and raising their child together.

This is good news, Nazir!

But a nagging doubt remained: how had he found her number, how did he know where she lived, and how had he learned that she was pregnant?

16:01

The Head of Campus Security was in his office pacing, as he shouted into the telephone, 'I don't care how busy you are, that machine isn't working! Your engineer was here this morning and it was working fine when he left, but now it's broken again. You need to send him back.'

'I'm sorry, sir,' the woman on the other end of the phone repeated. 'All of our engineers work to a tight schedule they are all busy today. I can check and tell you the next available appointment time.'

'Fine!' he sighed. 'When can I expect to see somebody?'

'One moment please,' the woman replied, before placing the call on hold.

He moved the irritating music, which was now being pumped through the phone, away from his ear and returned to his desk. His day was already busy enough, without having to chase up Vendor Services. He knew there would be a flood of complaints if the machine's fault wasn't fixed promptly.

'Yes, I'm still here,' he barked when the woman returned to the call.

'Well, sir, the earliest available appointment I can book for you is next Wednesday.'

'Next Wednesday?' he shouted. 'That's not good enough. I need someone here today; tomorrow at the latest. Don't you understand? I'll have a riot on my hands if they can't get their pre-lecture sugar fix.'

'I'm sorry, sir, unless there's a cancellation, Wednesday is the best I can offer you.'

'I want to speak to your supervisor.'

'My supervisor will tell you the same thing as me, sir. I am not trying to be difficult, I can only tell you what availability we have.'

'Fine, book the goddamned appointment, but I tell you this: when your servicing contract is up for renewal at the end of the year, I'll be looking elsewhere. Your service is terrible!'

He slammed the phone down in protest and hoped that the reaction had been loud in the woman's headset at the other end. He slumped down in his chair and let out a big sigh.

The phone rang on the desk.

'Hello?' he said wearily.

'Is that Highfield campus security?'

'It is, yes, who am I speaking with?'

'Hi, my name is Detective Sergeant Kyle Davies. I was told you would be able to help me with a delicate operation. I'm on my way to the Highfield Campus now and need a few minutes of your time while I look for...something,' Kyle continued. 'I can't say too much now. I'll be there in a few minutes; I need you to cancel any meetings you have for the next hour or so. Okay?'

The Head of Security acknowledged the command and hung up. Kyle had been picked up from the train station by two P.C.s in a patrol car and they were currently hurtling through Portswood towards the university. Mercure had confirmed that she had made contact with two of the remaining campuses and had units en route to each of them. She had decided to remain at the station to coordinate efforts. She had advised Davies that the new D.I. was flying in from Newcastle and was likely to be with them in the next couple of hours. Kyle wondered why he'd been made to catch a five hour train when it would have been quicker to have sanctioned him to fly. He didn't have time to worry about it at the moment, but he vowed he would sit down with Mercure when all this was over and demand to talk about his future. It was in his blood to protect and serve, but this recent snub was making him question the force he had grown to love. There seemed to be such politics operating at the highest level that he wasn't even sure if he wanted to remain in this career; not that he knew what else he could do instead.

The patrol car pulled hard to the left and screeched to a halt at a small brick building emblazoned with the words 'Campus Security'. Kyle ran from the car, his warrant card in hand, eager to commence the search for the next bomb. Regardless, of what tomorrow would bring, he was adamant the terrorist wouldn't win today.

16:12

Tracey Reed's teeth were chattering. It wasn't cold out; in fact, it was fairly mild for the time of the year. Even so, her teeth continued to chatter. It felt so unreal. Here she was: wife and mother of one standing on the street, waiting for a bus, so that she could deliver a briefcase, of God only knew what, to somebody she didn't know. Despite her son's captor telling her not to open the briefcase, she had tried to break it open, but the lock was coded and it would have taken too long to try and crack it.

The briefcase didn't feel particularly heavy, which suggested its contents were relatively lightweight. The address scrawled on a label tied to the handle, was for somewhere in Totton. She wasn't overly familiar with the area, so she had looked the street name up in a road map, which was now in her handbag. She had decided to catch a bus towards Totton's shopping precinct and walk the rest of the way there.

Tracey's role at the factory required her to wear a large apron over her day clothes, so she tended to wear jeans and a top to work. Having hung up the phone on the mysterious South African, she had thought long and hard about what she was to undertake. Regardless, of what was in the case, she knew she didn't wish to draw attention to herself. A woman in jeans and a parka coat carrying a briefcase would be more noticeable than a woman in a skirt and suit jacket, on her way home after a day at the office. Tracey had a smart outfit, which she reserved for interviews and funerals, hanging in the wardrobe. She had changed into that and applied some makeup, before heading out and walking to the bus stop.

She felt nervous about delivering the briefcase; anxious for Lewis' safety and a little bit apprehensive about the clandestine nature of her mission.

She had removed the severed finger from the fridge, in case Ian returned before she did and phoned the police. She had no idea whether what she was doing would get Lewis back, but she was certain that involving the police would result in his death. Despite their various arguments, she was still his mother, and couldn't bear the thought of any harm coming to him.

She saw the bus approaching and thrust an arm out to signal she wished to board. She saw the woman driving the bus indicate to stop. Tracey looked around, convinced she was being watched, but, unsure by whom. She allowed half a dozen passengers to disembark and stepped onto the bus. She paid her fare and took a seat about halfway back. She glanced at each remaining passenger as she walked past them, trying to assess if any of them worked for the South African or, worse still, the police. She had no idea what particular traits she was looking for; just a shifty look. She clutched the briefcase to her, determined that no mugger would be prising it from her fingers.

✳

Jean-Paul Retourget stepped onto the bus and thrust a five pound note on the driver's coin tray. His eyes were watching the back of Tracey's head, as she made her way along the bus towards a seat.

'Where you going to, luv?' the driver asked.

The question caught his attention and he looked at her. 'What?'

'I said: where do you want to go to? What destination? The further you go, the more it costs you see?'

Retourget wasn't familiar with the English public transport system. He expected a flat rate fee for travelling on a bus.

'How far do you go?' he asked.

'Well, the route ends in Totton, luv. We go past the train station on the way.'

'I'll go to the end,' Retourget confirmed, glancing up to see where Tracey had sat down.

'That'll be three pounds then, the driver answered, taking the note and replacing it with his change. 'Don't forget your ticket, luv,' she said, as he scooped up the money and headed away. He tore the ticket stub from the machine and marched to the rear of the bus so that he would have a good view of everyone inside.

He still had no idea who the woman with the briefcase was, nor the youth that he had witnessed being tortured. Al-Batani's claim that Richard

Eksteen was more than just a local trader, and was now somehow involved in a powerful underworld organisation had surprised him. He knew he had been foolish to underestimate Eksteen, and he was determined not to repeat the mistake. As far as he was concerned, the hit on his life was business. He didn't like the thought of anyone agreeing to execute him, but his vengeance had to be aimed at Santiago Hernandez, and not just Eksteen. Retourget had worked for some very powerful people in his time and it still troubled him that he too may have been mixed up in The Cadre's activities.

He had watched Eksteen's goons take the briefcase from the car lot to the woman's house. He had watched through a window, as they had left the youth's severed finger in her fridge and the briefcase on her table. The woman had arrived home shortly after. She didn't look like the sort of middle-man that he was used to seeing in such situations. She looked scared and fragile, but then maybe that was part of her act.

Who would think she was involved in drugs, weapons or money laundering? She looks like a housewife.

He was starting to think that there was a lot more to Eksteen's operation here on the south coast than he had first realised. If the South African had cohorts with this level of ability to integrate into society, there was every chance he was a major player in the area. Retourget knew he was taking a risk by focusing all his attention on the briefcase but, in his mind, the case had to contain drugs or, more likely, cash. Whether it would be sufficient to compensate for the lost commission was a different question but, if it wasn't, he knew where Eksteen would be and could pay him a visit in the morning.

I need to get that case!

16:22

Kyle Davies and the Head of Security, a man called Vallow, entered the Hartley Library. They had been searching for the device without success for nearly twenty minutes.

'This is hopeless!' said Vallow. 'This device could genuinely be anywhere.'

Kyle had been uncertain whether he should tell Vallow the truth about the threat to the campus or not. On the one hand, Vallow knew the campus inside and out, and it would make it easier to move from building to building having the Head of Security at his side. On the other hand, the man was not a trained professional and was just as likely to panic as any normal person.

He had opted for the former choice, and had spent a couple of minutes explaining what the device could look like to both Vallow, the two officers sent over by Mercure and two of Sid Travers' bomb disposal team. Kyle had told them to split into three teams of two and they had divided a map of the campus up between them.

'You see anything that might be a bomb, you call the rest of us immediately,' Kyle had warned. 'We are looking for unguarded bags, unattended laptops, anything that just doesn't…look right.'

'If anyone asks what you're doing,' Vallow had chimed in, 'tell them it's a routine drug search. It'll panic one or two of the students, but not nearly as much as telling them there could be a bomb on campus.'

One of the teams had taken the buildings around Salisbury Road, which included the Mathematics, Economics and Social Sciences blocks. The second team had been told to focus on the main block, which included the Geography, Computer Sciences and Student Union blocks. That left the library, Medicine and Engineering blocks for Kyle and Vallow to tackle. Each of the teams had stayed in contact, advising when a building had been deemed 'clear' and what building was next to be looked at.

Vallow had furnished Kyle with a map of the campus and he had been crossing through buildings as the 'clear' message was received. They were about a third of the way complete but, so far, nobody had reported finding anything. Kyle was beginning to think that Vallow was right: it was hopeless!

The truth was: Kyle had no idea how big the device would be. Mercure had told him the bomb outside the child-minder's house had been the size of an iPad. Travers had confirmed that the amount of semtex used then would have been enough to put a serious dent in the house as well as the school wall across the road. The terrorist had not said how big the university device was. He had to hope it would be bigger if they were to have any chance of finding it. Of course, it was also possible that the device would be at a different campus or even at the Solent University.

Kyle pulled out his phone to report into Mercure. 'Anything yet?' she asked.

'No, Guv. We're about a third of the way through with twenty minutes to go. Anything from elsewhere?'

'A sports bag was found at the Avenue Campus, but it only contained tennis equipment.'

'Do you think we should start the evacuation process?'

'I've just spoken with campus security at each location and they are ready to commence the evacuations when I give the green light. I've played down the scale of the device and advised that it is unlikely to cause too much damage.'

'Guv, we've no idea how big this thing is!'

'I'm aware of that Davies, but I don't want to cause widespread panic out there. It won't be conducive to our efforts. I'll tell them to commence evacuation in ten minutes, unless we find it in the meantime.'

Kyle didn't like her game plan, but knew better than to question her decision. 'I had a thought, Guv,' he said. 'You reckon that this politician is the target, right? Well, if that's the case then maybe the terrorist has planted the device near something related to her. You know, like a statue of her or something? Do you know if she's been honoured by one of the universities for anything?'

Mercure put the phone to her chest while she asked the politician.

'I'm afraid not,' Eve answered. 'I sit on the board of governors for both universities, but there are no busts of me, nor are there any buildings named after me. To be honest, my dealings with the universities amount to little more than a couple of monthly meetings.'

Mercure relayed the message to Kyle before hanging up.

'Any news?' Vallow asked as they completed their search of the second floor.

'Nothing yet,' Kyle replied glumly. 'Tell me, Vallow…have you had any new equipment delivered to the campus in, say, the last week?'

'Equipment?'

'Yeah, like large machinery, anything like that?'

'I'm not too sure, to be honest. It's mid-term and most new equipment arrives off-term, not during. To be honest, I wouldn't necessarily be in the loop regardless. The Dean might know…'

Kyle felt the pangs of hunger growl in his stomach. He hadn't eaten anything since the train and now he had built up a real…

'I've got it! How many cafés or restaurants are there on site?

Vallow thought for a moment. 'Well, the main restaurant is back in the building where my office is; downstairs. And of course, the bar sells snacks: crisps and nuts. How come? You hungry?'

'They've both been checked already. How many of the buildings have vending facilities in them? The terrorist said I would find the device if I had built up enough of an appetite. I didn't think anything of it at the time, but now I think it was a big clue to the location.'

'I see, well, the Union bar has a drink and snack machine, as does the Physics building at the far side of the campus. So does the Mountbatten building, near Salisbury Road. There's a machine in the main building too, outside my office, but you won't be able to get anything from that; it's been out of order all day.'

Kyle's eyes widened. 'It's out of order?'

'Yeah, it allows you to insert money and punch in the item's code but then nothing happens. The frustrating thing is, we had an engineer look at it first thing this morning, and then it broke right after...'

Vallow's voice trailed off as he made the same connection as Kyle.

'Holy fucking shit!' Vallow whispered.

'Couldn't have put it better myself,' said Kyle, tearing off in the direction of the Student Union building.

16:31

Sally rotated the big steering wheel to the left and eased the bus to a halt.

'Southampton Central train station,' she declared to the remaining passengers. She turned the engine off and pressed the button to open the doors.

Nothing happened.

She pressed the button again, but still the doors did not open.

'You gonna open these?' asked an irritated passenger in a traffic warden's coat.

'Just a minute, luv,' Sally said, pressing the button again.

'I haven't got all day, you know,' the overweight man challenged.

'I appreciate that, sir,' she smiled through gritted teeth, 'but the mechanism seems not to be working.'

'What d'you mean it's not working?'

'I mean exactly that: the button isn't working.'

'Maybe it's because you turned the engine off. No?'

Sally shook her head. 'The two aren't connected. The door should open and close when I press this button, regardless of whether the engine is on or off.'

'Well, humour me. Why not restart the engine

and try the button again?' the traffic warden persisted.

'I've told you: they're not connected. But, to satisfy you…' she said, trying to restart the engine. 'That's odd: the engine won't start now either.'

'Are you kidding me?'

No,' she replied. 'Look.'

Sally turned the key in the ignition, but there was no noise.

'Are you going to open the doors soon, please?' asked Nazir, blushing slightly. 'I need to…need to find a toilet.'

'They're stuck, apparently,' the traffic warden relayed.

'If you'll all just retake your seats, I'll radio the fault through to the office.'

'I don't fucking believe this!' he shouted.

'Hey! Watch your language, mate,' said Aaron, who had now moved forward to see what the hubbub was. 'There are ladies present,' he added, nodding politely to Nazir and Tracey.

The traffic warden turned to see who had dared admonish him, but on seeing Aaron's build and uniform, he backed down and returned to where he had been sitting.

'What seems to be the problem?' Aaron asked Sally.

'The doors are stuck and now the engine won't start. I believe the bus is…what's the technical term? Oh, yes: dead.'

Aaron returned to his seat as the driver picked up her mobile phone and dialled her boss at the bus depot. 'Hi George, It's Sally Trexal, here. I'm on the number four route and we're at the train station, but the bus has died.'

'Okay, received, Sally,' her boss replied. 'There's another bus due in the next half an hour, depending on traffic. Let the passengers off and refund the fares for anyone who was not due to disembark.'

'I would, George,' but the doors are jammed shut. Do I have permission to operate the emergency release mechanism?'

'Will they really not open?'

'The whole system is bust. Even the radio isn't functioning, which is why I'm calling you from my phone.'

'Okay, understood. You have permission to use the emergency release system. I'll make a note of it so it can be reset when the bus is back. I'll arrange for a tow truck to come and collect it. Is everyone on board okay?'

Sally eyed her passengers via the rear-view mirror, 'Yeah, they're understandably frustrated, but otherwise okay. Oh, but there is a pregnant woman in need of a wee.'

She heard George giggle down the phone. 'Thanks for calling through, Sally. Go get yourself a cup of coffee and we'll send a replacement bus for your journey back to Fareham.'

Sally hung up the phone.

'Well?'

She turned to see the overweight traffic warden in her face again.

'If you'll return to your seat, please, sir, I should have the doors open in just a minute.'

Sally waited for him to move away, before she

opened the door to her cabin and stepped out. She stretched her legs to relieve her aching calf muscles; it felt good to be out of that seat.

The emergency release lever was behind a small plate of glass in the wall closest to the door. There was a small plastic hammer secured next to the glass that she prised off before tapping it hard against the glass. It cracked slightly and then smashed when she hit it a second time. The mechanism was in place for situations where the bus was on fire and it was impossible to reach the cabin. The lever was pneumatically powered to open the doors when pulled up sharply. All drivers had to undergo bi-annual training on what to do in the event of a fire and needed to evacuate the bus swiftly. Sally gripped the lever and yanked it up.

The doors remained closed tight.

Puzzled, Sally returned the lever to its original position and tried again.

Still nothing happened.

There wasn't even the familiar hiss of the pneumatic system operating.

'Is there a problem, here?' Aaron asked, moving forward once more.

Sally smiled, relieved that the handsome man in uniform was asking, instead of the irritable traffic warden.

'Damn thing isn't working,' she sighed.

'It's pneumatic?' Aaron asked, examining the lever.

'That's right! It should open when the lever is pulled up, but it doesn't seem to be working.'

'May I?' Aaron asked, gripping the lever himself.

'Sure,' she smiled, noticing he wasn't wearing a wedding ring.

Aaron pulled the lever up but the doors remained closed. He pushed the lever down, then up and back down again several times, in an effort to pump the air around the system, but it was to no avail.

'I am getting really desperate,' called Nazir, standing to take the pressure off her bladder.

'We'll have to break the doors,' Aaron said, nodding towards the hammer in Sally's hand.

'Oh no,' she said, shaking her head. 'You can't do that. The company has policies for this kind of thing, and breaking the doors is not part of it.'

Aaron frowned. 'You serious? What's to stop me kicking the doors in myself?'

Sally shrugged her shoulders. 'What good would it do, luv? Even if you broke the glass, they are only small pains. None of us would fit between the metal frames.'

Aaron looked at the doors and acknowledged she was right. The concertina-effect of the door did mean that none of them would fit through the gap; least of all the pregnant woman or the tubby traffic warden.

'We'll just have to wait for the engineer to arrive,' Sally offered dismissively, climbing back into her cabin. 'Make yourselves comfortable.'

'What about me?' Nazir pleaded.

The quiet Frenchman from the back of the bus stepped forward and offered an empty cardboard coffee cup.

Nazir looked at the cup and back to the man. She sighed as she reached out and took it from him and waddled towards the back seats.

16:42

Ophion was staring through a pair of binoculars from a third floor window in an office block near Southampton Central train station. This floor was available for lease, according to the large board hanging from the side of the building. It gave him a perfect view of the bus he had immobilised, under which he had placed a large quantity of semtex. So far, everything was going to plan. All the passengers were still on board, and nobody had made a desperate attempt to leave, despite the faulty doors.

It had been Uncle Giorgio who had given him the nickname. It meant 'serpent' in Greek and it was a name he had decided to maintain in his current line of work.

Ophion's father had been too young to serve in the civil war of 1946, and had struggled to make ends meet on the island. His father had uprooted the family to Turkey when Ophion had been two or three. At the time, Turkey had been a land of relative opportunity for potential farmers, and his father had worked hard to secure a small piece of land, four goats and two calves. He had bred them quickly and, by the time Ophion was twelve, the small business had been thriving.

His father had been a bodybuilder in his spare

time, and the prizes he had received for winning local contests had kept their heads above water in the winter months. Ophion had spent a lot of time with his Uncle Giorgio, listening to the old man's stories of his travels around the world. It was like manna for an imaginative and impressionable young man who dreamed of something more.

It was Uncle Giorgio who had taught him how to kill.

He would take the young Ophion on small hunting expeditions, and they would poach chickens, and goats from neighbouring farms; never more than once a month, for fear of raising their neighbours' suspicions. Giorgio had shown him how to carefully stalk prey; how it was important to observe the habits of the target.

'You need to be like the snake: you need to understand how your prey will react; to plan your move,' Giorgio would tell him. 'If you move left, will the target move right? You need to be able to predict with total accuracy your opponent's next move.'

Ophion had practised and practised, until he had become proficient at poaching chickens and goats. Once he had mastered the technique, he had grown bored of it. Killing farm animals was no longer a challenge, and with it had gone the pleasure of the kill. Giorgio had recognised this instinct and encouraged Ophion to join the local armed forces.

'There are tougher targets than animals,' he would say, a telling look in his eye. 'An armed opponent is quite different.'

One evening, when Ophion was fifteen years old, a young immigrant man was caught breaking into one of the cattle sheds on the farm. The family dog had raised the alarm, but the young immigrant had escaped with a chicken tucked under his arm.

'He can't have gone too far,' Giorgio had whispered to Ophion, so that the parents would not overhear. 'Do you think you could track him?'

Ophion hadn't answered; instead he had fetched his small crossbow and sheath of arrows and the two men had snuck out, using the light of the moon to guide them. Ophion had followed the footprints through a corn field and out into the bordering forest. He enveloped his mind in that of a desperate poacher, and he had quickly considered and ruled out several places his prey would run to. He had narrowed it down to two locations. The two men had crept quietly to the first location, a small clearing in the forest, down a slope and near a flowing river.

'He will want to be out of sight and the river will give him water to drink and clean,' he had whispered to Giorgio.

'Very good,' the old man had replied, a broad smile on his face.

They had smelt the chicken cooking on a small fire before they had spotted the young man. He had been sitting with his back to them, huddled around the small fire for warmth.

'Should we apprehend him?' Ophion had whispered.

Giorgio had not replied; instead pulling the bow over Ophion's head and pointing at the young man.

Ophion could still remember the feeling of excitement in his groin as he had placed an arrow against the bow and taken aim. He had savoured the moment; the feeling of power. He had felt like a God; holding this thief's life in balance.

He had taken too long to release the arrow. The immigrant had sensed their presence and quickly leapt to his feet, turning to see who was watching him. Ophion had fired his arrow, but the immigrant had managed to duck out of the way. Ophion had looked round at Giorgio, with a feeling of panic and despair that he had failed the old man. Giorgio's eyes never left the immigrant as he pulled a small blade from a brace on his leg, and thrust it towards Ophion.

'You know what to do,' he had said, nodding towards the terrified immigrant.

Ophion had taken the knife in his hand. His feeling of power had dissipated and been replaced by fear. He had walked down the slope, ready to engage his prey. The immigrant quickly armed himself with the fallen arrow and the two began to circle the fire, waiting to see who would make the first move.

'Remember your training!' Giorgio had shouted.

Ophion had steadied his breathing and stared into the eyes of his prey. The immigrant had looked absolutely petrified; his body language revealing that he was not comfortable with confrontation. That made him unpredictable. Quick as a flash, Ophion had worked out how to overcome his prey and reached across the fire with his left hand, as if trying to grab at his prey's clothes. The immigrant reached out and grabbed Ophion's wrist, thrusting the arrow into it with his free hand. Ophion leapt across the fire and plunged the blade up and under the immigrants arm. The prey fell to his knees, the fight gone from him.

'Finish him off, boy!' Giorgio had shouted.

Ophion had grabbed the immigrant's hair and lifted his head, before pulling the knife out and running it across the man's exposed neck. He could still remember the feeling of the man's warm blood spurting out and trickling over his fingers, before he had allowed the body to fall into the fire. By offering out his weaker arm, like a chess master sacrificing a pawn, he had managed to catch his prey off guard and strike the killer blow. It had taken him under thirty seconds to kill the immigrant, but the feeling of satisfaction had remained with him forever.

Giorgio had stayed quiet as they had walked back to the farm. Once they were back, he had said, 'Tell nobody about this. I will clean up the wound in your arm.' Although the old man had never told him directly, Ophion had seen the proud look in his uncle's eyes and known he had done well.

Ophion now felt the mobile phone in his pocket vibrating. He pulled it out, knowing exactly who it would be.

'I want a progress report,' the scrambled voice told him.

'Everything is still on track. The bus is at the train station and my contact on board is awaiting my instructions.'

'Do you think the police suspect the final outcome?'

'Not yet. I imagine they will be considering possible targets for the final bomb, but they won't have considered that it could be mobile. I'm guessing they will have identified a list of possible target buildings. Everything is running smoothly.'

'Good.' There was another pause on the line before the client said, 'It's time.'

16:43

The bomb disposal expert from Travers' team had been examining the vending machine for the last fifteen minutes. Vallow and Kyle had reached it fifteen minutes earlier and had called the remaining two teams to the building. The three uniformed officers had been evacuating students from the vicinity, while Kyle had been interrogating Vallow.

'You said that a fault had been reported on the machine?'

'Yeah. Several students complained that the machine accepted their money, but once they had typed their item's code in, the machine refunded their money instead of providing the item.'

'But you said an engineer was here this morning. Did he not fix the fault?'

'The machine was working fine until the engineer arrived. The fault wasn't reported until after he had left.'

'Was the engineer's visit scheduled?'

'Of course it was,' Vallow said. 'The bloke was dressed in the proper uniform, arrived in a company van and flashed me the correct credentials. There was no reason for me to question his presence.'

'Can you describe what he looked like?' Kyle asked.

'Tall…I think…he had dark hair, maybe…I didn't get a great look at him,' Vallow answered glumly. The truth was: Vallow had been too preoccupied with trying to catch up on emails that he hadn't even looked at the engineer's identification properly.

'Did he have any distinguishing features? Did he talk with a recognisable accent? Come on, Vallow, give me something!'

'I don't know!' he pleaded.

'What about security cameras? Do any point at the vending machine?'

'Yes!' Vallow declared excitedly; pleased that his own incompetence might pass. 'I can get the feed up in my office; do you want to go and check it now?'

Before Kyle could answer, the man from Travers' team was beckoning him over. 'There's something you need to see.'

Kyle rushed over to the machine to see a timer had now appeared on the machine's display. A clock was ticking down from sixty seconds.

'What did you do? Why is it counting?' Kyle demanded.

'I haven't touched it!' the man in Kevlar replied. 'It started by itself.'

Kyle glanced at his watch and realised it had been an hour since he had spoken with the terrorist. What was it he had said?

I'm sure you'll be able to figure out the deactivation code by the time you find it.

'Try typing one, two, three, four,' Kyle urged, remembering the Sudoku puzzle.

The naval officer did as he was instructed. 'It

wants three digits, Sarge, not four.'

'Okay, try one, two, three.'

'It's still counting down.'

'Okay, try three, two, one.'

'Still counting, Sarge. Any other ideas?'

'He said I'd be able to figure it out. This guy thinks I'm stupid, so what would he make the code?'

'It would have to be something easy then? How about zero, zero, zero?'

'Try it!' Kyle demanded.

'Sorry, Sarge, it's still counting.'

'Dammit! Thirty seconds left.'

'I think we better bale out of here. There's no knowing how much explosive he's packed into this machine. We should get as clear from the area as possible. The fire service is on standby if it's a big one.'

Kyle hated the idea that the terrorist had beaten him, but he knew it was better to retreat to fight another day than to die in battle. He started to run towards the exit. Vallow was holding the door open for him. 'If only there was a phone a friend option, right?' Vallow said.

Kyle's eyes widened as he realised the answer. He turned so quickly, he almost lost his footing. He charged back to the machine and typed in the most obvious answer he could think of.

Nine.

Nine.

Nine.

The timer stopped and there was a whirring noise followed by a clunk as an item dropped into the collection drawer. Kyle breathed a huge sigh of relief and opened the drawer.

'A phone?' said Vallow, who had also returned to the machine. 'I don't get it.'

Kyle turned the phone over in his hands. 'I guess it's so the terrorist can call me,' Kyle said examining the menus.

'You don't think that…that's the…bomb?'

Kyle hadn't even considered the possibility that he was currently holding an explosive device. 'I don't think it can be. The various built-in menus are working and I'm not sure there would be room for semtex as well as a processor and battery.'

The phone vibrated to life. A withheld number was calling it. Kyle again remembered the terrorist's words:

I will call you in an hour with the next device.

He had assumed that the terrorist would call his own phone again.

'Hello?' Kyle said, connecting the call.

'Detective Davies, you have thwarted me again,' the scrambled voice mocked. 'You're obviously smarter than I gave you credit for. Congratulations! You are still in the game.'

'Game? What game? These are people's lives you are threatening!'

'Oh please, Kyle, don't pretend you aren't enjoying the thrill of the chase as much as me!'

'Enjoying it? I am doing my job. That is all. How do people like you sleep at night?'

'I sleep fine, thank you, Kyle. You are still being so hostile towards me. Who knows what rewards will come your way if you solve this thing? You should appreciate the fact that I've kept you in the game as long as I have! I could easily have exploded devices all over the city and not told you about it. Then how would things be? Huh? You would all be running around like headless chickens, trying to figure out what is going on. I have kept you in the loop. I have made you the focus of the investigation. I am the reason that you will be seen as the hero when all this ends.'

'You mean when I catch you, dipshit!'

'As I say, when this is over, you will be the hero of the hour: the man who saved the students and passengers.'

'What passengers?'

'Oh right, I forgot, you don't know that yet. Well, your reward for deactivating the university bomb, is to know the final target...there is a bomb in the city that will detonate at seven p.m.'

'I know that already. Where is it?'

'I am guessing your D.C.I. has been compiling a list of targets? Has she not figured it out yet?'

'I'm only going to ask this once more: Where. Is. The. Bomb?'

'It is on a public bus, somewhere in the city. You have two hours to figure out where the bus is. I can tell you that the bus is in operation currently and that there are several passengers on board, one of which is holding the detonator. You will need to identify which passenger has the device to stand any chance of stopping the bomb exploding.'

'What happens when we work out which one it is?'

'That's simple, Kyle: you kill that person.'

'Kill? Are you crazy? We're the police! We can't

kill a member of the public on the whim of a madman!'

'How else will you prevent the detonator switch being activated? Hmm? If you kill the right passenger, you will save the lives of everyone on the bus and in the immediate vicinity. If you kill the wrong passenger: the bus will explode. If you kill nobody: the bus will explode. These are my terms. I will call you one final time before the deadline to see what you have decided.'

Ophion disconnected the call.

17:00

Ten thousand pounds.

It had seemed such a vast sum of money when it had been offered to her a week ago. Now, in the cold light of day, she wondered whether she should have pushed for more. It had been a generous offer and she knew she would have regretted turning it down; particularly considering the news she had received two months before. It felt like she had been on a run of bad luck all year.

Did I break a mirror or something?

She asked herself this question every day. She had never been one for superstition, but there had to be a reason for all the bad news coming her way.

'First stage lung cancer,' the doctor had said, plain as day.

'Lung cancer?' she had repeated. 'But I don't even smoke! There must be some kind of mistake.'

'The good news is,' he had started.

'Good news?' she had interrupted. 'What possible silver lining can make this news good?'

'Let me finish! The good news is: we believe the affected cells we have found can be removed. Then, a few short bursts of radiation, and you should enter remission. It really is lucky that you came in when you did. Had the cells been allowed to metastasise, you may not have been so lucky.'

There was that word again: lucky.

I have cancer: how is that lucky?

'I'll give you some leaflets on what is growing inside of you and the various available treatments. The operations and radiation therapy can all be carried out for free on the NHS, so you don't need to worry about the cost,' the doctor had said, smiling thinly.

That had been that; she'd left the surgery to allow the doctor to break similar or maybe worse news to the next frightened patient. She had walked home that day, tears streaming down her face.

By the time she had reached home, she had told herself to be more positive. Whilst the news was anything but lucky, the truth was: it could have been worse. She had tried to phone Johnny, to tell him what she was going through. If anything could have brought him back to her, surely the guilt of this would. He hadn't answered her call. Had he just been busy or had he ignored her? She had left him a message asking him to call her urgently, but after three days had passed without a return call, she had phoned again.

'I've got cancer,' she had told his voicemail service. 'I thought you should know as…anyway, give me a call back, please? I really need someone to speak to.'

Johnny had moved out a month before she had developed the cough. He had claimed he didn't love her anymore and needed to move on with his life. She had refused to believe him at first.

How can someone fall out of love with

somebody?

Two days after the voicemail message, she had spotted him in a local supermarket with another woman. This one was much younger, with thick black glossy hair and a massive beaming smile. She could see why Johnny liked her. She had decided against confronting them, although she could tell from their body language that the two had been together for far longer than six weeks.

So, single, alone and now dying of cancer, at least she had still had a job that she enjoyed.

'I'm sorry, Sally, we've got to make these cuts. You haven't been with us as long as some of the other drivers and you are probably least familiar with all the routes we cover. Then there's the amount of time you had off sick last month…look, it wasn't an easy decision for us to make.'

Sally had stared back at the bus company's Operations Manager, awe struck.

'The good news is,' he had continued, 'the redundancy package is a year's salary, plus you'll be able to take any contributions you have made to the staff pension scheme to a new pension provider in whatever your next job is. You're lucky to get such a generous package.'

How am I fucking lucky?

She had wanted to bellow it at him, but had known better. Her mother had raised her to stare adversity down.

So, single, alone, dying of cancer and now about to be made redundant; she had been craving any kind of genuinely good news she could find.

'I want to pay you ten thousand pounds to help

me play a prank on one of my friends,' the strange-sounding voice had told her on the phone. 'He is getting married in a couple of weeks and has always thought of himself as some kind of action man. He's always bragging how brave he is and what he would do in a precarious situation. My friends and I want to test his bravado with this prank. All you have to do is play along with what happens on the day. Act a bit dumb to the situation, and whatever you do, keep him on the bus.'

'I'm not sure,' she had said. 'it sounds a bit wrong. What if he reacts badly and ends up damaging the bus? I could lose my job.'

'He's not a violent man,' the voice had assured. We expect him to fall on his knees and beg for mercy. We'll install a small camera at the front of the bus somewhere to capture the humiliation, which we'll then play back on his wedding day. It'll go fine. Look, my friends appreciate the risk you'll be taking, which is why we've clubbed together and can pay you ten thousand pounds for your participation. We'll even pay the money up front.'

Ten thousand pounds and all she had to do was play along: it was easy money.

Finally, my bad luck is over!

Sally, now sitting in her bus and staring back at the passengers via the rear-view mirror was not sure any of them would see the funny side of what had happened so far. A couple of them looked very angry and would probably put in a complaint with the bus company, and then her involvement in the prank would be exposed. But what was the worst that could happen? It's not like they could sack her.

She wasn't sure which of the men on the bus the brave bachelor was, but she suspected it was probably the one in the uniform. At least he was handsome and good-natured. The tubby traffic warden looked like he hadn't had sex in a very long time and the rugged Algerian one who had remained quiet since boarding just didn't seem like the marrying kind.

'Where the hell is this engineer?' the traffic warden shouted. 'I have an important meeting to get to.'

'I'm sure he is on his way,' Sally pacified.

'We've been waiting for nearly half an hour already. Can you not phone in and find out where he is?'

'Okay, okay,' Sally lied, pretending to call the depot.

Before she could relay the fake message, the bus' radio crackled to life and a deliberately slow voice began to speak. 'Ladies and gentlemen, I apologise for keeping you trapped together here for so long. You are about to be involved in a social experiment. Although this is just the start of your journey together, what will happen tonight will stay with you for a lifetime. You have each been carefully selected to participate in tonight's experiment based on your age, sex, background and beliefs.'

There was a stunned hush across the bus, followed by nervous glances: is this for real?

The voice continued, 'The driver will now take you to a specific location for the experiment to commence. I apologise if you had previous engagements to attend to today, but these will now be cancelled for the foreseeable future. Before you all grow angry with the situation, I can assure you that you will be well-compensated for the part you play tonight. I can also promise you that this will take no more than two hours of your time.'

'How does he think you will drive?' the traffic warden asked Sally. 'He obviously doesn't know the bus is fucked.'

As if on cue, the engine roared to life, catching Sally by surprise.

'I have programmed the satellite navigation system with the chosen route for this evening and would appreciate if the bus driver would now follow this route to its conclusion. As for the remaining passengers, please relax and enjoy the sights as we commence our tour.'

The voice crackled off and the radio returned to its previous silent state.

Sally pushed the indicator down and prepared to pull out. Behind her she could hear the passengers angrily shouting, clearly not happy with what they had heard. Sally ignored the protests and imagined how she would spend the ten thousand pounds.

17:05

'The bomb is where?' Mercure practically shouted into the phone.

'It's on a bus somewhere in the city, Guv. It's mobile, so we still don't know what the target is.'

'Did you look at the footage from the security cameras? Can we identify the engineer?'

'I'm afraid not, Guv. The camera does pick up the engineer, but he is wearing a baseball cap and his head remains down. The camera is pointing at his back the whole time he is servicing the machine. He can clearly be seen placing the semtex packet inside the machine, along with the mobile phone he called me on, but other than telling you that he is at least six feet tall, I can't tell you anything else.'

'Right, Davies. I want you back here to help coordinate this thing. We are going to initiate the GBS command protocol. The Detective Superintendent will be Gold, I'll take Silver but I want you as my Bronze. You've been nothing if not resourceful today, and your skill set will be best used at an operational level.'

'Understood, Guv,' Kyle replied, disconnecting the line.

'Right, team,' Mercure began, addressing those officers in the incident room. 'We now know the terrorist has placed a bomb on a bus somewhere in the city. This threat is very real. The device will detonate at precisely seven p.m., which gives us just under two hours to find its location. First things first, Gillespie, before Davies gets back here, I want you to take operational control. I need you to call in all available officers. Those about to finish their shift need to stay on. We will pay overtime. Also, get late shift in early; we're going to need all the help we can get. See if the Portsmouth and Bournemouth operations can lend us a hand too.'

'Yes ma'am,' D.S. Roger Gillespie replied, picking up the phone.

'We need to coordinate with the local fire and ambulance services. Barrett, you have a brother-in-law who's a paramedic, right? I want you to be liaison there.'

D.C. Hugh Barrett acknowledged the command and picked up his phone.

'Beth, I need you to get on to the local bus companies. Find out the location of each of their buses. If they have GPS tracking, see if you can get them to upload the feed to us, will you?'

D.C. Beth Taylor nodded.

'Listen carefully, people. This office is now Silver Control. Once we pinpoint the bus' location and target, we may move location. Capshaw, I want you and Barnes to prepare three mobile command units and have them ready to go at a moment's notice.'

D.C.s Oliver Capshaw and Neil Barnes hurried out of the incident room.

'I want a map of the city up on this board ASAP. Once we know the locations of each vehicle, I want them and their routes up on the map. Understood? We need to see if there are any major targets along current routes, as that could give us a clue to what this bastard is looking to hit. It'll also show us if any vehicles have deviated.'

'What do you want me to do, Guv?' asked D.C. Emma Jarvis.

'Emma, you've got a good analytical mind. I want you to draw me up a list of possible targets in the city. I want you to put yourself in the mind of this bastard and think about what sites you'd hit. He's been building to this all day, so I believe it'll be somewhere big. I still think this guy is political, so he will want the target to be as big as possible so that his message gets heard. I am not going to let this bastard win; not on my watch!'

Satisfied, that her team was organised, Mercure calmly left the room and walked to her office to call Detective Superintendent Peter Gulliver and break the news.

'Understood, Jan,' Gulliver replied when she had explained what had happened. 'I've just arrived home. I'll grab a sandwich and explain to my wife that I'm needed back at the office and I'll head back to the Headquarters building. I'll be at least forty minutes, depending on traffic, but my mobile will be on and I want you to phone with updates. It sounds like you've made a good start with structuring the work. I need to contact the Chief Super and explain everything. I think you are going to need to set up communication channels with the media. Who is your sharpest and brightest bod? You should make them responsible for relaying information. You can take the stage when we have major breakthroughs, but with all this activity, it won't be long before the media outlets are asking us questions. We don't need another shit storm like that politician caused earlier. We need to be seen to be on the front foot, Jan. is that clear?'

'Sir,' she acknowledged, still reeling from Eve Partridge's interview with the radio journalist earlier.

Mercure returned to the incident room and was pleased to see that a large map was now hanging from the noticeboard at the front of the room. There were now half a dozen more officers milling about, some talking into phones, others plotting bus locations and routes on the map.

'How are we progressing, Beth?' Mercure asked.

'First Bus has confirmed that all their buses now provide free Wi-Fi to passengers. This means they can pinpoint the location of any given bus. Unfortunately they can only check one bus at a time, so we will not be able to see a true picture of what is where, but the lady I've been speaking to at the depot is providing me with regular updates for each vehicle that is operational. Do we want them to let the drivers know about the situation? The lady suggested she could tell the drivers to eject all their passengers and return the buses to the depot. That way, we would limit casualties and would know exactly where the buses are.'

Mercure shook her head. 'It's too dangerous. If the perpetrator with the detonator becomes suspicious of our actions, they could detonate the device ahead of schedule. We need this bastard to think he's in control, right up to the moment where we diffuse the device and catch him.'

Mercure spotted Eve examining the map,' Can I help you with something?' Mercure asked.

'Sorry,' Eve said. 'I just find it fascinating to watch. All the team pulling together, it makes me think you might actually catch whoever is behind this.'

'You mean you have your doubts?'

Eve smirked. 'Let's be honest, Jan, you've been somewhat fortunate so far today, wouldn't you agree?'

Mercure could feel her blood beginning to boil. 'Fortunate? How so? Have there been any explosions in the city today? Has there been any loss of life? No. A terrorist has been holding the city to siege for ten hours and yet we have thwarted his every move.'

'Oh please,' Eve laughed, 'the only reason there have been no casualties is because he hasn't wanted there to be. Do you really believe you have had any control over today's events? Do me a favour! This terrorist has had you running around in circles all day, and you're still no closer to identifying who he is.'

'Think what you like!' Mercure dismissed. 'We will catch this bastard, I assure you. Now, get the hell out of my incident room!'

'Where do you expect me to go? I'm the one he wants to get, don't forget.'

Mercure bit her tongue to stop herself saying what she really wanted to. 'Just go to the canteen, Eve. I don't want you interfering with my investigation.'

Eve felt her cheeks redden, but she picked up her handbag and did as she was told.

17:10

Retourget stared down at the two word message on his phone: Call me.

Al-Batani was as paranoid as they came: he didn't trust electronic communications, as he knew all too well how easily they could be intercepted and manipulated. He had remained off the grid for so many years and now here he was sending a text message to the former legionnaire. It didn't make sense in Retourget's mind, but he was smart enough to know that his old friend wouldn't go to such an extreme without good reason.

Retourget scanned the faces of his fellow passengers, wondering if any of them could be part of The Cadre's little operation, sent here to execute him. He doubted it very much but he knew the importance of not ignoring the impossible. He was sitting at the very back of the bus, and the closest person to him was Eksteen's mule, but she was three seats in front.

He plugged a small set of headphones into his phone, and discreetly placed one into his ear; moving the headset's small microphone close to his mouth. He dialled the number that had sent the message and waited for it to connect.

He spoke in a whisper when he heard Al-Batani's

voice, making sure he did not identify the man by name. 'Qu'est-ce que c'est?'

'Call me on a public phone,' Al-Batani admonished.

'It's not possible,' Retourget whispered back. 'I am nowhere near another phone.'

'What is going on? Why are you whispering?'

'I'm not alone. I don't want to compromise us.'

'Very well…as before, what I am about to tell you is highly classified…we believe The Serpent is in Southampton! The UK authorities have told Interpol there is a terrorist attack on the city imminently and they suspect The Serpent is behind it.'

Retourget's mind raced. 'What kind of attack?'

'The police believe he has planted a bomb somewhere in the city and they are currently searching for it.'

'Why? He's a gun for hire, a paid assassin, he's no terrorist!'

'I know he isn't. I've been reviewing the file we hold on him. He is an expensive, but reliable killer; no more than that.'

'What else can you tell me about him?'

'He has more than eighty kills to his name…that we know about…the method of killing varies from victim to victim…he seems quite adept with a knife, but has used poison, bombs and guns too. He is one of Interpol's most wanted. As soon as his fake identity flagged up last night, they dispatched several agents to the UK to try and apprehend him, but their search was focused on London. Nobody expected him to strike Southampton.'

'You think The Cadre is behind this?'

'I would assume so...although I am not sure what they will gain from a terrorist attack there.'

'Me either...is this their style? Pretending to be terrorists? Is that in their M.O.?'

They don't have a modus operandi that we can identify yet...they do what it takes to achieve their ends. Did you find the South African yet?'

'Eksteen? I did...I'm following one of his operatives now.'

'What do you think they are up to?'

'I wish I knew...the woman I am following is carrying a briefcase...you don't think...'

Retourget adjusted his position so that he could see Tracey Reed better. She was gazing out of the window closest to her, clutching the briefcase tight to her chest. She looked nervous.

'What is it?' Al-Batani asked after a moment.

'Is there anything in the file to suggest that The Serpent has any female associates?'

'He has no known associates listed in the file...he is a loner...he doesn't have friends. Why?'

'Eksteen's associate is a woman. I've been following her for more than an hour and she is sat on the same bus as me...she is carrying a briefcase...'

'You think the bomb is in the briefcase?' Al-Batani interrupted.

Retourget considered the size of the article. 'If it is, it can't be very big...I mean a bomb that size would cause some mess, but that would be all...what are they up to?'

Before he could consider a response, he overheard the man in the naval uniform talking on his phone. What he heard made him curious.

'Mohammed, I need to go.'

'What is it? Is the bomb on the bus?'

'I'll let you know when I figure it out…I may have a lead on The Cadre's plan.'

17:12

Each of the passengers on board the bus felt pangs of frustration at having the next two hours of their lives dictated, but as there was little they could do about it; the consensus was to go along with it for now. The woman driving the bus hadn't said much since the radio message had faded. She had been told to follow the directions in the satellite navigation system and she seemed to be doing as she had been instructed. They seemed to be on some kind of magical mystery tour and, thus far, had driven up Hill Lane and past Southampton's General Hospital.

Aaron's mind was elsewhere. He was tempted to rip open the present and check the contents of what Paul had provided him, but he was conscious that he didn't know who any of the passengers were. Although it seemed unlikely, he didn't know if any of them could be undercover government agents, waiting to catch him in the act of revealing military secrets. The present was on his lap and he was nervously drumming his fingers on the lid when he felt his mobile phone vibrating.

'Aaron, it's Harry,' his cousin said cautiously. 'What are you up to?'

Aaron wasn't even sure how to begin explaining

his current predicament so settled for, 'It's a long story. How you feeling? Has you hangover kicked in yet?'

Harry laughed and winced at the same time. 'I can feel it coming. What about yours?'

Aaron considered the question. 'Old naval trick: drink two glasses of water to replace lost fluids and eat a slice of plain bread to soak up excess alcohol. Works a treat! You should try it.'

'Maybe I will. Listen, the reason I'm calling: some woman phoned here about half an hour ago asking to speak with you. I told her you had left, but that I could pass a message on. She told me that she knew my father. I realised it must have been the woman who slipped you dad's will, so I let her speak. She told me to tell you that you need to look into some company called Parvon Trading. I tried to ask her why and what it related to, but she said it wasn't safe to say any more over the telephone. She hung up before I could ask anything else.'

'You think it has something to do with Troy's death?'

'Given what she told you earlier, I can only assume it does. Anyway, I typed the company's name into a search engine and it's some kind of investment firm based in southern Spain, but with offices throughout major cities in Europe and in Casablanca. I opened their website and it looks pretty classy, to tell the truth. I read their prospectus and they seem to be a bank for the mega rich. I mean, they state the minimum investment sum they accept is, like, two million Euros.'

Aaron whistled through his teeth and joked,

'Maybe we should bank there when your dad's estate pays out.'

'The website states they are a multimillion pound investment firm with expertise in private banking and developing markets. I don't really understand what this would have to do with my dad though.'

'It would explain why there were so many banker-types at the crematorium. Remember? It looked like a bankers' convention. You told me you thought he did dirty work for powerful people; maybe he worked for this company. What did you say they were called? Parvon Trading?'

'But if he worked for them, why would they have him killed?'

'Do you remember your dad's email? He said he had done things he wasn't proud of and that he thought his life was in some kind of danger. What if he was working for this company and discovered something bad and threatened to blow the whistle?'

'But what kind of thing? What kind of criminal activity could bankers get up to?'

'That's a rhetorical question, right? The sky's the limit. Maybe they're a front for money laundering. Maybe they are guilty of insider trading. It could be anything.'

'Excuse me,' said an accented voice. Aaron looked up and saw Retourget hovering over him. 'Did I hear you say Parvon Trading?'

'Do you mind?' Aaron shot back. 'This is a private conversation.'

Retourget ignored the rebuttal and sat down in the seat directly behind Aaron.

'Hold on a second, Harry,' Aaron said, before

lowering the phone and clutching it to his chest. 'What's your problem, pal?'

Retourget eyed the man in the naval suit carefully, not sure if this was a trap or an insight into why The Serpent was threatening the city.

'My name is Jean-Paul Retourget,' he began, offering out a hand. Aaron shook it, noticing how softly-spoken the Frenchman was. 'I am a man with many connections. I overheard you mention the company Parvon Trading. I know it well and I would urge you not to invest your money there.'

'Why not?' Aaron asked suspiciously.

'What do you know about the company?'

'They are a private bank investing in developing markets.'

'How did you hear about them?'

'What is that to you?' Aaron challenged.

Retourget snickered. 'This is not your usual high street bank. Do you understand? You cannot just walk in off the street and deposit your savings. You have to be introduced by the right people. I'm curious: who introduced you?'

'As I said: what's it to you?'

'I have introduced a number of clients to the opportunities that Parvon Trading afford. They can guarantee you a return of twenty percent within five years. It is the best interest rate anywhere in the world. What's more, they guarantee you that return, regardless of the New York Stock Exchange. Impressive, non?'

'You work for Parvon Trading?'

Retourget shook his head. 'No, no, no. This is not a company you work for. I have introduced people to their services and in return I received a generous commission for facilitating the transaction.'

'It's a front, right? That's what you're suggesting?'

Retourget shrugged. 'They are not a bank I would use personally. Before you think about investing with them, I would think very carefully. They will make you sign a confidentiality agreement and a contract guaranteeing that you will not withdraw your investment before a set date. These are powerful people and are not to be messed with.'

'It sounds like a warning.'

'It is a warning! They offer the investment of a lifetime...and sometimes that is as long as it lasts. So I ask you again, how did you come across this company?'

Aaron weighed up his options and then decided to be honest. 'I think my uncle worked for them. Do you know a man called Troy Cross?'

Retourget shook his head, but Aaron could have sworn there was a glimmer of recognition in the Frenchman's eyes.

'My uncle was murdered a couple of weeks ago and I suspect Parvon have something to do with it.'

'It would not surprise me...the men who operate it have a dismissal policy that is unique in the industry.'

'What do you mean by that?'

'Let's just say they have ways of making their problems disappear; nobody speaks out about the company and lives to tell the tale. If your uncle had carried out work for them and is now dead, I would warn you against looking any further into his death, unless you want to end up in a grave yourself.'

Retourget returned to his seat at the back of the bus, allowing Aaron to return to his call.

'Where are you now, Harry?'

'I'm still at home. Why?'

'Tell me you didn't access that website from your own computer?'

'Of course I did. Why?'

Aaron closed his eyes and sighed. 'You need to get out of the house, Harry. Your dad said he had taken precautions to keep you and Toby out of harm's way and that you were not to look into his death. I have a horrible feeling that by looking at their website you may have put yourself in grave danger.'

'You're kidding, right? What can they do?'

'If they're as powerful as I believe, they have probably already tracked your IP address. When they see your name, they'll put two and two together and realise you are related to Troy. You need to get out of the house. Now! Where is Toby?'

'He's staying at a friend's house tonight.'

'Good. Go and get him and check into a hotel somewhere out of the city. Don't use a credit card. You have cash?'

'Sure, I have about ten grand in the safe. What's this all about?'

'I believe that Parvon killed your dad and will look to tie up any further loose ends. Just get your brother and lay low. For me, please?'

'Okay, okay, I'll do it.'

Aaron hung up the phone and for the second time that day wondered exactly what Uncle Troy had been involved in.

CROSSHAIRS

17:25

The canteen at the Police Headquarters building was unsurprisingly empty, with all manpower focused on locating the errant bus and its target. M.P. Eve Partridge found a seat at a table out of ear-reach of the two older women who were standing in the small kitchen waiting for anybody to come in and order some supper. Eve had ordered a cup of coffee and slowly drank it before pulling out her phone and redialling the last number in her phone list.

'Paul, hi, it's Eve,' she began. 'Where are you at the moment?'

'I've just returned to the office,' the P.A. said. 'I had an errand to run in town; I hope you don't mind?'

'That's fine, Paul.'

'Where are you now, anyway? I've been looking for you all afternoon. Are you at home now?'

'I'm still at the police station. Things have developed somewhat since this morning.'

'Oh really? Have they identified the nutter who wrote you that letter yet?'

'What? No. Apparently this terrorist, whoever he is, has planted a bomb on one of the city's buses and is planning to detonate it at seven o'clock outside of some kind of high profile target.'

'Holy shit!' Paul exclaimed, before quickly apologising for the expletive.

Eve was feeling a similar reaction, so she didn't judge him for the outburst. She would hate to admit it but, the truth was, Paul was her only real true friend these days. He was the one person she spent most of her time with; he had become her confidant. He knew most of her dark secrets, and whilst he might not agree with some of her policies, he always stuck by her. Sure, she had 'friends' she had known for a number of years; people she occasionally met for lunch or dinner, but they weren't true friends. They were just acquaintances. Paul had been there when things were at their worst. She had no idea how she would have coped without him.

'How are you holding up?' he asked.

'It's a situation I'm not in control of,' she admitted. 'How do you think I feel?'

Paul chuckled. 'You must be at your wit's end! You need to release your inner control freak.'

'I wish I could, but Mercure has frozen me out again. I think she's only keeping me here because the Detective Superintendent insisted she protect me.'

'Do you want me to come down and be with you?'

'You should be getting home, Paul. It's already after five.'

'Nonsense! I'm not asking as your P.A. I'm asking as your friend, Eve. I don't mind. I'd like to keep close to the action.'

Eve couldn't help smiling. 'I would really appreciate seeing you right now, Paul.'

'Well then; that's settled. There's a couple of bits and pieces I need to sort, but then I'll trot on down.'

'Great. I was wondering...do you think I should do another interview with Karen at the radio station?'

'Didn't the D.C.I. go ballistic the last time?'

'Of course she did; I told my constituents what she was trying to keep quiet. I think they deserve to know about this latest incident even more. Don't you?'

'I was the one who told you to speak to Karen in the first place and that is the reason Mercure has frozen you out now. I wouldn't want to see you repeat that mistake and end up in her bad books even more.'

'Don't blame yourself, Paul. Do you realise I've had ten 'thank you' emails from constituents today? When have I ever received complimentary feedback? I spoke out and received a positive response.'

'Oh my God! That's amazing!' Paul gushed.

'I know, right? Look, the truth is, Mercure is probably doing the right things and following police protocol, but I still think the residents of my city deserve to know that there is some crazed asshole out there threatening them. She shouldn't be trying to keep this under wraps.'

'You're right, Eve, as always. Maybe the pressure is getting to Mercure a bit. No?'

'Exactly!'

'Are you thinking what I'm thinking, Eve?'

'I'm not sure...what are you thinking?'

'Television!'

'Television?'

'That's right. You've spoken on the radio already. That's old news now. You said it yourself; things have developed from this morning. This bus-thing is massive! The city needs a hero to stand up and steady the ship through this tempestuous storm. The city needs you, Eve. I have a couple of contacts at Meridian and the local BBC news desk. This should be the top story on this evening's six o'clock news! The people need to know what is happening.'

'Mercure would probably lock me up!'

'No she wouldn't. Her methods aren't right and, if someone of influence was to point out the error of her ways in public, maybe they would turn to a woman who has been at the heart of this story since it broke. A woman with strong project management skills. A woman democratically voted into public office by the people of this wonderful city. A woman who can lead and motivate the police force into catching this psycho!'

'Do you think you could arrange it in time?'

'I could have a journalist and camera with you in under twenty-five minutes, Eve. Look, what happened in France seriously dented your credibility, but this your opportunity to rise like a phoenix from the ashes. Someone, somewhere, clearly wants you to be the centre of attention; what's wrong with making the most of the opportunity? This is your chance, Eve: your chance to win back the respect of the people who voted for you. Come election time, they'll remember the pivotal role you played in bringing this terrorist to justice.'

Eve took a deep breath. 'Okay, Paul, set it up. Get me on the television news tonight and I won't let you down.'

'That's my girl! I'll make some calls now. This is just what we needed, Eve!'

17:48

Sally pulled up at the traffic lights, waiting for the filter to turn green so she could turn right.

'Do you think we get food as part of this experiment?' the overweight traffic warden asked the bus in general. 'I'm bloody starving!'

Tracey Reed had been anxiously glancing at her wrist watch since their captor's message had played nearly an hour earlier. She was worried about Lewis, but she had no way of contacting the South African to advise that she would be late in delivering his package. She needed to get off the bus and back on track with her journey, but she didn't want to draw any attention to herself. For all she knew there were drugs or worse in the briefcase and, if she began to act suspiciously, one of the other passengers might demand to see the contents of the case.

Just keep your head down till this is all done.

Retourget was still watching Tracey with great interest. She was looking nervous and was the only passenger who hadn't spoken since the mystery tour had started. He desperately wanted to know what she was delivering for Eksteen but didn't want to draw attention to himself yet.

When the time is right, I know what to do.

Nazir had overcome the humiliation of having to

pee into a cardboard coffee cup. Samir was probably at the train station now, wondering where she was and why she had stood him up. She was actually pleased to keep him waiting as this would test the true nature of his feelings.

If he really loves me, he will wait.

Aaron continued to drum his fingertips on the lid of the present Paul had given him. It had been a strange day all in all. He hadn't cried at the crematorium as he had expected he would. He would miss Troy for sure, but he knew better than to grieve for the dead. He had witnessed too much death in his time to let it affect him. His plan was to review the documents and files tonight and to forward them to the exposé website in the morning. He had already met the website's leader on two occasions, and she had promised to do the story justice. He hoped he wasn't making a huge mistake by speaking out. He had grown accustomed to naval life and wasn't ready to choose a new career path just yet.

He wasn't planning to expose inadequacies in the Royal Navy, however. His issue wasn't with his own service. Mel, his brother in arms, would still be alive today if The Army ground crew on that day had been better equipped. The dockets he was going to leak criticised the higher-echelons of The Army; not The Navy.

I hope they don't court-martial me for this.

Sally saw the green filter light appear and pulled the bus to the right and into their destination. Leisure World had been built on a disused industrial estate and housed a casino, cinema complex and a large night club, as well as a couple of restaurants. It also had a very large car park. Sally had been to the site with her ex-boyfriend once, but had never imagined driving her bus there. She was wondering whether this was going to be where the prank was to be carried out, when the engine suddenly died, leaving the bus parked directly outside the entrance to the cinema and nightclub complex. The bus' overhead lights dimmed and they were left in semidarkness.

'Leisure World?' the traffic warden exclaimed loudly when he saw where they had stopped. 'What the hell is going on?'

As if by answer to his question the radio crackled to life again, and they heard the voice of their captor. 'Ladies and gentlemen, I would like to thank you for your patience and can now confirm we have arrived at our final destination. Having watched you for the last hour, I feel certain I made the right choice in selecting each of you to participate in this social experiment. I am sure some of you have questions, but would ask that you allow me to finish explaining the terms of this experiment before asking them.'

The passengers looked at one another, puzzled expressions on their faces.

'There is a large amount of explosive material hidden on this bus. Within the hour, the vehicle will be surrounded by armed police officers and members of the emergency services. The local police are aware of the threat to your lives and are currently searching for you. I am certain that you will be found soon. The device on the bus is set to detonate at precisely seven p.m. this evening. There is nothing you can do to prevent this: it is inevitable. However, not all of you have to die for this experiment to be a success. I have set the police a challenge that, if they complete it, will mean that the doors to the vehicle will be unlocked and you will be released.'

Aaron's eyes narrowed as his impulses began to search for an escape route.

'Please do not waste your time or energy trying to plot an escape,' Ophion continued. 'There is a small camera hidden at the front of the bus capturing your every move. If I see anybody defy my orders, the bomb will be detonated by me. Is that understood? To repeat: if you try to escape, I will see and the bomb will explode. If you sit quietly and allow the police to solve the problem I have set, you will survive. This is the social experiment.'

'He can see us, but probably can't hear us,' the traffic warden mumbled to Aaron, keeping his face staring forward, and his lips hardly moving. 'You look like a resourceful man; you need to get us out of here.'

'In case there are lingering doubts about my power or the magnitude of the situation, one of you will die now,' Ophion declared. 'But who should it be? The man in the uniform? The fat man sitting just in front of him? Perhaps I should kill the pregnant woman or the man hiding at the rear of the bus. Maybe it should be the woman holding the briefcase. What do you think? Who should die first?'

Nobody moved.

Nobody spoke.

'Perhaps it should be Sally. Ladies and gentlemen, what do you think? After all, she's the one who has driven you here. Does she deserve to die? If you think she deserves to live, I will need one of you to stand and exchange places with her.'

Sally grabbed the radio and pressed the transmit button before jabbering into it, 'What the fuck? We had a deal. What about my money?'

There was static on the radio before an electric surge was released under Sally's chair. Her body juddered about as the charge entered her body. There was a whirring noise emanating beneath her, but this was barely audible over the sound of Sally's shrieking as her body thrashed against the pain. The traffic warden looked away; Nazir screamed; Aaron moved forward to see if there was anything he could do to help. Tracey and Retourget stayed where they were, transfixed by the sight befalling the bus driver. The bus was filled with the smell of burning flesh.

17:50

Marshall Lancaster, the BBC's renowned 'Man in a Crisis', a title he had grown to despise in recent years, had been heading back to London when he had received the call. He couldn't believe what he had been told.

'A second bomb in Southampton? On a bus? It's going to be detonated at seven?'

He had ordered the pimply intern to immediately turn the vehicle around and head back to the BBC building in the city. The call had come at just the right moment, as they had been about to join the M3. Lancaster and his two-man crew had been sent to the city earlier that afternoon to report on the device located at the school. A second device in as many hours had to suggest that the two incidents were linked and that meant he would be the face that broke the news to their many viewers.

Lancaster had worked in the BBC newsroom since 1997, but his enforced retirement was rapidly approaching. Having grown up in Margate, the son of a local fisherman, he had never expected to have a career lasting as long as he had. It was a career filled with awards and commendations; the University of Durham had even awarded him an honorary degree for services to the industry. The certificate was framed and hanging in the downstairs toilet for all visitors to see.

He hated to admit it, but his career had been in decline for a couple of years. No longer was he the face of the six o'clock news; he had now been relegated to stories of interest on the network's News 24 channel. At least he was still working, and being paid a reasonable wage, but, since the move, he had noticed fewer and fewer people recognising him in the street, and that served as a reminder that his life was slipping away. The decline had started at an awards ceremony three years ago. He had been nominated in three categories and was confident of securing at least one statuette for his reporting of the prison break at Belmarsh prison, when convict Mark Baines had escaped. It had been Christmas weekend and he had been the one to break the story. The ratings had been the highest on record for the festive period. A young journalist, working for Channel Five, at another table had been given a special mention for a report she had delivered looking at public attitudes to homelessness. Lancaster had leaned over to the head of network and questioned the young woman's journalistic integrity. She had overheard and retorted, 'Sorry, who are you? Didn't you used to report the news during World War Two?'

The next day, the head of network had called him in and told him they were going to make some changes. The head had some concerns that the news was ignoring the younger demographic and so they were going to bring in a new Special Affairs journalist. He had assured Lancaster that there was a job available at the News 24 channel.

Oh great! He had thought.

Everyone in the industry knew that News 24 was the equivalent of a pasture where aged cattle grazed until death. The day he had walked into the newsroom, he had been amazed by how many faces from the past he had recognised.

But this story: a bomber terrorising the southern city, and a device due to explode imminently, well this was going to thrust him back into the limelight. He had been promised an exclusive interview with the city's M.P. who had been close to the day's events. The interview would be shown on every news programme on each of the network's channels. He was giddy just thinking about it. The call had come twenty-five minutes earlier and now here he was, once again staring into the camera lens, ready to address the nation.

In her office, only five minutes up the road, Mercure was watching the interview unfold. They had received a tip-off that Eve Partridge had fled the station and was now tucked up safely at the studio, waiting to reveal her side of events. As much as Mercure wanted to stop her, there was nothing she could do, apart from watch the interview and hope the M.P. was kind.

Lancaster gave an introduction to explain what had happened earlier and the exclusive story that a second bomb was due to explode imminently. Mercure wondered just how many people in the city were watching.

'I am joined now by Eve Partridge M.P.,' Lancaster said to the camera. Eve's face filled the screen. 'She has come forward to provide an update on today's unfolding events. Welcome, Mrs Partridge.'

The M.P. smiled into the camera and nodded her acknowledgement. 'Call me Eve.'

'What can you tell us, Eve? Is it true?'

Eve's smiling face turned to an expression of anxiety; her brow furrowed. 'I am afraid it is very true, Marshall. As we speak, the police are carrying out an extensive search for the bomb and the man behind today's atrocities.'

'So the incident at the school earlier this afternoon is linked to this latest development?'

'Very much so,' she nodded. 'The police have been looking for this man since early this morning. This latest bomb is just one of a series of terrors the city has witnessed today.'

'Yet the police are yet to hold a press conference, or share any of this information with the public. That strikes me as odd.'

'As it does me,' Eve agreed. 'I believe the public have a right to know if they are in immediate danger, yet the person heading up this investigation wants to keep it very low key.'

'That person is Detective Chief Inspector Janet Mercure, is that right?'

'Correct, Marshall.'

'And you have doubts about her ability to handle such an investigation?'

'I do. It is a volatile situation and the increasing stress that she is feeling as a result of these acts, must be overwhelming.'

'But she's doing a good job, right? I mean, the

device at the school was discovered and diffused before anyone was injured, right?'

'This terrorist, whoever he is, has been feeding the police with information all day. I think it is more luck than judgement that nobody has been harmed thus far.'

'These are quite strong allegations you are making here, Eve, can you back up what you are saying at all?'

Eve smiled at the camera. 'Yes I can, Marshall. For starters, I received a letter at my home this morning warning of today's events. I took this letter to D.C.I. Mercure immediately and she dismissed it as the words of a fanatic. I told her that she was underestimating the contents of the letter but she wasn't interested. Maybe if she had given it the attention it deserved, they would have caught this man by now.'

The camera switched to Lancaster who was nodding empathetically.

'When this terrorist phoned Mercure to warn her about the device at the school, rather than evacuating the area and telling the public of the very real danger they were in, she wanted to keep it all quiet. That kind of disregard for public safety is criminal in itself.'

'Is that why you arranged an interview at the local radio station?'

'That's right, Marshall. I felt compelled to warn my constituents of the threat to each of their lives. These are people we are talking about here, Marshall! They have the right to know if they are in danger so that they can make the necessary arrangements to protect themselves. What gives Mercure the right to choose who lives and dies?'

'Why do you think she's not been more open with the public? I mean, even now, we are hearing that the police are refusing to comment on whether there is a bomb somewhere in the city.'

'That's an excellent question, Marshall; one I don't have an answer to. Maybe she is hoping she can solve the crime on her own and earn that next promotion. Who knows?'

Mercure was grinding her teeth as she felt the knife plunge deeper into her back.

'The real question we should be asking is: why haven't they caught this madman yet?' Eve continued. 'They have been investigating since nine a.m. but are no closer to identifying who he is, or why he is doing what he is doing.'

'How can you be certain that no progress has been made, Eve, if you don't mind me asking?'

'Because I've been in that Major Incident room all day, Marshall. I've been watching them floundering about all day. I mean, it's not her fault. I am sure she is a very talented woman.'

'But maybe this is just too much for her?'

Eve smiled. 'They are your words, Marshall. What this operation needs is someone strong to come in and take the reins. We need to find this terrorist and stop him causing any more harm!'

Mercure switched the television off. As character assassinations went, that one was top drawer. The phone on her desk began to ring.

'Mercure,' she sighed, putting the phone to her ear.

'Jan, it's Peter Gulliver.'

'Sir,' she acknowledged, adjusting her posture.

'I've just been listening to Eve Partridge's interview on the radio news. I have to say, Jan, I'm very disappointed.'

'With respect, sir, she doesn't know what she is talking about. I can…'

'That's not the point, Jan. She has made us look stupid. She is a figure of respect in the city and she has put us firmly under the microscope. Everything we do here on in will be dissected for all to see, so we need to get a result. Is that clear?'

'Sir,' she acknowledged, knowing now was not the time for argument or recrimination.

'What progress have we made in locating this bus?'

'We are still searching for it. We have drawn up a list of possible targets along the known routes and have patrols stationed at each target. As soon as we find it, I will head to the scene and set up a mobile command post.'

'We have little over an hour, we need to work faster and smarter, Jan. Listen, I'm in the car, about five minutes away from you. From now on I want you to ratify every strategic decision regarding this incident with me. Is that clear?'

'I don't need you to hold my hand, sir. I am more than capable of the Silver Commander duties.'

'I am sure you are, Jan, but do you think the public would agree with that statement? There's another thing; I want Eve Partridge involved in the strategic decisions as well.'

'Sir that goes against all protocol' Mercure

pleaded. 'We can't involve a civilian in this kind of operation.'

'I disagree, Jan. You said yourself that you thought she was somehow the target of this madman's campaign. She has a good knowledge of everything that has happened today and, despite what you may think of her, she is a resourceful woman. Maybe a fresh pair of eyes on matters wouldn't be a bad thing.'

'I must protest, sir.'

'It's too late, Jan; I've already made contact with her P.A. They will be with you as soon as she finishes the interview. You will involve her in matters. She is now the self-appointed face of this operation. We need her on our side. Is that understood?'

'Yes, sir,' Mercure said through gritted teeth.

18:01

'Right then,' shouted the dishevelled man as he strode purposefully into the Major Incident room. 'Who's in charge round here?'

'Detective Chief Inspector Janet Mercure,' she replied, 'and you are?'

'Good evening, ma'am. You spoke with my D.C.I. on the phone earlier,' Tony White confirmed, removing his warrant card and handing it over to her.

'Tony? I wasn't expecting…'

'You have a nutter running around the city letting off bombs. Well, nutters are my speciality, ma'am. I'm here for whatever you need.'

White's sudden appearance had caught her off guard, but she led him through to her office.

'Take a seat, Tony,' she said opening a cupboard in her desk and pulling out a small bottle of gin. 'Can I offer you a glass?'

'I don't usually drink on the job, ma'am, but if you're having one then it would be rude to decline.'

The truth was: he had already consumed two bottles of Newcastle Brown during the flight down, but the gum he was chewing seemed to be hiding the smell.

'That's good to hear,' she said, offering a smile. 'I

wouldn't normally encourage you to break that rule…but it's been a long day. Welcome to the team!' she added, raising her glass and passing his.

White threw the shot down his throat and savoured the burn, but regretted the decision when he saw her sipping hers.

'Sorry,' he offered guiltily. 'It's how we do it where I come from.'

'What have you heard about today's incident?'

'Well, as I said, I've heard there's a nutter in the city and that you were a bit low on manpower.'

'I won't deny, today has been one kick in the teeth after another. In all my years, I've never known an incident like it.'

'So you definitely think the threat is real? It's not some sick joke?'

'Oh no, it's definitely real, but I can't help thinking there is something much bigger going on in the background that we don't know about.'

'Like what?'

'I wish I knew! The events have been so carefully planned, and we've been one step behind this terrorist the whole time…I'm probably just being paranoid…'

White thought about the blueprints in McManus' desk earlier, but decided it was too soon to admit the real reason he had accepted the transfer.

'Has he said why he is doing all this? Do you think religion is involved?' White asked.

'It's political, that much I know. He has threatened one of our local politicians, but I don't trust her motives either. Whatever's going on, someone wants her to pay for her mistakes'

'Personally, I think Guy Fawkes had the right idea of what to do with politicians,' White smiled. Mercure smiled back.

'I thought you had an active investigation you were working on?' Mercure said, changing the subject

'I did...I mean I do...we raided a suspected front for an illegal casino this morning, only to find out someone had tipped off the bastard we were after...' White quickly apologised when he noticed Mercure frowning. 'With respect, ma'am, I'd rather be getting up to speed with the investigation, if you don't mind?'

Mercure nodded, accepting that her much needed break was over inside a minute. 'You're quite right,' she said putting her glass down. 'I'll introduce you properly to the team and they can brief you on what is happening.'

'Who is the acting D.I.?'

'Unofficially, D.S. Kyle Davies has been holding the fort. He's on his way back in. He's a competent individual, but I should warn you he was very interested in your new role too, so tread carefully. Oh, and Tony, call me Guv, please.'

Mercure and White stepped into the Major Incident room and saw a hive of activity. Mercure called Beth Taylor over. 'Beth have we got a probable location yet?'

'I've got it narrowed down to two possible routes and we are tracking four vehicles on those routes,' Beth replied, pointing at the map.

'What's that one?' White asked studying the map.

'Which one?' Beth asked.

'This one here,' White said, pointing at a bus near the bottom of the map. 'It's in this industrial space but away from any of the routes.'

Beth compared the bus' identification number to the list on a pad of paper. 'It's okay, that one is broken down. The driver called in an hour ago to say the engine had failed, so they have taken it off route while it waits for a recovery vehicle to collect...'

The three stared at the map and looked back at each other.

'That's Leisure World, Beth,' Mercure pointed out, deflecting her own embarrassment for not noticing it. 'That's on our list of probable targets, right?'

'It was, Guv, but we dismissed it as it wasn't along any of the city's bus routes.'

Mercure knew in her gut, they had made the breakthrough. 'Right team, this is it. We have the probable location of the attack. I want us to initiate the mobile command units. I want all of you downstairs, dressed in full body armour and in the vans within three minutes. Beth, I want you to remain behind with D.I. White and fill him in on everything that's going on. I also want you to continue to check the status of this bus; let me know if it moves or anything changes. Tony, D.S. Davies is due back soon, I want you to run post here until he arrives.'

'Understood, Guv. I'll let the Gold Commander know what is going on too.'

'Guv, that politician and her P.A. are back. They're down at the front desk, they want to know whether to let them back in,' shouted a voice.

Mercure wanted to tell them to leave her outside so the terrorist could get her, but knew better than to question Gulliver's command.

'Tell them D.I. White will go and collect her,' Mercure answered, nodding at White, before she disappeared out of the room with the rest of the team. 'Watch them, Tony,' she shouted back over her shoulder.

White smiled at Beth and told her he would go and collect them. She gave him instructions for how to reach the front desk and returned to her telephone conversation with the bus company. White was descending the stairs when he noticed a woman walking towards him. 'I presume you are D.I. White?' the woman demanded.

'Aye, that's right,' he replied.

'I'm Eve Partridge,' she replied. 'The desk sergeant said you were coming down but I thought I'd save you the job.'

Fair enough, he thought.

'It's nice to meet you,' he said, thrusting out a hand, which she shook. 'Where's your P.A.?' he asked, noticing she was alone.

'He said he was going to stop off in the canteen and pick us up a coffee,' she replied absently.

A thought sparked in his mind.

Could it...

'You know your way up to the Major Incident Room, right?' he said quickly.

'Yes,' she said. 'Why?'

'Because I don't want your P.A. to get lost,' he replied, turning and running down the stairs.

18:09

Ophion switched the car's engine off and rotated his neck, enjoying the sensation as it clicked. This particular job had required months of planning. Observing and learning Denby's schedule and frequented haunts; arranging for the necessary tools, like the semtex, to be delivered; developing an escape route. He had been meticulous in his organisation of events. As a rule, he never formally met his clients. It was his rule, not theirs.

He felt the phone vibrating in his pocket and swiftly removed it.

'Yes?'

'You have certainly proved your reputation today,' the client said. 'I wasn't convinced that you would be able to undertake everything demanded of you, but I'm pleased to have been proved wrong.'

'Who recommended me to you?'

'A friend explained what you could do, and suggested I contact you for this role.'

Anonymity.

It was what had made Ophion so successful over the years. He couldn't blame the client for his discretion.

'I thought you should know,' the client continued. 'The police have worked out where the bus is. They are en route to its location as we speak.'

'It took them longer than I expected. I was about to phone that detective and give him a clue to its whereabouts,' Ophion admitted.

'This is probably the last time we will speak, so I wanted to ask you to confirm that you have carried out my instructions to the letter.'

'I have told you before: I am a professional. I have carried out everything you have asked of me. Everybody associated with the McKenzie case is dead. The solicitor's body was discovered at lunchtime. The only other person to have seen the file is his secretary. She is currently on board the very bus that is primed to explode. What's more, she has the only physical copy of the McKenzie file on her person. I have uploaded a virus to the firm's network, which will wipe out any digital traces of the file, so it will be as if it never existed.'

'Good; and the other thing?'

'The French fixer is on board the bus too. I don't understand his involvement in this thing…'

'He is an unwanted complication. Life will be easier if he is not around. He is lucky to have lasted this long. Do you think the police believed that they can prevent the device exploding?'

'Everything I have told them today has come true, so they have no reason to question my word. Whether they actually shoot one of the passengers is uncertain, but they know that is the choice to be made.'

'Good. Are there enough random passengers to disguise the real intention of the bus?'

'There are six passengers in total, including the

driver. She has already been dealt with, so that leaves them five to choose from. It's enough.'

'The website was accessed by an unknown laptop earlier this evening. Have you managed to trace the I.P. address yet?' the client asked.

'I have. I am outside the property as we speak.'

'Do we know who accessed it?'

'The property is in the name of a young man called Harry Cross.'

'Why do I recognise that name?'

'His father, Troy used to work for the company.'

'The ex-navy guy? The one…'

'Yes, the one I disposed of in Monaco.'

'It seems too much of a coincidence. Do you think the son knows anything?'

'There's only one way to guarantee his silence.'

'So you will take care of it?'

'I will, but it will cost you extra…he was never part of the original target list.'

'The money will not be a problem; do what you need to, but make it clean. I don't want any trace back to the bus. Is that understood?'

'Agreed. He is a young man, grieving for his father; he will die of a drugs overdose.'

'Perfect! You have done well.'

'The rest of my money: it is ready to be transferred?'

'I will email you confirmation of the account it will be transferred from. The money is scheduled to travel to your offshore account at eight p.m. UK time.'

Ophion disconnected the phone and withdrew a small bag from his coat pocket. He unzipped it to check the contents. The syringe, containing the rust-coloured liquid, glistened.

What is one more death?

He promised himself a well-earned break in the coming weeks, with all the cocktails and rent boys his money could buy.

18:21

'Aaron, it's Paul, answer your phone, please? Look, I've changed my mind, I don't want you to release the information I gave you. If Eve ever found out what I had done, she would have my guts for garters! You understand? I made a mistake in selling you the information. Technically, what you are holding is mine, and I want it back. You can keep your money. I am not prepared to lose my job over this.'

Paul hung up the phone. He had tried ringing Aaron twice now, but both times the messaging service had taken his call. He was sweating as the day's events took their toll. The last thing he needed now was the naval man sharing those documents, which could easily be tied back to him. What had he been thinking?

He wondered whether to phone his solicitor to see if he could take out an injunction against the website that Aaron was planning to use to expose the dirty little secrets, but he knew the firm closed at five p.m.

There's no use crying over spilt milk, his mum would have said. Well, there was if you caused the milk to spill by violently kicking over the bottle.

Paul dialled the number again but hung up as

soon as heard the familiar recorded voice tell him the phone was not connected. He started towards the exit of the canteen, surreptitiously placing the phone back in his trouser pocket.

'You must be the P.A.?' a loud Geordie voice boomed.

Paul looked up and saw a tall man in a dishevelled suit standing by the canteen's door.

'Yes, I am,' Paul replied. 'Who might you be?'

'I'm Detective Inspector Tony White, but you can call me, sir. Who was on the phone?'

Paul's eyes widened. 'Phone? What phone? I wasn't on the phone.'

'Just playing Angry Birds then, were ya? Why else would you be placing your phone back in your pocket when I walked in?'

'I don't know what you're talking about,' Paul bluffed, trying to walk past him.

White placed a hand on Paul's shoulder and pushed him backwards. 'Just a minute, I haven't finished talking to you.'

'Please don't put your hands on me. I know my rights; I've done nothing wrong.'

'Correction: I can place my hands wherever I like, for this is my castle and I am the King!' White boomed. 'Whilst you are a guest in my castle, you will obey my rules and do whatever I tell you. What's more: you will do it all with a big smile on your face! Do I make myself clear?'

Paul's eyes widened again and he gulped audibly to register his submission.

'Good. Now, I will ask again, who were you phoning? What was so important that you had to place the call in a dark corner of my castle? Hmm?'

'I was dealing with official council business, okay? I am not at liberty to disclose all the details to you. It is to do with Eve's campaign.'

White eyed him cautiously. 'Are you lying to me, P.A.? I mean, you wouldn't do that in my castle, would ya?'

Paul took a breath and stared him right in the eye, hoping that his body didn't give him away. 'I am telling the truth. That was about Eve's campaign. Who did you think I was speaking to?'

Before White could offer an answer, Beth Taylor ran into the canteen.

'Guv,' she said, 'the bomber…he's back on the phone. He wants to speak to whoever is in charge. I can't get hold of the D.C.I. as they're still setting up at Leisure World. You are the ranking officer.'

White nodded and the pair of them tore out of the canteen. Paul took several deep breaths and then slowly followed them back towards the Major Incident room.

White grabbed the phone and breathlessly yelled. 'Yeah?'

'You are not D.C.I. Mercure. Who are you?'

'I'm Detective Inspector Tony White. What's your name?'

'My name is not important…'

'That's a funny name; your parents not like you or something? Should I call you 'Mr Not Important' or just 'Not' for short?'

'You're a comedian? Have things really sunk so low?'

'My mother always told me laughter is the best

medicine. What did yours teach you? How to dress up dolls?'

'Where is Mercure?' Ophion demanded.

'She can't come to the phone right now, I'm afraid as she's busy chasing some nutcase who is threatening to detonate a bomb in the city! Sorry if that's inconvenient for you.'

'Where is Kyle Davies? I will speak to him if Mercure is away.'

'Detective Sergeant Davies works for me, so I would be happy to pass on a message.'

Ophion chuckled. 'Do you find this confrontational approach produces better policing?'

'I don't know; do you find hiding bombs like a cissy gets you off?'

'I'm growing to like you...what did you say your name was?'

'Detective Inspector Tony White.'

'Well, D.I. White, your attempts to antagonise me were amusing, but all you have achieved is making your job harder. I had phoned to identify one passenger who definitely doesn't hold the detonator. It would have narrowed your choice from six to five, but now, I don't think I'll bother. When Mercure fails to shoot the right passenger and the bomb explodes, be sure to tell her your role in the operation's failure, won't you?'

'Why don't you pop in and tell her yourself? I'm sure the two of you could chat for hours.'

'I sense you are somebody who uses humour as a defence mechanism, did you have an unhappy childhood?'

'That's an interesting observation. I had a shit

upbringing, but it doesn't stop me being the best copper I can be. How was your upbringing? Did your mam make ya wear pretty dresses?'

Beth Taylor, who was listening into the conversation from a secondary device, mouthed the letters W, T and F in White's direction, a puzzled frown on her face.

'White held the phone down to his chest for a moment. 'My gut tells me it's a man we are dealing with; probably a homophobe. I'm trying to rile him into accidentally giving us a clue to his identity.'

'I will not be drawn into a debate about my mother, despite your best efforts, D.I. White. I am growing bored of this conversation. Please advise D.C.I. Mercure that she is not to interfere with the bus in anyway. If my passenger suspects anything underhand is going on or sees anybody approaching the vehicle, they will detonate the device.'

'Will he?'

'He or she is fully aware of their responsibilities. My rules are clear. It is a game of roulette: shoot the right passenger and win the game. Don't shoot, or choose the wrong candidate, and the bus explodes. Is that easy enough for your Neanderthal brain to comprehend, D.I. White?'

Ophion hung up the phone and placed it back in his pocket. He picked up the small bag containing the syringe and left the car. The house was a decent size and the windows looked quite secure. He would have to find a suitable place to break in.

18:28

Leisure World was a hive of activity. The entrance to the site was cordoned off, and police vehicles had been stationed at all access points to the West Quay Road. Overhead a helicopter was circling the perimeter with a large spotlight brightening the darkest corners of the large car park. The cinema complex had been evacuated, and Mercure had ordered that all nearby shops and businesses be evacuated too, including the furniture store across the road. Police officers were stationed at pedestrian access points. Since Eve Partridge's interview had been screened on the BBC News 24 channel, the police presence at Leisure World had tipped off the media that this was the probable location of the device.

The bus was still parked right outside the entrance to the cinema complex. The two mobile command units had been stationed at the entrance to the car park, about one hundred yards from the bus. From here, Travers and Mercure had a clear view into the bus using binoculars. The first mobile unit contained various schematics of I.E.D.s that Sid Travers team were pouring over on the off-chance that they could get close enough to try and diffuse the device.

'I don't want any cameras filming the bus or our movements!' Mercure had told her officers. She wasn't prepared to sit back and wait for the deadline to arrive; they were going to advance on the bus and tackle the device, if they could locate it. One of Travers' men was currently looking at an exploded diagram of the bus, trying to determine where the bomber could have hidden the device, and estimating how much semtex may have been used. Everything that had happened today was pointing towards this final event, which made Mercure feel like this device would be bigger than the other two they had encountered. If that were true, there was no way of knowing just how big a mess the explosion would cause, which was why she was determined not to let that happen.

Mercure was sitting in the second mobile unit: the tactical unit. She had a map of the former industrial site and had marked the locations of all her men. She was reviewing the locations for weaknesses when there was a knock at the door. The door opened and Kyle Davies entered.

'Davies, good, where have you been?' Mercure demanded.

'It took longer than expected to resolve things at the university, Guv. I had to brief campus security and arrange for the vending machine to be collected. I headed back to the station but was told you had found the bus and that you were here.'

'Did you meet Tony White?'

'Briefly, Guv. He told me to tell you that the terrorist phoned again to warn us not to try and interfere with the bus. He said that if his contact on the bus suspects we are doing anything underhand he or she will detonate it.'

Mercure considered the news before saying, 'I don't care! I am not going to let that bomb explode. I will do whatever it takes to stop him winning.'

'But how, Guv? If the person with the detonator sees us...'

'We will cause a distraction...if we can get all of them looking one way, we can sneak a couple of Travers' men in on the opposite side.'

'And what if he has cameras on the bus and spots us? The risk is too great!'

'You have any better ideas, Davies?'

'How about we post an image of each passenger online and ask the public to come forward and vouch for them?'

'The switchboard is still jammed with people phoning after that silly bitch gave her interview. It's not a bad idea, Davies, but I don't think we have the time. Besides, the terrorist may have pre-empted such a move and may have people on hand ready to vouch for the real threat.'

There was another knock on the door as Capshaw walked in. 'Guv, Gold Commander is on line one for you.'

Mercure waved him away and answered the phone. 'Yes, sir, we are in position. I can confirm we have six people on board, three male and three female. One of the women, whom we believe is the driver is slouched over the steering wheel...well, I don't know what that means, sir...for all we know she could be the one we are looking for...I don't know what else she could be doing...I'll have to put you on speaker…'

Mercure pressed a button on the phone and replaced the handset. 'Can you hear me okay, sir?'

'I can hear you fine, Jan. So, I want you to tell me what you can see. We are going to need to draw up basic profiles for the people on that bus. We have half an hour to try and figure out which one has the detonator.'

'You're not actually contemplating ordering a kill shot, are you?' Davies interrupted, unable to believe his ears.

'Who's that?' Gulliver demanded.

'Davies, sir. Sorry, I was briefing D.C.I. Mercure when she received your call.'

'That's okay, Davies. After your heroics at the university, you deserve to be in the loop of this conversation. In answer to your question, a decision has yet to be made on whether to give in to the terrorist's demands. We would prefer to explore all alternative avenues first. Nevertheless, we have to show we are prepared. We have to do everything by the book. If we draw up a profile on each passenger, it might help us figure out this man's motives.'

'Davies, use the binoculars and describe each passenger one by one. I'll jot some notes on the whiteboard and we'll go from there,' Mercure ordered.

Kyle scooped up the binoculars and focused on the passenger closest to him.

'There is an African male at the rear of the vehicle, maybe Algerian judging by his skin tone. Hair: dark. Clothing: Black overcoat. He is sitting alone and doesn't appear to be interacting with the other passengers. He seems calm; collected.'

'Right, we'll call him Target-one. Who's next?'

'Target-two is an Asian female. Dark hair, business suit, pregnant.'

'Pregnant?' Mercure questioned.

'That or...' Davies didn't need to finish the sentence.

'Sir,' Mercure continued, 'she could be the one.'

'Guv, being Asian with a bump doesn't automatically make her a suicide bomber,' Kyle challenged. 'Besides, for all we know, the target is only holding a switch; the semtex could be anywhere on the bus.

'I'm just saying it's a consideration. Who's next?'

'Target-three is a white male: overweight and wearing a traffic warden's uniform. Age probably in his early to mid-thirties. He looks moody, if that helps.'

'Anything else?'

'I'd say it's more likely that he's wearing a bomb vest than the pregnant girl, judging by the size of his coat. That or he is very overweight. He seems to be shouting at his fellow detainees...as if he's trying to rile them or something. I'd say he's the most likely suspect at the moment.'

'Okay, we'll put a question mark next to him too. Next?'

'Target-four is another white male. This one is in his late twenties, wearing a naval uniform. His hair is light brown and he looks clean shaven. He is sitting next to a present of some sort.'

'Present?' Gulliver enquired.

'Well,' Davies continued, 'there's a large box on

the seat next to him. Your guess is as good as mine, sir. Would you really go to a birthday party dressed in full naval uniform?'

'So he is another for consideration,' Gulliver dictated.

'There's another white female towards the back of the bus. Again, she's dressed in business attire. Finally, we have a white female slumped over the steering wheel. She hasn't moved once since I started looking at the bus. I think it's the driver, judging by the uniform.'

Mercure snatched the binoculars and checked for herself.

'Davies is right, sir. She isn't moving...wait a minute...the pregnant woman...Target-two...I met her earlier. She's the secretary of the solicitor who was found hanging in his apartment at lunchtime. What the hell is she doing on there? It can't be a coincidence.'

'We need to get ears and eyes on that bus, Jan,' Gulliver continued. 'I presume snipers are in place on the roof of the complex?'

'Just waiting for the call to confirm they are in position, sir.'

'Good. Brief them on our targets. I want sight of each of them in case of sudden movements.'

'We could see if a directional microphone would allow us to listen in on what they are saying. It won't be ideal, but might help.'

Mercure nodded. 'See if anyone nearby can read lips too.'

Davies nodded his understanding and left the vehicle.

'I need to know if I have the green light, sir,' Mercure said, once the door was closed. 'When the time comes, will I have permission to give the order?'

'There are too many options at the moment, Jan. You need to narrow that list down.'

'But if it gets to six fifty-nine and we've not disarmed the device or individual, do I have the authority?'

'It's being discussed as we speak, Jan. I'll let you know when we've reached a decision. In the meantime, try and get closer to the bus. We need to find that device.'

18:41

Aaron glanced at his watch. The police had been anxiously milling around for the last thirty minutes but, so far, had made no attempt to approach the bus.

'Why aren't they fucking doing something?' the traffic warden demanded again. 'Why aren't they trying to diffuse the bomb?'

'The voice said he had given them a puzzle to solve. Maybe that is what they're doing. Maybe the puzzle is connected to the device somehow and if they can solve it, we'll be released,' Nazir reasoned.

'I'm not ready to die! I don't deserve to!' the traffic warden continued.

'You think any of us do? You think just because I'm Muslim, I should die? You think any of us deserve to be here? We're all as anxious as you, but shouting isn't helping.'

'Fuck this!' he suddenly declared, moving towards the door. 'I'm getting off this fucking bus.'

'No!' Aaron shouted, leaping forward and dragging him back to his seat. 'If we try and leave, we all die.'

'We're dead anyway,' he replied dismissively. 'What's the difference if it happens now or in twenty minutes? We're all fucked! The police aren't making any move to save us. Hell, I can see snipers on the roof pointing their weapons at us. What's that all about?'

'Maybe they think one of us will detonate the device,' Aaron suggested. The thought stuck in his mind.

What if they're right?

His eyes scanned each of his fellow captives.

Which of you is it?

Aaron moved to the front of the bus and faced them. 'One of us may not be as friendly as we appear. There is only one reason the police would deploy snipers to target us...they think one of us is going to set off the device. So, this is that individual's opportunity to come forward and do the right thing. Give yourself up and I am sure they will go easier on you. Who is it? Which of you is the real threat?'

'Well don't look at me! I'm just a traffic warden. Why the hell would I want to blow up a bus? Where's my motive?'

'What are you implying?' Nazir challenged.

'All's I'm saying is: if you look at history, what is the common reason for terrorist bombings? Religion!'

Nazir wanted to slap him hard in the face, but decided to remain calm. 'I have nothing to hide,' she said, standing and turning so that everyone could see her. 'If anyone wants to feel my bump, to confirm I am actually pregnant, go ahead.'

'This is getting us nowhere,' Aaron continued. 'I don't want us to accuse each other and develop reasons for our suspicions. Let's each take it in turn to prove our innocence. I'll start. My name is Lieutenant Aaron Cross. I serve in the Royal Navy and am home on leave to attend my uncle's funeral. In that present box is paper and a memory stick,' he added, pointing at the box.

'Open it up then,' the traffic warden fired back.

'Okay,' said Aaron, moving to the box and pulling the lid off. He showed the contents to the rest of them. 'Happy? Right, traffic warden next.'

'Very well, my name is Warren. I am a traffic warden and I am on my way home.'

'What's in the bag?' Aaron asked, pointing at the satchel looped over the man's shoulders.

'Nothing. It's what I use to carry my lunch in.'

'Hand it over,' Aaron continued.

The traffic warden reluctantly did as he was told. Aaron unzipped it and peered inside. He reached his hand in and removed a small metallic flask. The traffic warden shrugged. 'It's medicinal.'

Aaron placed the satchel on the floor.

'Her next!' the traffic warden demanded.

Nazir was still on her feet. 'My name is Nazir Ahmed; I am a legal secretary and I have no parcels or bags,' she said, raising her shirt to reveal her bump. She was surprised by how much bigger it looked now, compared to this morning. 'If you wish to feel my bump, go ahead.'

'That's okay,' Aaron replied. 'Who wants to go next?'

'My name is Tracey Reed. I'm on my way home from a day in the office. I have a briefcase, but it contains confidential client files, so I am not at liberty to open it.'

'Bull shit!' Retourget shouted from behind her. 'You work for Richard Eksteen!'

'What's going on?' Aaron challenged. 'You two know each other?'

Tracey turned to see who had questioned her, but did not recognise the Frenchman's face. 'I think you must have me confused with someone else. I don't know you.'

Retourget grinned. 'You're good, lady. I have been following you since you left your house this evening with that briefcase. I know that a South African businessman called Richard Eksteen deposited that case at your house earlier on today, because I was there when he did. Is Eksteen the bomber? Is that it? You are the one?'

'Me? What? No...I...'

Tracey was suddenly conscious that all eyes were on her. In a panic, she threw the briefcase forward. 'Open it, please? I don't know what the combination is. I don't know what is in it, I was just told to deliver it to the address on the handle.'

'Who is Richard Eksteen?' Aaron asked.

'I don't know,' Tracey fired back. 'All I know is what the South African told me to do.'

'Eksteen is a local drug importer,' Retourget explained. 'He is from South Africa, so he must be the man she spoke to. Pass me the case.'

Aaron scooped it from the floor and passed it to Retourget. The Frenchman removed his knife and ran it between the locks. After some jiggling the two locks snapped open.

'Some security!' he said, lifting the lid to reveal two bags of white powder and an envelope stuffed with cash. 'You are his mule?'

'No,' Tracey cried. 'I was just doing as I was told…'

'Whose is that?' Retourget interrupted, pointing at a manila-coloured file on the floor.

Everyone looked to where he was pointing.

'Oh that's mine,' Nazir said, picking up the McKenzie file. 'It's a case I'm working on: McKenzie vs Parvon Trading.'

Aaron shot a glance at Retourget as he heard the name. The Frenchman was nodding back at him. Aaron snatched the file from Nazir and began to flick through it.

'Hey,' she shouted, 'that is confidential!'

'What's the case about?' Aaron shouted. 'I need to know. Come on, who am I going to tell?'

Nazir considered their current predicament, before sighing. 'A Scottish investment firm, McKenzie Investments is suing a European investment company for stealing customers.'

Nazir paused to see if she had given enough detail but decided to continue when she saw blank faces staring back at her. 'A senior partner at McKenzie left last year and went to work for the European firm, Parvon. The plaintiff is claiming the trader stole a list of clients when he left the company, who have subsequently moved their investment business to the defendant company. It's not all that exciting.'

'Do you have the list of clients that it's claimed he took?' Aaron asked.

'Sure, I have a full list of both companies' clients. Why?'

'Give it to me, please?'

Nazir reluctantly passed the two lists of clients to Aaron who began to read them eagerly.

'Holy shit!' he declared when his eyes stopped on one name in particular. Before, he could finish the thought a voice boomed through a megaphone. 'This is Detective Sergeant Kyle Davies of the Hampshire Constabulary. I want every person on the bus to move towards the driver's side of the bus, facing the window. You are all to put your hands on your heads with your fingers interlaced.'

18:58

Mercure was on the phone to Detective Superintendent Gulliver, who had taken up position in her office back at the Headquarters building. 'I need a decision, sir. There are two minutes and counting until the device will detonate.'

There was silence on the other end.

'Silver Commander to Armed Response: do we have all targets in sight?' she said, holding the walkie-talkie close to her mouth.

'Armed Response to Silver Commander: we have eyes on all targets. They are still standing at the window with their hands raised. Waiting for your orders, over,' replied the sniper commander.

'Jan, are you there?' asked Gulliver.

'Silver Control receiving, over.'

'We want you to provide an update on the targets again,' Gulliver instructed.

Mercure sighed and began to recite the information she had already shared three times in the last thirty minutes: 'Target-one Retourget: a French-Arab male, early forties, in dark clothing. He hasn't interacted much with the other passengers so we don't believe he is a realistic suspect. Target-two is Nazir Ahmed: an Asian female in her late twenties. She is the secretary of the dead solicitor we found earlier, and her presence here feels too coincidental for my liking. We believe she is a probable suspect. Target-three is Target-three refused to give his name when asked. He is a white male in his thirties, who has a bulge beneath his traffic warden's coat. He is a possible candidate for lead suspect. Target-four is Aaron Cross: another white male in his thirties, dressed in a black naval uniform. We have observed him opening the box in his possession and showing it to the other detainees, maybe as a warning of what he has. We have determined he is also a probable suspect. Target-five is Tracey Reed: a white female in her late forties, dressed in business attire. We don't feel she is a realistic suspect, as the case she was carrying has been opened and did not contain any explosives. We have learned from those on board that the bus driver was executed on arrival. We believe Targets one and five are just in the wrong place at the wrong time. I need a decision on Targets two, three and four, over.'

The line was muted once more, while Gulliver and the Chief Superintendent discussed their options.

Kyle knocked at the door and entered. 'Any decision yet, Guv?'

Mercure shook her head.

'What did Sid's team find?' he continued.

Mercure had commanded Davies to instruct the passengers via a megaphone fifteen minutes earlier, to stand facing the windows on one side of the bus. That had given two of Sid Travers' bomb disposal team time to move in close at the opposite side and undertake a quick assessment of the bus. It had also allowed him to ask the passengers their names.

Mercure frowned. 'Nothing! They've pulled back now and reported that there is no bomb outside of the vehicle; it must be inside with the passengers. They have checked the holds beneath the bus, as well in the engine compartment, but there's no trace of any explosive. They also reported there is no obvious transmitter or receiver. Sid said he would have expected one if the bomb was to be detonated remotely from outside of the bus.

'That means that the bomb is either on a timer, connected to a remote inside the bus as the terrorist has claimed, or doesn't even exist,' Kyle reasoned. 'I mean, Guv, have we even considered that possibility? What if this whole thing is a ploy to get the police to shoot an innocent victim, even though there is no real threat to life?'

'You think I haven't considered that, Davies? This guy has had us on the ropes all day and we are still no closer to identifying him, let alone finding him.'

'D.I. White has reached out to Interpol to see if they have managed to locate or identify the assailant known as The Serpent and is waiting for a response. Did you get hold of your contact at MI-5?'

'It was a dead end, as I thought it would be. I've said all along, this is not about religion; this is political!'

'You still think Partridge is the target? I don't see how this incident will impact her. Besides, White told me she doesn't think we should shoot. She thinks it will be political suicide for whoever gives that order.'

Mercure shrugged. 'What choice do we have? Rely on the word of a crazed madman or ignore it? We're screwed in public regardless. If we shoot the wrong person and the bus explodes, he wins. If we shoot nobody and the bus explodes, he wins.'

'I cannot believe we are even considering this!'

'Gold Commander?' Mercure shouted into the phone. 'This is Silver Control, deadline is sixty seconds and counting. I need your decision now, please.'

'Received, Silver Control,' Gulliver's voice boomed back. 'No decision has been reached yet, over.'

'Silver Commander to Armed Response,' Mercure said into the radio, 'do you still have eyes on all targets? Any changes?'

'Armed Response to Silver Commander,' the radio crackled, 'we still have eyes on all targets. We...wait...there's movement on the bus, Silver Commander. The naval officer has moved away from the window and is walking to the front of the vehicle.'

'Do you have a shot?' Mercure shouted.

'Negative, he is out of view...the traffic warden has moved forward too and appears to be shouting at him...wait...the traffic warden is still in scope...'

'What is the naval officer doing?' Mercure cried, exasperated. Is he about to detonate that bomb?'

'Can't say, Ma'am,' the radio crackled. 'He is out of sight.'

'Then get round so that you can see him. I want eyes on him. What the fuck is he doing?'

'Gold Commander to Silver Control,' Gulliver

said into the phone. 'What is going on down there?'

'The man in the naval uniform has moved from the window, sir,' Mercure fired back. 'We've lost sight of him.'

'Armed Response to Silver Commander,' the radio crackled. 'The traffic warden is now moving to the rear of the vehicle with his arms over his head. He is shouting something. Should we take the shot?'

'Stand down!' Gulliver shouted into the phone. 'I repeat: stand down! Do not take that shot!'

'Armed Response to Silver Commander, should we engage? Twenty seconds till deadline. Ma'am? We need a response…'

'Stand down, Jan, do not give that order! Do you copy?'

'Silver Commander, we need an answer now!'

'This is Gold Commander. Do you copy?'

If we shoot nobody and the bus explodes, he wins.

'Silver Commander to Armed Response: take out the traffic warden!'

THE AFTERMATH

19:11

'To confirm the latest here in Southampton,' reporter Marshall Lancaster said, staring long into the lens, 'minutes ago there was the sound of a gunshot, swiftly followed by what can only be described as the sound of a large firework exploding. As yet, it is unconfirmed whether the shot was fired by the police or by one of the passengers they have been monitoring on the bus for the last hour. In the moments following the explosion, several ambulances and fire engines were allowed access through the police perimeter, though none of those vehicles has re-emerged as yet. The decision to operate a media blackout during this crisis has left us with only speculation as to what is going on. Earlier today, local M.P. Eve Partridge told us that there was a bomb on a bus somewhere in the city and that the police were trying to identify the vehicle's location. Then, just under an hour ago, we received a tip-off of significant police activity here on West Quay Road. Upon arrival, it quickly became clear that the Leisure World complex had been identified as the likely location for the terrorist's device. As I stand here next to the cordon tape, I can tell you I can hear a hive of activity behind me, but for now, I cannot tell you what is happening.'

✳

'I need you to tell everybody to stay back from the doors at the front of the vehicle,' the fire officer shouted through the burning rear of the bus. 'We are going to use a large saw to cut through the doors so that we can gain access to you. Can you see if anyone is hurt?'

Nazir could not see anything through the thick grey smoke filling the bus. She could hear the man's voice coming from the rear of the bus, somewhere beyond the thick orange flames. She had a ringing in her ears that was impossible to ignore. Her head ached like never before and the smoke-driven cough was only making matters worse. She moved her hands about in an effort to make contact with any of her co-detainees. She was certain she could feel a leg to her left, but it wasn't moving.

'We're about to start using the saw, now,' the fire officer shouted. 'We need to get you out of there as quickly as possible. Keep your head down and if you can find something to cover your nose and mouth with, then do so.'

Nazir did as she was instructed and ducked her head down. The last few minutes had passed by in a flash and her brain was struggling to process everything that had happened. The police had commanded them all to stand in front of the windows with their hands on their heads. She could remember Aaron saying he could see snipers on the roof and that it was likely the police thought one of them had the detonator. He had been pretty good at trying to keep them all calm.

'Everything will be okay,' he had kept repeating. 'If we do as they say: everything will be okay.'

She couldn't say why, but she had believed him; maybe it was the sincerity in his voice? She could remember thinking: this is the end, and in that moment she was filled with a deep sadness; not for her own life, but for that of the unborn child she was carrying. Motherhood had not been her choice but, now that the gift had been bestowed upon her, she didn't want to waste the opportunity. She remembered vowing that if she managed to escape the bus alive, she would make it her life's work to raise her child in a loving home.

The traffic warden had begun shouting that he didn't want to die; that he didn't deserve it and questioning why the police had not managed to locate and disarm the device.

'It must be inside,' Aaron had muttered and then asked, 'where would you hide an explosive device in a bus?'

Nazir had noticed him close his eyes as if he was trying to visualise the layout in his head, and then all of a sudden he had declared, 'I know where it is,' and had rushed forward to the driver's booth and yanked the door open. He had unceremoniously pulled the driver's lifeless body from the seat and allowed it to fall to the floor.

'I've found it,' she had heard him yell. 'Keep looking forward; don't give them a reason to shoot you! The bomb is on a timer and is set to go off in twenty seconds. If you stay still, they won't shoot you.'

'What if you can't disarm it?' the traffic warden had shouted. 'You shouldn't touch it: you'll kill us all.'

'I am trained to diffuse I.E.D.s,' Aaron had shouted back. 'Trust me: stay still.'

But he hadn't listened. 'Why should I?' he had demanded, lowering his arms and moving forward.

'Stay back,' Aaron had shouted. 'I have fifteen seconds to stop this thing. Stay where you are!'

Still the traffic warden had ignored the instruction. 'If the device is at the front of the bus, then the safest place for all of us is at the rear. The police won't shoot. Everybody move to the back!'

'No,' Aaron had pleaded. 'Stay where you are. I can do this!'

Nazir had been glaring at the traffic warden, wishing him dead when she had heard the window crack and a bullet bed itself into his neck. She could still picture the blood as it had spurted from the wound, as he had fallen to the floor. She had been about to scream when there was the most almighty bang and suddenly the back of the bus had become engulfed in flames. She had instinctively ducked her head down and to the right, as the flames had spread across the vehicle's ceiling towards her. The blast must have temporarily knocked her out, as her next recollection was the fireman shouting.

Above her now she could see a beam of light growing around the rim of the door as the large saw cut through the hinges. It looked like they nearly had it open and, as the door fell away, she saw a group of unfamiliar faces peering through, bathed in a bright light. She blinked against the brightness and saw that she was slumped next to Aaron and that it had been his leg she had felt. His eyes were closed and he didn't appear to be moving. To her left was Tracey, who was starting to raise her head. The small group of people at the door stepped back and were replaced by a new crew, this one dressed in green and carrying oxygen masks. They strapped a mask to Aaron's face and pulled his body out. Two more green uniforms stepped to the door and asked Nazir if she could walk. She crawled towards them and, when they were within touching distance, she allowed them to take her arms and lift her from the vehicle.

'I'm pregnant,' she managed to whisper before passing out.

19:15

Mercure extinguished the cigarette beneath her shoe and headed back into Mobile Command Unit Two.

'Ah, Guv, there you are,' said D.C. Capshaw, who had remained inside to man the phone. 'I've got the Gold Commander on the phone asking for an update.

Mercure nodded reluctantly and waved Capshaw out of the vehicle.

She had been dreading this call but knew it was inevitable. The three survivors who had been pulled clear of the wreckage were now all conscious and receiving treatment in the back of ambulances. Against the paramedics' instructions, Mercure had stationed two detectives at each vehicle, taking hurried statements from the victims. She had insisted that the statements be taken separately, on the off-chance that one of the three had in fact detonated the device. Whilst Mercure continued to cling to the hope that the terrorist had not misled them, she knew she was fighting a losing battle. Target-four, whom she now knew to be serving Lieutenant Aaron Cross, had advised that he had managed to diffuse a timed device under the driver's seat, but that a secondary bomb had detonated at the rear of the bus; in all likelihood courtesy of a timer switch as well. He had also explained that the driver had been electrocuted shortly after the vehicle had arrived at the site.

The other two survivors, a legal secretary and a factory worker, had thus far corroborated the naval officer's story.

'Mercure,' she sighed, putting the phone to her ear

'What the bloody hell is going on down there? Report immediately!'

'Details are still a bit sketchy, sir. I can confirm that a device did explode at the rear of the bus, but that a second device was successfully disarmed by one of the passengers at the front of the vehicle.'

'Disarmed by a passenger?'

'Target-four, sir. He is Royal Navy and is trained to disarm I.E.D.s. If it wasn't for him, we would probably have six victims now instead of three.'

'The news is reporting that a gunshot was heard shortly before the explosion. Tell me you didn't give that order, Jan.'

Mercure closed her eyes and took a deep breath. 'Yes, sir, I did give that order.'

'On whose authority? I gave you an explicit order not to proceed!'

'On my authority, sir! A decision had to be made and I took it.'

'The chain of command is in place for a reason. You disobeyed a direct instruction.'

'You're damn right I did. It was an impossible situation. Target-three made a move consistent with detonating the device. There was a choice to be made and I did it. You were delaying the decision and someone had to take control. I did that! I gave the order to take out Target-three before he could set off the device.'

'But it was the wrong call, Mercure! We know that this terrorist lied to you: none of the passengers had the detonator. The bomb was always going to go off at seven. You killed an innocent man who was panicking in a tense situation. We are not permitted to take human life on a whim. I was strategic command. The strategy was not to give in to the terrorist's demands. He's made us look foolish!'

'You don't understand the situation, sir. With the greatest respect, you have only become involved in today's events at the end of what has been a challenging situation. You haven't spoken to this man; you don't understand his thinking…'

'And you do?' Gulliver interrupted. 'If you understand him so well, how did you not see that he was stringing us along? We have killed an innocent man because the chain of command was not followed.'

'We don't know yet that Target-three wasn't heading to set off the device,' Mercure lied, determined to make her point.

'Well, if that's the case, how did he do it? You shot him before the device exploded, so how did a dead man set it off? Hmm?'

Mercure remained silent.

'You give me no choice, Mercure. You are hereby relieved of your position as Silver Commander with immediate effect. You acted irresponsibly and your reckless decision-making has endangered the lives of those around you as well as prematurely taking the life of an innocent man. I want you to go home straight away and meet me in your office at nine a.m. tomorrow morning. I warned you that we had to do everything by the book and that our every move would be scrutinised under a microscope. The shit is going to hit the fan, Mercure, and I can promise you I will make it my duty to examine your actions in this whole debacle today. Is that clear?'

'Sure,' she sighed and dropped the phone back in its cradle.

She remained sitting, staring at the wall, replaying the day's events in her head when an urgent knock at the door caught her attention. Kyle Davies burst through breathlessly.

'We've got a break, Guv,' he declared. 'I've been speaking to Lieutenant Cross…he told me that all this…it's to do with a law suit…a UK investment company was suing a money laundering front…some badass people…he thinks he knows who is behind today's events…'

'Calm down, Davies,' said Mercure, whose interest was piqued. 'You're not making any sense.'

'Sorry, Guv…it's a long story…I'll explain it all later, but we need to move now…Cross said he recognised one of the names involved with the money laundering…Paul Burns…'

'Burns? Eve Partridge's P.A.?'

'Exactly! He is one of the clients who knowingly invested funds in the laundering front. What's more, Cross said a 'P. Burns' is listed on the company's articles of association. He said all the evidence is in a file on the bus.'

'Have they got the fire out yet?'

'Not yet, but they're getting closer. We can tell them to look for the file when sifting through the debris. In the meantime, I think we need to detain Burns for questioning.'

'You really think he has the audacity to arrange something like this?'

'Why not? A criminal mastermind's greatest disguise would be in the quivering shell of a man scared of his own shadow. It's the Keyser Söze effect. Think about it, he's clearly got the funds, judging by the figures this investment company was posting. Let's say, for a moment, that he's more involved in this front than just investing his own capital. A legal suit against the company suddenly puts it heavily under the spotlight. The last thing he wants is the authorities looking any closer at their details. So how does he make it go away? He kills anyone who has had any dealings in the case. Simon Denby was acting for the plaintiff and he mysteriously committed suicide. His legal secretary, whom you met earlier and who had the file in her possession is on a bus destined to be destroyed.'

'Okay, but how does Eve Partridge fit into all this? Why leave photographs of her at the stadium?'

'You said it yourself: this thing is political. Maybe he's had enough of being in her shadow. He organises today's events and lays the blame at her door. The press already knows that she was the target of the terrorist, so eventually she will be held culpable. Maybe he doesn't agree with her policies. Who knows? I think it warrants further investigation, don't you?'

CROSSHAIRS

19:20

'Hi, it's Aaron, right?' Nazir said, peering around the side of the ambulance door. 'I know we met on the bus, but I thought I should introduce myself properly. I'm Nazir.'

Aaron lowered the oxygen mask from his face and smiled at her. 'It's nice to meet you,' he coughed, before replacing the mask.

'I wanted to come over and thank you. What you did...well you saved my life. If that second bomb had detonated...I...'

'You're welcome,' he said, lowering the mask again. 'To be honest my motives were pretty selfish: I was trying to save my own skin as much as anybody else's.'

She smiled at his modesty. 'They'll probably give you a medal for what you did.'

'I only did what anyone else would have done.'

'You shouldn't be so modest, Aaron! You risked getting shot and blown up to disarm that thing. It's incredibly brave. You're a hero,' she coughed.

Aaron blushed slightly. 'I'll let you buy me a coffee some time and we can call it quits, okay? How are you? Is the baby okay, you didn't break any bones did you?'

'I'm fine,' she said, shrugging her shoulders. 'A

bit of smoke inhalation, but no major damage. They want me to go to the hospital and have an ultrasound just to double-check everything is okay with the baby. I feel fine, considering I was just in the most stressful situation of my life. I'll probably write pages and pages in my diary tonight!'

'That's good. I'm pleased you're okay.'

'What about you? Are you going to be okay?'

'What? This?' Aaron said, pointing at the oxygen mask. 'They told me I needed some extra oxygen in my lungs, that's all. They said I'm okay to go as soon as I feel up to it. Just a few bumps and bruises thankfully…do you know if there were any other survivors?'

'Yeah…that woman with the case: Tracey I think her name is…she was pulled clear too. Can you believe the police actually shot that traffic warden? Apparently there was mass confusion when you went forward and so they thought he was making a move to detonate the device. Not that it would have made much of a difference; he would have died in the explosion a second later anyway. That Frenchman didn't make it either. I guess we were the lucky ones.'

'Everyone has their time,' Aaron smiled. 'I learned that a long time ago. When your ticket is punched, you just have to smile and accept your fate. It wasn't our turn today.'

'I like that philosophy…kind of a live life for the moment thing.'

'I'm not philosophical, Nazir…I've seen too much death for that. No, when my time comes, I will face the consequences of the choices I have made in my life.'

'Do you have a place to stay tonight? I heard you say you were back for a funeral?'

'Yeah, I have a flat here in the city…it's not very big, but I'm hardly ever there so it serves a purpose. You okay? You got anyone to go home to tonight?'

Nazir thought about the phone call she had received from Samir earlier, and shrugged again. 'I'll be okay…I better go…do you have a card with your telephone number on? It's so I can buy you that coffee.'

'I don't, I'm sorry. I have a pen if you want to write it down?'

Nazir smiled and held a hand out. Aaron felt in his trouser pocket and pulled out the pen, before reciting the number. Nazir scrawled the numbers on the back of her hand, before returning the pen and walking away.

*

'What do you mean, he's not there? Where the hell is he?' Kyle shouted into the phone.

'He took off about ten minutes ago,' White replied. Him and that M.P., they said they were going to go back to her place to wash and change and would then come back to the station afterwards. She seemed really scared to be honest; I think she thinks she's next on this killer's list.'

'I think the P.A. is the one who's been behind everything today.'

White couldn't help laughing. 'Have you lost your

mind? He couldn't organise a piss up in a brewery! He's no killer!'

'I think he hired someone to carry out the killings. It's a long story, but there is strong evidence pointing to his involvement. We need to find him.'

'I'm not sure how things are run down here, but I think you're barking up the wrong tree. That said, I'm happy to sit back and watch you make a tit of yourself, if that's what you want to do.'

Kyle turned and looked at Mercure. 'Burns is out there and he has Partridge. I don't think this thing is over yet.'

'Kyle, look...there's something I need to tell you...I've been relieved of my post...there's every chance I will be suspended from duty in the morning...and I could lose my job over what has happened here today...I don't expect you to feel sorry for me, but I do want you to know I have seen a new side to you today. Jack Vincent told me he thought you would make a fine officer one day, and I can see what he meant. You're young and you will get further opportunities to prove you are ready for the role of Inspector; I'm sure of it.'

'Guv, I...don't know what to say.'

'Tony White knows what it is to play the game; learn what you can from him. If Burns is behind this thing, he is the only one who will be able to identify the terrorist he bankrolled today. Get Burns and make him talk. The public need to see somebody hung for today's attacks. The force needs to catch someone to restore faith in the service. I'm relying on you to deliver that.'

Kyle's eyes narrowed. 'Don't worry, Guv, I'll get

the slimy bastard, I swear!'

19:36

'You're free to go,' the paramedic said, smiling at Aaron. 'You'll probably be coughing up smoke for a couple of days, but there's no long-term damage done. You may have a slight concussion from where you bumped your head, so if you begin to feel nauseous, or the room starts spinning, you may need to pop into A&E and get it checked out.'

Aaron smiled back and stepped out of the ambulance. 'Thanks for taking care of me.'

He wasn't sure what to do next. The police had already taken a brief statement from him, but he didn't know if he would be needed for further questions. He needed to speak to Harry too, to check that he and Toby were somewhere safe. He pulled the phone out of his pocket but saw a big crack down the middle of the screen.

Just perfect!

He must have landed on the phone following the explosion.

'Excuse me? Aaron?'

He turned and saw Tracey standing behind him.

'Hi,' he smiled. 'Look…before you say it; you're welcome. You don't need to thank me for saving your life. Please, I don't like all this attention.'

'That's not what I came to say. I need your help.'

'My help? With what?'

Tracey looked around to see if anyone could overhear them and then beckoned him to follow her. When they reached a quiet corner, away from everyone else, she began to tell him her story.

'The reason I was on that bus was that I was supposed to deliver this briefcase,' she said revealing the case in her hand.

'You can't take that! The police might need it as evidence.'

'Listen to me! Please? When I got home from work today, I was told that my son had been kidnapped and would be killed if I did not deliver this case by seven o'clock. Well, I've missed that deadline now because of all this...I'm worried that my son has been killed.'

'Listen, Tracey, I'm the wrong person to speak to. You should be telling the police this, not me.'

'You don't understand! The man said he would kill my boy if I involved the police. If there's a chance he is still alive, I don't want to jeopardise it by telling the police. Besides, they've got their hands full with all this.'

'So what is it you want me to do?'

'Look, you seem like the kind of man who can handle himself, right? I want you to come with me and help save my son.'

'I'm in The Navy but I'm not a marine.'

'Please, Aaron? I'm desperate. The Frenchman told me the name of the man who took my son: Richard Eksteen. He owns a second-hand car dealership in the city. Please come with me and maybe put the frighteners on him. He's a real lowlife. Please, Aaron?'

'What else do you know about him?'

'There were drugs and cash inside the briefcase, so I would assume he is a dealer of some sort. I think this was maybe a bribe or a payment for something.'

'And you were told to deliver it somewhere?'

'That's right. The name and address on the handle.'

Aaron lifted the label and read the name and address.

'Jesus Christ! You were supposed to deliver this to Paul Burns! He's the one that caused all of this! You need to go and tell the police immediately!'

'I can't do that! He will kill my son!'

'I'm sorry, Tracey, but your son has clearly got himself involved with the wrong people. You need to let the police handle this!'

'They cut his finger off,' she wept. 'I found it in my fridge. They said they would return him piece by piece if I didn't do as they said. I'm desperate. I don't want my son to die! Have you never been in desperate need of help?'

Aaron remembered back to the night of his sixteenth birthday and what Uncle Troy had done for him: Discipline, son: that's what you need.

'You're asking me to go head first into a situation I know little about and confront a man who could be armed, dangerous and surrounded by bodyguards...do you realise that?'

Tracey bowed her head to hide her tears.

'Please don't cry, Tracey...you don't understand the gravity of what you're asking...'

It's not a job. It's not even a career. It's a way of life. The navy will make you a man. You want to make something of yourself? I'm giving you the chance.

'Okay, okay!' he said, closing his eyes. 'I'll help, okay? I'll help you…but we do it on my terms. Right? First of all you need to get that briefcase to the police.'

'I can't…if they ask where I got it…'

'Say you found it on the bus…tell them it belonged to the Frenchman and he told you to make sure it got delivered in case he died…they need to know that Paul Burns lives at that address. You understand? You tell them or I don't help.'

'Okay, okay, I'll take it to them now.'

19:57

'What a crazy day!' Eve Partridge said, as she unlocked the front door and flipped the porch light on. 'I feel truly exhausted!'

'It has been a bit more stressful than our usual kind of day, hasn't it?'

'Did you have any issues with re-arranging today's meetings?'

'No; not after that radio piece you did at lunchtime. I guess people got the message that your priorities had changed.'

'Good. I'll go upstairs and pack a few things to take with me. Please make yourself at home and fix yourself a drink.'

Paul moved through to the living room and admired Eve's vanity wall: covered in photographs of her meeting visiting dignitaries and celebrities. He opened the door to the drinks cabinet and poured himself a large sherry.

'Can I fix you a drink of anything?' he shouted up the stairs.

'I'll have a gin and tonic,' Eve shouted back. 'Be generous with the gin measure!'

Paul mixed the drink and left it on a coaster on a nearby coffee table.

'Your husband not home yet? That's a bit odd,

no?'

Eve descended the stairs with a small holdall in her hand. She had changed from her business suit into a pair of leggings and sweatshirt. Paul couldn't help noticing how different she looked.

'Neil's away on a business trip,' Eve said, as she took a sip from her glass and walked out to the back garden. There was a cool breeze blowing but it was otherwise fairly mild.

'Whereabouts? Do you think he's heard about today?' Paul asked, following her outside.

'Well, the events are being captured nationally, so I suppose there's a chance they are being reported abroad too. Who knows? To be perfectly honest, we haven't been on the best of terms in recent weeks; he's been having an affair with one of the neighbours and I think he's in love with her.'

'Oh gosh, Eve! I'm so sorry...but if I'm honest, I think you could do better anyway. Just you wait, when all this settles down, you'll have eligible bachelors queuing up to date you.'

'Thanks, Paul, I don't know what I would have done without you for this last year. You really have been my saviour!'

'Ah, no, you're going to make me blush, Eve.'

'Is everything okay with you? At the station earlier, you seemed troubled by something.'

'It's nothing...nothing to worry about, I'm fine,' he lied.

'Come on, Paul; tell me what's troubling you. Hell, you've had to put up with enough of my shit, the least I can do is return the favour.'

The sound of a police siren in the distance caught

their attention. Paul's eyes widened and he took a long gulp from his drink.

'Is everything alright, Paul? You look like you've seen a ghost.'

The sound of the siren grew closer.

'Oh God,' he said, his mind racing.

How do they know? How do they know where we are?

'Paul, whatever's the matter? You're starting to worry me.'

'Oh God, Eve, I've done a bad thing, I mean, a really bad thing.'

Eve followed him back into the living room and poured more sherry into his glass. 'What's going on, Paul?'

'They're coming for me, Eve. The police. They're after me!'

Eve looked at him, puzzled. 'What would the police want with you?'

'Before I tell you, you need to know: I never meant to hurt you. That's not what it was about...I...just...I couldn't sit back and let it happen...I'm so sorry...'

'Paul, you're not making any sense. What did you do? What couldn't you let happen?'

'I leaked some confidential documents to someone. I know I shouldn't have, but his motives seemed so sincere...I've made a terrible mistake.'

'Paul, what did you leak? What have you done?'

'It must have been the voicemail I left; that must be how they know. Oh God, I was so stupid!'

'Paul, take a deep breath and tell me everything. I'm sure that whatever you have done, we can deal

415

with. You're my P.A. and friend; I will help you no matter what.'

'Back when you were on the Parliamentary War Committee I saw some documents relating to the finances of the war in the Middle East. I couldn't believe how they were prepared to cut the military budget and deny our men the equipment they needed. I made a copy of those documents...I don't even know why...I was just so disgusted that these other politicians on their fat bonuses would endanger those men and women defending our country...'

'What did you do with these copies?'

'I sold them to a guy who wanted to blow the whistle on the whole thing...he said he would keep my name out of it, but...'

The siren could still be heard through the open door.

'Oh God, I can't go to prison...I couldn't handle it...help me, Eve...please?'

Eve slammed her glass down on the table. 'Go out the back, Paul. At the end of the garden is a small forest, it will provide you with cover. I'll tell the police officers that you aren't here and that I haven't seen you. There is a fence at the end of the treeline, which will take you to a farmer's field, and then it's about three hundred yards back to the main road. Wait for me there and I will come and collect you, and then we can sort a way out of this mess. Go now.'

Paul wiped the tears from his face and tore out the door, grateful that she had taken pity on him.

19:59

'I guess this is the place,' Aaron whispered, crouching down at the bumper of an old Volvo. 'You sure Eksteen is the name the Frenchman gave you?'

'Positive. He said Richard Eksteen is the man who had my son. He said he witnessed them attacking a young lad inside.'

'Well, it looks all closed up now. The lights are off and, unless I'm mistaken, there are shutters down inside. Do you know where else this guy could be?'

'Please, can we look a bit closer?'

Aaron didn't like the thought of being noticed hanging about outside a car dealership, in case someone passing called the police.

'Come on,' he said, climbing over the small brick wall that ran around the perimeter of the property. Tracey followed suit and, keeping low, they made their way over to the glass shell of the building. Peering through a gap in the shutters, Aaron noticed a light on in the back office.

'We may be in luck,' he said, pointing through the gap. Tracey adjusted her position so she could see where he was pointing. Aaron moved further along the building to where there was a larger gap between shutters. 'Oh he's there alright,' he chuckled. 'I think it's safe to assume his bodyguards probably aren't.'

'What makes you say that?'

Aaron pointed again and, when Tracey reached his location, she saw exactly what he meant. From where they were crouched, they had a good view into the office through the main window. Inside, a man in a shirt and tie had a woman bent over a desk. Tracey blushed when she realised what she could see. Aaron crawled around to the main entrance of the building, but found that the large glass door was locked. 'No obvious way in,' he said. 'Do you want to wait for them to finish and catch him when he comes out? We could still call the police and let them deal with him.'

'No! I told you, my son is dead if we call the police. Is there really no way in?'

'Not unless...' Aaron began and then looked around. 'Come with me,' he said, crawling back towards the Volvo. 'Are you one hundred percent certain that this is the man who has your son?'

'I trust the Frenchman.'

'The reason I ask; if we break into this building and threaten the owner, we'll be breaking the law. I want to make certain that you are prepared to face any consequences.'

Tracey looked him in the eye and said. 'Please, Aaron, he's my only boy. I am prepared to face the full wrath of the law if it saves him.'

'Okay,' said Aaron shrugging. 'I need you to find me a large rock or brick or something. Go now; be quick.'

Tracey moved away as instructed and within sixty

seconds had returned with a house brick from a neighbouring wall. 'Will this do?'

Aaron looked at the brick and smiled. 'That'll do fine. Now stand back for me.'

He removed his naval jacket and held it over the passenger window before smashing the brick into it. Tracey jumped at the sound of the glass breaking.

'You think they heard it inside,' he asked.

Tracey shook her head.

Aaron reached through, unlocked the door and slid in. Tracey watched in amazement as he used the brick to break off the plastic cover beneath the steering column and pull out three bundles of wire.

'Where did you learn to do this?' she asked.

'I wasn't always all about Queen and country,' Aaron smiled. 'Believe it or not, I was a bit of a shit when I was younger.'

He set about twisting the two battery cables together before striking them against the exposed ignition wire. The engine sputtered to life and he gently pressed his foot on the accelerator.

'Are we going somewhere?' she asked.

'Not exactly,' Aaron said putting the automatic gear box in reverse and carefully placing the brick on the accelerator. 'You might want to step back.'

Tracey moved to the front of the vehicle and watched, as Aaron released the handbrake and dived from the vehicle. It shot backwards, smashing the showroom's large glass window on impact and tearing the metal shutter from the wall. The car carried on moving until it stuck on a parked car inside the showroom. Aaron charged in after the car, hoping that the element of surprise would catch

Eksteen off guard.

'What the fu…' the South African began, as he stormed from the office, his trousers down around his ankles. Aaron didn't allow him to finish the sentence, instead striking out and catching him square in the jaw. Eksteen stumbled backwards, yelping as he did. The woman from the office emerged to see what all the noise was about.

'Back in the office, luv,' Aaron suggested. 'This is no concern of yours. I mean you no harm. This little shit, on the other hand…'

The woman didn't wait to hear the end of the sentence, before rushing back into the office, barricading the door with a chair.

'You're making a big mistake, pal,' Eksteen said, feeling his jaw for damage. 'You have no idea who you're messing with.'

'You're wrong there, Dick. I know exactly what kind of a man you are, and I've beaten tougher men than you. Now, we can do this the easy way or the hard way; I don't mind which.'

'What do you want?'

'Tell me where Lewis Reed is and I'll let you go back and finish off what you were doing.'

'I don't know that name,' Eksteen shouted.

'Don't lie to me, Richard. You'll make me mad, and you don't want to see me when I'm mad.'

Eksteen pulled his trousers up and fastened the belt, before suddenly lunging at Aaron. The two men fell backwards onto the bonnet of a nearby car, before tumbling to the ground. Aaron was the first to recover and he leapt onto Eksteen and punched him twice in the face before applying two shots into the man's midriff. With the wind knocked out of him, Aaron was able to drag Eksteen to his feet and manoeuvre him to the still-running Volvo.

'Tracey, would you mind popping the bonnet?' he said politely. Tracey obliged, and lifted the lid high, before securing it in place. Aaron put Eksteen in a headlock and began to push his face down towards the car's battery.

'Stop! Stop!' Eksteen yelled, as he felt his cheek warming.

'Where is Lewis Reed? I won't ask again.'

'He's in the boot of the BMW; over by the office,' Eksteen whimpered.

'The blue one?'

'Yes, yes.'

'Where are the keys?'

'In the office.'

Aaron nodded at Tracey who ran to the office door and begged the woman inside to unlock the BMW with the remote. The sound of the car unlocking followed and Tracey lifted the boot lid. Lewis thrust his arms out and around her neck, tears streaming down his face.

'I'm so sorry, mum,' was all he could manage to say.

'It's okay, Lewis. I'm just so glad you're okay,' she said, letting her tears flow. She glanced over at Aaron and mouthed the words, 'Thank you.'

Aaron released his grip on Eksteen's face and kicked the man's legs out from beneath him. Eksteen landed on the floor in a heap.

'Lewis, what was it like being in that boot?' Aaron shouted over.

Tracey helped her son from the car and supported him as they moved over to Aaron.

'It was horrible,' he said. 'I'm embarrassed to say...I wet myself.'

'So do you think a similar fate would be a suitable punishment for Mr Eksteen here?'

'I don't care,' Lewis said. 'I just want to go home.'

Tracey hugged him close and kissed his forehead.

Aaron grabbed Eksteen by the wrist and dragged him across the floor toward the BMW, before manhandling him into the recently vacated boot.

'I think you need to have a long, hard think about your life choices, Dick,' he said. 'I'm going to help you with that. If I hear that you've troubled this family again, I will return and I won't be so forgiving.'

Aaron slammed the boot lid down and asked the woman in the office to throw the key out. She obliged and Aaron smiled as he locked the car and walked through the hole in the showroom's window. Tracey and Lewis followed behind.

'What now?' Tracey asked.

'I think you should get his finger checked out,' Aaron said, nodding at the missing digit. 'Make sure it's not infected.'

'What about him in there?'

'Don't worry about him,' Aaron smiled again, dropping the car keys into a drain. 'He won't bother you anymore.'

20:01

The sound of tyres on gravel indicated the police had arrived outside. Eve glanced at her reflection in the mirror and took a couple of deep breaths to steady her nerves. She needed to appear calm and collected if they were to believe that Paul wasn't here. She couldn't believe he would leak sensitive material. He had always been so trustworthy; this was out of character.

She opened the door and fired a look of bewilderment at the two plainclothes officers. 'Can I help you with something, Sergeant Davies?'

Davies was surprised she knew his name and quickly pocketed his warrant card. 'Good evening, Mrs Partridge. This is Detective Inspector White; we're looking for Paul Burns. Do you know where we might find him, please?'

'Goodness, no,' she replied. 'He's not here I'm afraid.'

'Do you mind if we come in?' said White, pushing past her.

'Well I suppose not,' Eve replied, stepping to one side.

'Has he worked for you long?' White asked, striding through the hallway and into the living room.

'Paul? Yes; he's been part of my team since I was first elected,' Eve replied, struggling to keep up with his pace.

'And has he always been your personal assistant?'

'No, not always,' she sighed. 'He was a volunteer on the campaign at first, but he demonstrated an aptitude for planning and organising so I took him on full-time. He isn't just my P.A. I don't know what I'd do without him.'

'I see. Was it his decision for you to do the interviews today?'

'It was a joint decision; I felt it only right that the people of the city be informed about what was going on.'

'But did he suggest the idea?'

'I can't really remember who suggested what,' she lied. 'I'm sorry Detective Inspector, it's been a very long day and I'm very tired, can you tell me what you want, please?'

White eyed her cautiously, unsure of how much to say. There was something about her demeanour he didn't trust. The silence was interrupted by a knock on the door. Davies opened it and two P.C.s stepped in. 'We've checked the immediate perimeter and there's no sign of him,' one of them said.

Davies told them to wait outside.

'What is it you think Paul has done?' Eve asked, alarmed by the additional officers' appearance.

'Have you noticed anything strange about Paul recently? I mean, has he been acting differently?' White asked.

'No, not that I can recall.'

'And have the two of you had any major

arguments recently? Is there any reason why he might be holding a grudge against you?'

'A grudge? Paul? No. Certainly not! We have the occasional disagreement...in fact there isn't a day goes by when we don't disagree about something, but that's just work. I don't understand your interest in him. Can you just tell me what is going on, please? What is it you think he has done?'

'We're not really at liberty to share details of an open investigation with you at this time,' White replied, hoping his vagueness might elicit additional details.

'Look, D.I. White, you're new around here. Maybe you're not aware, but Peter Gulliver has already asked me to act as civilian oversight on all major investigations going forward. You can trust me. I'll find out at some point. Please just tell me what's going on?'

'What you drinking?' he asked, nodding towards the nearly empty glass in her hand and ignoring the question.

'Gin and tonic. I'm sorry, do you want a drink?'

'No, not on duty, thank you,' he lied, ignoring the craving. 'Gin and tonic, you say?'

'Yes, that's right,' she replied, looking to Davies for a clue about where the question was heading. Davies returned the puzzlement.

'I'm just curious,' White continued, striding across the room, 'if you're drinking G&T, who's been on the sherry?'

White lifted the glass that Paul had left on the coffee table near the back door.

Eve's eyes widened.

'Where is he, Mrs Partridge?' White demanded.

'He's not here…I swear.'

'Don't mess us about, okay? We believe Paul Burns is the crackpot behind today's events; we need to speak to him urgently.'

'Paul? No. That's absurd…that's impossible. He was with me when your terrorist-person called.'

'We have reason to believe that he hired somebody to place the bombs and make those calls,' Davies chimed in.

'Where is he?' White demanded.

'I don't believe…'

'There is significant evidence linking him with a money laundering operation on the continent,' Davies explained. 'It seems he has been leading something of a double life. He lied to you, Mrs Partridge; he lied to all of us. Remember the letter you received this morning? I am one of you. I walk amongst you but you do not see me. It's Paul, I swear to you. Please? Help us find him before he does something stupid.'

Eve slumped down in a chair, her world rocked.

'This isn't your fault,' Davies continued. 'You weren't to know he had an alternative agenda. Help us bring him in so we can understand why he did all this.'

'Okay, okay,' she said. 'He was here…about three minutes ago. He ran out the back door when he heard the siren approaching…he's heading for the trees at the bottom of the garden; it leads out to the main road. If you hurry, you might still catch him.'

Davies called for the two P.C.s to come in and sit with her while he and White tore out the door and sprinted for the trees.

20:06

White had made it out of the back door first, but Kyle was younger and fitter, and soon swallowed the gap between them. This left him with a dilemma: did he pull ahead in the hopes of catching up with Burns, or did he hold back and maintain pace with his new D.I. They'd hardly made it fifty yards down the stretch of lawn and already White was showing signs of fatigue and breathlessness. Kyle looked at him once more, and decided catching Burns was more important than sparing his new boss' feelings.

Partridge's house was built on a hectare of land. The five bedroom property was big enough, but paled in comparison to the stretch of grass that led to the forest at the end. Kyle pulled a torch from his pocket and shone it at the ground as he ran. There was dew on the grass making it difficult not to slip. The lawn was in need of a mow, but that meant the flattened grass made it possible to see any tracks left by Burns. He could hear the wheezing White five yards behind him. As the trees appeared in sight, the trail ended. The clearing was massive and Burns could have shot off at any angle or could have been hiding somewhere in the trees.

He's spooked, Kyle figured, which means he'll probably run in a straight line.

'This is D.S. Kyle Davies in pursuit of suspect Paul Burns. I need a chopper and search light at my location, over,' he shouted into the radio when he reached the first tree, pausing to wait for White to catch up. The D.I.'s face was covered in sweat and his cheeks had reddened significantly.

'You okay, Guv?' Kyle asked, taking a couple of short breaths himself.

'I'm fine…I'm fine…you called it in?'

Kyle nodded. 'You want to go in or wait for backup?'

'You think the suspect is armed?'

'No idea, Guv. I doubt it.'

'You happy to risk it?'

Kyle smiled. 'I am if you are, Guv.'

'Right, you go in that way, I'll be a few yards to your left. Tread carefully and listen for any sound. Agreed?'

Kyle nodded and the two men headed into the trees, their torches held at eye-level.

'Paul Burns,' White shouted. 'My name is Detective Inspector Tony White. I am here to arrest you. Stop being a prick and come out and see me. Don't make me add a resisting arrest charge to your sheet. Eh?'

There was no response.

'How far do you think this forest stretches?' Kyle whispered.

'God knows! You hear anything?'

'Not yet. You?'

'No. He's either stopped for breath or we're too far behind him,' White whispered, before clearing his throat. 'Paul Burns,' he shouted again, 'this is your last chance. This forest is surrounded. There is no escape for you, son. Do us both a favour and give yourself up. Things will go easier for you in the long run.'

Kyle continued forward slowly, the occasional small branch snapping beneath his feet. The ground was hard, meaning there would be little visible trace of which direction Burns had run in. The sound of White's breathlessness to his left was making it difficult to hear anything.

'Okay, Burns, you can stay where you are now. We have a chopper overhead using heat detection radar,' White bluffed. 'I am in radio contact with the crew and they are helping me pinpoint your exact location. Apparently, we're getting closer, so don't do anything stupid.'

'You think he believes you?' Kyle whispered.

White shrugged. 'He may not even be in here, but we've got to try something,' he whispered back.

Suddenly there was the sound of a bush rustling about twenty yards ahead of them, swiftly followed by the sound of twigs snapping. Burns was running.

Kyle didn't wait for the command and tore off in the direction of the noise. White tried to follow but found himself stuck in a net of brambles. He kicked and thrashed until he was free and then he sprinted after his colleague. Kyle shone his torch ahead in an arc, looking for movement, to ensure he was heading in the right direction. He didn't see the divot in the ground until his foot had caught in it, and he'd tumbled forward, dropping the light. White didn't see the fall and was soon tumbling over Kyle's outstretched legs.

'I've got you!' White shouted, flipping Kyle over and pinning his hands behind his back.

'It's me, Guv!' Kyle shouted.

White released his arms. 'What the hell are you doing on the floor?'

'I tripped, Guv.'

The two mean jumped back to their feet, but silence had once more returned to the forest. Kyle looked around, trying to get his bearings. They were too far from the house to see any lights and the intertwined branches overhead all looked the same.

'What direction are we facing?' Kyle asked.

'Eh? What?'

'Which way is the house? Which way was he running?'

White shone his torch around before declaring, 'Shit! I don't know!'

'He must be hiding somewhere again, but he could be anywhere. We're going to have to wait for the helicopter.'

'Shit!'

'We don't have a choice, Guv.'

'Burns, if you do not get your arse out here now, I am going to be very pissed off!' White shouted at the trees. 'There is no escape! Stop wasting everybody's fucking time!'

'I can't go to prison!' a timid voice shouted out somewhere to the right.

White and Kyle glanced at each other, before slowly advancing.

'Prison is inevitable, Burns,' White called back, more softly this time, not wishing to reveal he was moving closer.

'I don't deserve to go to prison,' Burns cried back. 'All I did was…'

'We know what you did, Burns. I don't want a statement from you until you've been properly cautioned. It's okay…if you tell us everything at the station: it will be okay…you never know, you might even avoid prison.'

Kyle shot him a look of astonishment. White shrugged and mouthed. 'Got to try something.'

Another rustle of leaves to their left caught their breath. Kyle spun round with his torch to see a large hare shooting across the ground, from one bush to another. The movement must have spooked Burns too as he leapt from the bush he had been cowering behind, and ran blindly towards the trees ahead of him. He ignored the pain of twigs and brambles as they slashed at his legs. He felt exhausted, but the adrenalin kept him moving. Then he saw it: the fence Eve had mentioned.

Beyond that is freedom.

Twenty yards behind him, White and Kyle were tearing through the woodland, their torches lighting up the figure of Burns as he leapt at the metal fence before him.

A sudden flash of bright light caused Kyle and White to stop and shield their eyes. The flashing light was interspersed with a shriek like neither of them had heard before. Just as suddenly the flashing and shrieking stopped, followed by a thud as the body of Paul Burns crashed to the floor.

White and Kyle approached the body carefully, the smell of burned flesh entering their nostrils. White moved his torch over the fence until he spotted what he was looking for: a small yellow sign indicating the fence was electrified.

'Poor bastard,' he said.

'There goes our chance of catching the bomb maker,' Kyle exclaimed.

'You better radio it in. You never know, we might get lucky; he might have kept a diary. At least we caught the brains of the operation. I'm sure we'll catch the bomb maker with some good policing.'

Kyle cursed the moon, as he picked up his radio and reported the death of their chief suspect.

20:20

Ophion had broken protocol; returning to the scene of a previous crime was something he had sworn never to do. He had made it his unofficial mission statement. Yet here he found himself, back in the room where he had woken some thirteen hours earlier. He wouldn't have returned if there had been any other way.

The 'Do Not Disturb' sign was still on the door handle where he had left it and, on entering the room, he was pleased that the curtains were still drawn closed and the room had indeed remained undisturbed. The young man's cadaver was still sprawled on the bed, though the victim's eyes had started to bulge slightly. Ophion wasn't squeamish. In truth, he had never stuck around long enough to watch what happened to the men and women he killed; he had always tried to move on quickly.

The young man's blood had formed a reddish-brown shadow on the sheets around the body, undoubtedly from the hole in the man's forehead. If only the young man had left when he had been given the chance, he would still be alive now; but Ophion was not one for regret or remorse. He had killed the man to cover his tracks. At least he thought he had.

Ophion had checked the room twice while he

had been dressing; looking for any sign that could link the police back to him. He had scrubbed the bathroom clean, ensuring no stray hairs could provide them with any D.N.A. He had checked to ensure that he had his three passports, in case he needed to make an emergency exit. He had placed those in his jacket pocket. As he had held the small pistol to the back of the rent boy's head, he had been certain that he had collected everything and was leaving clean.

That was until half an hour ago when he had been about to pay for some petrol in a small petrol station across the city. He had decided to use the credit card that matched the profile of the businessman he was claiming to be on this trip to the UK. He had several profiles and back stories that he could rely on, so when he was at passport control, he could confirm he was here on business and what his business was. That meant he needed to maintain this profile during the trip, for example paying for bills and petrol with the correct card.

He had opened his wallet to find the card, when he had noticed it was missing. Having not used the card since the previous evening, this had come as something of a shock to him. Ophion was blessed with a highly developed memory, one of the reasons he could speak a dozen different languages. He knew he had collected the card after his meal the night before. He knew he had definitely returned it to the wallet; a wallet that he had not opened since. There was only one other person who could have come into contact with his wallet.

Ophion turned the volume on the television set

up, to disguise the sound of him ransacking the room. The victim's clothes were still strewn across the floor, so he searched those first, looking in the pockets of the man's trousers and in his shoes, but it wasn't there. He then began a systematic search of every nook and cranny of the room, including under the bed, in case the card had somehow fallen out of the wallet. But he couldn't find it. Ophion's eyes scanned the room, looking for anywhere he had yet to check. They fell upon the body. The young man's dressing gown was now a dark pink colour and it clung to his body like a wet towel. He peeled a layer of it back to locate the pocket and carefully placed his fingers in. There was nothing in the first pocket, but in the second, he found it.

So the little shit stole my credit card!

Ophion could feel the sticky blood on his fingers where they had touched the fabric of the gown and he quickly washed them in the sink in the bathroom, before scrubbing the basin once more. As he returned to the room, he saw that a news programme was on. He recognised the scene immediately. The male reporter was framed by large search lights and police tape, and a small banner at the bottom of the screen informed him that a bomb had been detonated at the Leisure World complex. He continued to watch the report.

'We are hearing unconfirmed reports that there were in fact two devices on the bus, intended to kill all six on board, however, one of the passengers managed to diffuse one of the devices, and so three of them have walked free and have been helping the police with their enquiries.'

Ophion glared at the television set.

He had failed in his mission. He had never failed to carry out a client's instructions to the letter. His reputation depended on it. His career would be over if it ever leaked out that he had left loose ends.

He continued to watch the report, desperate to know who had walked free. He had a horrible feeling that he knew what the answer would be.

'The police have not revealed the identities of the survivors, but have arranged a press conference for ten p.m. this evening, which would suggest that they have either made a breakthrough in what has been a real test of their manpower today, or they will be appealing for public help.'

There has to be a way I can find out.

'These are the pictures we brought you earlier,' the reporter continued as pre-recorded footage replaced him on the screen. There was the sound of a gunshot followed by a loud bang, before screaming followed and nearby people ran in hysteria. 'What you can hear in that footage is what sounds like a gunshot and an explosion, although Detective Superintendent Peter Gulliver wasn't so forthcoming on exactly what had happened, when we spoke to him half an hour ago.'

The image on screen changed again and a man in a police uniform and fitted hat appeared on the screen with a microphone in front of him.

Ophion's eyes widened as he saw the confirmation he needed. He rushed over to the screen and, ignoring the main picture, concentrated on a small image in the top right-hand corner of the picture. A young Asian woman could be seen leaving the scene.

So you survived, Miss Ahmed. I will not make the same mistake again.

He pulled the phone from his pocket and dialled 999 to report what he had left in Nazir's flat, but the line failed to connect and a recorded message told him the switchboard was busy and to phone back later.

He knew what he needed to do. Nazir was the only one who could realistically connect the dots that would lead back to the client. It was possible she had already spoken to the police, but he would make sure she couldn't tell them anything else. He scanned the room for a final time and left again, ensuring the 'Do Not Disturb' sign was still in place.

20:21

'Just pull up anywhere here, mate,' Aaron told the taxi driver, when they arrived in Lowford. He paid the fare and climbed out. His back was aching, as the impact of the explosion began to take its toll. The thought of a hot shower and some good food kept him going.

The last time he had spoken to Harry, he had told his cousin to get away from the house and to go somewhere safe with Toby. As he walked up the path to the front door he was pleased that his cousin had taken the advice. There were no obvious lights on inside and the door felt secure when he pushed on it. He had bought a cheap pay-as-you-go phone from a supermarket on the way over. He pulled this from its box now and slipped in the sim card from his damaged phone. It took a moment for the phone to power up and when it did he skipped through the set-up process. He wouldn't have this phone for long, he had decided, but it would get him through the next couple of days, until he chose a better replacement.

He stifled a yawn as the welcome screen appeared. He couldn't believe how tired he felt, given how early into the night it was. Part of him was hoping Harry had been smart enough not to share where they had gone, but part of him hoped for some sign that they were safe.

The phone flashed up to tell him he had a voicemail. He dialled into the service and listened. He heard the voice of Paul Burns frantically telling him not to share the information he had leaked. Not that he had any choice. The box containing the leaked papers had gone up in smoke, and the chances were that the memory stick was now toast too. At the very least, it would be in the possession of the police and he didn't want to have to answer the awkward questions that might arise if he tried to claim it back. He decided to keep the message in case the police wanted to listen to it. He saved the message and was surprised to hear he had a second message.

'Hey cuz,' he heard Harry say, 'it's about half past six and I was just phoning to find out where you are. Did your meeting go okay earlier? Did you get everything you hoped for? I'm still at home at the moment. I know you said you thought I might be in danger, but I think you're panicking for no reason. Even if somebody was monitoring the website for Parvon and, even if they could trace my IP address, it doesn't mean they would be able to locate my home address. They certainly wouldn't be able to identify my name, so I can't see how they would tie my search back to my father. For that reason, I've decided not to go anywhere. Toby is at his friend's house across town and he seems happy there. I'm sure he is safe. So, get yourself back here and we'll have another go at that bottle of tequila, okay?'

There was a pause on the message. Aaron

checked his phone to see if he had lost connection, but the screen told him it was still playing. He turned the phone's volume to the maximum so he could try and hear why Harry had stopped talking.

'Who are you?' he heard Harry shouting, though the voice was now more distant, as if the phone had been dropped without disconnecting.

'What are you doing in my house?' Harry's voice continued. 'How the hell did you get in?'

There was another pause, followed by the sound of glass smashing. Aaron listened intently, wanting to scream out, but knowing it was useless. He looked up to the living room window, where the message had to have been recorded two hours ago, but the lights were off.

His heart skipped a beat, as he heard his cousin pleading. 'Oh God, don't. Please, mister...I don't know anything...'

There was a second petrified shriek, and then the sound of someone picking up the fallen handset.

'Listen closely as I will only give this warning once,' said a deep and emotionless voice. 'Desist your investigation into Parvon Trading immediately, unless you wish to meet the same fate as your cousin and uncle. You are dealing with powers beyond your imagination. I am a black plague, spreading death wherever I go. Do not give me a reason to come after you. I know who you are, but you don't know me. You will not see me coming.'

The message ended and Aaron forced himself to replay it. He looked back up at the window, knowing that he needed to confirm his suspicions. He kicked over the plant pot on the doorstep and found the spare key. He quietly slipped into the house and tore up the stairs, being careful not to touch anything. He found Harry slumped on the sofa, a tourniquet around his right arm and a used syringe on the floor in front of him. Aaron felt for a pulse in his cousin's neck, but didn't find one. Forcing back the tears he ran from the room, back down the stairs and out into the street. He wiped the key clean, and placed it back under the plant pot, before pulling out his phone to call for help.

As he did, he saw that an unknown number was phoning him.

'Hello?'

'Aaron? Hi, it's Nazir Ahmed...from the bus...I'm sorry, I didn't know who else to call.'

He temporarily forgot about what he had just witnessed, relieved to be speaking with a friendly voice. 'That's okay, Nazir. How can I help?'

'Well, it's...I just got home and...and my flat...I think someone has been here...'

'You've been burgled?'

'No...well, yes...I mean, I don't think anything is missing but...there is stuff on my table that wasn't here this morning...I think...I think someone is trying to frame me for what happened on the bus...I'm scared, Aaron...can you come over?'

Aaron looked back up to the living room window. There was nothing more he could do for Harry at this moment; but he vowed he would not let his cousin's death go unpunished.

'I'll come straight over,' he said, and made a note of her address.

'Hurry, please,' she said before hanging up.

He dialled the emergency services and, when connected to the ambulance service switchboard, he covered the mouth piece with a handkerchief and put on a voice.

'My elderly neighbour won't answer his door; I think he might have had a heart attack. You must come quickly.'

He gave the address, before hanging up the phone. He knew the paramedics would be able to get in touch with the police when they located the body. It served him better to be far from the scene when that happened. He jogged down the road and phoned for another taxi.

20:48

There was nothing Nazir Ahmed wanted more than to curl up in bed, close her eyes and go to sleep. She felt exhausted and had been stifling yawns for the last hour, refusing to give in so early in the evening. The pregnancy was taking its toll, but the stress of the day had not helped. She had left the Leisure World complex an hour and a half ago and had headed to A&E for an urgent ultrasound of the bump.

'Your daughter is absolutely fine,' the nurse had declared, before realising what she had said. 'Oh God, did you know the sex yet? I'm so sorry...'

Nazir smiled. 'I found out this morning. Don't apologise.'

'Phew! Well, her heart beat is strong and I have no reason for concern.

The nurse considered her for a moment. 'And how is mum? You look exhausted.'

'It's been a long day,' Nazir smiled, grateful for the concern. 'It's nothing a long soak in the bath and an early night won't cure.'

The nurse had called a doctor over, who had concurred with what the nurse had said and then she had been on her way. Arriving home, she had headed to the kitchen to make a cup of decaffeinated tea. She had felt hungry, yet too tired to really cook anything, so had made a cheese sandwich and devoured it in seconds. It wasn't until she had walked into the living room that she had sensed something was wrong.

On the table by the window, she had found a couple of fan heaters in pieces, a couple of schematic blueprints, and a soldering iron. She had approached the table slowly, wondering firstly what the machinery was doing there, and then who had left it on the table. She knew as much about electrical engineering as she did about origami; that is to say: nothing! She had quickly moved from room to room to see if anything else was out of place, but everything looked as she had left it. Even her small container of savings was where she had left it; hidden under the bed. It appeared nothing had been taken and yet someone had been here and left the gear.

She knew not to disturb any of the evidence, for fear of contaminating it, so had taken a seat as far from the table as she could and had sipped her tea, while considering what to do. She had wondered what could have been in the heaters that had been dismantled. It was only when she had thought about what the scene reminded her of that she had grown scared. She had immediately tried to phone the police, but the switchboard had been engaged. As she had hung up the phone, she was actually relieved that they hadn't answered.

I'm being set up, she had concluded.

She had glanced at her watch to check the time and that was when she had seen Aaron's number scrawled on her hand. She had phoned him and was relieved when he had answered and agreed to come round. She hadn't moved since placing the call, even though her cup was empty and she wanted another drink.

A knock at the door caught her attention.

Thank God: Aaron is here.

She walked to the door and began to open it. By the time she realised it wasn't Aaron, it was too late. Ophion shoulder barged the door, knocking Nazir back and out of his way.

'Who…who are you?' she managed to ask, as he carefully closed the door behind him, turned back and smiled broadly. The look of excitement in his eyes was difficult to ignore and sent a shiver down her spine.

'Who are you? What do you want?' she repeated.

Ophion shook his head. 'No questions, Nazir. I don't have the time or the patience to talk with you. The quieter you are, the quicker it will be.'

'What will be?'

He pulled out his trusty blade and allowed it to glisten in the overhead light.

Nazir screamed and ran through the nearest door, slamming it behind her. She pushed her body up against the door, determined not to let him in, but he was stronger than her. The door reverberated as he barged it. She pushed harder against it, but as he barged it a second time, she heard the wood of the door frame splinter as the door opened, sending her sprawling across the room.

'Don't make this more difficult than it has to be. If you scream and draw attention to your situation, I will be forced to execute anyone who comes to your aid. Is that clear? Do you really want to cause others to die?'

'Are you the one who left that mess on my table?'

Ophion observed the small scene he had crafted earlier. He tutted mockingly. 'It looks like someone has been building incendiary devices in this room. I bet if the police searched your computer they would find several interesting sites in your internet history. Tut-tut, Miss Ahmed, what have you been up to?'

'It's you, isn't it? You're the one who spoke to us on the bus! You're the one who has been terrorising the city all day!'

'If you really believe that, then you know I will have no hesitation in killing you now.'

There was something horribly sinister in the man's face. He looked like he had seen a lot of death in his time and had become tolerant of it.

'Why did you do it? What did you have to gain?' she continued.

Ophion considered her. 'What is the answer to ninety-nine of a hundred questions? Money.'

'You're a hired killer! You're employed by Parvon Trading,' she concluded.

'Now where did you learn about that company?'

'I know all about what Parvon have been doing. It's all recorded in the McKenzie...'

Nazir paused as a chilling thought dawned on her. 'Oh God...you...you killed Simon...'

'Denby knew too much. My employer wanted him gone, so I killed him. It seems my employer wants you gone too. You were supposed to die on that bus, Miss Ahmed. That's why I phoned you, pretending to be that Bollywood playboy you love. Like he would be interested in someone like you…'

Ophion lunged at her, but she managed to roll away from his grasp and used the armchair to get back on her feet. The assassin grabbed at her neck with a vice-like grip; his leather gloves squeezing the life from her. She fought against him, but his grip remained strong. She could feel the oxygen draining from her and knew she needed to release his hand or die here and now. She kicked her right foot out and caught him in the groin. His fingers released their grip instantly and he doubled over in pain. She rushed back to the door, but knew he would be on her before she made it to the front door. He was already upright again and was twirling the knife in his hand. Looking to her left she spotted a table lamp and yanked it from the wall, thrusting it in his direction. He ducked out of the way and the lamp flew past him into the window, smashing the glass and crashing to the ground below.

I need a weapon.

Nazir ran to the kitchen, reaching for a chef's knife from the block on the side. She could hear him striding in behind her. She was certain that he would win a knife fight, but she wasn't prepared to surrender her life, nor the life of her baby just yet. Seeing the blade in her hand made him smile even more.

'I'm going to enjoy this,' he grinned.

Nazir thrust the knife out in front of her, hoping he wouldn't enter the protective perimeter. He lashed a hand out, which connected with her wrist, sending her knife flying across the room and into the kitchen sink.

The front door swung open and slammed into the wall behind it. The sudden noise caused Ophion to turn and see who was intruding on his fun. Nazir was relieved to see Aaron standing in the doorway, a look of anger on his face.

'The naval officer. You're the one who disarmed my device, aren't you? Pity; you wrecked a perfectly good plan.'

'You're the fuck who killed my cousin and my uncle!' Aaron declared, recognising the voice from Harry's message.

'You're Troy Cross' nephew? Oh this gets better and better. My client will pay me more when I get rid of you too.'

'Haven't you heard? The police have your client in custody,' Aaron bluffed. He sure hoped White and Davies had apprehended Burns. 'It's all over. They're on their way over here now to arrest you too. Burns has squealed, you see, told them everything they need to know about today, and about you.'

'I don't think so, Mr Cross. My client knows very little about me. Besides, I'll be long gone before the police get here and find your dead bodies. How fitting that they'll find two of the survivors surrounded by bomb equipment. They'll hold you responsible and close the case. Maybe it is a good thing that you disarmed that device after all.'

'There's one thing you've forgotten,' Aaron said.

'What's that?'

'Now Nazir!' Aaron shouted, and before Ophion could react he felt the blade of a small chopping knife thrust into his right shoulder, severing a nerve. He felt his hand go numb and he dropped his own knife. Aaron moved closer to him and kicked the discarded weapon away, before punching him hard in the face. Ophion felt the pain, but he wasn't going to give up that easily. He lunged at Aaron, causing the two of them to crash to the floor. Ophion was the first up and pinned Aaron to the floor. With his good hand, he began to rain punches down on the prone sailor, who used his arms to try and block the blows, all the time wriggling, trying to escape the hold. Nazir quietly approached Ophion from behind and crashed a frying pan down on the back of his head. He lashed out and sent her crashing into the living room door. Feeling a trickle of blood on the back of his neck, he knew he would have to retreat. The closest exit was the broken window, but it would involve a jump of twenty or so feet to the ground. As he looked out, he saw the top of a tree, swaying in the cool breeze, just below the window line. If he could make it to that he would be free.

Ophion kicked out at Aaron, catching him square in the jaw, knocking him back. Checking that Nazir wasn't going to trouble him further, he pulled the small blade from his back and tried to assess how much damage it had caused. He felt woozy, but Aaron was starting to stand once more; there was no time to rest. He watched his prey, looking for the best method of attack.

'Just go!' Aaron shouted. 'Leave us alone. Your reign of terror is over; there is no need to kill us.'

Ophion didn't want to accept the response. Retreating was not an option.

'You should have died on that bus! Instead, you will die here and watch her die too.'

Ophion stepped forward, the small knife in his hand ready to strike out.

'There's one thing you're forgetting,' Aaron began. 'Now!'

Ophion turned quickly, expecting to see Nazir making a move against him again. He didn't expect to see her still unconscious on the floor. He turned back, just in time to see Aaron lunging at him. The two men crashed back into the hallway. Still Aaron drove him back until they were outside of the flat. Ophion tried to thrust the blade towards him, but Aaron's hand was wrapped tightly around his own and the blade wouldn't budge. The killer's body slammed hard into the handrail in the corridor. He dropped the blade and tried to fight back. His punch was weak and barely connected. Aaron kicked out, striking him in the face, causing him to lose his balance and fall backwards down the stairs. His head crashed against the wall, then darkness.

∗

'Is he...' Nazir asked as she approached from the doorway a moment later.

'He's not moving...I'd be surprised if he wasn't dead after a fall like that.'

'How did you know I was in danger?' she asked as they moved back into the flat.

'I nearly got clobbered by a falling lamp,' he smiled. 'I figured you needed me.'

'What will we tell the police?'

Aaron considered the question. 'We tell them the truth. We found an intruder in your house when we arrived here and he attacked us. I fought with him and he slipped while trying to flee. Maybe it's time to get hold of D.S. Davies and tell him that story. What do you think?'

Nazir nodded and smiled at him. 'You know that's twice you've saved my life today. I guess I'm going have to buy you more than a coffee now.'

'I'd settle for a plate of beans on toast right now; I'm famished.'

'Me too. I'll see what I can whip up.'

'You should rest in your condition. I don't mind cooking.'

'That's very kind. You're a good man, Aaron Cross.'

'If you knew some of the things I'd done in my time…'

Nazir placed a finger to his lips. 'I don't believe in living in the past. You're here now and there's nobody I'd rather have with me.'

He looked into her eyes and recognised the longing he was feeling too. He leaned in and kissed her tenderly.

20:59

'If there's nothing further we can do, Mrs Partridge, we'll be on our way,' Kyle said, standing up and draining the remains of his coffee.

'You're certain that there is no danger to my life now? You said you thought Paul wasn't acting alone; what's to stop his partner coming out of the shadows and coming after me?'

'We've just been told that we've got him too,' White said, purposefully striding into the room.

'Really, Guv?' Kyle asked, surprised at the admission.

'Uh-huh. It seems he paid a visit to the house of one of the survivors and tried to finish the job, but slipped as he left and broke his neck. Silly twat!'

'Guv!' Kyle admonished, nodding at Eve.

'It's okay,' she smiled. 'I work in politics, I hear worse all the time.'

'You understand: we'll need to take a formal statement about Burns down at the station, in the morning,' White continued. 'But for now, I think you can sleep easy. The forensics officers will continue working at the bottom of the garden into the night, but they'll see themselves out when they're done. No need for you to stay up if you need to get to bed.'

'I never imagined this was how my day would turn out,' she sighed. 'For all his faults and twisted psyche, I will miss Paul's company.'

'It's understandable for you to feel remorse,' Kyle offered. 'He pulled the wool over everybody's eyes; you probably feel like you could have helped him had he just come clean, but it's pointless thinking like that. You're better off moving on quickly and closing this chapter in your life. Tomorrow is a fresh page in the manuscript of life.'

'What a lovely sentiment,' she said, smiling warmly. 'I might use that when I run for re-election. Would you mind?'

'Why should I mind? It's not mine; I read it somewhere I think.'

'Well, if there's ever anything I can do for you gentlemen, please don't hesitate to ask,' Eve added, showing them to the door.

'There is one thing,' Kyle said as he exited. 'D.C.I. Mercure is going to come under a lot of scrutiny for what happened today…can you do what you can for her? We haven't always agreed on her decisions, but she's a decent copper.'

Eve smiled. 'I'll do what I can, I promise.'

Kyle and White thanked her and walked towards the car. Their next stop was Nazir Ahmed's house to speak to her and Aaron about what happened to The Serpent.

'Some first day you've had,' Kyle said as he climbed into the driver's side.

'Whey aye, I think we deserve a pint. You find the nearest boozer and the first round is on me.'

'What about the dead terrorist?'

'He's not going anywhere. We'll go there after.'

'Tell me,' Kyle paused, 'what's the real reason you've moved down here?'

White wasn't sure how much he should say about his vendetta against McManus. 'I'll tell you over a pint,' he offered.

Kyle started the engine and pulled away.

Back in the house, Eve poured herself a generous glass of red wine and sipped it. Loading up her laptop, she saw she had received multiple emails requesting she appear on news programmes in the morning. She replied to each one, welcoming the opportunity to speak to her constituents; eager to unite the city following the day's terrors. They needed a leader and she was more than ready to fulfil that role. She closed her inbox and located the number she was after, punching it into a pre-paid mobile phone she kept hidden in a drawer.

'Sí, dígame,' a familiar voice said.

'Hola Santiago! Como estas?'

'Señorita Partridge, I wondered when I might hear from you. You are well?'

'I am very well, gracias. Everything went according to plan; we are clear to proceed with the next stage.'

'The McKenzie case is gone?'

'Yes. The file, and everyone associated with it in the UK, has been taken care of. Unfortunately, I had to burn the Parvon Trading name in the process, but if I'm honest, I think it was growing too quickly anyway. We will move the monies and declare the company bankrupt in the morning. We'll then start a new front for our purposes.'

'Another bank?'

'Maybe not a bank this time…I think we need to be more creative than that.'

'Will it not seem suspicious when Parvon ceases trading?'

'Not when we leak a story to the press that the main director of the company was involved in the terror attacks on the UK today and was killed while trying to make his escape.'

'You killed your P.A.?'

'Not directly, although I did switch on the electric fence after he had fled from my house. I was fortunate that he decided to run instead of dealing with the police.'

'And you think they will believe that he was behind everything?'

'I'm confident that the backstory will stand up to scrutiny. I've saved enough files on the server under his name to point suspicion, as well as using your local businessman to issue him with a bribe. That was a good idea, by the way.'

'I'm happy to share my list of contacts whenever you need them.'

'I'm not sure I like Eksteen,' Eve admitted. 'I think he is sloppy and greedy. I think you should curtail that relationship. We'll replace him with one of our own.'

'Consider it done. You have someone in mind?'

'Not yet, but I know someone who will.'

'Who?'

'My silent partner. I'll bring him out to Bogota when I visit next month.'

'You think it is safe to come?'

'My visit to Rio has been on the agenda for over a year, to tie in with the World Cup. I am pretty sure the Home Secretary will still want me there. From Brazil, I'll travel via back-channels to see you. Nobody will be any the wiser, I assure you.'

'Who is your partner?'

'His name is Jock McManus. He's a Glaswegian businessman who controls crime in the north of England. He will import your product to our shores. He has a number of senior officials in his pockets and will distribute throughout Britain.'

'You trust him?'

'McManus is a smart man, but he knows which side his bread is buttered: he realises the bigger picture and will toe the line, I can assure you.'

'What about local law enforcement?'

'You don't need to worry about that. McManus controls the north and I'll cover the south. I've just been invited to act as third party oversight for Hampshire for all their major cases. I will be able to steer any investigations away from our operation and to our competitors. Within twelve months, we should have a monopoly on the cocaine market in Britain, meaning we can set the price as we want it.'

'I admire your confidence. What about the woman who was leading the police investigation? Do you think she will steer clear of your affairs?'

'Mercure is finished; I've seen to that. If she's lucky, she'll escape a prison sentence, but her career in the force is definitely over. She won't cause us any issues. I'm meeting with her boss in the morning; I'll make my views on her performance quite clear. I think today has proved my versatility to our mutually beneficial agreement. I am certain that my exposure today, and in the days to come, will ensure I am re-elected to my seat next year, and who knows from there! Maybe a place in the next coalition cabinet.'

'We should end the call now. I look forward to seeing you again. You have done well, Eve. Welcome to The Cadre.'

She switched the phone off and removed the sim card. She remained in the chair until the wine glass was empty.

Tomorrow is a fresh page in the manuscript of life.

This thought brought a smile to her face as she climbed into bed and closed her eyes: she couldn't wait to start this new chapter of her life.

THE END

Aaron Cross will return in
DOUBLE CROSS.

ALSO BY STEPHEN EDGER

Integration

THE OFFER
Mark Baines is a Team Leader in a call centre. He dislikes his job and dreams of the day he can afford to give up his job and buy the house of his dreams. Following a terrifying burglary at his home, he is contacted by a group prepared to pay him one million pounds in return for a favour.

THE CATCH
The offer seems too good to be true, and he begins to worry about what they might expect in return. The group calls again and tells him to integrate their laundered monies through the bank he works for, but he refuses. When Mark's girlfriend Gabrielle goes missing and his brother is attacked, Mark begins to realise just how far the group will go to get what they want.

EVERYONE HAS THEIR PRICE
As the game begins and the pressure mounts, Mark finds himself risking everything he has to find Gabrielle and save his own life before the group and the police catch up with him.

INTEGRATION
Blackmail, murder, suspense, conspiracy and money laundering: *Integration* is a British crime thriller set in the murky depths of the finance industry.

ALSO BY STEPHEN EDGER

Remorse

'I didn't mean to kill her. That is the first thing you need to understand about me...'

FAIRY-TALE LIFE
John Duggan had it all: married with a beautiful four month-old daughter; Manager with a career on the up; nice house in a good area of Southampton.

BEHIND CLOSED DOORS
His wife is cheating on him; his daughter's relentless screaming deprives them of sleep; he drinks too much.

ON THE EDGE
Unable to deal with the mounting pressure, he hires a private investigator to spy on his wife. But Johnson Carmichael has troubles of his own.
As the conclusion of Duggan's trial looms, he must come to terms with what he has done and why he is facing a life behind bars. He is about to learn a valuable lesson: not every fairy-tale has a happy ending...

REMORSE
Betrayal, revenge, regret and suspense: *Remorse* is a gritty British thriller exploring what fathers will do when driven to desperation.

ALSO BY STEPHEN EDGER

Redemption

LAST YEAR

Mark Baines was blackmailed into integrating two hundred and fifty million pounds of laundered money through the bank he worked for. The same group framed him for murder. Now serving two life sentences in a maximum security prison, the future looks bleak.

BREAK OUT

A siege at the prison allows Mark to escape with a mysterious group who know everything about him. They are searching for a secret passage buried somewhere in the heart of London, and they believe Mark is the key to finding it.

UNDERWORLD

Ali Jacobs is undercover with a Russian mafia family in London. She is shocked when her path brings her into contact with Mark again.

Kidnap, car chases, and an uneasy union with underworld figures mean Mark is in a race against time to prove his innocence and find redemption.

REDEMPTION

Kidnap, torture, blackmail and revenge: **Redemption** is the breath-taking follow-up to the acclaimed *Integration*.

ALSO BY STEPHEN EDGER

Snatched

Approximately one hundred and fifty thousand children go missing in the U.K. every year. That's one child every three and a half minutes.

ABDUCTION

Every parent's worst nightmare: seven year-old Natalie Barrett is snatched walking home from school. The police begin a desperate hunt to find her before it is too late. They fear the worst when a body is located near a golf course.

THE FALLOUT

Sarah Jenson is Natalie's teacher. When one of the detectives on the case is suddenly killed, Sarah believes the events may be linked and begins to search for answers. She is in a race against time to discover the true identity of the perpetrator before Natalie winds up as another statistic.

UNANSWERED QUESTIONS

Where were Natalie's parents when they should have been collecting her? Why was Natalie so scared of her Uncle Jimmy? Could a convicted sexual offender from Sarah's past be involved?

Children not found within the first seventy-two hours, rarely return home alive. Sarah knows the clock is ticking...

SNATCHED

Abduction, terror, suspense and sorrow: **Snatched** is a breath-taking British crime thriller set in Southampton.

ALSO BY STEPHEN EDGER

Shadow Line

THURSDAY NIGHT
The pilot of a routine flight from Paris deliberately crash lands the plane at Southampton airport. Miraculously, there are no fatalities, but who is the man in the Panama hat risking his life to save all on board and who is the mystery eighty-third passenger?

FRIDAY MORNING
An insurance broker carrying an automatic gun opens fire on his colleagues before turning the gun on himself. What motivated him to take such drastic measures and where did he get the weapon?

SATURDAY MORNING
A student enters the West Quay shopping centre with a bomb strapped to his chest. He takes control of the complex and begins to preach from the Qur'an. Why is he bringing his terrorist act to Southampton and why did he choose today?

IN THE SHADOWS
Charged with leading the three investigations, D.I. Jack Vincent is under enormous pressure to deliver results.

SHADOW LINE
Murder, espionage, suspense, terrorism and a face from the past: **Shadow Line** is the thrilling follow-up to *Redemption*.

ALSO BY STEPHEN EDGER

Trespass

VICTIM

September 1989: Beth Roper is a single mother struggling to earn enough money to take care of her four year-old daughter, Lauren. One night, she is followed home by a stranger who forces his way in and brutally assaults her whilst her daughter sleeps in the next room.

ATTACKER

May 1993: Known deviant, Nathan Green is on trial for the violent assault of two women and the murder of a third. The trial forces the victims to confront the man whose eyes they will never forget. He is eventually sentenced to life in prison, but it doesn't feel like justice for one of the victims.

ACCUSER

November 2013: Following her mother's passing, a now adult Lauren Roper hires Private Investigator Johnson Carmichael to prove that it was Nathan Green who assaulted her mother back in 1989.

With no evidence, no witnesses and only the fragile memory of the client to work with, this is a case Carmichael doesn't want. However, when he begins to ask questions and his life is threatened, he learns there is more to Lauren's claims than first thought.

TRESPASS

Fear, murder, revenge, and suspense: *Trespass* is a gritty thriller examining the horrifying effects of sexual assault.

ALSO BY STEPHEN EDGER

Complicit

REUNION
Connor Price is a young man meandering through life without purpose. He receives a chance phone call from Dylan Taylor, his best friend from school and they agree to meet up. Dylan offers him money if Connor will go with him to a meeting. Connor is suspicious but Dylan assures him it is nothing illegal.

ON THE RUN
Connor's world is turned upside down when he witnesses Dylan execute two Russian gangsters at the meeting, and then steal their bags full of cocaine and cash. When Dylan disappears, Connor is left to face the music alone, and becomes the target of the drug dealer, loan shark and Russian mafia who Dylan ripped off.

NO ESCAPE
The Chairman of a secret organisation known as 'The Cadre' is hunting Dylan as well. He has terrifying plans for Britain's future and will stop at nothing to achieve his goals. He uses the members of his organisation to exert the necessary pressure to get to the truth.
Connor is fighting for his freedom, his future and his life. Who do you turn to when even the police are after you?

COMPLICIT
Politics, espionage, conspiracy and finance: **Complicit** is the breath-taking follow-up to *Crosshairs*. This is the second book in 'The Cadre' series.

ALSO BY STEPHEN EDGER

Double Cross

LOOKING FOR ANSWRS
Aaron Cross is hunting for the men responsible the death of his uncle. He finds himself retracing his uncle's final movements in Mexico. Dylan Taylor is still running from The Cadre whilst searching for his missing girlfriend. When Aaron's and Dylan's paths collide, little do they realise how much they are going to need each other if they are to survive and finally stop The Cadre's plans for a New World Order.

IMPOSSIBLE ODDS
D.I. Tony White and D.S. Kyle Davies are also trying to prove who really masterminded the terrorist attack on Southampton. Their chief suspect is MP Eve Partridge, but with the whole country and The Cadre supporting her, their chances of building a case are remote at best. With nobody they can trust but each other, they set out on a dangerous journey to deliver justice.

NEW WORLD ORDER
It seems like nothing will stop The Cadre achieving their plans for world domination. But they didn't account for the four men with nothing to lose, who cannot be bought and will risk everything in the pursuit of freedom.

DOUBLE CROSS
Politics, terrorism, conspiracy and suspense: *Double Cross* is the non-stop thriller that concludes *Crosshairs* and *Complicit*. This book is the final part in 'The Cadre'

series.

Made in the USA
Charleston, SC
24 August 2015